LOOM OF THE LAND

Loom of the Land

BY *Eleanor R. Mayo*

REBEL SATORI PRESS
New Orleans • MMXVIII

Originally published by
William Morrow & Company

ISBN: 973-1-60864-129-1

Published in the United States of America by
Rebel Satori Press

For Ruth

LOOM OF THE LAND

The law will punish man or woman
  Who steals the goose from off the common;
But lets that greater villain loose
  Who steals the common off the goose.

THE MORNING after the big storm was one of those wind-washed, clear, fall days when things are so sharp they look as if they existed only in silhouette; as if they'd been burned out of their background, leaving their bulk nothing but a hole and not really there at all. October, after delivering one final smashing blow at Christian Ridge, was going out in a blaze of blue and gold, blowing out on a clean northwest wind.

If the day hadn't been so lovely, the desolation of the roadstead wouldn't have looked so complete. The clean light magnified damage. The big sardine boat that lay on her side on the ledge under High Head, exposing the black gap in her bottom where the planks had been ripped away, looked like a foundered dinosaur. Farther down the shore, on a small pebbly beach, there was a big lobster car that had torn loose from its moorings. One end of it had been smashed in and its dark hold yawned emptily.

The shore looked cluttered and untidy. All kinds of minor wreckage had been spewed up far above the normal high-water mark and made a dreary looking mess in the grass and around the small alders that grew down to the beginning of the beach.

Russ Walls parked his big old Buick in front of the house thinking that Stan or Jake could put her in the barn later. He was too anxious to see Grace to bother with it himself right now. He went up across the lawn under the big chestnuts and in the front door. He shed his overcoat just inside the door and threw it at the newel post, not stopping to see whether it hit what he'd aimed it at or not. He didn't bother to take off his hat, he just kept going through the hall and the dining room and out into the kitchen where he knew he'd find her.

Grace was at the sink, her broad competent back turned to

him and he stood in the doorway watching her for a moment before he said anything.

On his way back from Augusta, when he turned south from Freehold onto the road home, he had begun to feel queerly depressed and inexplicably sad. He called it restlessness because inexplicable things didn't exist; sadness was an emotion that belonged exclusively to children, poets, and women; and he had nothing to be sad about. But still the look of the land made him feel depressed. Fall was a season that made the land look old; the flat fields, lying used and empty now under the low sunlight, made him feel tired just to look at them. And he *was* tired.

Those visits to Augusta wore him out. It was hard for him to be on his guard all the time against men who were as smart or smarter than he. He had become too accustomed to men who weren't as smart and the week of constant strain told on him.

October was a bad time of year anyhow, he told himself with an impatient movement of his shoulders. Everything was over, all the crops were in, things just lay around waiting. And he couldn't think of anything that looked more dismal than a cornfield waiting for snow.

Now that he was on his way home, he found himself longing for a sight of the Ridge and for a word with Grace. For the first time he realized how much he missed them both and he straightened up in his seat, tightening his big hands on the wheel, straining to get his first glimpse of the high blue shoulder of the Ridge to the south. There the land never had time to be tired and he liked that—it was too busy going up or down hill.

He noticed himself moving slightly in the seat, almost as if he were trying to make the old Buick go faster when he knew quite well that her gentle lumbering waddle never reached more than forty-five. Finally, though, she'd started down the last long hill and past the first few outlying houses and Russ, immediately feeling better, leaned back, relaxed and content. Here was his place and he was glad to be back in it.

Now standing in the dining-room doorway grinning at his wife's oblivious back, Russ said, "Hello, old girl."

Grace let out the scream he'd expected and turned on him fiercely.

"Russ, you devil," she said, half-angry, but too pleased to see him to show it much. "Why on earth didn't you let me know you were gettin back? I haven't got a thing special in for dinner. We're just goin to have a pick-up."

"Pete sake," he said, "can't a man come home when he wants to without lettin the whole world in on it? This any way to treat me when I been away? Think you warn't glad to see me."

"Well, I am," she smiled broadly, "and you know it, too."

She came over and kissed him heartily, holding her wet hands away from him so as not to get water on his good gray suit. Russ didn't let go of her immediately. The firm solid feel of her wide hips and strong back was so good that he grabbed her, wet hands and all, and kissed her soundly. Grace was really blushing when she moved away.

"My lord, Russ Walls," she said, "what a way to act—and you over fifty."

"That's all right, old girl," he looked at her appreciatively. "There's times when you can make me feel twenty and you know it." He put his head back and let out his big laugh when she started blushing again. "And when you do that," he added, "you don't look much older yourself."

"I don't know what you're talkin about. I'm not doin anythin."

"You're blushin like a school girl," Russ said. He looked with pleasure at her wide warm-colored face under its bun of snowy hair. "Honest, it's a wonder people don't think you bleach your hair just so's to look younger'n you are."

"Russ—" She made a half-hearted, coquettish swipe at him

and turned away. "The kids ever hear you, they'll think we're both crazy." Her wide flat-lipped mouth kept quirking into an unwilling smile.

Russ sighed, suddenly depressed again. He took his hat off then and hung it on a hook behind the door.

"I dunno but what the kids think I'm crazy, anyhow," he said and immediately sounded as old as he was. Grace glanced at him over her shoulder.

"You tired, Russ?"

"Ah, not very. I'm just sort of flat. City always does that to me. How anyone could ever be happy livin in a place like that I don't know. They even put fences around their trees."

"Nemmind. You're back now."

"And some old glad to be, too." He settled into a straight kitchen chair and started taking off his low shoes, his big-boned ankles looking thin in the light socks. He reached in behind the stove and brought out his larrigans, with his heavy wool socks tucked into their high legs.

"Certainly feels good to let your feet spread out again," he said.

"Anythin special happen this time?" Grace asked, more to make conversation than because she was interested. She felt much as Russ did about cities and she didn't have his necessary incentive to show interest.

Russ looked at her calculatingly, his bright hard blue eyes suddenly thoughtful.

"How'd you like to be a Congressman's wife?" he asked. Grace's whole back went stiff before she turned slowly from the sink to face him again. This time her face was completely sober.

"What've you done, Russ? You haven't got yourself into anything, have you?"

"Maybe you don't realize what an honor it'd be," Russ said, his expression giving her no clue to his seriousness. "Think of

6

the women who'd give their eye-teeth to have a husband in the legislature. Maybe even live in Washington sometime."

"Maybe," she said cautiously, waiting to see what he was leading up to.

"I been thinkin—maybe that's all I'm good for now I'm gettin along. The kids growin up and all makes me feel my age."

"Hnh. Long's you talk that way I don't worry. It's when I hear you goin around claimin you feel like a spring chicken, I'll start thinkin you're old. Till then, I'll know there isn't a thing wrong with you."

"You mean you wouldn't want to live in Washington?" Russ said evenly.

"Russ." She turned on him, her good natured face exasperated. "Now, you come right out an tell me what you've done. I don't want any more of this hintin around. What're you up to?"

"Couple of fellers want me to run for state senator next fall," he said, his good temper completely restored by her reaction. "Didn't know what to do. Thought I might mull it over. May be a good idea. Thought you might be tired of livin here, maybe like a change."

"Russ," Grace said heavily, "you know perfectly well I never get tired of livin here. I was born and brought up here an I like it. You were yourself. Besides, bein your wife the way you are now's about all I'm up to. If you go to Augusta or anywhere else to live, you'll go alone."

"Why, Grace!" He looked a little surprised, as much as he ever let himself look. "You mean that?"

"No, of course I don't." Instantly contrite, she turned soft. "I'd go with you. But I wouldn't like it an I don't believe you would, neither."

"Ayup," Russ said. "That's just what I told them. Said I wouldn't like it, m'wife wouldn't like it, and I was damned if I was goin to do it."

Grace looked at him obliquely, her face amused.

"You certainly do like to get a rise out of me, don't you?"

She went past him to the table, dodging with the ease of long practice the big hand he put out to catch her.

"Go on, now," she said. "I want to set the table for dinner. Go on and change your clothes. You won't feel human till you do. Pa's in the front room, I think. Or else he'll be out in the barn. Anyway, he'll want to see you."

Russ started upstairs, shedding his tie. She's right, he thought, hauling the white shirt off over his head. I'm not human all dressed up in that monkey suit. But he was careful about hanging the gray suit on its hanger so there wouldn't be any wrinkles in it when he needed it again. He tucked the legs of his heavy pants into the loose tops of his larrigans, shrugged his suspenders up over the bulky shoulders of his red and black plaid shirt, and went downstairs again.

There was nobody in the front room so he kept on out to the barn. The packed dirt of the yard was hard and dark brown with dampness underfoot; but when he crossed the patch of grass he noticed how the earth gave spongily and water oozed up around his feet at each step. That storm yesterday must have been a regular ripsnorter here, he thought, seeing the sodden look of the kitchen garden, tomato vines dead and pulpy—even the unpulled turnips looked pounded down and dejected.

Nat was in the barn. Russ could hear his father-in-law's thin reedy voice going on about something, but he was still too far away to distinguish the words. It was hard to tell whether the old man was alone or not because, as far as conversation went, he didn't need company.

Russ came silently up to the open barn door and stood there for a moment. Even with his own family and in a situation as simple as this one, he liked to know what it was all about before he had anything to do with it—he liked to know and not have other people know he was finding out.

The light inside the barn was murky and at first he had to strain to make out what the old man was doing. He had a couple of heavy planks laid out in the form of a huge kite in the empty space where Russ's Buick usually stood. Beside them lay a long newly peeled spruce pole and there was a coil of stiff bright warp hung over one of the headlights of the new car.

Stanny was standing back to the door watching his grandfather closely. Russ glanced once at his youngest son's thin scrawny back and looked quickly away, not bothering to hide the faint disgust in his eyes.

Nat was talking a mile a minute, but he wasn't talking to Stanny. He wasn't talking to himself either, Russ knew. At the moment he was actually talking to Will Hutchins, but he was using Stanny's name for convenience sake and because Will, at the moment, might be miles away—he certainly wasn't anywhere within the sound of Nat's voice.

"Stanny," Nat said. "I said, Stanny, you old cooter, you put it over on me about that rifle. I admit I never thought to look see if she hed a firin pin. You knew I wouldn't, neither. But they ain't anythin you can tell me about fishin rods. By god, Stanny, I said, you try anythin more funny on me an I'll pull every one of them goat whiskers of yourn out, one by one." He straightened up. "What's the magazine say to do next, Stanny?"

Stanny, who had been paying no attention to the tirade, realized suddenly that the last sentence had been actually addressed to him, and went for the magazine that lay open on the running board of the car. He picked it up and glanced up over it to see his father standing in the open doorway. He jumped and then tried to look as if he hadn't.

"Hello, Pa."

Russ nodded, not bothering to speak, and came in to stand with his hands doubled on his hips, staring down at the contraption.

9

"That you, Russ?" Nat got up slowly and started brushing dust off the knees of his neat shiny black trousers.

"Umph," Russ said. He looked the situation over carefully while both Nat and Stanny tried to appear unconcerned. "What for the lord sake you makin now?" he said finally. "A flyin machine?"

"It's goin to be an ice boat," Stanny said quickly before the old man could answer. "That pole there's for the mast."

"I warn't askin you," Russ said, his voice more impatient than rude. Then he stood waiting for Nat to answer him as if Stanny hadn't spoken. Stanny flushed and looked down; the thin fingers of his brown hands holding the open magazine were shaking, so he put it down and shoved his hands into his pockets.

"They was an article in that magazine tellin how to build one," Nat said. "I didn't see but what one'd handle jest about like a cat boat. I thought we might try it."

"Well, where am I goin to put the Buick?" Russ said. "You can bet I'm not goin to leave her outdoor till it's cold enough to use an ice boat."

"No, no," Nat said hastily. "We jest started it in here because it was stormin yesterday. We'll take her out in the yard right now. Come on, Stanny."

He grabbed one end of the crude timber frame and stood waiting for Stanny to take the other. Stanny just stood looking from his father to the old man, not moving.

"Well, go on." Russ jerked his head impatiently. "Muckle on there an get that thing outa here. You expect your grandpa to stand there holdin it all day?"

"He's all right, Russ," Nat said gently, trying to smooth things down. "It was my idea. He jest gets excited, that's all."

"I don't give a damn if you build twenty ice boats," Russ said loudly, a little ashamed of himself. "Break your cussid neck, likely. I just don't want them kickin around where they're in the way."

He stood in the barn door watching them carry the frame out to the level place under the apple trees. Stanny came back to get the mast and the coil of rope. When he dodged out the door past Russ, the dragging end of the pole took his father just above the ankle. Russ swore and moved pointedly well beyond reach of the stick.

"I'm sorry," Stanny mumbled, without looking at him, and Russ, suddenly angry for no particular reason because it hadn't been a hard knock, stood glaring after him. Stanny stood the pole against the trunk of the Northern Spy, hung his warp over a sawed-off branch, and disappeared around the corner of the house.

Nat came over to the barn slowly, his bent back looking somehow pathetic, although there was nothing in his face that asked for sympathy. His well-tanned skin was covered with wrinkles, but they weren't the usual soft wrinkles of old age. He looked as hard and solid as a nut and his long clean-shaven sanctimonious-looking upper lip was shut down firmly, making his under jaw stick out. He's mad, Russ thought with a rueful grin.

"The idea, a man your age building a kid's toy like that. Probably plannin on usin it yourself, too, aren't you?" Russ made a feeble attempt to get Nat's mind off what was bothering him.

"What if I am?" Nat said tartly, coming alongside and glancing up at Russ. "When the day comes I won't feel like doin somethin like that, you can tell them to bring the wagon for me—I'll be dead."

"Well, when you crack your skull, don't come howling to me."

"I ain't never howled to you yet, Russ."

"Guess maybe you haven't at that."

Unwilling respect and a sort of backhanded liking for the old man's peppery courage made Russ grin. To his relief there was an answering twinkle of light in Nat's eyes. But he saw that Nat was still determined on coming out with whatever he'd set his jaw about and Russ thought he knew what it was.

"Look, Russ," the old man began cautiously, "I don't think you treat that kid right. You act like he was always doin somethin wrong or goin to. That ain't no way to treat a kid."

"Oh, god," Russ said angrily. "I don't know. Every time I look at him seems as if I'd like to haul off an let him have it. He's so cussed meachin."

"Well, it's your fault if he is," Nat said. "You treat a hound dog the way you treat Stanny, he'd meach, too. Whatta you expect? He's only a kid. What is he? Fourteen. Kid that young, he's sensitive. And you don't take no trouble to hide the way you feel."

"I know it." Russ turned his back on Nat and took a couple of steps away from him. "I can't seem to do anything about it. I can't change the way I feel."

"Yes 'n I know why you feel that way. He's little, that's every cussed thing you really got against him. Judast, here you've got three other kids that's every one of them jaysters. Just because you scraped the bottom of the barrel on Stanny ain't no excuse to go treatin him like it was his fault. Way I see it, you're the one to blame."

Russ turned back to face him, flexing his huge shoulders.

"How d'you get that way? I don't see as you could call me exactly little."

"No, you ain't." Nat squinted judiciously and with a good deal of appreciation at Russ's six-foot-three. "But I can remember your father; he warn't what you could call a big man. And Stanny looks a good deal like him, too. He was always a handy sort of feller to have around. You take a little man, he can do a lot of things a big one can't. Usually he's a lot quicker on the headwork, too."

"Well, don't ask me where Stanny was when the brains were passed out," Russ grunted. "Behind the door, I guess. He doesn't show signs of being even ordinarily bright."

"He's bright enough when *you* ain't around," Nat said. "You got him to where he don't even know what his name is the minute you heave in sight."

"Scared of his own father," Russ said bitterly. "That's a fine thing. I don't see any of the others bein scared of me."

"Perfectly good reason," Nat said. "They ain't a one of the others ain't big enough to look you right in the eye, darn near. And I notice when you can look a man in the eye, you ain't so apt to be ascared. You wait, though. Someday Stanny'll surprise hell out of you."

"If he does," Russ said ambiguously, "he will. Come on. We better get in to eat. Grace was startin dinner before I come out."

Nat fell into step with him and out of some consideration that he didn't recognize himself, Russ took care to see to it that the old man wouldn't notice how he shortened his stride.

"You have a good time in Augusta?" Nat asked.

"Not very. Never could have a very good time in a city."

"Yeah. I traveled around some myself before I settled down an I never found a place could come up to this. Not for me, anyhow."

The two men stopped for a moment outside the shed door and stood looking silently down the sloping shoulder of the Ridge. Below them and a little to the south, beyond the double row of houses that was the village, the sea began and went on and on out into distance. Today the water was a brilliant and hurting blue and the line between it and the sky was clear, but in certain lights from this back door, it seemed to Russ as if everything ended right there beyond the village. You couldn't make out whether it was water or air—it looked as if everything just dropped off into nothing beyond the houses.

He turned to glance up at the Ridge and already its deep shadow had started down its side although the sun looked to be almost directly overhead. The high whaleback of the Ridge always looked gloomy and dangerous, as if it leaned out over them, as if a single touch would be enough to send the heavy spruces and the red rocks roaring down to cover them all.

He had often wondered why it was the people had built this house facing the Ridge instead of looking off over the water. Probably because the road ran between the house and the Ridge and folks were so used to building their houses facing the road they never thought of it any other way. There had been times when he'd had half a mind to pick the old place right up bodily and turn it on its foundations so they could look out over the water from the front windows. He was pretty sure he never would, though.

It was an old house and it had always stood where it was. It looked sort of comfortable and settled down. Be a shame to move it. Grace always said, too, that she liked being able to see the water from her kitchen window. And besides, to Russ, there was something a little shocking in the idea of his back door opening on the main road. He was used to spending a good deal of his time in the kitchen and around the back of the house, and he'd feel as if everyone who went by could see him and what he was doing. And no man would feel right having to go out his front door to get to the backhouse. He guessed he'd better leave her where she was.

Usually a man's feeling for his own house is hard to analyze, especially if the house is an old one. It's a combination of pride of ownership; customary depreciation because, being old, it always needs repairs; a half-inarticulate intention to have something better some day; a queer affection because he usually realizes he never will have anything better.

Russ felt only the first one of these because all the others had been satisfied and had dropped away from him when he'd acquired the house. Here he was, owning and living in the oldest house on the Ridge, from the kitchen window of which he could look down on the roof of the house where he'd been born. There it was, down there in the village, one indiscriminate small roof among others just like it.

Age mattered—old things were always the best. That was why, although he'd bought a new car when Grace kept after him, he left it sitting in the barn and used the old one. Newness meant insecurity and age meant accomplishment, soundness, and a graciousness that he needed.

He thought of the house like that—an old house where people had lived for more than a century. If they had been his people perhaps he wouldn't have had his deep necessity for the knowledge of age. They hadn't been, but he was still too pleased, even now, with the way he had come into possession of the house to mind deeply.

Russ and Aaron Billings had been close friends when they'd been young men, such close friends that their financial affairs were subjects for conversation between them and, in a village like Christian Ridge, a friendship stands a lot of strain before it reaches that degree of intimacy.

When Aaron left the house and Russ moved his family into it, they were no longer friends. It didn't bother Russ. He was on his way up and he didn't have time to be bothered. To get along in the world you had to be a sharp dealer and there was nothing wrong with that as long as you kept it legal. He had been aware at the time that people wouldn't think much of a man who'd buy up a mortgage the way he'd bought up Aaron's, but his own calm assumption of right had made them forget about it long ago.

They had forgotten it as Aaron had apparently forgotten it and as Russ never would have.

By god, he thought, if it was Aaron'd done it to me, I'd have had his heart out.

He turned and went into the house, leaving Nat to latch the shed door and follow him. When he went in through the door to the kitchen, he bent his head to keep from cracking his forehead against the low lintel. His family was sitting patiently around the table waiting for him and the heaped dishes in front of Grace steamed gently, bearing silent witness to the fact that when she said pick-up meal, she didn't really mean it.

"Well," she looked up, "I'm glad you two finally had sense enough to come to dinner. I set out to call you but Stanny said he thought you'd be right in."

"Would have been sooner," Russ said, splashing hastily at the basin in the sink, "only we got talkin."

"I never saw the woman could out-talk a couple of men," Grace said. She smiled at her father as he slid hastily into a seat beside her and glanced around the table at the three kids. Every time he looked at the kids, Nat felt like laughing. Not about Stanny, but the three oldest ones. Jake and Mary sat across the table from him, but Gene wasn't there. He usually took his lunch with him and wouldn't be home until suppertime. Russ scraped back his chair at the head of the table and sat down, the chair creaking uncertainly under his weight. Nat had a pretty good idea that the two across from him had sat down in much the same way and with the same result.

It wasn't that the three oldest kids *looked* so much like Russ —actually they didn't. Gene was as tall as his father but light. Mary, she was dark and tall and she had brown eyes the way Grace's folks had. Jake, the middle one, came closest to his father in coloring, but he was the shortest one of the three and thick through the chest like a young bull.

It was the expression, the look of their eyes, their grandfather thought. If it had been any man but Russ, it would have been embarrassing for him to sit down to the table and find three pairs of eyes with his own exact expression staring back at him. Being Russ, Nat was pretty sure he enjoyed it. Yes, he thought, they don't look too much like him, but you'd know whose kids they were, all right.

Russ glanced at Jake and Mary briefly, said hello, and started to eat. He was hungry and not interested in talking at the moment, so he didn't look up at Grace until he came to

16

little mouthfuls. When he had finished and pushed his plate away from him, he leaned back in his chair, pulled out his pipe, and lit it carefully, before glancing down at Grace to say something. But she beat him to it and he saw that she'd been waiting for him to finish.

"Russ, I was up to see Hat today."

"That so?"

"Well, I was wonderin. Since Ma died, she's been sort of rattlin around in that big house all alone. She won't admit, though, she's lonesome. Wild horses wouldn't drag it out of her, but I know she is."

"What you want me to do," Russ grinned wolfishly, "go up an keep her company?"

Grace glanced quickly at Stanny before she laughed, but Stanny's eyes were on his plate and she got the idea from the closed look of his face that he wasn't even listening to what his father said.

"Now, be serious," she said. "I was thinkin, we got that big room upstairs next to Jake's. Since you finished it off, I haven't used it for anythin but storage. Why don't we—"

"You mean," Russ said when she stopped, "you want to ask her down here to live?"

"Well, yes, I was thinkin of it."

Nat looked up suddenly, his old face pleased.

"I think that'd be real nice," he said. "Hat always was an easy woman to have around. Even if she is my own daughter, I'll say that."

"Well, I dunno, Grace," Russ said thoughtfully. "Mind, it's not I don't want her, but how d'you think you'd get along, two women in the house?"

"I don't see why Hat an I can't live together now. We did all the time we were growin up."

"I was *always* thankful," Nat said, "neither one of you girls took after your mother."

"I dunno but what it'd do Hat good to get the chance to

live in a decent house again," Russ said. He looked at Nat and added hastily, "I don't mean that one warn't. But it couldn't have been very interestin for Hat, livin there alone all the time the old lady took dyin."

"Just like her, too," Nat put in. "She was contrary about everything she ever did. I dunno but she was a little extra contrary about dyin. If Hat hed the good sense I give her credit for, she'd of got out of there long ago."

"Honest," Grace said, smiling, but managing to sound serious, "it's a wonder the two of you don't have Ma hauntin you, the way you talk. I should think you could let her rest, now she's dead."

"I doubt if she gets much, even now," Nat said. "Probly spends all her time spinnin."

Stanny snorted suddenly and choked over a mouthful of milk. The fine spray hit the front of Russ's shirt. Russ sat looking down at it in the moment of horrified silence, then he looked at Stanny and opened his mouth. Before he could say it, Nat caught his eye, and Russ shut his mouth again so suddenly the snap was audible.

"I'm sorry," Stanny said. "I choked."

"So I see," Russ brushed hopelessly at the milk, but he added, "Nemmind. It's all right."

Grace, who had been holding her breath, let it go again. In the ensuing silence, Russ made his escape, knowing he hadn't really got away from the problem of Hattie. As soon as Grace thought he'd calmed down enough, she'd be after him again, hammer and tongs. He managed, with adroitness, since he spent the whole afternoon around the place, to keep out of her way till suppertime.

THE GROUP of men who were standing in the sun in the lee of the packing room on the fish wharf surveyed the wreckage of the harbor philosophically. Their faces weren't expressive, but their voices sounded tight and worried. Aaron Billings had come down from the Ridge early that morning to see just how much damage had been done along the shore and he'd found just about what he'd expected.

"I see a couple of floats down by the coal wharf slipped their moorins, too," he said, nodding toward the narrow unprotected harbor mouth where several other wharves thrust their spider legs out into the brilliant blue of the water.

"It's no wonder," Gene Walls said. "I don't know when I've seen a tide come up that high. Joe Blair was tellin me it lifted the door clean out of the trap on the floor of his bait shed and that floor's a good ten feet above high-water mark."

He nodded his head sagely and stood squinting out across the harbor, trying to make out what boats were at their moorings and what boats weren't. In the bright sunlight, his rawboned long young face looked unfinished to Aaron, or as if something hadn't been added to it yet. Maybe it wouldn't look like that, he thought, if I'd never seen Russ.

"Perley Watson have any lobsters in that car?" he asked, jerking his head in the direction of the car that lay smashed and empty on the beach.

"Well, you know Perley, he cars when everyone else's sellin. Somebody was tellin me this mornin, he's been carrin for the last couple months. He must of had near two thousand pounds," Gene said. "His boat went adrift, too, if that warn't enough bad luck. Nearly stove her bow in on a ledge—Perley got to her just in the nick of time."

"Ralph Kelly was tellin me," Aaron said, "he thought he heard someone knockin on his door in the middle of everythin last night. He said they was so much hell breakin loose he couldn't be sure, but he went to open it anyhow. And there was his punt scrubbin her bow on the doorstep for all the world like a dog wants its head scratched.

"He said anyone didn't believe him could come an see. She's still settin there, high an dry."

They laughed, but for them it was quiet laughter.

"Well," Gene said thoughtfully, "maybe a couple more storms like this'll be what it takes to persuade you guys the old man's right when he says we need a breakwater out there."

To avoid looking at Aaron, most of the men turned and glanced out at the harbor. The long narrow waterway could just as well have been a river. It opened out due northeast on the breadth of unsheltered ocean. It was like a funnel for a good northeasterly. Wind came ripping into it and up its full length, unchecked by even so much as an island. Up inside the harbor the wind always seemed stronger as if the narrowness of its enclosure accentuated it. The only safe mooring in it, in a storm like last night's, was the almost land-locked pool that grew off like an enlarged teat from the southern shore, a quarter mile inside the harbor mouth. But the summer people had built their houses in the thick growth of spruces around the pool and there was no access to it from the landward side. Their big cabin cruisers rocked gently and safely in the lee during a northeaster, while the lobster boats and draggers heaved wildly at their moorings in the unshelter of the harbor main.

"Well, I ain't so sure," Art Ferguson said slowly. He glanced up the shore to where the big white *Mary C. Ferguson* lay, her missing garboards leaving a black space against her clean green bottom. "It'd take more than a breakwater to do *me* any good. The old *Mary C.*, she was way up the harbor here. It wouldn't of made no difference to her whether they was any breakwater."

He blew the straggling hairs of his dun mustache away from his upper lip with an impatient whoosh and his pale brown eyes popped slightly with pure rage against the elements.

"Goddam it, lookit that sky! The way it looks, you'd swear there hadn't been a cupful of wind around here in weeks."

"It would of made a difference all right, Art," Gene said. "And I'd be willin to bet good money Perley's car wouldn't be up there on the beach empty now. No, an them boats wouldn't a been kissin each other out there in the harbor last night, neither, if there'd been any kind of a lee."

"Ah, you young-ones," Art waved his hand. "You're always willin enough to spend good money, but none of you ever got any suggestions how to make it. Buildin a breakwater out there would put this town in debt for years."

"I've heard that argument before," Gene grinned. "But when you stop to think how much money was lost right here in the harbor last night, an count up how many times it's happened in the last twenty years an probly will again, you'd still be better off."

Art, on hearing his pocketbook appealed to so solidly, looked uncertain and more than half convinced; but Aaron, watching him curiously, knew quite well that Art wasn't going to admit it in front of him.

"Ah," Art said, "big talk. I ain't got the time to stand around here listenin to you clapper-jaws. I got work to do. An by god, Gene," he added, remembering that he himself was paying Gene to stand around shooting off, "so've you."

After Art had gone bustling away with Gene in his wake, Aaron stood leaning against the sun-warmed red shingles listening to them have it over. Far below him, under the wharf, he could hear the lazy swell that was all that remained of yesterday's easterly, smashing in against the mussel beds. The sky was clean even of gulls except for one that quartered languidly upwind, its wings motionless, its head down, watching what went on beneath it on the flats. There was a faint smell of ripe fish in the air when he breathed deep and he grinned, thinking it was as small a thing as that that had kept him from being a fisherman now, that had kept him out of the spot most of these boys were in. The smell of bait had always made him sick, and still did when it was strong enough.

He looked half-asleep, but behind his squinted eyes he was doing some hard thinking. Maybe Russ was right, maybe he'd been right all along. Maybe a breakwater out there at the mouth of the harbor would be just enough to kill the force of the wind and waves that made a shrieking vortex of the narrow arm of water. They'd never know till they did something about it. The town could afford it. Art was right when he said it'd put them into debt for years, but if it made any difference in the way they were getting cleaned out every five years or so, it'd be worth it. He had opposed the breakwater from the very beginning, but when he thought it over coldly, he figured it was probably because Russ had been so hot for it.

He'd left his truck at the garage that morning to have the oil changed and now, still occupied with his thoughts, he said good-by and started off uptown on foot. When Aaron was halfway up the hill, Bill Martin got up unobtrusively from the crate he'd tipped back against the shed and followed him, coming up with him silently just after Aaron reached the main road.

"Godsake, Bill." Aaron glanced around, his face startled. "Whyn't you say somethin? I thought I was all alone. What'd you of thought if I'd started talkin to myself?"

Bill's smooth brown face cracked into wrinkles that rayed out from his eyes and mouth when he smiled.

"Probly thought you was no crazier than I *ever* did."

"Hunh," Aaron looked quizzical.

"That's no insult," Bill said sagely. "I've seen a lot of crazy men I'd trust sooner'n I would a lot of sane ones. You'd be surprised."

"I don't know whether I would or not," Aaron said. Then he shut up, waiting to see what Bill wanted. He knew Bill hadn't tailed him up the hill for nothing.

"Spose Russ put Gene up to startin talk about that breakwater again?" Bill said finally, looking straight in front of him.

"No, I don't believe so." Aaron sounded judicious. "What'd you *think* about that, anyhow, Bill?"

"Well, I tell you, it's beginning to make sense to me. I seen this same thing happen too often. Maybe we oughta do somethin about it before all the folks move away an start fishin out of some other harbor. They's smaller things than that turned better places into ghost towns. But, I dunno—it grizzles me to do anythin like that because Russ wants it."

"It'd really be for your benefit. He don't stand to get much good out of it."

"I know it—that is, I guess it would. But I been holdin off all these years just because he *was* so hot for it."

"I was thinkin just a minute ago," Aaron said, "I dunno but what that was my reason, too."

"That so?" Bill looked at him curiously. "I sort of figured Russ must see somethin pretty good for him in it or he wouldn't be so het up to start a job like that."

"D'you ever know him to be dishonest?" Aaron asked, coming out with it, point-blank.

Bill looked suddenly cautious, as if he were wondering how much he could say without getting himself into trouble.

"Don't worry," Aaron said. "What you say to me ain't goin any further. An I hope I can feel the same way."

"I ain't one to do much talkin as a rule," Bill said. "No, I don't know's I ever knew him to do anything you could call dishonest under the law—but he's had some pretty sharp dealings I guess. I never figured what he did to you could be called honest."

"For godsake," Aaron stared. "You mean that's still goin around? That was all of fifteen, twenty years ago."

"Well, you ain't forgot it, have you? A man'd do a thing like that to a friend, well, it don't take much to imagine what he'd do to somebody he didn't care nothin about."

23

"Well," Aaron began carefully, "no. I hadn't forgot about it. But I don't know's I let it bother me much now." A thing like that was hard to forget if it happened fifty years ago, no matter how long ago it happened, you didn't forget it, it just got dimmer and less important—but it still rankled.

"No, I don't let it bother me," he said. "I figure what's the use. It's over now and here we are, me an Russ, havin to work together a lot. It don't pay to let it bother."

"That's as may be," Bill said. "Maybe you don't. I don't care one way or the other. But I can tell you, it put me off Russ for good. I wouldn't trust him any further'n I can heave a bull by the tail."

"You feel *that* way," Aaron said, trying to sound no more than normally interested, "what makes you go on votin him back into office every year? You got a good chance of puttin him out an gettin in somebody you could trust."

Bill shrugged.

"He's been in there too long. Besides, I don't know's I *really* think he'd do anything. I go on votin for him, but it's just because I figure so many other people will anyhow, it wouldn't make no difference whether I did or not. And as long as he is First Selectman in spite of me, well, I'd just as soon be able to tell him to his face I voted for him."

"Ayeh," Aaron said. "I see just what you mean."

"Well," Bill said as if he'd got a load off his chest, "that's the way I feel about it. But I been thinkin this business about the breakwater over, Aaron. I just thought I'd tell you I was willin to jump either way you did."

"I'm glad to know that, Bill."

"Ayup," Bill said. Then, as if he'd never mentioned Russ, he started talking about the weather. "Looks like we was goin to have a late fall."

"I dunno." Aaron went through the customary procedure of looking at the sky—cloudless and dazzling blue—that tented up over the dark hump of the Ridge. Against that blue, the spruces, a mile or more away, looked close and separate as if they were cut out of metal and stuck against the sky. "Never can tell what the weather's goin to do here. Sometimes I wonder if the Ridge, stickin up like that, don't influence the weather we have, make it a little more finickin than weather other places."

"They say a lot of gun firing, big guns'll make the weather change," Bill said. "I wouldn't wonder a thing like the Ridge could, too." He glanced up at its whaleback soberly. "I should think you'd get nervous livin right under the damn thing the way you do, Aaron. How d'you know it ain't goin to come slidin down into your lap some day?"

Aaron laughed.

"It never slid down on my old man. If it held out on him I wouldn't be surprised it would on me."

"I shouldn't wonder. Looks solid enough, don't it."

The town began with a few scattered houses, each with its apple trees and barn and garden—solid and established-looking. The houses were closer together near the center of the village and the Ridge Road was an informal demarcation; beyond the turn the stores began: the yellow front of the dry-goods store, the red front of the A & P, the tan front of the drugstore. If all the stores had been gathered together they might have filled one city block. The largest building of all was the Masonic Hall, big and square and gray. It had three full floors and housed all the town offices as well as the rackety old auditorium where the junior and senior classes gave their school plays and where all other business and entertainment in town was conducted.

They passed the road that led to the Ridge in companionable silence and went on toward the drugstore. Aaron, glancing up, noticed the old Buick parked in front of the Masonic Hall and knew that Russ must be back in town.

"Say, speak of the devil," Bill said suddenly and they stood in front of the drugstore watching the tall figure come out of the Masonic building and climb into the big car. When Russ went by them, he was going slow and the old Buick, swaying and creaking like a genteel dowager, slowed still more. They saw his profile, heavy and sharp, before he turned to look at them and lift his hand. Bill raised his own hand in answer, but Aaron only jerked his head, keeping his hands in his pants pockets. The car picked up speed as it drew away from them.

"He must have driven all night," Aaron said thoughtfully. "Just got back from Augusta."

"Augusta, hanh? He go down pretty often?"

"Not very. Once or twice a year."

"Wonder why."

Aaron shrugged.

"Hnh," Bill said. He turned to go up to the post office. "I'll see you, Aaron," he said over his shoulder. Aaron, still thinking busily, stood watching him go.

It was nearly four-thirty that afternoon when Aaron drove his light pick-up up along the Ridge Road toward home. He parked the truck in the lean-to shelter he'd built on the side of his barn and started toward the house. There was a shadowy suggestion of dark in the still bright sky. The sun was down behind the Ridge and its long shadow lay deeply blue across the fields above the road, reaching almost to his feet as he stood there looking at it. He turned slightly, the half-turn necessary for him to look up the road toward Walls's. He could see the big white gable of the house clearly now that some of the leaves were gone off the huge chestnuts. As he always did, he remembered himself as a kid, playing on the back doorstep under those trees, waiting impatiently each fall for the first chestnuts.

He was hungry and, with the long nights setting in, he liked his supper early. When he went into the kitchen the room was empty but there were potatoes frying on the stove and he sniffed deeply. When she heard the shed door shut, his daughter came quickly into the kitchen.

"Hello, Pa," she said.

"Hi, Sis." Aaron tossed his cap at the hook behind the stove and to his amazement it hit just right and stayed there.

"Thought you'd be turning up pretty soon." She smiled at him and went over to the stove. For a moment Aaron stood looking at her with pleasure. He liked to watch her walk— she didn't hit hard on her heels the way most women did—and he noticed as he always did that she was really a good-looking girl.

Ralph came in from the barn with two brimming milk pails, set them down on the shelf that ran around one end of the kitchen level with the sink and, taking a glass from the cupboard, dipped it full from one of the pails. Aaron shuddered a little, watching him drink. Must be still warm—couldn't see how Ralph could do it; it would have made him sicker than a dog. Ralph emptied the glass and put it down. His face was red from the nip of the air and he had a mustache of milk along his wide curling upper lip.

"Good for you," he said. "Chock full of vitamins."

"Ralph, you stop," Annie said, "you won't want any supper."

"Well, I do, I want some right now," Ralph said fiercely. He grabbed the frying pan but she snatched it out of his reach. "I'm goin sportin tonight and I'm in a hurry."

"Mary Walls?" his father said.

"Ayup." Ralph sat down at the table, picking up his knife and fork, and stared at his sister until she gave up with a shrug, half-amused, half-testy, and fed him.

THE MOMENT Gene Walls set foot in the house that night he knew his father was home. There was no apparent evidence of Russ's appearance. His Buick was in the barn where Gene couldn't have seen it; Grace had long ago taken the overcoat from the newel post and hung it in the front closet; and there was nobody in the front rooms when Gene came in. But his over-sensitized mind felt the difference in the atmosphere of the house immediately. It felt as if a certain loose freedom had gone out of it. It felt tight and explosive, like a place that has stopped being geared for several people and is suddenly geared for one.

Gene went back out the front door noiselessly and around to the back. Everyone was sitting at the table when he went in and Russ looked up and nodded to him.

"Hello, son."

"Hi," Gene said. " 'D you have a good time?"

"So-so." Russ swallowed his mouthful and leaned back. "Kind of late, aren't you?"

"My regular time." Gene's voice was muffled in the towel. "You must have started supper early."

"I got hungry," Russ said.

Gene sat down without speaking. Grace smiled at him when she passed his loaded plate, but nobody else said anything. Russ had been the only one he hadn't seen that morning.

Russ finished first, got up and started for the living room and his paper, hoping to get away before Grace caught him and made him commit himself about Hat. She didn't bother to stop him, she just got up and came after him. When she got to the front room door, Russ was already sitting in his big chair with the paper in front of him; but somebody else had got to it first and it was so mixed up he couldn't find his way in it.

"Who the devil's been messin around with my paper?" He stared up at her truculently. "I never saw the beat of it. Isn't there anyone in this house can read a paper from front to back like a decent civilized human bein?"

"You might's well stop there," Grace said calmly. "You know you can't read it till you put your glasses on, anyway.

I wouldn't a let anyone touch it, but I didn't know you were comin today. Besides, I want to talk about Hat."

"What more is there to say?"

"Nothin for me," Grace said. "I've had mine. You say now whether or not you'd mind."

"Well, if that's all. I'd just as soon as not have her come here to live. I always liked Hat—guess maybe because she's a lot like you. How do the kids feel about it?"

"Why don't you go ask them? They're still in the kitchen."

Russ got up with an elaborate show of patience and went back out to the kitchen. Before he reached the door he could hear their voices having something over, but he knew they'd stop talking when he went in. They did. Gene was standing with one foot on the fire-box shelf, smoking a cigaret. When Russ came in, he reached down slowly and put the half-smoked cigaret into the stove.

"I should think you would," Russ said. "Don't you know those things aren't fit to smoke? My god, when I was your age, I was smokin a man-size pipe."

"Russ," Grace said behind him.

"Your Ma says I should ask you all what you think of havin your Aunt Hat come down here to stay. You're oldest, Gene, what d' you say?"

Gene looked down at his big hands, flexed the fingers once or twice, and said in a voice that sounded like an echo of Russ's own, "Well, I don't care."

"You mean you don't care to have her here?"

"No." Gene didn't look at his father. "I mean I don't mind havin her come. I always liked Aunt Hat."

"There's one," Russ said. He turned on Jake who was still sitting at the table beside Mary. "What about you?"

"As long as she don't snore, it won't bother me," Jake grinned.

"Well, Mary?" Russ said. "You're next."

"The emancipation proclamation," Mary said. "I've got a vote. Sure, let her come, we're still outnumbered."

Jake got up suddenly and walked over to stand looking out the window with the air of a man who doesn't want to be too close when the bomb goes off. Russ stared at her dangerously, but she kept her eyes down and there was no expression on her face. Finally he turned to Stanny with a nod.

"Well, Stanny?"

"Me?" Stanny said and, when Russ didn't answer, said quickly, "Yeah. Sure."

"I know how you stand, Nat," Russ said. "Guess I better go up and have a talk with Hattie. I hope you all remember she's got the biggest voice in this. It ever occur to you she wouldn't want to come?"

He went out the door, slamming it behind him, without waiting to see what Grace would have to say to that. Besides, he wanted some excuse to get out of the house. Those kids, he thought, what ails them? It bothered him to go into a room where his own children were and have them stop talking like that. It made it look like they were talking about him. They probably hadn't been, but he didn't like the way they stopped.

He forgot them, though, and his long thin lips quirked up into a smile as he went out to the barn for the Buick. He was thinking of the day when old lady Hanna had found out he wanted to marry Grace. The old lady hadn't ever been very tight-mouthed about anything. When she'd had something to say she came right out with it and if it was unpleasant that suited her all the more. She'd said then she couldn't see how he planned to support himself, much less a wife. He'd done better than that, Russ thought, and a good deal of his satisfaction could be traced to the fact that Mrs. Hanna had known for several years before her death that he was not only supporting Grace and his sizable family, but was also paying the bills of the Hanna household.

As soon as he'd gone out of the house, Mary got up from

the table and went over to Gene, holding her hand out, palm up.

"Cigaret please, Gene."

"Just because you're old enough to vote," Gene grinned, "that's no sign you're old enough to smoke, too."

He took the package out, though, and handed it to her. Mary lit her cigaret, holding the match for Jake who had decided there wasn't going to be an explosion and had come over just in time to get a cigaret from the pack before Gene snatched it away.

"Anythin for free, an I'm interested." He looked up at Gene through the smoke.

"What a bunch of panhandlers." Gene took his own light from the match.

"Three," Jake yelled, and blew, but he was too late. Gene leaned back triumphantly with the cigaret glowing.

"Thought that'd get a rise out of you."

Watching the three of them there, Grace had to smile. Gene was standing back to her squarely and it might have been Russ himself if he hadn't been so light. Jake and Mary were both tall enough, but Jake was so thick he didn't tower the way Gene did. Sometimes Grace thought it was a shame Mary was as tall as she was. You take a girl just a hair under six feet and there aren't many men who'll be able to top her. Sometimes she wished Mary hadn't shot up so, but there wasn't much you could do about a thing like that. They were three nice-looking kids, if she did say it. She stopped in the middle of the floor, a dish in each hand, and looked at them again. Behind her, her father snorted slightly.

"Thinkin what a good job you done?"

Grace didn't answer him, but she was smiling a little when she went into the pantry.

Nat and Stanny were alone at the table and Stanny, now that his father had gone out, was making up for lost time on the cake. He'd finished off three pieces and was reaching for his fourth when his grandfather stopped him.

"You still hungry, eat some more solid food," he said mildly. "Cake tastes good, but it'll give you pimples."

Stanny grinned, brought his hand back empty, and finished his glass of milk at a gulp. He had his cap on and was halfway through the door when Grace called to him from the pantry.

"Where you goin, Stan?"

"Just down to the movies."

"Well," Grace poked her head around the door to look him over. "You look decent? You get home right afterward, now."

"Ayup." Stanny's voice floated back through the closed door.

"These kids," Gene said. "They'll walk down there every night in the week to go to a movie. They have to have a bus to go to school, though. We never had a bus."

"You sure have had a hard life, Gene," Nat said. "I don't see how you ever lived to grow up, you've had it so hard."

"Leave that stuff to Pa." Jake glanced at his older brother. "You sound so much like him it ain't even funny."

"Who's got a better right?" Gene carried it a little further. "Why, when I was a boy, I got up at five o'clock and milked twenty cows before breakfast."

"Gene—" Grace's voice jerked their heads around toward her. It was so seldom she used that particular icily even tone that Gene knew he'd gone too far. "That's enough of that. You know I won't put up with it."

"I'm sorry, Ma," Gene said. He went out, grabbing his own cap from the hook. Outside the door he hesitated and came back, just sticking his head into the kitchen. "Guess I'll go down myself, Jake. Want to come?"

"Could you wait a minute till I shave?"

"You shaved once today," Nat said.

"I'll wait down by the road," Gene said. "Hurry up."

Jake disappeared, ignoring his grandfather. Mary and Nat,

alone in the kitchen listening to his pounding feet, looked at each other with amusement.

"Must have a new one," Nat said, speculatively.

"He always has."

There was a muffled crash from the second floor.

"My god," Nat said, "that boy's as graceful as a cow on ice. What you spose he's done now?"

"I've got to the stage," Grace said, coming out of the pantry, "where I just don't hear it any more. Time was I used to get duck bumps every time Jake was out of my sight. He never came back without a black eye or something. But I guess he's tough."

She started the dishes at the sink and Mary took a towel from the rack to help her. They were busily clearing away when Jake came back downstairs. He'd put on his best blue suit and his firm young face was bright red where he'd scraped it with a too-dull razor. When he went by them the smell of shaving lotion swept back like a veil behind him.

"Full grown man using perfume," Mary began in an accurate imitation of Russ's voice, before she thought and glanced quickly at her mother. Grace was looking down at the dishpan, but her mouth was shut tight and her cheeks were pink. Jake said something insulting over his shoulder to Mary and went out. After he'd gone there was silence, only the sound of dishes clattering in the soapy water.

Finally Mary, unable to bear it any longer, said, "I'm sorry, I didn't think."

"You kids," Grace started. "You do that altogether too much. The only thing is, I don't ever want him to hear you. I don't ever want him to know you mock him like that. Someday I'm afraid you're going to forget an do it in front of him—then I don't know what would happen."

"He'd just laugh," Nat said soothingly. "He wouldn't think nothin of it." `

They let it go at that, but each one of them, alone with his own conception of Russ which made him three separate people, knew that none of those three would just laugh.

THERE WASN'T room for Jake's Ford inside the barn what with Russ's two cars, so he kept her out in the field under the big old Red Astrakhan tree. He pounded out across the dead grass, piled into the rackety little roadster, and flung her down the driveway. She rattled to a stop at the intersection and Gene, who'd been waiting there, got in. He sat watching with amusement as Jake hauled the car out of the drive and started her down the Ridge Road toward the village.

"I should think drivin would make you tired," he said, grinning.

"How's that? Nothin to do but sit back."

"Way you go at it, I sometimes wonder if you don't forget there's an engine there to do the heavy work."

Jake, feeling a little foolish, relaxed in his seat.

"You—" He started to say something, hesitated, and then finished it. "You said anything to the old man yet?"

"What about?" Gene asked.

"About your leavin?"

"Fat chance I've had. The only time I see him was at supper."

"Well, you mentioned it to Ma?" Jake persisted.

"You know I haven't or she'd have said somethin to him an I don't want it to get to him second-hand. He'd just get mad before I had a chance to talk."

"What you goin to do if he gets mad anyway?" Jake wasn't looking at him. His eyes were glued to the road.

"I dunno," Gene shrugged. "I dunno but what I'm better off to stay right here till—"

"Till what?"

"What you so curious for anyhow?" Gene said sharply, knowing he'd said just what Jake had expected him to say.

"What bothers me," Jake said, ignoring Gene's show of temper, "is what's gonna happen to us. Here we are, the pair of us. You're twenty-five an I'm twenty-three. Anyone else's kids that old would have a place of their own, be supportin theirselves, maybe even be married. But what're we doin? Just sittin around lettin him take care of us. What're we gonna do when he passes out?"

"What d'you mean, lettin him take care of us? We're both workin, aren't we?"

"Yeah," Jake snorted. "We're both workin, but who're we workin for? Who pays me my wages? He does."

"Well, he don't pay mine," Gene said acidly.

"Maybe you think he don't." Jake's voice was casual. "You remember four years ago when Art built that addition onto the factory? Well, where d'you think he got the money? That was when Pa bought an interest in the business. You see what I mean?"

"That's a lie," Gene said. "Whoever told you that's a christly liar."

Jake shook his head.

"You probly wish he was."

"Is there anythin," Gene said bitterly, "in this whole damn town that he hasn't got a say in?"

"If there is," Jake said seriously, "I'd give a lot to know what it was. If there's any money in it, he's in it, too. Way it is with me, I got things figured out. I think I'm wise to stay where I am."

"How's that? You're in the same spot I am, far's I can see."

"Well, I stand to get somethin out of it." Jake fumbled for what he meant to say. "I figure, by rights, that the place'll come to me. He knows you ain't interested in it an I am. I put too much of me into it to back out now. Me, I get along with the old man a lot bettern'n you do. I figure I treat him square an he'll do the same by me—an besides, he can't live forever."

Startled, Gene looked at him thoughtfully. It was so seldom Jake said more than ten consecutive words that his talkativeness now was amazing in itself—but it surprised Gene to find out Jake had been doing some thinking about his own future. Somehow he hadn't expected Jake would.

"You, it's different," Jake said. "You ain't got anythin to hold you there. In your place, I'd get out—but fast."

RUSS COASTED the Buick to a stop in front of Hattie's house. There was a dim light in the kitchen and he went quickly up the path to the back door and went in without knocking. She was out in the shed and he stood waiting for her, towering in the middle of the room. When she came in Russ was struck again with her physical resemblance to Grace. They were both big women, but Hat hadn't gone as white as Grace had. There was still enough black in her hair to let you know what color it had been. She had a pail of water in each hand and Russ didn't move to take them. She smiled at him, put the buckets on the wooden shelf by the sink, and sat down.

"Well, Russ, see you're back."

"Ayup." He went over and sat down himself, in one of the straight chairs that stood beside the table.

"Have a good time?"

"Good's could be," he said. "I never take to cities much. Never go unless I have to."

"You feel the same way Pa does." Hat put up her hand to tuck the strands of loose hairs into the neat pug at the back of her head. "Whew! I ain't as young as I once was. Either that or the old cow's taken to drinkin twice as much."

36

"Hat, you ever thought of havin anyone here to help you, now your Ma's gone?" Russ thought he saw an opportunity to lead up to his subject.

"My lord!" She put back her head and laughed. "You talk as if poor Ma was any help to me. Why, I ain't doin no more now than I was when she was alive. Nor so much, when you come right down to it."

"Hmm. Well, at least she was company for you. It must be sort of lonesome here alone."

"What're you comin at, Russ?" She peered at him sharply. "I can always tell when you're havin an idea. It sticks out all over you. Now out with it."

"Hanh," Russ showed amusement in his characteristic snort. "I can't put anythin over on you, Hat. Never could. Well, me an Grace was talkin today. She's run afoul of the idea that you're lonesome here. Thinks you might like to come down an live with us. Maybe rent this place."

"Pity sake." Hat's mouth fell open in amazement. "I certainly don't know what give her *that* idea. *I* never did. For the lord sake, I'd go crazy not havin my house an my chores. I'd be back inside a week."

For a second disappointment held him silent. He'd started thinking about this proposition on his way up and the idea had come to be his own so that her refusal was a personal affront.

"Pretty independent, aren't you?" he said in the easily smooth tone he used only when he was angry. Hat recognized it and, knowing the reason, flushed slightly, but she didn't sound mad.

"I spose you mean I'm not in much of a position to be."

"Well, are you?"

"Maybe not right now. But you know perfectly well, Russ, if it hadn't been for Ma, I would be. I'd never of let you do as much as you have for us."

"Well," Russ said again. He was temporarily restored to

37

good humor and feeling pleased with himself, remembering how much he'd done for the Hannas. "I know that, Hattie. But I don't see quite what you plan to do. You can't live on here an keep up this place all alone, you know. And I'm afraid I can't see my way clear to maintainin two places much longer."

That'll get her, he thought triumphantly.

"I'm glad you brought that up, Russ," Hat began slowly. Her wide face, in the lamplight, looked thoughtful and not at all afraid. "I was wonderin how to tell you. I feel the same way. I don't want you to think you got to support me any longer. Now I've got more time to myself, I intend to do a lot of things."

"What for instance?" Russ's eyes seemed to fade a little under his heavy brows. "You plan to go out an get yourself a job in an office or somethin?" He said it deliberately trying to make her feel foolish. She smiled slightly and shook her head.

"No, I don't believe I'll try that yet, but I was thinkin. I've got the hens an the cow. What with the garden truck I can sell in the summer I can make out all right."

"What I'd like to know," Russ said angrily, "is where you think you're goin to sell enough stuff out of your garden to make anythin? Everyone here on the Ridge has their own garden."

"I made a deal with the peddler who comes around. He said he'd take all the fresh things I could spare." Pleasure in her own perspicacity and remorse at having to go against him mixed in her face.

"Well," he persisted, "that's next summer. What're you goin to do for money all winter?"

"I got about a hundred and fifty dollars," Hat said. "I been squeezin pennies."

Russ scowled heavily.

"I see you've got it all planned out. Without sayin ah, yes, or no to anyone."

"I thought you'd be pleased," Hat said. "I thought I'd get everythin fixed so I could tell you about it an you'd be pleased."

"It don't really matter to you whether I'm pleased or not, does it?" He got up and went over to stand staring down at the stove. He couldn't quite see why this whole thing was making him so mad. He couldn't understand why it bothered him so to have her go and do all this arranging without a word to him.

"Well, in a way it does," Hat said hesitantly, her eyes troubled. "I certainly didn't think it'd make you mad."

"I'm not mad."

"Well, after all you've done for us, Russ," she said, "I don't want you to think I don't appreciate what you've done. Why, if it warn't for you, I guess me and Ma would have lost the house long ago. I want to pay you back, too, as soon's I can."

"I don't want it," Russ said. "You don't owe me anythin."

He felt baffled as if, in some obscure way, she had betrayed him. And he felt flat and disappointed.

"Yes, I do, too. I owe you a lot an don't think I'll forget it."

"You don't owe me a penny," Russ said. He went over to the door quickly, trying to get out of the room before she could see how his face looked. He knew himself it must be twisted with his anger because it felt stiff and unreal. But he couldn't leave without saying something more to her. As he opened the door, he glanced back at her troubled face, pleased that at least she *was* troubled.

"Not a goddamned cent," he said distinctly, and went out shutting the door quietly behind him.

Russ was too disturbed to go home then and face Grace's inevitable questions. So he went downtown and spent the evening in his office clearing up the correspondence that had collected while he'd been away. Much later, and still angry, he locked the office door and headed for the Ridge.

The short drive home smoothed him out a little and he wasn't thinking of anything much when he put the car away and came back to the big rolling door to stand for a minute smelling the weather. There was a dampness in the air that had nothing to do with rain or fog—it was the feeling of fall. The big stars were brilliant and close-looking, so bright they almost shut out the smaller ones. To the west Russ could sense more than see the Ridge; and to the east, the falling away of land to the water. He liked the sensation he got from living on a little plateau between two extremes of country.

The brisk northwest wind had died as the sun went down and as he stood listening sounds came clearly to him through the windless dark. Somewhere down the road, a dog was howling mournfully; behind him in the chicken house the hens stirred restlessly; one of them made a querulous sound and settled down again.

When he went into the kitchen Grace was sitting at the table writing a letter and she looked up at him.

"Where have you been, Russ? I thought I heard the car five minutes ago."

"Some old curious, aren't you, missus? I've been smellin the weather."

"I thought maybe you'd taken up star-gazin in your spare time." She looked back at her letter, trying not to smile.

Russ started to lock the door, but she stopped him.

"You'd better leave it open. Gene and Mary haven't come in yet."

Russ glanced at the clock.

"It's twelve o'clock."

"I know it."

"Where the devil do they go, rantin all over this hour of the night?"

"Oh, Russ, pity sake, they're both old enough to take care of themselves. We don't have to go worryin about them."

"I'm not worryin about Gene," he said, "but what's a girl find to do this late? Everythin's closed up."

"Ralph came for her an they said somethin about goin to Freehold. There," she said as the car lights made an arc of brightness on the wall, "that must be them now."

"Ralph Billings?" Russ said before the door opened. Grace nodded as Mary came in. She stopped by the door, looking a little startled to find them both there waiting for her.

"What's the matter?" she said. "Anything wrong?"

"Not's I know of," Russ said. "Didn't take you long to say good night to your boy friend."

"He's not my 'boy friend,'" Mary said heavily.

"Probly gets mixed up an thinks you're his," Russ said. "You always wearin those pants."

Mary glanced down at her corduroy slacks. When she looked up again, she was smiling, her irritating, secret-looking smile, and Russ saw that he'd lost his momentary advantage.

"Ralph doesn't mind them," she said easily. "He hasn't mentioned it."

She went past her mother, touching Grace's shoulder lightly with one hand.

"Good night, Ma," she said and disappeared into the other room. Both Russ and Grace were silent, listening to her go up the stairs to her bedroom. When the door shut behind her, Russ sighed heavily. Grace lifted her head.

"It's every bit your own fault," she said tartly. "Seems to me you ought to be able to get along with your own kids."

"I get along all right."

"Trouble is, you're all too much alike," Grace said as if he hadn't spoken. "You're all pig-headed an stubborn and every one of you cut off'n the same pattern. Sometimes you make me so mad I could yell."

"Bedtime," Russ said. He went out, leaving Grace to ad-

41

dress her envelope before she turned out the light and followed him up the front stairs.

When she went into the bedroom, Russ was in bed and at first she thought with amazement that he was asleep and wondered how he could drop off like that. When she got in beside him, she realized suddenly—she didn't know quite how because he didn't move—that he wasn't asleep. He was just lying there waiting to talk to her about something.

"Russ?" she said uncertainly.

"Yeah."

"Did you go to see Hat?"

"Yes, I did." The explosion of his voice made her jump slightly. "And of all the damn fool stubborn women, she takes the cake. Do you know what she told me?"

"How could I?"

"She said," Russ began, "she said she'd rather stay up there an support herself sellin eggs than come down here and live with us. That's your sister for you."

"Oh, Russ, I don't believe she said anythin like that," Grace said easily. "That don't sound like Hat to me. She knows how much you've done for her these last years. I don't believe she'd say that."

"Well, maybe she didn't in so many words. That's what it amounted to, though. She's goin to stay there."

"I don't know's I'm awfully surprised." Grace sounded thoughtful. "Hat always was an independent soul. I guess she just doesn't want to be beholden to you for any more than she is."

"Well, why not, that's what I can't see. I'm willin to give her a good home. She's gettin along. She's not goin to be able to work the way she does forever."

"I don't believe she ever thinks about that."

"She ought to," Russ said sharply. "I can tell you, when she does an comes beggin to me, there's goin to be a lot said."

"I don't know's she ever will come beggin to you, Russ.

42

Not after tonight if you talked to her the way you're talkin to me." Grace turned over heavily. "I don't see why you're lettin a little thing like that bother you so," she said. "It's not really as important as all that, is it?"

"I spose not," Russ said reluctantly, seeing that he was letting his impotent and surprising anger betray him. He lay there in silence for a moment, then began on something else.

"How long's she been goin around with him, anyhow?"

Grace groped for a moment before she came up with the meaning of what he'd said.

"Ralph? Oh, they've been runnin around together since they were both knee-high. You know that, Russ."

"I don't either," he said angrily. "If I knew it, I wouldn't ask you, would I? You think it's serious?"

"I never stopped to think about it," she told him. "I figured if it was, Mary'd tell me sooner or later."

"Well, I don't know's I think much of it."

"Ralph's a nice boy," Grace said defensively. "Nothin extra maybe, but he's a good boy an you needn't go off half-cocked about it just because he's Aaron Billings's boy, neither. You've known for a good long time that Gene and Annie Billings were thinkin about gettin married and you've never had a thing to say against that."

"Gene never seems to get any furtherer in his thinkin," Russ snorted.

"No hurry," Grace said gently. "They're all young yet. I'll be just as happy if they *don't* all get married as soon's they're old enough."

"Just the same, it's different with a girl," Russ said. "I just as soon have Gene marry Annie. She's always looked like a good solid one to me. But I don't know's I think much of Mary goin around steady with this Ralph. Got a good mind to speak to her about it."

"Oh, go to sleep, Russ," Grace said. "You don't know any-

43

thin against him, do you? Well, then, go to sleep. Just forget about Hat an you'll feel better about everythin else."

"What d'you mean?" Russ reared up on his elbow to see her, but Grace wouldn't answer him and presently he heard her breathing grow steady and knew that she wasn't going to say anything more.

RUSS, sitting alone in his inner office, heard somebody come in through the outer door and speak to the girl. Then her high voice said something, and immediately afterward, Aaron Billings tapped on the inner office door and came in. He was wearing his overalls and a heavy gray wool work shirt. He had a limp cap thrust so far back on his head that the cracked visor pointed straight up.

Russ looked up from his desk and nodded shortly.

"Sit down, Aaron. Be right with you."

He had been writing a letter and he kept on with it. In the stifling airlessness of the close little room, the scratching of the old pen he used was loud. He drove it across the plain white paper with the whole force of his big fist behind it. Once the pen spluttered and the point went through the page. Russ said "Dammit." Finally he signed his name, folded the letter, and stuffed it into the envelope he had addressed and ready. Then he leaned back in his chair and looked at Aaron over the flap of the envelope; the unoiled swivel squeaked protestingly under him.

"Well, Aaron." He put the envelope on his desk and rubbed his closed fist once or twice along the sealing. "What can I do for you?"

"Like to talk to you if you ain't too busy," Aaron said. He hadn't bothered to take off his cap and he was leaning back in his own chair, his knees crossed. Somehow he managed to give the impression that he'd never before found such a comfortable chair as the rickety old golden oak one he was sitting in now.

"Sure," Russ said. "I've always got time. This business or pleasure?"

Aaron grinned a little.

"Probly both," he said. "First for me, the last for you."

"Sounds interesting."

"Yeah. Well, I tell you. I been thinking."

"About what?"

"You still interested in getting that breakwater?" Aaron said.

"You know as well as anyone how I been workin these last few years to get folks to see the need of building one," Russ said and stopped there, as if it weren't necessary to say anything more. But when Aaron started to speak, he added, "I know, too, it's your influence as much as anyone's kept it from goin through. That right?"

"Yeah," Aaron nodded. "That's right. I always figured it was too expensive, a project like that in a town this size. But, well, I'd be willin to withdraw my objections next time you bring it up."

For a moment the two men sat in silence regarding each other cautiously over the cluttered desk top. Aaron's face was a perfect blank and Russ's might have been a mirror. They were almost like two tomcats, waiting to see which way the other would jump. Then Russ, beginning to visualize the ramifications of what Aaron had just said, started to feel the expansiveness that always gave him confidence when he'd won a point. The expansiveness in this case was greater because the point was one he'd been belaboring for years and had never expected to have solidified for him in this particular manner. Here was a straightforward offer of support and, so far as he could see, an honest one—although it came from a man whom he had recognized as his enemy. Momentarily, the enmity was

45

replaced by something that was almost gratitude, something part relief at having won, and smacking a little bit of loss because his good fight was dying. But the gratitude won out.

Maybe he's not such a bad guy, Russ thought; and then he remembered that he actually disliked Aaron only because he had once done him what might have been interpreted as a wrong. After all, Aaron was the one to feel inimical; and here was Aaron man enough to come forward and admit he'd been wrong. Well, Russ thought, if he can do it, I can.

His thoughts must have reflected themselves a little in his face because he could see Aaron begin to relax.

"I think you're bein smart," Russ said easily. "And there's somethin to be said, too, from your point of view."

"How's that?"

"Well, this is what I mean," Russ began slowly. "You're the only contractor in town big enough to put in a bid on a job like that. Course, there'd be bids from out-of-towners, too; but you'll admit anyone here would be more apt to want to see you get that job. Ever think of that?"

"Good god, yes," Aaron said. "I've thought of it ofen. But I always thought, too, it was a pretty big job."

"Well, you could handle it, couldn't you? You just have to consider all the angles." Russ picked up his pen and started raying out strokes on the corner of the aged blotter he'd been unable to find a moment ago. "I know I'd be one would rather see you get it than some company from out of town, providing, of course, you could submit a bid that was reasonable."

"When you stop to think, that puts a different light on the matter, don't it?" Aaron said.

"Thought it might." Russ waited.

"Well, what you want me to do about it?"

"*I* don't want you to do *anything*," Russ said. "You just go ahead the way you planned—that's all. After that, it's up to the Selectmen."

"Ayup," Aaron said. For a moment there was a dispirited beaten air about him, but it disappeared as he looked up. "Yeah, all right, Russ. And thanks."

"Don't thank me." Russ waved his hand. "If you're interested, there'll be a special town meeting soon's we can call it."

"I'll be there, all right."

"Hanh." Russ made the nasal snort of sound through his big nose that meant he was pleased and threw himself backward in the whining chair. "I knew you'd see it my way some day, Aaron. Since the storm the other day I'm pretty sure a good *many*'ve come to see it my way. It's only good sense. Besides, havin work goin on, too, makes the place look prosperous."

He got up and came around the desk and Aaron, refusing to let Russ look down at him, stood up, too.

"You get your bid in when the time comes," Russ said. "See it's a good one, not to steep. It'll have a good chance for my vote and a lot of others, too."

Aaron smiled and nodded.

"Come along down to the drugstore," Russ said. "I'll buy you a coke."

As they went through the other office, Russ grabbed his hat off the rack and glanced at his secretary.

"Dunno when I'll be back. Soon's you finish up what you're doin, you can go home."

She nodded and sat listening to their heavy feet creaking down the narrow staircase. Her sharp, pastily wan face was topped by a cap of perfect bright curls, each one like a little snail. She sat tapping the smooth top of her typewriter table with nails, each one of which protruded a quarter inch beyond the tip of the finger, each one a shining bloody shell.

Florence Rice had a normal curiosity, she liked to know what went on around her. If she hadn't been so aware of Russ's distaste every time he looked at her, or if she hadn't known she owed her job to the fact that her father, now dead

47

a year, had been a good friend of Russ's, she wouldn't have tried to satisfy that curiosity with abnormal intensity.

She got up and went over to the hall door, opening it a crack. She heard the heavy front door of the building, two stories down, swing shut. By moving quickly into Russ's office, she caught a glimpse of the backs of the two men as they crossed the road and disappeared into the drugstore. She knew enough of the gossip in the village to know there was no love lost between them, and she knew, too, that in her year here in this office, Aaron Billings had seldom come into it.

She went back to the door and glanced cautiously into the outer office to make sure she was alone and that the hall door was still open so she could hear anyone coming up the stairs. Then she crossed to Russ's desk and stood staring down at the mass of papers, but there was nothing there she hadn't seen before and nothing that explained Aaron's visit.

Back at her desk, she put her typewriter away, and went rapidly down the stairs and out the back door so Russ, in the drugstore across the street, wouldn't know she'd gone as soon as he was out of sight.

NOBODY but Aaron Billings would ever know what his afternoon had cost him. Having to go to Russ and, in honesty, admit his own mistake—he would as soon have gone to the Devil for the same reason. Russ left him at the corner late in the afternoon and Aaron, climbing into his own truck, noted with particular awareness the difference between the worn old leather seat and the soft plushy feel of Russ's Buick.

For a while that afternoon, standing on the shore looking out over the proposed site of the breakwater, the two men had reached a closer accord than they had ever known before. It was partially because they each had a deep feeling for the place; each in his way felt as strongly about the land and the town and the harbor, and for a moment they had been more nearly in communication, nearer a ground where they could meet each other equally.

Under the spell of Russ's expansiveness, Aaron had felt good, responsive, pleased about what he'd done. But now Russ, and Russ's voice, and Russ's words were in his memory and Russ himself had gone, and Aaron felt the spell slipping. Looking back on that afternoon, he saw that he'd let himself fall for it again. Russ had always been able to talk circles around him; sometimes Aaron wondered if Russ's mind just moved faster than his, or was it only his tongue. But anyhow, with Russ gone, he began to think clearly again.

Even after the way I know him, he thought, he could talk me into anything now. I'd just go ahead and let him. Quite suddenly, and because of his own inability to withstand Russ's persuasiveness, his old hatred boiled up in him more strongly than it had for years. Remembering Russ's talk this afternoon, his outgoingness, Aaron remembered clearly a time when he had talked and Russ had listened and what the result of that had been.

In the back of his mind, Aaron had been keeping for years now a memorandum that read: Someday I'll get him.

I'd like to, he thought resentfully; I'd give my eyeteeth to get him. But what do I do? Stand around and nod and agree with him like a fool while he talks.

Suddenly the words made a pattern just inside his eyes. I talked a long time ago and he listened and he got me. This time, he talked and I listened.

What did he say? What had he been saying all afternoon? Maybe he spilled a little too much.

Now he was beginning to recall actual phrases Russ had used, actual words. And they could sound dangerous.

'You're the only one in town could put in a bid on a job as big as that.'

49

'Anyone here would be more apt to want to see you get that job.'

'It'll have a good chance for my vote, and a lot of others.'

"By the lord harry," Aaron said, his own voice loud enough to make him jump. "By the lord harry, I bet I got him."

He hadn't noticed the actual words much when Russ had been saying them to him because he knew Russ well, recognized that expansiveness, that good fellowship. He knew that particular mood of Russ's that made him spill a sort of pseudo-political double talk—made him say things that didn't mean any more than if he'd said, 'It's a fine day.'

But, Aaron thought, if I was to repeat those words to somebody else, with *my* expression, it'd sound bad, awful bad. He grinned, and on his pleasant face, the grin wasn't nice. You have to be patient, he was thinking. If you're patient, sooner or later you get your chance. By god, I believe this's mine.

When he reached the house, he found Mary Walls sitting in the kitchen talking with Annie. She was usually somewhere around but he couldn't recall having seen her lately. Having in mind the idea that had just come to him, it was hard for him to look her in the eye, but he did it, and carelessly, casually.

"You're quite a stranger, ain't you?" he said.

Mary nodded, smiling at him the way you smile at a person you like.

"I've been busy."

"Ain't got a job, have you?" Aaron who had heard Russ's views on working women often enough to know them well was frankly interested. Mary, reading accurately from his face what he was thinking, grinned wryly and shook her head.

"Nothing like that. I have to provide my own amusement."

"I've often wondered what you girls find to do with your time." Aaron looked from one of them to the other. "Me, I'd go crazy with nothin more to do than you have. I spose you spend a lot of it, though, sittin around gossipin." He hesitated and then added with conscious gallantry, "I mean durin the day, of course. Come night, a couple of good-lookin girls like you, I guess you find your time pretty well taken up."

"We-ell," Mary drew the word out, rising without effort and through habit to the lure, knowing what was expected.

Aaron, satisfied that his social obligations had been fulfilled, took the morning paper from the table, glanced at the head-lines, nodded again, and disappeared into the other room.

"What *do* you do with your time, anyhow?" Annie said, crossing over to sit in the chair at the other side of the table. Mary could see her face, in deep shadow and accentuated high light, looking at it across the flame of the lamp.

"Oh, you know. I've told you how I spend it mostly. Out in my Aunt Hat's shed." Mary lit a cigaret and sat watching the smoke coil up through her fingers. "I can't tell them what I'm doin, though. Either Pa would have a fit and fall into it, or decide I'd gone completely crazy."

"Well," Annie said. She picked up a sock from the basket that stood waiting beside her and thrust her balled fist into the leg. It came out through the toe, having met no resistance whatsoever. "There," she said, and held it up for Mary's in-spection. "That's Ralph for you. Honestly, I never in all my life saw anythin like the way that boy goes through his socks. Now you can see what you'll be in for." She said the last few words tentatively, watching Mary's face as she spoke, and finding no change of expression there.

"In for?" Mary looked over at her blandly.

"Well," Annie bridled slightly. "After all, when you marry a fellow you have to expect to darn his socks for him."

"I never said anythin about marryin Ralph."

"Foof! You two think you're pretty smart. Never lettin on anythin. You can't fool me, though. All I have to do is look at Ralph's face when he's with you. I've known him long enough to know."

Mary sighed slightly and looked away from Annie's curious

eyes. This was a familiar conversational gambit and in return she was expected to say something about Gene. It was a more serious form of the teasing that high school kids did, she thought. It was like a couple of sophomore girls getting off in a corner to decide to their own personal satisfaction who was the best looking boy in the class. She supposed, although she didn't know, that Gene and Ralph must occasionally bandy the same sort of half-teasing, half-serious banter. It seemed to her sometimes that every personal relationship she had, no matter how slight, was based in some degree on that preoccupation with sex that Annie's intent eyes revealed. It's not me as a person she wants to talk to, Mary thought; it's just me as my brother's sister. I can't sit here and talk to her about *things*, I have to talk about people—and she understood what Aaron meant when he said they sat around gossiping. In a way, that was exactly what they did, only they gossiped about themselves.

"Of course," Annie went on a little tightly, "when you *do* have to spend your time mendin socks and doin housework, you won't find much time to fiddle around with pictures. Besides, I don't think Ralph would think much of it, if he knew."

"Well, he doesn't know, does he?" Mary could feel her determined smile beginning to slip a little. "The only way he could find out would be for you to tell him and you gave me your word you wouldn't."

"I know it." Annie bit off a thread and the little snap of its taut parting was loud in the quiet room. "I did. But if I thought it was havin a bad effect on you, I don't know but what I'd break my word. For your own good."

"What on earth are you talkin about?" The smile was gone now. The look Mary turned on her made Annie flush a little. "I don't think I understand what you're talkin about."

"I mean," Annie looked beleaguered, "artists are usually queer. I'd hate to see you gettin that way. Or gettin to think you were too good for the rest of us. I'd hate to see Ralph get hurt."

"Look." Mary stood up suddenly and she could feel the corners of her composure begin to slip. "I don't know what you're drivin at, Annie, but whatever it is, I wish you'd come right out with it instead of hintin around like this. And besides, how on earth d'you know artists are queer and who said I *was* one? And what d'you mean, gettin to think I'm too good for the rest of you?"

Annie looked a little startled when Mary got up, and it made her feel small to sit and look up the way she had to to see Mary's face. For a moment, seeing it heavy and foreshortened, almost as if it threatened her, she felt frightened, but something drove her on to say what had been bothering her.

"Well, you take this summer. You haven't been near us all summer. But we're plenty good enough for you now your ritzy summer friends've gone." Her smile was friendly, but there was enough half-concealed resentment behind the words to make them come out sharply.

Mary went slowly over to the window and stood looking out into the windy darkness. She'd been on the verge of losing her temper, but she wasn't any more. It was as if she could feel that cold wind pouring over her, smoothing her down; she could imagine herself out in it, how it would be like a great black river of cold pouring down out of the northwest, over the silvered spruces of the Ridge, having the smell of winter and of ice. She stood thinking how far it must have come and over what land. It seemed to her she could sense the land going north from her, and the way it must be hard and clean and cold—dark mysteries of land under the moon, looming, lost, forbidden, field after wood-surrounded field with the frost-stiffened grass brittle under the pads of rabbits. She thought of the deer feeding on frost-crisp apples in the deserted orchards, their horns clicking against the low-growing boughs, the way they tossed their heads to sift the scent of danger from the friendly wind. The night was cold and clean and inhuman and what was she doing here, looking out at it through glass.

She had forgotten Annie so completely that her voice, coming a little harshly, made her jump.

"It's true, isn't it? We weren't good enough for you when you could hobnob with your summer people. And I don't know anyone who's said the things you have about *them*."

"Why, no." Mary turned slowly to face her. "No, it's not true."

"I certainly didn't see you bringin any of your fine friends around here."

"*That's* true." Mary began to smile a little because she couldn't help herself. It was suddenly so obvious just what was wrong with Annie. "I didn't. Mostly because I didn't have any 'fine friends.' There was just one and she wasn't what you mean when you say that."

"She was too good for us."

"Ralph liked her," Mary said, unable to resist the temptation, her eyes on Annie's face. "Ralph thought she was nice."

"I—" Annie started to speak, then realized what Mary had just said and shut her mouth tight before she opened it again. "Hmph, he never said anything to me about meeting her. I don't believe he ever did."

"Well, he did," Mary shrugged. "Probly figured it wasn't anythin to say anythin about."

"You heard from her since she went away?"

Mary shook her head.

"I thought so! That's the way they all are and you might as well find it out. You never meant anythin to her. They come here and take up with somebody amusin, that's all. They pretend to be friendly as anythin, to think you're just as good as they are, but once they go away, they forget about you just as if you'd never lived. You'll never hear from her again, you mark my words."

"Well, so what?" Mary's face was expressionless, but she'd begun to seethe under the surface. "What of it? I don't see what you've got to get so excited about. You certainly won't be the one to lose out by it if I don't. So why get excited?"

"There you go." Annie drew her yarn tautly and with neat exactitude across a gaping hole. "You certainly have developed a temper the last little while; sometimes I wonder how Ralph stands it. I guess you're different with him."

"Ralph," Mary said. "Ralph, Ralph, Ralph. Sometimes I think that's all you ever think about. Ralph or Gene and what they think and how they feel. Sometimes I get so goddamned sick and tired of hearing about Ralph and about Gene that I could howl."

"Your language certainly hasn't improved much, either." Annie looked up at her judiciously.

"Well, what's wrong with it? D'you mean Ralph wouldn't like that, either?"

"If you're going to come down here just to be unpleasant," Annie said, "why, you might as well go home. I don't have to sit here in my own house and be talked to like that."

"Oh, honestly," Mary said. She stood for a moment in the middle of the floor groping for words and not finding any. "Honestly," she said again and turning went out the entry door and closed it carefully behind her.

There, she thought, thrusting her hands into her windbreaker pockets and starting off up the road with a deep sense of relief—relief to be out and away from it. I've done it again. It seems as if I couldn't go into that house without ending up fighting with her and over the silliest things, too. Will you tell me what difference it makes who I know and she doesn't?

And besides, if it was Ralph or Gene who tried to paint, they'd have the pictures out in the parlor and the whole family'd gather around to exclaim and say how wonderful. Because it's me and I'm a girl, it's a waste of time and I ought to be darning socks.

55

It wasn't true and she knew it—if either Ralph or Gene had felt like painting a picture, he'd have been ashamed to admit it, much less expose the finished product to the possible ridicule of his family; but she was so angry it suited her to be put upon. Resentment of everything boiled up in her like sand in a spring.

She was too angry to go, as she'd planned, miles along the road, coming back late at night along the moon-shadowed side of the Ridge. She was too mad to do anything but go home and go to bed. She stamped up the drive and into the kitchen. Gene was sitting at the table reading and he looked up at her with sleep-heavy eyes, squinting to make her out.

"Hi, Toots," he said, choosing unfortunate words, "you look madder than a wet hen."

"Well, I am," Mary said, "and it's all your goddamned fault."

Grace appeared in the door of the pantry like an affronted fury.

"Mary Walls!"

Mary glared at her, said "Ha" loudly, and disappeared into the dining room. Gene looked at his mother, his face blank with amazement.

"Pete sake," he said. "What d'you spose ails *her*, hah?"

"I certainly don't know," Grace said. "Maybe she had a fight with Ralph."

Luckily Mary had been going fast enough to be well out of earshot by the time her mother had explained the burst of temper to her own satisfaction.

She had gone up the stairs two at a time, slammed her bedroom door behind her, and flung herself down on the bed with a jounce that made the springs jangle alarmingly.

There was really another basis for her temper—she had begun to think herself some of the things Annie had put into words. It did seem as if Lucy might have taken the trouble to write at least a post card—unless she was the way Annie had made her out, just another summer person looking for something to take up her time. But somehow Lucy hadn't seemed like that.

Lucy had been a piece of luck. She'd come wandering along the shore one morning and Mary hadn't heard her until she'd looked up to find Lucy standing behind her obviously looking over her shoulder and apparently not at all embarrassed about being caught at it. Instinctively, Mary'd grabbed at the canvas panel she had dropped against a rock and her hand had smudged it badly.

"Now, it's too bad you did that," Lucy'd said. "Anyone with half an eye can see what you're doing and you might just as well have left it there and let me have a good look at it."

"I—I didn't hear you coming."

"I took care you wouldn't. I thought probably you'd do something as childish as that. You look pretty much the sulky sort. I thought I'd sneak up on you and then you went and did it anyway."

"Well, I'll be—" Mary began, anger overcoming embarrassment.

"Tst. There. I didn't mean to make you mad." Lucy grinned and suddenly the foxiness of her face disappeared and it was warm and friendly looking. "Don't go flying off now. Be sensible and stick it back up there till I can get a good look at what you've left of it."

Surprised at herself, Mary had done as she was told. She propped the panel up against its original rock and stood back, her eyes on Lucy's face. The face was noncommittal now and there was no way for Mary to know what this peculiar stranger was thinking. She moved back slightly and then she just stood there looking. Once she indicated a sharp-angled shadow and said, "What made you make that line so dark?"

"I don't see why I shouldn't?" Mary said stiffly.

"No reason at all." Lucy's momentary stare had been surprised. "I just wondered."

"That's the way it looked."

"Well, I don't know any better reason."

After that she'd kept still until Mary could stand it no longer and said, "Well?"

"What d'you want me to say?" Lucy turned to face her.

"I don't know. What're you thinking?"

"That's a dangerous question to ask anybody. If I said it was good you'd know I was a perfect damn fool. It's crude, and unfinished, and fumbling."

Crushed beyond all reason, Mary stood staring at the painting. She couldn't even look at the woman who'd just said aloud what she'd been thinking herself.

"Here, wait a minute. For the love of god, don't look like that. If you just painted that picture there, you know perfectly well everything I've just said's the truth," Lucy said. "But, look here, I'll say this, too. Your way of using your color is interesting. You ought not to look as if I'd hauled your sky down on top of your head. You ought to look pleased. There's hope for you if I can find *one* good thing about it."

Mary took a cigaret out of her shirt pocket and lit it with shaking fingers.

"You don't think much of yourself, do you?"

For a surprised instant, Lucy stared, then she began to laugh.

"Ha," she said. "A spark. Well, I'll tell you. There's no reason why I shouldn't. I've spent thousands of dollars I couldn't afford and as many hours learning how to make that opinion a valid one. And I've done it, too. But, of course, there's no reason for you to admit its validity. For all you know, I may be one of these crack-pot maiden ladies who go around painting seascapes on scallop shells."

"Maybe you are." Mary's face had looked sullen and hostile and her eyes had taken on the cold look her father's always had when he was displeased.

"Well, I'm not." Lucy smiled again and quite suddenly Mary had felt her anger run out of her. "My name is Lucy Simmons and I make my living doing that." She jerked her thumb at the offending painting. "Only better. Or I couldn't live on it, see? What's your name?"

"Mary Walls." Mary let it go at that.

"Well," Lucy made a beckoning gesture with her hands. "Come on. Give. What do you do? How do you do it?"

"Me? I don't do anything," Mary remembered saying. "I don't do anything but sit around and wish I was somewhere else."

"Oh, like that?" Lucy raised an eyebrow. "Married?"

Wondering why she wasn't offended at questions like these from a total stranger, Mary shook her head.

"I thought not," Lucy said. "From what I've seen of the married women in this town, they don't find much time to sit around on the shore trying to paint. Got a job?"

Mary shook her head.

"Well, if you won't tell me, you won't," Lucy said. She turned back to the picture and then, as if the idea had stung her, spun back again. "Walls!" she said loudly. "Walls. I see a great light. I'll bet you dollars it was your father who rented me that little shack I'm staying in at what I might say was an exorbitant price. Big man. Huge. Six feet two or three. Sort of drawly talker until he gets interested. Eyes that feel like icicles. Your father?"

"That's Pa." Mary had to grin a little at hearing Russ so pinned down.

"Ha. I'll bet he doesn't know how you spend your time, my girl. Not if the way he looked at my paraphernalia was any indication."

"All right," Mary said. "You can stop there. Keep it up and you'll know more about me than I do, myself."

"I doubt it very much," Lucy said, but it seemed to Mary that her eyes were nearly as sharp as Russ's, although a good deal more friendly. Somehow that made it an unoffensive sharpness.

The second time she'd seen Lucy it was as if they'd known each other forever. The third time Lucy had invited her down to the rough shack in the young spruce growth along the shore a little to the south of the fish wharf to look at the things she'd been doing that summer. Seeing them had given Mary an altogether new attitude toward Christian Ridge; it was like seeing her home for the first time. They were, for the most part, landscapes; but there were a few she couldn't put a word to. A grotesque piece of driftwood with nothing behind it but a stylized sea and sky; a rough tor of granite, red and huge, with that same background; a perfectly round pink stone, sea-washed and smooth, on sand with a strip of kelp cast up alongside it and the tracks of some sea bird wandering across the sand.

Lucy had found her staring at them fascinated.

"I was just trying to illustrate a theory of mine," she said. "It's not so much what you put in, but what you leave out, that makes a thing interesting."

She'd laughed, too.

"It's not these that keep me in bread and butter, though."

The way she'd produced the paintings, matter-of-factly and with perfect confidence, had been a revelation to Mary. She could never have done it—her instinctive grab at the wet panel that first day had shown her that.

"Well, now you've seen these, how about showing me what you've done besides that one I saw the other day?"

"I wipe most of them out," Mary said, feeling the beginnings of nervousness. "I couldn't show them to anyone. I wish to god I had your confidence."

"I'll tell you something that might help you out," Lucy said. "I really don't have it myself. But I've spent a good many years convincing myself I'm good. I find when other people sense what's apparently self-confidence, pretty soon they'll begin to think there's something in it and decide maybe you're right. See what I'm trying to say?"

"Well, maybe."

"I'll tell you what. Why don't you trail around with me a while? Try to paint with somebody else around. Besides, I'd like to see how you do what you do."

"I couldn't," Mary said shortly, knowing that she wanted nothing more than to say she would. "Not with you knowing enough to do that."

"If you're going to be like that, I don't want you. But you'd better try it once just to see what happens."

"Would you show me how you paint that way?"

"No," Lucy'd said. "I won't. And you let me catch you trying to copy my style and I'll drop you like a hot potato. If there's some technical thing you want to know enough to ask me, I'll tell you if I can. But style's a thing that belongs to *you*. In the first place, I've worked a long time for mine. In the second, you've got one of your own, even if it is unformed. For pete sake, don't be ashamed of anything that's as much your own as that is."

That summer had been a queer time, a tantalization and a fulfillment. Lucy refused to volunteer any information, but if Mary asked her for something, it was always there and the little she learned to ask for seemed to make her see only how much more there was to know and how little of it she had suspected. It seemed to her that she was suddenly awake after having slept all her life. It was like finding new miraculous eyes that saw through things instead of bouncing off the surface. She began to see skeletal form instead of mere outline and found her hand even less competent when she discovered the difference between the two.

In early October, Lucy had gone.

"Let me know," she'd said, "when you decide to come to New York."

"What makes you thing I'm coming? And where'll I get

61

the dough?" Mary had scowled, seeing the end of a blissful summer and knowing quite well she'd never see nor hear of Lucy again.

"You'll come," Lucy had said. "Someday something'll happen and you won't be able to help yourself. As for the money, you'll beg, borrow, or steal. But you'll come."

Money, Mary grinned without amusement, a mere drawing back of her lips. Pa'd probably *give* me a *house* if I got married—but money to go and learn how to paint? Ha! I suppose I ought to have the gumption to earn it myself, but there's nobody here would give me a job, knowing him. And I wouldn't dare take it if they would.

GENE kept telling himself he was several kinds of a fool to let anything Jake said bother him as much as he was letting it. Before you can let a man's opinion bother you, Gene thought, you've got to have some respect for the man; and his feeling for Jake was far from respect. It might even have been contempt if he hadn't felt sneakingly that he had to like Jake because they were brothers.

During the few days Russ had been in Augusta, Gene's resolve had gone out of him. He had basked in the freedom of his father's absence and let himself be lulled into that old familiar and very young feeling of security, of everything-will-turn-out-all-right-if-you-just-let-it-alone.

But the minute Russ came back the security vanished, leaving Gene so aware that everything wouldn't be all right that he was completely incapable of trying to find his way out of the mess. It was going some, he thought, when you couldn't live in the same house with your own family, not and be comfortable; when you went around feeling as if the floor under your feet had turned into egg shells. And what's the way he felt.

Then, on top of everything, Jake, who never saw anything beyond the end of his nose, had had to go and have a streak of intuition, and had said just what was needed to set off Gene's already tight nerves.

He couldn't seem to get the words out of his mind. "Anyone else's kids that old would have a place of their own," Jake had said. And he'd said it just at the time when Gene had been ripe for it. He held on to it, kept hearing it over and over. And each time Jake's heavy young voice got heavier, older, more accepting, until it seemed to Gene he could hear the way Jake would sound twenty years from now when he said the same thing. Only then Jake would say the words the way you said, "It's a fine day," evenly and without really hearing yourself say it.

At the end of the week, he was still skittering around in his mind, trying to screw his courage to the point of telling the old man he wanted to get married, to go away, to get out and take care of himself. It was a slight thing that brought his resolution to a head and afterward Gene was surprised to realize that the resolution must have been there all along and it had taken this inconsequential thing to harden it.

At noon on Saturday he stopped in at the wharf office to get his pay. The girl handed him the envelope and slid the receipt over the desk for him to sign. He picked up the pen, fastened to the desk by a short length of beaded chain, and scrawled his full name on the blank line at the bottom of the slip. Then he stood staring at it. For the records he had to use his full name, something he never did commonly and never before had he even noticed the words he wrote. But he noticed them now.

Russell Eugene Walls, Jr., Gene felt his lips move as he tried the name over once. He did it again and looked up to find the girl watching him, her head slightly to one side. Flushing angrily, he snatched up his pay envelope and went out of the office, feeling her questioning gaze come after him like something with feet.

When he turned into the main road, Ralph Billings hailed him.

"Gene, goin home? I'll give you a lift."

"Thanks, son." Gene climbed into Ralph's new Chevvie, slumping down in the front seat, his long legs hitting the dash.

"Annie was sayin just the other day, she thought you must be sick," Ralph said.

"Me? I'm never sick."

"Well, she said you hadn't been down to the house for goin on a week."

"I been thinkin things over," Gene said and let it go at that. Ralph glanced at his abstracted face and let him alone, taking it for granted that Gene meant he'd been thinking about Annie.

Gene had forgotten, he thought, just why it was he never used his full name. He had almost forgotten when he started insisting his name was Gene, not Russell, not Junior, but Gene. Now that he stopped to think about it, though, the memory was so strong it surprised him. He would have said he'd forgotten about it completely, but there it was in his mind so clearly he could even see himself the way he'd been.

He shook his head, thinking, my gosh, you wouldn't expect a kid that old to be so cussed stubborn. And why would a kid just starting school bother to be so stubborn about a thing like that? It didn't make sense. But he could see himself—he couldn't have been more than six years old, if that. A tow-headed kid in short wool knickers and a pullover sweater, his best clothes; he'd been dressed up for his first day of school.

"Ralph," he said suddenly, "can you remember the first time you went to school?"

"You mean when I started the first grade?" Ralph eyed him obliquely.

64

"Ayeh."

"Hunh," Ralph snorted, his wide pushed-up face amused. "My gosh, when I think how much I learned in school and forgot, then you come along expectin me to remember the first day I ever went! Boy, you must think I've got a memory like an elephant."

"You mean you can't remember anythin at all about it?" Gene insisted, wanting Ralph to admit that he could so there wouldn't be any reason for him to think it queer that he himself could remember it so clearly.

"That was near twenty years ago," Ralph protested. "No, of course I can't remember it. Pete sake, I can't even remember what teacher I had."

Gene, groping through his own mind, got a little comfort from the fact that he couldn't either. He couldn't remember her name or what she looked like, only her voice asking him what his name was and the silence after her voice stopped and he refused to answer.

She'd asked him three times, each time getting a little stiffer. Finally she had said, looking at him coldly, "Well, here's a big boy, nearly six years old, and he doesn't even know his own name."

It was so real to him now that Gene could feel the way his face had started to get hot when the kids around him began laughing, that shouting jeering laughter of children who turn so easily on one of their own.

"I *do* know my name," he could hear himself shout, his voice thin and piercing. "My name is YOU-geen."

The laughter around him had stopped suddenly.

"What's the matter?" The teacher had peered near-sightedly down at her class.

"His name ain't Eugene," one of his tormentors announced. "His name's Russell."

The word had goaded him into a raging fury and to this day, recalling how he'd felt, Gene couldn't see why.

"It ain't Russell," he'd said. "It's Gene. And if anyone calls me anythin else, I won't answer."

He hadn't either, he remembered, grinning a little. He found out later that his teacher had gone to Russ to find out what his name really was. For two weeks she'd persisted in calling him Russell, and for two weeks he'd sat at his desk, his hands folded on the scarred top, saying nothing, refusing to answer. They had been two weeks of sharp and absolute misery, the complete sagging misery without hope that only children know because they can see no end to it.

But he had known immediately the second time she went to Russ. When he'd come straggling home from school that night, Russ met him at the kitchen door. One look was enough to tell Gene his father was angry and he felt himself grown smaller, remembering how little he'd felt looking up at Russ's big face.

"Your teacher says you're not behavin," Russ said.

"I'm behavin," Gene said. "She just won't call me by my right name."

"What'd you tell her your name was?"

Gene said nothing.

"If I'd wanted you to be called Gene," Russ said, "I'd have named you that first. Your name's Russell Walls, Russell Eugene Walls; Russell's your first name. That's what you're goin to be called, see?"

Gene still said nothing.

"Well, are you goin to answer when she says your name?"

"I—not if she says Russell."

Squirming slightly in the seat beside Ralph, Gene thought he could feel the grip of Russ's big hand on his shoulder. He thought he could feel the sharp slash of the smooth razor strap across his backside.

"Now," Russ had said, breathing hard, his eyes bulging slightly the way they did when he lost his temper, "you goin to behave and answer when she says Russell?"

66

Gene had managed to jerk out an uncertain "Yes." But he hadn't answered to the name. He saw to it that it wasn't necessary. The next two days he'd spent down around the shore, leaving the house early enough so that Russ would think he'd gone to school and coming home ravenous at night. He was beginning to think he was being successful when they caught up with him. There was another session with the razor strap, but afterward Russ had looked at him with a thin tight smile.

"That lickin was for playin hookey," he said. "If you want to be called Gene so bad, from now on she'll call you Gene. But no more hookey."

His teacher had called him Gene from then on; and the other kids had called him YOU-jeen, in their scraping thin voices until it got worn out and was no longer a joke. Then they just called him Gene and forgot about it. And he had thought *he'd* forgotten about it.

Ralph pulled the car to a stop and Gene climbed out.

"Funny," he said, "the things you remember."

"Like what?" Ralph looked at him. "That what you been doin? I didn't know but what you weren't feelin good."

"Hell," Gene said explosively, "I feel fine. I feel wonderful. Tell Annie I'll be down tomorrow night, will you?"

"Yeah, sure."

"Oh, and thanks for the ride, Ralph."

"That's okay." Ralph waved his hand and shoved the car into gear. Gene went quickly up the drive to the house.

There was nobody in the kitchen when he went in and he'd thought he'd seen the bright blue of his mother's dress out by the hen-yard. He splashed some water into the basin in the sink and washed hastily, wiping his hands nearly dry on the roller towel that hung beside the shed door. Then he went into the pantry and started rummaging around for something to eat. He didn't hear Grace come into the shed, but when he took the heavy cover off the stone crock where she kept the cookies, he heard her voice right outside the pantry door.

"Get out of my cookie jar."

"For pete sake," Gene said, "I could have sworn you were so busy out there you wouldn't be in for another hour."

"You can't put anything over on me, you young devil," she said fondly.

"My lord, Ma, you make me feel about ten years old." Gene stuffed a handful of the thin dark molasses cookies into his shirt pocket, took another handful, and came out to sit beside the table and watch her.

"I should think you'd *feel* about ten, stuffing on cookies before you even have your dinner. You won't want a thing to eat." She glanced at the clock and gasped. "Where the time goes! I don't wonder you're hungry. I get out there workin around the yard and I never think it's anywheres near dinnertime."

"You ought to be the one to run the place," Gene said. "I believe if it warn't for feedin us, you'd be outdoor all the time."

"Well, it's probly a good thing I've got someone else to think about," Grace said. She started slamming cupboard doors and set the frying pan on the front of the stove. "I'd starve myself to death if I was livin alone the way Hat does. I haven't got any more idea of time than the man in the moon."

It seemed to Gene, waiting aimlessly around the house, that the afternoon would never pass. He sat around the kitchen for an hour or so after he'd finished his dinner, until Grace, who'd stumbled over his feet once too often, turned on him in good-tempered shortness and drove him out. He stood on the back steps for a minute, hands in his dungaree pockets, staring down the road toward Billings's. He had half a mind to go down and see if Annie was home. Then he shook his head. No, he didn't want to do that till he'd seen and talked with Russ. Annie had been after him lately, saying they ought to do something definite one way or the other, and Gene had been staying out of her way until he could tell her he'd done it.

He bent his head far back and stood staring up through the chestnut branches into the clear deep blue of the sky until it made him dizzy and he wasn't sure whether he wasn't looking down into deep brilliant water where there was no bottom. The only clouds were a few tenuous cirrus wisps over the saw-teeth of the spruces on the Ridge back. The still brilliant air made the shadows of things look hard and each little hummock of grass out across the field had its sharp dark echo tapering out from its base.

There was chill in the quiet air, even without a wind. Gene could feel it through the heavy wool of his jacket. He shook himself like a dog coming out of water, plunged off the doorstep, and went rapidly down over the bank and around the corner of the house.

He glanced at the neat wood pile, kicked thoughtfully at the chopping block, and decided to split a little kindling. The ax was just inside the open door of the root cellar and when he went to get it, he saw that Grace had most of her vegetables in and what he couldn't see he could smell. The cabbages, hanging by their stalks from the beams, looked like great featureless pale heads swinging in the gloom. He could see dimly the row of barrels along the back wall and knew they were filled with apples and potatoes. And everything there had its own distinctive aroma. Under it all lay the cool loamy dirt smell of the floor, packed hard and brown underfoot.

A cellar like this one made him feel suddenly that maybe it wasn't so senseless to stick around a little place like the Ridge all his life. At least here a man would always be able to keep himself in food if he wasn't too lazy to go after it. There was plenty to be had for just a little work. Maybe he'd never get anywhere—not what an outsider would call getting anywhere —but it must give a man a good deal of satisfaction to face a long winter with this much food to get by on.

He knew that at intervals all summer and almost steadily for the last two months, Grace had been busy preserving and canning. There wasn't anything they raised in the garden or brought up from the shore that she didn't try at least once to can for winter.

Even knowing that, he was surprised by the rows of gleaming jars in the preserve cellar. There was a faint flicker of light from the cobwebbed narrow window set into the stone wall and it was reflected back to him from the rows of glass that went endlessly around the other three walls. The shelves ran from the floor to the low ceiling and all of them were full. Feeling an immense respect for the amount of work his mother must have put in to achieve anything like this, Gene closed the door and went out to the chopping block, taking the heavy single-bitted ax from alongside the outer door as he passed.

There was just enough frost in the wood to make it split easily and he split it fine for kindling, filling the box until his mother made him stop, complaining that she'd have no room left for stove wood if he kept on. After that he piled it in the little jog in the wall halfway down the steps. Finally she came to the kitchen door and stood looking down at him.

"You're restless as a cat today," she said. "What ails you, anyhow?"

"Nothin much," Gene said. "I can't seem to settle down."

"Nothing wrong, is there?"

"Nope," he shook his head. "I just want to see Pa about somethin and was tryin to think how to say it."

He could see from her face that she was bursting to ask him what it was, but she didn't. She disappeared for a moment and when she came back she had a big market basket.

"Here." She handed it down to him. "Go on out there and pick me up some of those windfall crabs. I can't bear seein them layin there to rot."

When he took the basket and went out, Grace turned and went into the pantry so she could watch him out the window.

She'd thought at first the way he was flipping around today had been just another sign of natural restlessness. Now she stopped to think of it, though, Gene's restlessness lately hadn't been natural. There was something more than just spirits about it and whatever it was it was evidently coming to a head.

She wanted to ask him what was wrong, make him tell her —but she knew he'd made up his mind to talk to Russ first. And besides, whatever it was, Russ wouldn't like it if he thought she'd known about it before he had.

"If you haven't anythin to do this afternoon," she said when Gene brought the basketful of crab apples in to her, "why don't you go out and help Jake? He's puttin some patches on the barn roof."

Jake was. The weathered dun of the barn roof looked as if it had the measles where Jake had replaced a couple of shingles here and half a dozen somewhere else. All the rest of the afternoon, they worked together in companionable silence and in the purely mechanical work, Gene got so engrossed he managed to forget that he was waiting to talk with his father. When Russ came home that night, neither of the boys heard him until he was standing directly beneath them.

"See you got a new hand, Jake," he yelled. "How much you payin him?"

Jake grinned down at his father, his ruddy face made redder by the brisk air.

"He's not much good. He's only workin to get experience. I let him."

"Not a bad system at that," Russ said. "Keeps down the bills, anyhow."

He waved his hand and went on into the house. Watching him go, Gene could feel his face turning numb and tight with apprehension. Russ wasn't going to feel like that later and Gene wasn't looking forward to it.

LATE in the afternoon, Stanny left the house where he'd been loafing in his room since he'd eaten his lunch, quietly, so as not to attract Grace's attention and have her root him out to do something for her. He heard her come to the foot of the stairs twice to listen, trying to find out if he was in the house. Once she called him, but he lay still on his bed, holding his breath, as if letting it go would break the charm and bring her up the stairs. But each time she turned away without coming up.

It had been chilly in his room because the upstairs part of the house was hard to heat. There was only the small radiator in the floor over the air-tight stove in the room below and he had to keep one of the thick braided rugs over that so she wouldn't hear the occasional rustlings he made. He hadn't been doing anything all afternoon, just lying there on the bed, hands under his head, staring out the window.

Against the sky outside the chestnuts were beginning to show their bones clearly—even though there were leaves left on the trees, they had lost all the thick summer obscurity and were almost transparent now. He thought he could see through them as if they were made of thin clear yellow glass —only their veins were hard still and opaque. The windless day made the illusion of glass even clearer; the leaves hung motionless into the brittle hurtingly clear air, preserved intact and immovable in an atmosphere that looked too rare to breathe.

For a while he lay watching the sunlight creep across his floor, from gray-painted boards to braided rug and along to boards again. It reached the white iron foot of his bed and started crawling up along the rough cloth of his pants. The steady progress of the direct light fascinated him and he kept feeling less substantial and more weightless, as if he had gone out of his own body; but presently the steadiness itself started to make him nervous. It was inexorable and awful and he began to think it would kill him if he lay still long enough to let it fall across his face. That light on his bare skin would be death.

Possessed, he went down the stairs and out the front door at top speed, bringing his mother into the hall to stand staring after him as he spun across the field to the road and went racing up the Ridge field to where the first spruces began. She watched him until he disappeared into the trees and went, shaking her head, back to the kitchen. Now he must have been up there all afternoon, she thought. He must have heard me calling him and he just sat there and never said a word.

The minute he crossed the road, as if he had stepped onto enchanted ground, Stanny changed physically. He was instantly six feet tall and he could feel the thin air reaching deep into his chest that was broader and deeper than his father's. He had the long thin muscles that, like fine steel bands, conceal instead of reveal their power—and he could feel them moving in him as if each one had a separate life and he was nothing but the covering, the container. His feet went surely, smoothly over the tough hummocky grass, and the oiled regular swinging of his wide shoulders made him feel good. He was running with his head back and the wind of his own speed lifted his hair from his hawklike profile.

When he passed in among the first trees, he was a ghost, spiriting his agile winding way among the smoke-blue trunks. Nothing could see him pass. He reached out and touched the screaming red squirrel at the side of a big spruce—the squirrel that screamed because it sensed his coming and couldn't see him, didn't know where he was until he touched it and it went out from under his invisible hand like a thin tongue of exasperated fire.

Power welled up in his nonexistent body, diaphanous as fog, and he went up the side of the Ridge, the steep beetling thin-earthed rib of the Ridge, like a puff of smoke and as easily.

When he reached the top and the trees narrowed and shortened and thinned out around him, he was death with light in one hand and dark in the other—his feet spraddled on top of the world. The thinly bleating crows were his lightning messengers, the piping squealing fish hawk was harbinger of his coming.

But it was cold and the stirring fingers of the beginning night wind tore the robes of his might away from him and plastered his thin shirt against his skinny shoulders. And he was winded, with a sharp pain in his chest, and his ankle hurt where he'd barked it against a rock. And his power went without giving him time to be used to its going.

So he stood shivering, his shoulders drawn up against the beginning of cold, watching fascinated the slow creeping of the shadow of the Ridge toward the wide comfortable roof of his own house—the roof under which he could have been warm and happy, and would have been fed. Because he was up in the eye of the wind, far above it, a little of his exaltation came back to him. He was momentarily the lonely wanderer, pausing on the edge of darkness on the distant peak watching the night come down over the safe habitations of men—men who didn't have the wilderness calling in their blood, men without the insane disease of the mind that sent them out to wander, friendless and alone, with madness and elation for their company. In a moment he would smile, a fine, half-sad smile for something that could never be, and pass on, leaving the material signs of his fellow man far behind him. Perhaps someday, somebody who had once known him would see him, standing on a distant blue ridge somewhere, looking down, always looking down. Perhaps that somebody would even call out to him—it would be one of his old schoolmates, grown to the full ripeness of golden womanhood—she would see him and his immense loneliness would strike deep into her heart, wrenching the cry out of her, the voice of her heart. For him. But he would be incapable of answering, would turn away with that same fine sad smile, with longing in his eyes perhaps, but longing that could never be healed, that must go on tearing with its wolf-teeth at his solitary heart. He must always turn away and she must always see him go, must stand and watch him disappear like smoke, like mirage, always, always alone.

Alone he stood, wrapped in his silence, to watch the night come down. He saw the last red-gold light fading from the chestnuts; he watched the darkness creeping up their trunks until it forced the light, like some brilliant blood, out of the tips of their last finest antenna. He saw the shingles of his father's house glow warm enough to heat his own chilled mind, and fade to ash and cinder. Then he looked up to see that the sky above him was as clear and thin as a great blue-white bubble of invisible crystal. It was sky for itself alone, there was no purpose behind its luminous clarity, there was nothing left in it it could give to the earth. Then he decided that the night came up, not down. It was something that grew out of the earth itself, it was what lay beneath the flat motionless silver of the water and came creeping out over the land when the guardians were asleep.

But now it was creeping up on him, too, and the awful loneliness got too much for him and he had to get back under the shelter of that roof just as fast as he could go. He went headlong down through the woods again, only too corporeal; he raced gasping, with heavily thudding feet across the Ridge field, feeling the purple tide lapping around his ankles, around his knees, gripping his waist, holding him back from the safety and the human voices he needed to hear.

The night pursued him across the road and up to his own back door and when he slammed it and leaned panting against the heavy boards with the beating of his heart shaking his whole narrow body, he could hear darkness like an animal scratching outside, gently so as to fool him. Gently so he wouldn't realize what it could do to him if he dared to step outside the door.

Russ pulled open the inside door to the kitchen and stood

there staring at him and Stanny felt the terror in his own face pinned down by the impatience of his father. He could sense Russ's mood like a blow from a hammer inside his head and knew that Russ had already heard about the way he'd been acting today and was disgusted and contemptuous.

"What's wrong with you, anyway?" Russ said. "You like to took the roof right off the house, bangin the door like that."

"I don't know what ails him today," Grace said from somewhere inside the kitchen. "That Stanny, isn't it? My lord, Russ, what gets into that boy I cannot say. Will you tell him to come in here and fill this wood-box before I have to get his grandfather to do his chores for him?"

"Get in there and fill the wood-box," Russ said with unnecessary explicitness. He stood to one side and pointed majestically at the ailing wood-box; and Stanny, with his last shred of identity cowed into a quivering mass of jelly somewhere low in his stomach, slunk by him and went down the cellar stairs to get the wood.

But now the night was just darkness and something to be sworn at, softly, through the held-back weak tears that made him gulp.

"Goddam it to hell," Stanny whispered between his teeth because it was dark and he hit his barked ankle against the corner of the stone chimney foundation.

Gene didn't get his chance until after supper. If he'd followed his impulse, he'd have had his say out just as soon as Russ got home. But when he went in, Russ was already in the kitchen and apparently planning to stay there. Nat was sitting by the table waiting for supper and Gene couldn't have said what he wanted to say with his grandfather listening.

When Russ got up from the table and disappeared into the front room, Gene shoved his chair back and went after him. He didn't look at his mother, but he knew as well as if he had that her eyes were following him anxiously. He could almost feel her holding him back, as if she had some sort of mental rein on him.

Russ was just taking the paper off the table and he stood still with it in his hand when Gene looked in and said, "Pa, can I talk to you?"

In the second before Russ nodded his head, Gene stood there in the doorway looking with resentment at the unruffled paper that had been on the table untouched all day until Russ came to read it.

"What's it about?" Russ took off his heavy glasses and stuck them into his shirt pocket.

"Me."

"Well, suppose you tell me what's *wrong* with you."

"Nothin wrong," Gene said. Then, seeing that Grace had come to the kitchen door and was watching him, he shut the door carefully. He could feel his Adam's apple bobbing convulsively and knew he couldn't help it. He seemed to have more saliva in his mouth than he knew what to do with. That made him know he was nervous. When he looked at Russ, though, common sense told him that Russ was only a man like other men. But his own mind said: Not like other men.

"Guess you know I'm plannin on bein married," he blurted, determined to get it out before he dried up altogether.

"Why, I probably knew you had it in mind," Russ said slowly. "Been travelin around quite steady with Aaron's girl, haven't you?"

There was no reason why Russ shouldn't have known who the girl was and every reason why he should, but Gene was surprised.

"Got eyes and ears." Russ answered the question before he asked it. "Sit down."

Gene lowered himself carefully into a chair and was immediately sorry because Russ stayed on his feet and it was hard enough to talk to him when you could look him in the eye.

"Want to get married soon?"

77

"Soon's I can," Gene said, seeing his situation slipping away from him.

"I'd be the last one to object—that what you're ascared of?"

"No—I'm not scared."

"Well, then, what is it?"

"I was figurin on movin out and gettin my own place," Gene said boldly. In all the imaginary conversations he'd had with Russ on this particular subject, he'd worked around to the point gradually, but Russ wasn't letting him do it that way. He felt relieved, cheated, and a little belligerent. Then he looked at his father and knew for the first time what actual effect the six words would have on him. Judast, he thought, what's wrong with him? For an undefended minute, Russ's face showed what he felt, but it was only a minute and he had both face and voice under control again when he repeated slowly, "Movin out, huh?"

Gene nodded.

"Aren't you happy here?"

"It's not a question of whether I'm happy or not," Gene said. "When a guy gets married, it stands to reason he wants to get out and start a place of his own."

Russ took his glasses out of his pocket and stood tapping them thoughtfully against his broad thumbnail. The quick flashing of reflected light across the lenses caught and held Gene's stare.

"Only when he has to," Russ said.

"Well—what does that mean?"

"I'll tell you what it means," his father said deliberately. "Just this. You're my oldest son. I'd sort of planned on havin you carry on here after I go—see?"

Gene looked at him as if his ears had played him false.

"I don't know the first thing about runnin this place," he protested wildly.

"You could learn. You could afford to hire a man that did."

"But Jake's been handlin the place. He'll think—well—"

Somehow this talk of the time when Russ would be gone was just what Gene needed to make him sure he was dreaming all this. He couldn't conceive a time when Russ wouldn't be there to be asked what to do. "I guess we all thought the place'd go to Jake," he said.

"Been talkin it over, hanh?" Russ's voice was satirically polite, but his eyes were angry.

"No," Gene lied stoutly. "He never mentioned it—neither have I. But it just looked like he'd be the natural one to get it."

"I hired Jake," Russ said. "I pay him. So long's I do, Jake isn't any more than a hired hand and you'll do well to keep that in mind."

Once he'd stated the case clearly, Russ's expansive good humor came back like a jovial flood. Gene, when he'd been a kid, had always visualized God's face as having very much the same expression Russ's did at this moment.

"I know it's not very pleasant to talk about dyin," Russ voice started to sound smooth, "when you come in to talk about marryin. But I've got to go sometime, and when I do I'd like to go knowin my oldest son was carryin on here. This is an old place, Gene, and a good one. I know you kids don't bother much about tradition—but it just seems better it should go to you and that's the way I planned it. What d'you say?"

All the time he'd been standing there talking, there'd been a part of Russ that was standing off to one side listening with a cynical amusement. It wasn't that he didn't mean every word he was saying, he never said anything he didn't mean to —but he had never even thought of this before, much less given it the careful consideration he intended Gene to think he had.

He had never thought that he would die—he didn't believe now that he would. He had the vaguely usual idea that he alone was immortal. He realized that everyone he knew would die—Gene, Grace, the other kids—sometime. But he thought of that eventuality as a time when he would be left alone, not as a time when he himself might have been dead for years.

79

It was just that he couldn't bear to think of the breaking up of his family, the family he'd started. He couldn't imagine any of them living anywhere but under the roof he provided for them. And if he himself had been Gene, this offer would have held him. He had no doubt that it would hold Gene.

"Well—" Gene let out his breath in a long half-whistle. "I don't know."

As he hesitated, Russ said, "Of course, I'd expect you to let your Ma live on here—as long as she lives, and the others till they want to go."

"Yeah," Gene nodded. "Sure."

"Then you like the idea?"

"I dunno why not," Gene said. "It never occurred to me before, but I dunno why not."

"Then it's all settled." Russ picked up his paper.

"Yeah, sure," Gene said again. He got up and got as far as the door, hearing his father settle into his chair behind him, before he remembered that actually nothing had been settled, he hadn't accomplished what he'd come for. He wasn't any further ahead than he had been when he first came in. That's how he does it, Gene thought.

"Hey."

"What the devil's wrong with you?" Russ's eyes were amused.

"Well, I said I wanted to get married. Right away. All this is all right, but it isn't gettin me any furtherer."

"Haven't *got* to, have you?" Russ bent his head forward a little, ready to be either angry or amused as the mood took him.

"No." Gene avoided the predatory glance. "It's not like that."

"Well, if you're in such a confounded hurry, go ahead," Russ said. "Bring her here. There's always room for one more in this house. I guess she could get along with your Ma, couldn't she?"

"Annie could get along with anyone."

"Do that, then," Russ said complacently, as if he'd arranged everything perfectly. "There's even that extra room that warn't good enough for your Aunt Hat. If she's got new fangled ideas and wants a room of her own, why she can have that. Though, I don't know's I'd think much of it."

Gene felt his ears getting warm. He did plenty of that kind of thinking himself and somehow he didn't want to—not about Annie.

"Okay," he said shortly. "That's okay."

He went out, leaving the door open, and went upstairs to dress. He wanted to talk to Annie before his own first enthusiasm wore off—something made him wonder just how she was going to take this.

When Gene reached Aaron's back door he wasn't walking as fast as he had been when he'd left his own. His excitement had worn down until he could look at Russ's proposition the way Annie would, coldly, wondering where the catch was. He had begun to be a little surprised at himself, too. Here, just a couple of hours ago, he'd been so hot to get away from the old man and out of his house he could hardly wait to tell him he was going. For the last two years he'd been building up to this moment.

Now he was feeling like a pricked balloon, cheated out of his triumph. Russ had taken his occasion away from him so neatly and with such an air that Gene was just beginning to realize what he'd lost.

He pulls out all the old tear-jerkers, Gene thought, beginning to be angry, and what do I do? Dance to his damned tune just the way he knew I would.

Resentment changed Gene physically. His face looked heavy and younger—all the youthfulness in it was pushed sullenly forward and all the maturity blurred. Annie wasn't going to like this one bit, he knew, and he had a battle with her to look forward to. Essentially Gene was peaceful—situations like this made him uncomfortable and, because of his own dis-comfort, a good deal crueller than he normally was.

He went in without knocking and stood in the doorway until Annie who was looking out the kitchen window turned around. The immediate lighting of her face disarmed him momentarily.

"Hello, there. I thought it was Ralph or Pa."

"Well, it's me."

"What's the matter with 'me'?"

"Glad to see me?"

"I don't know's I'll tell you whether I am or not," she teased. "It's been so long since you've been around I've al-most forgotten what you look like."

"Oh, is that so?" Gene grabbed at her. Somehow Annie managed to let him catch her easily and at the same time give him the impression that she had done her best to evade him.

"Darling," she said breathlessly, "I *am* glad to see you."

"That's much more like it." Gene bent his bright head to kiss her and it was so right and so inevitable and so long since he last had that he wondered how he could possibly stay away from her more than a day at a time.

"I won't ever forget about that," she said softly and her lips were so near his he could feel them move. But when he reached for her again, she moved away, this time decisively. "I can't," she said. Feeling his own breath coming thickly in his throat, Gene knew what she meant.

When she went into the other room and sat down on the sofa, Gene leaned slouchily against the door jamb instead of going over to sit beside her. He remembered suddenly why he'd come and had begun to feel sullen again.

Might as well have it out and over with, he thought. He looked away from her and stared with concentration at the bowl of artificial orange flowers on the high old sideboard. He could see her face reflected at a peculiar angle in the long low mirror behind the flowers.

"They've been there a long time," she said finally. "And you've seen them before."

"Annie," Gene began desperately, knowing that he wasn't going to tell her the way he should—there wasn't going to be anything subtle about it. Once he got started, his own disquiet would be great enough to make him blurt the whole thing out.

He started and it was just as he'd known it would be. Gene wasn't particularly sensitive, but it seemed to him he could hear each word hit the wall of resistance she'd built—and perversely, that made him blunter.

Annie heard him through in silence and when he stopped talking her silence was as audible as his voice had been. She didn't look at him and her hands were clasped tightly in her lap, so tightly that each knuckle made a small shiny white knob.

"Well?" he said desperately, against her immobility.

"No."

The word dropped into the air of the stifled room and left rings of feeling spreading out after it. Gene thought he could sense them washing over him and the intensity she'd put into one word scared him a little.

"Why d'you feel like that?" He sounded more impatient than he felt. "Here we've got a chance to start out with more than I could ever scrape together on my own and you won't even listen."

"I've always told you I'd never live with your family."

"Will you tell me why? You've never given me any reason. Is it because of the way my old man never got along with yours?"

"That's silly." She looked at him and away quickly. "No, it's just that I don't believe young married people ought to live with their families. It always ends in a fight."

"Oh," Gene said impatiently. "You can't tell me the way

you feel is just because you're afraid of in-law trouble. That's just as silly."

"I know it."

"Well, then, what the devil *are* you tryin to tell me?"

"I don't know," she said loudly, staring at him as if she couldn't focus her eyes. "That's it. I just don't know. I never told you why because I don't know why. It's just that you're the only one in the whole family without something wrong with you."

"Wrong?" Gene sounded as if he'd lost his breath.

"I can't be comfortable with any of them but you, Gene. They make me feel as if they were cripples. If they were hunchbacks or blind or something, I'd feel the way I do. They all feel so—oh—dark."

"For pete sake." Gene gaped at her. "Are you tryin to tell me my whole family's crazy?"

"It's just a feeling." She sounded as if she wanted to cry but wasn't going to let herself. "I can't help it. I can't live there, Gene, and if you want me you've got to realize that. Why, I'd be out of my mind inside a week. Even when Mary comes down here—the way she is—she just sits around lookin. I get so nervous I could scream."

Annie stopped talking and for a fleeting second felt as if she'd betrayed Mary, but whatever she did to Mary it wasn't as important as what happened to Gene and to her.

"Why didn't you tell me before?" When he went over to stand looking down at her, Gene felt outside of himself and he was so angry he could hardly see her—so angry he was still, and anger with him was a violent emotion.

"I couldn't—" She looked up at him hopefully and he watched the hope fade. "And I can see it was the wrong thing to say now."

"Yes, I guess it was," Gene said over his shoulder. He had to grope like a blind man to find the kitchen door and he let himself out slowly and carefully, as if he were very old. He

84

wasn't listening, but he knew Annie wouldn't call him back.

He hadn't wanted to go and leave her like that. But the compulsion that had forced him out of the room, carried him sightlessly down the drive. Aaron, who was coming up to the house, spoke to him and turned to stare when Gene went by him as if he'd been a hole in the air. Shaking his head, Aaron went on up to the door and Annie met him just inside.

"For godsake," he looked at her, "what did you say to Gene? I don't think he even saw me."

"I don't know why he went off like that. I didn't say much more than I've said before."

"You better marry that boy and settle him down before he does himself a hurt."

"For the last two years we've been planning to get our own place," Annie said. "Tonight he acted as if we'd never even talked about it. He says Russ wants him to stay there and take over that place when he dies. Gene's going to do it."

"That would be somethin," Aaron smiled tightly. "His grandchildren in that house, and have them be mine, too."

"You'll never live to see it," Annie said. "I told him I wouldn't."

Aaron put his arm around her shoulders and walked her into the kitchen. He started to say something about lovers' quarrels being easily patched, but when he looked down at her he couldn't say it because she was crying silently and he'd never seen her cry before.

JAKE came in at twelve o'clock. Up in the little room under the eaves, Gene lying flat on his back on Jake's bed heard the rattling old car come to a stop under the chestnuts. Then he heard Jake come quietly in the back door and start in through the hall. I bet he doesn't make it, Gene thought, just as Jake's heavy too-cautious foot hit the first stair with a crash that shook the walls. He's the clumsiest devil I ever saw. Gene grinned tightly.

Jake hauled open the door, which stuck and came away with a jar, shaking the very wall. He got halfway into the room before he saw Gene and stopped.

"Pete sake," he said, "what're you doin here?"

"Just waitin for you." Gene got up slowly and went over to stand, stooping beneath the sloping ceiling, looking out the window. "Been to Freehold?"

"What if I have?" Jake came in and shut the door carefully. He kept his eyes on Gene's back as he crossed the room to the vacated bed and sat down on it. Still watching Gene, he started unlacing his heavy shoes.

"Have a good time?"

"What's the matter with you?" Jake said impatiently. "You drunk?"

"I don't sound it, do I?"

"Well, I ain't sure *how* you sound. You sound pretty darn queer to me."

"Maybe I'm just as queer as the rest of the family, only it doesn't show on me so often."

"Will you, for godsake, tell me what you're talkin about?" Jake took off one shoe and, in an excess of impatience with something he couldn't understand, flung it across the room. The thud of the heavy boot against the wall brought Gene around to face him.

"I just found out tonight people think this family's crazy," he said. "I just had the pleasure of sittin around hearin somebody tell me we were all batty as loons."

"I'll begin to think you are," Jake said, grinning, "if you don't come down off'n your rafter an tell me what's up."

"There was somethin else I found out, too," Gene said.

"Yeah?"

86

"Yeah, I found out I'm every bit as cussed mean as the old man himself."

"All right," Jake said shortly. "I know how you feel about him—you don't have to tell me again. But he's treated me all right, see? I'm doin all right."

"You only think you are." Gene came over to stand, spraddle-legged, looking down at his younger brother. "You don't know the half of it, kid. And to prove how mean I am, I waited up to tell you about it."

"Well, why don't you? If they's anythin I ought to know, I'm willin to listen."

"Hanh." Gene snorted his amusement, throwing his head back, and his momentary resemblance to Russ was so great that even Jake was struck by it and sat staring.

"Look at me," Gene said. "He put his mark on me, all right. I looked like him then, didn't I?"

"Well, I dunno who's got a better right."

"Right? Right! You don't think I want to do things the way he does—or even look like him, do you? Listen!" He bent over, bringing his face on a level with Jake's and the word hissed with the force of his breath. "Let me tell you. Because of him I have to spend half my time tryin to be like I'm not. It's natural to me to act the way he does, and I don't want to. I'd like to take everything in me that comes out of him and rip it out, see? Why, sometimes when I do a certain thing, I *feel* the way he looks. My face *feels* the way his looks."

"Jesus," Jake said. More than usually insensitive, Jake seldom bothered to try to understand the way other people felt. But there was something so naked and hating in Gene's face that he felt as if hate become alive hammered against him. "If you feel like that why d'you stay here? We talked all that over. Get out."

"No." Gene's face relaxed into a smile, but it was a smile that set Jake's teeth on edge. He sat there staring, his other shoe dangling from his big hairy hand. "I've found out how to get back at him," Gene said. "I've found the way, see? He'll be dead when I do it, but it won't make any difference. I'll have the satisfaction of knowin what I did to him and how he'd feel if he knew it."

"What," Jake started to ask and the word came out in a dismal croak so he wet his lips and started over again. "What're you goin to do? You haven't gone foolish, have you?"

"Foolish?" Gene considered the word as if he'd never heard it before. "Why, no. The beautiful part of it all is, he'll help me get my own back, see? He wants me to keep his name goin, to keep his place goin. And I'm goin to do everythin I can to rub him out. He'll be dead then and he can't stop me. He'll never be able to stop me again."

"Look," Jake said. A glimmer of what this was all about had started to penetrate his mental fog. "Will you tell me in words of one syllable, what gives?"

"Why, sure." Gene made his tone magnanimous. "I'll endeavor to bring a little light to that thing you call a brain. Now, listen carefully. He's got this place, see? It's old, isn't it? He's proud of it. He's been figurin ever since he got it, how a place like this'll go in his family for generations. What he has in mind is startin a sort of dynasty, see? Like a king."

"Yeah," Jake said dazedly when Gene stopped. And then he wished he hadn't because the sound only started Gene off again and he looked as if the taste of each word was pleasant.

"He didn't even worry about how he got this place, just so's he got it. You know that, everybody knows it. He saw what he wanted and he took it. Well, when I get this place, I'm goin to sell it. I'm goin to kill his name cut here just the way I'd erase a word written down. And if he was only here to see me do it, it'd be worse to him than if I'd killed him. Inside ten years after he's dead, people'll forget he ever lived. Him and his tradition! Him and his inheritin'"

Jake's mind had stopped assimilating what Gene said after the fourth sentence. It seemed to him the sound in his ears was nothing but a muffled jerky roaring. He couldn't see very well. He got up, lurching into the small night stand by the bed and nearly tipping it over. Gene grabbed at the light and restored it to a firm base. He made very sure it was steady, making more of a job out of it than it was, before he looked at Jake again. By that time Jake had his voice back, but Gene could see just how mad he was. His anger made his whole face swell and redden; it made his eyes look smaller and brilliantly red; it made the veins in his short thick neck stand out and Gene could see the blood pounding angrily in them.

"What d'you mean 'When you get this place'?" Even Jake's voice was shaking.

For a moment Gene's sanity came back to him and he wished he hadn't started this thing. He wished he could have stopped the whole business before it had even begun. But then he remembered how much he'd lost himself, this night, and was again ready and willing to hurt somebody else more than he'd been hurt himself.

"Oh, yes," he said. "It slipped my mind. I forgot to tell you that's how well he's treatin you. You don't stand a chance, bud. The place is comin to me. I'm the oldest. You're lookin at the original crown prince. You? Why, you're nothin but a hired hand around here. *He* thinks so. That's how it is."

Gene stopped and took a careful backward step away from Jake. He found himself wondering just what Jake would do. He'd never seen that particular look of blinded brute anger before and he found it frightening. Jake looked like a goaded bull, his head seemed to sink into his shoulders, and Gene could see it swing slowly from side to side, the way a bull's does. And when he listened, he could hear Jake's breath loud in his throat.

"You're gonna take it, too, ain't you?"

"Take it?" Gene looked surprised. He stopped wondering

how far he could push Jake before he'd let go. "Why, sure. Wouldn't you, in my place?"

Jake gave his head a vicious shake and the fog behind his eyes cleared up a little leaving him an altogether too clear view of his brother.

"I never realized what a pair of sons of bitches you two were," he said. "You knew what I was plannin on doin here. You knew because I told you. And you said you was clearin out. And now you got the nerve to stand there and tell me you're goin to take this place, that you're goin to get it. Not me."

"That's right. And there's somethin else. I won't sell it to you, either, because your name's Walls, too."

"I ought to kill you, playin me a double cross like that. How long've you been plannin this? How long did it take you to work me out? Oh, you must've gone at it pretty sly. But I'm dumb. Maybe you didn't have to be so sly. Maybe I just thought bein your brother was enough to make sure I'd get a square deal from you. Maybe I thought bein his son was enough to guarantee it from him."

"Why, Jake," Gene said. "I don't know when I've heard anythin so appealin. You really ought to go in for politics. You could rival the old man on a different line, of course. He gets em the smooth way. You could touch a man's sense of justice. Between you, you could get em goin and comin."

"Is that all you got to say?" Jake's strangled voice got tighter.

"It isn't necessary to say any more, is it?"

"I guess it ain't. I guess I don't want to hear any more out of you. I'm afraid I'd be sick."

"Well, all I've got to say is, you must have an awful delicate stomach."

Jake stood looking at Gene as if he couldn't believe what he saw. His eyes got sicker and sicker and Gene, staring him down, saw that he'd won without violence and felt a little disappointed. He was surprised, too, at himself. He had never thought he could find it in himself to enjoy a situation like this, but now, suddenly, he could understand Russ. He knew now what satisfaction Russ got out of being able to pull a string here and seeing a man fall off his fence there, and knowing just what went on between the two.

There was a stir in the next room and Stanny's voice came plaintively through to them.

"Can't you two shut up and let me get some sleep?"

At the same moment they heard the door of Russ's bedroom open and a second later his bare feet padded up the hall. When he pulled open the door to Jake's room and looked in, they were both staring at him like two kids who'd been caught stealing jam.

"What the devil're you two talkin about?" he said. "You woke me up an now your Ma's awake, too."

He'd been half grinning with sleepy exasperation when he opened the door, but as his eyes grew used to the light and he could see their faces clearly, his grin disappeared. Even standing there barefoot, with the loose hem of his short nightshirt flapping around his bony shins, Russ was impressive enough to make Gene wish again he'd never started this.

"So I'm nothin but your hired hand?" Jake said in a curiously quiet spaced voice.

"For the love of god." Russ stared angrily at Gene. "I never thought I'd have to tell you to keep your big trap shut. I thought you'd have the sense."

"What are you goin to do?" Jake asked him when Gene couldn't find the words to say anything, "just keep me on like a horse, and turn me out to pasture when I wear out?"

Russ didn't even glance at him this time.

"You go spillin your business all over the lot, you got to expect trouble," he glared at Gene. "Act like a fool. Sometimes I wonder if you kids got the sense to get in out of the wet. Things like this make me wonder."

91

"Well, I—" Gene said.

"Well, you—" Russ mimicked cruelly. "Come on," he jerked his head impatiently toward the door. "Get in there an get to bed. I want a word with you. As for you," he turned on Jake, "you go to bed, too."

He spun around and disappeared and Gene, not looking back, followed him. Russ was waiting by Gene's bedroom door.

"Now, for pete sake," he began before Gene stopped moving, "be reasonable. Don't say any more to him. He'll forget it."

"She won't have me," Gene said miserably, going back to the root of his behavior. "Annie won't live here—she won't marry me."

"Hah," Russ snorted. "Good thing you found it out in time. Go find yourself a girl knows a good thing when she sees it. Now get to bed so's I can get some sleep."

He padded off down the hall to his own room, but turned just before he closed the door.

"Just as glad you aren't marryin Aaron Billings's girl, anyhow," he said, yawned deeply, and pulled the door to, leaving Gene alone in the dark hall.

WHAT he had done to Jake acted like a mental catharsis for Gene. He didn't sleep much that night, what with his own thoughts and the unsteady thudding of Jake's feet. He wasn't even sure which of the two made him more uncomfortable. His thoughts weren't pretty and somehow they were all mixed up with the noise Jake was making. That uneven blind clumsy sound was somehow very like the noise he would have expected Jake to make when he was miserable, if he had ever expected Jake to be miserable. He never had. He'd never realized that a person like Jake *could* be. When he stopped to think it over, it seemed to Gene he hadn't even thought of Jake as being able to feel anything but a sort of dumb exuberance that came from physical well-being and mental inertia.

It was a good deal like listening to an animal in pain—there didn't seem to be any object in it; it was nothing but an aimless noise. And knowing that he had inflicted that misery made him feel the way he would have if he'd gone out, without reason, and used a two-by-four on a horse. Jake was like an animal. All the violence he understood was physical; anything that went beyond that left him unarmed and writhing.

Security, Gene thought, that's what we all want. That's what Jake thought he had here. And I'm the one that knocked his security right out from under him—me, who didn't even want what he wanted. Here he's been working for it for years and I get it handed to me on a silver platter —with a few conditions.

Gene went to work Monday feeling emptied out and as if somebody had hit him over the head. All his momentary illusions about his own importance to his father had gone like tissue paper in a high wind before those last few words Russ had said to him before closing his bedroom door. Those last few words he'd said easily, between a show of temper and a yawn, as if they weren't really important and as if what lay behind them weren't worth considering and never had been.

"Just as glad you aren't marryin Aaron Billings's girl, anyhow," Russ had said, and yawned, dismissing easily and without thought the girl who was the most important person in Gene's life. Just how important she was Gene knew when he thought of his whole life without her. Lonesomeness was a comparative state, you were either more or less lonesome no matter what you did with your life because there was so much of it nobody else could ever touch. But when the person you wanted around wasn't there in the part of your life they might have occupied, then you began to realize just how lonesome one person could be.

There were other lonesome people—Jake, now. Jake was lonely. Jake always would be because he had no way to communicate with anyone else. He was going to be even lonelier now. Stanny? Gene thought of Stanny with a stabbing of guilt. There was that kid, cut off from all of them, unthought of, unheeded. But Stanny had his grandfather—they were friends the way it's hard to be friends with your own family, the way you seldom are friends with anyone else. Gene had seen their friendship working, they were together for hours at a time without having to say anything to each other, and he hadn't understood it before but now he thought he was beginning to.

No, he needed somebody to talk to, but it had to be someone who was as alone as he felt. He needed a push. He wanted advice from somebody who had his own capacity for misery because he couldn't put words to it for himself. But it had to be somebody he could respect or it wouldn't work.

It was typical of his mother that he never thought of her —the blast of Grace's perpetual motherhood could never come near his particular disease.

He was going home after work when he thought of the person he could talk to and was surprised because he hadn't thought of her before. She had the key to the whole thing and she would be able to listen to him. She'd talk back, too, he knew that. She never had much, but he knew this time she would and the lightening of his mind told him she was the one.

Gene stood hesitating outside Mary's door that night. More than once he lifted his hand to knock and let it fall again. He stood there in the wide old hall, listening for something, waiting for some sign to tell him what to do. What if she told him something he didn't want to hear, what if she didn't tell him he ought to do what he wanted to do but couldn't without help?

He had been building up to this moment since he'd first thought of going to her and he had already invested what she would say with such importance that it didn't occur to him he wouldn't have to do whatever she'd tell him to. He felt as if he had no more mind of his own left. After he'd left Jake Saturday night, he'd felt relieved, as if he'd managed to get rid of the part of him that was like his father, that had been backing up in him all the years he'd spent in this house. But with it, momentarily, had gone a part of himself, too. He had no resolution left; he felt weak and mentally washed out.

So he stood there trying to knock on her door, knowing that she was alone just on the other side of the wall. He lifted his hand again and tapped lightly, twice, on the door, thinking: If she doesn't hear that, it'll be a sign. I'll go away. I won't talk to anyone.

But he knew she'd heard it even while he was thinking. He heard her get up off the bed, the springs creaked slightly, and come across the room to open the door. She hauled it open and stood peering out at him from the light of the room, trying to adjust her eyes to the dusk of the hall.

"Mary," Gene said. "I—you busy?"

"No." She stood aside and he went by her nervously. Once inside he stood looking around him, realizing with surprise that he'd never been inside this room since it had been her personal place. The small table by the head of the bed was bare except for the green glass reading lamp, a reddish pottery ash-tray, and a package of cigarettes. He saw the book she'd been reading, face down on the pillow, before he turned to look at her.

Mary hadn't moved from the door and when he turned he surprised her staring at him levelly, her eyes dark. For a second he felt he'd been wrong; the stare made them mortal enemies, it made them hate. But it was only for a second and when she smiled she was familiar. Now there was only curiosity and a half-amused speculation in her face.

"What'd you do to Jake?" she asked suddenly, trying with something else to gloss over the strangeness they both felt. "He's been goin around like a bear with a sore head all day."

"Well," Gene went over and took a cigaret from the open package on the table, "that's partly why I've come in here. I wanted to talk about that. I done somethin I'm ashamed of."

"Oh?" Keeping him still with her eyes, she went over and sat down on the bed. But she got up a minute later to get a folder of matches from the bureau and Gene stood staring at her face, trying to read into it the power he'd thought she might have to help him out. It was a hard face to read. It was closed and smooth like all their faces, well shut away. We go around trying to hide ourselves from everyone else, he thought. The purely physical look of her head, the features foreshortened, the heavy shadows of lip and nose cast by the direct flame of the match bothered him, made him feel that she was a stranger to him and that he was a fool to be here.

"Didn't you hear the ruckus we kicked up Saturday night?" he said, painfully, trying to get back on a matter-of-fact footing when she settled back on the bed.

"Must have been late."

"Oh, about twelve, I guess."

"I was sound asleep."

"Well, anyhow, it's all mixed up with what I wanted to talk to you about. I—well, hell, I got to talk to somebody."

"So you picked me?" Mary asked with a flip upward note in her voice. Sensitive and quick to notice scorn, Gene glanced at her defensively, but he could see that his coming in here had pleased her; she was using the flipness for a defense herself.

"Well," she said, "you might sit down."

He sat beside her on the edge of the bed so she couldn't see his face unless he wanted her to. He started telling her about what had happened that night, dragging it out slowly at first, trying to make it as horrible as it had really been and as it seemed to him now. The words came slowly until he got interested in trying to say how he'd felt like Russ, and then his voice took on a quicker note and he groped less often for the right word. When he finished she didn't say anything until finally he turned to her.

"Look," he said, "it must be somethin wrong with us. We wouldn't want to do things like that unless there was somethin wrong. Even the girl I love tells me we're all crazy."

For the first time he looked full at her face and its immobility stopped him short. It was painful to watch somebody try as hard as she did to dredge up a smile, but she couldn't make it reach her eyes and they were sick and puzzled and a little frightened. That look hardened him, gave him back a little of the cruelty he thought he'd lost.

"What's it all about?" He thrust his head forward. "Why won't she live in the same house with you—with any of you?"

"Did she say exactly that?" Mary said carefully.

"Just about." Gene stared down at his hands, hanging limply between his knees. He felt as if the effort he'd have to put out to move them would be almost too much to bear.

"I don't know," she said. "It's some silly notion."

"It's not silly and it's not a notion. Not when it's enough to make her say she won't marry me because of my family. Here we've been plannin on gettin married for the last two years and now we've got the chance, she won't do it because of my family."

He was a little surprised at what she said then. When she looked up at him her face was frozen into a hard smile, but her eyes looked hopeless, as if something were dying in them and he stood helplessly by letting it die.

"Maybe she's right," she said softly. "Maybe there is something wrong with all of us."

He watched her reach out and take another cigarette from

the package, forgetting the one that was burning out in the ash tray. Her long brown fingers shook slightly when she lit the match and bent her head to it.

"Take her away from here," she said evenly, looking up at him, her eyes squinted against the smoke. "Get her away from the Ridge where she won't ever have to see or talk to any of us but you."

"But there's the place."

"You don't want this place. You don't want it anyhow because of Jake. I can tell from the way you told me about him that you couldn't ever take it. Don't you see what Pa wanted? He doesn't want any of us to get away from him ever and he's buying you that way. Get cut quick while you still want to."

Mary smiled at him and Gene could feel his own lips go taut with the instinctive imitative gesture you make when you try to help somebody out by doing just what they're doing, even when you know it won't make any difference.

"That's what you wanted me to say too." She reached out slowly and tilted the lamp shade until the direct light was no longer on her face. "Well, you've got it. Now get out."

Gene got up off the bed slowly, feeling like an old man, feeling physically stiff. But the sensation went immediately, melting like snow before the blazing fire of his own new resolution that she'd put the match to. He wanted to say something to her to make her see how he felt, to say he was sorry he'd hurt her. He knew he had hurt her, but he couldn't see why it should have been so bad. At the door, he turned to try to say what he felt he should, but she looked up again, sensing his hesitation and the hatred came back between them like a glassy wall.

"Get out," she said.

Twenty minutes later he came quietly down through the warm empty kitchen to the back door. Standing there, he turned to look back just once at the room he was leaving, remembering a little of what it meant to him. His whole life, all the while he'd been growing up, centered around that kitchen. He saw the moonlight shining on the water pail in its corner by the sink and, smiling a little, he went out wondering just how many times he'd filled that bucket from the well down by the old garden before Russ had had the pump put in.

ANNIE sat straight up in bed and stared at the window. The night was so still that she could feel her ears stretching to find a sound in it; she could hear silence now, but there'd been something unusual a moment ago, something strange enough to wake her out of the beginning of sleep.

She got up and went over to the window. There was a weak moon shining palely through low gray clouds and everything looked washed out and grayed down. Down in the valley and spreading out over the harbor there was a sea of mist that had a phosphorescence and seemed to writhe slowly as she watched it. The Ridge alone had any look of reality, looming darkly in the west, and she looked at it with that mixture of dislike and grudging pleasure people seemed to take in that great excrescence of the land. It made her think of a huge body lying there, not dead and safely quiet, merely asleep. Its red granite skeleton tautly held together with flesh of leaf mold and top soil and gravel—its great veins the taproots of the trees writhing slowly downward through the dangerous flesh into darkness.

Angrily she glared at it, thinking, it'd take more than a ground mist to blot *you* out.

When she looked down in the yard again, Gene was standing there watching her window. He was so still that she looked twice to make sure her imagination wasn't playing her

99

tricks; then she knew it wasn't by the way relief flooded up in her making her body warm in the chill air. She leaned forward feeling the ridge of the window sill cut cruelly across her suddenly hardened breasts.

"Annie?" His voice was so low she had to strain to hear him.

"What're you doin down there?" Relief made her sound harsher than she'd meant to.

"Look," Gene said. "Don't say anythin. I just came to tell you it's all right, see? Everything's all right."

"Wait." She leaned out the window. "I've got to talk to you. Don't go away." She started for the door and turned back to make sure he was still there. He was—the dim moonlight turned his smooth head to silver. Her knees felt weak as she hurried down the stairs to let him in. The key stuck in the lock the way it always did and by the time she got the door open, her breath was coming so hard she sounded as if she were crying.

Gene was waiting in the shadow of the house and when she threw the door open he slid in past her and hauled it to, quickly.

"You're crazy," he said. "Anyone ever see that and they'd have it all over town by mornin."

"I've *been* crazy since you were here last." She turned on him like a cat. "You ever go off like that and leave me again, I'll never speak to you—I'll—damn you, Gene."

"Hey." He caught her wrists and brought her about to face him, feeling the warm quickness of her breath against his cheek. "What's the matter? I didn't go anywhere. I just wanted time to think things over, that's all."

"I thought you weren't coming again. I thought you were mad. Can't you understand, you big lug. I love you and I thought the way you went off you weren't coming back."

"You never said you loved me before without me sayin it first."

"I have now," she glared at him. "And if you do that again, I'll kill you."

"Lord," Gene said in a whisper, "you're almost throwin off sparks."

"Come on in the kitchen. Tell me what happened."

"I've left, that's all. I'm not goin back."

"Did you talk to your father?"

"Yeah, but it was Mary really made up my mind for me."

"What did she say? Did you tell her what I said?" Annie sounded breathless.

"Yes, I did." He spoke slowly, remembering Mary's face when he'd told her. "She said you were right—I should get out—and take you with me."

"That's what *Mary* said?" She sounded as if she couldn't quite believe him.

"Yeah. Look, I don't get what this is all about. What's Mary got to do—"

"Nothing." She laughed and it sounded too loud to him. "I'm sorry about her, that's all. *For* her, I mean. She hasn't got anythin to do with us, Gene."

"What're you doin?" he whispered hoarsely, hearing her coming through the stillness of the sleeping house.

"We're all right now, aren't we?" she asked and her voice sounded dreamy and was so much closer than it had been that it made him jump and shake. "Aren't we?"

"Yeah, sure," Gene turned toward the door. "But I've got to go. Right now."

"No," Annie said. "I've got you now and you aren't going to get away again." She hesitated a minute. "There's a bed made up in that little room next to Ralph's. You go on up there and get to bed."

"Sure it's all right?"

"Don't be silly." She gave him a shove. "Go on."

He heard a door open and the scratch of a match. She lit the lamp and held it out to him; Gene took it and when she went past him, reached out and took her too. The way she came to him, quick and hard, made him know she'd been hoping he would.

"Kiss me good night first," he whispered. The lamp tilted crazily and he was glad he had only one free arm—if he'd had both of them he wouldn't have been able to let her go again.

"It won't be so long before you can come, too," he said softly.

"I'll come tonight if you want me to."

"It's not long to wait. But if you don't beat it now I won't be able to let you go."

He stood there waiting until he heard her go up the front stairs. Lying later on the narrow bed, Gene happened to think that if he'd planned this, he couldn't have picked a better place to come for his purpose. He was glad it had turned out the way it had, knowing that it wouldn't take Russ long to learn that he'd gone straight to Aaron Billings—that he'd gone there and been taken in.

SOME MEN can sense opposition in a crowd as finely as if it were articulate, and it stops them dead. Russ didn't work that way. He always sensed the opposition and it was like a blare of trumpets in his mind. It was like a thin bitter smoke of excitement to him, so acute that his nostrils widened, involuntarily, recognizing it.

So when he opened the door to the auditorium that morning and walked in to face the men who were sitting around waiting for something to happen, he felt instantly flaccid and his mind refused to keep any longer the interest that had burned steadily in it.

Aaron, or someone, had done his job almost too well. Russ glanced up toward the stage where Aaron, sitting in a straight chair tipped back against the wall, was looking out across the murky room with the air of a man who is satisfied with the world and everything in it. When he saw Russ, Aaron let the front legs of his chair come back to earth with a bang, got up, and came leisurely down the hall to meet him.

"Everythin all right?" Russ said unnecessarily. And because everything was so obviously all right, his tone was a little short.

Aaron glanced at him and nodded.

"Okay, on *my* end," he said.

It was, too. As the morning wore on Russ, more and more bored with the ease with which the whole thing was going along, had to admit grudgingly that Aaron must have had more influence than he'd given him credit for. The discussion went swimmingly. Whenever it showed signs of bogging down, somebody with a glib tongue retrieved it so ably that Russ found himself with little to do but sit back and wait. It was as if all the mortar had been removed from a dam and now the water itself was only too anxious to finish the job.

Russ sat back in his chair, shuffling through the batch of papers before him and trying to keep his mind on what was happening on the floor. It was hard for him because his incentive died with the death of his opposition—and he found his eyes watering and his jaws clenched in a mighty effort not to yawn.

Grinning wolfishly in an attempt to hold it back, he lifted his head and looked out over the hall, trying to spot individuals, wondering which ones Aaron had primed and how he'd done it. Russ's mind was held temporarily by the always fascinating speculation: What did Aaron have on so many men to make them come over to his side with a rush?

The attendance was better than they had a right to expect. Usually these special meetings, coming as they did in the middle of the business week and sometimes unexpectedly, were pretty light. But this time the town must have shut down for the morning. There were even a few women sitting in the back of the hall and apparently feeling as uncomfortable as they looked.

There were enough people present to warrant a written vote, he thought. He was supposed to be acting as moderator himself, but the meeting was going so peacefully that he'd just let it take its course. At last it had been hashed over to everyone's satisfaction and as the silence fell, Russ caught Aaron looking at him again and got quickly to his feet to call for the vote.

After that it had just been a matter of waiting: waiting until the long line of shuffling men passed the ballot box; waiting until the scrubby slips of paper were counted; waiting until the result was announced; waiting until it was all over.

But this waiting hadn't been as tedious for Russ as the meeting itself. One of the men in the line had been Gene. He'd looked up just as he thrust his ballot into the box and for a long, dangerously inimical moment father and son had tried to stare each other out of countenance. Russ won and, apparently completely relaxed but mentally alert again, sat watching Gene go back down to his seat and settle into it without looking up again at the platform. As he watched, Russ's long front teeth were barely showing in that tight grin, but his eyes were two icy pieces of opaque blue glass with no light visible through them.

He'd heard Gene go out of the house last night and he knew that Gene hadn't come back. There wasn't any way of telling *how* he knew. He'd fallen asleep soon after the door closed, thinking, Let him go; and had slept soundly until morning, but he knew as well as if his senses were awake and aware even when his body slept that Gene hadn't come back.

In the morning, Russ had been looking forward to a good battle at this meeting and his anticipation had been strong enough to make him forget about Gene—or not so much forget as tuck the whole affair back into his mind for future reference.

Now, cheated of one satisfaction, he remembered another.

Where the devil's he been all night? he was thinking as Gene sat down. He was sitting staring unseeingly before him when Aaron came up with the result of the vote on a scrap of paper. Russ glanced at it disinterestedly, got up, and announced it.

"Bids'll be accepted durin the next week," he said. "That's not much time, but now we've got started, I'm sure we all want to see this thing put through just as fast as we can do it. Besides, it'll be worth our while to have it done before the summer people come, so's there won't be any mix-up. They won't want to fiddle around out there in the harbor with a lot of barges and stuff like that. Meetin's adjourned."

Aaron came over and stood idly beside the table watching the hall spill its contents out the wide door. He leaned over and tapped the scrap of paper with a hard forefinger and his eyes were meaningly on Russ's face.

"Not bad," he said. "Ninety-four for, thirty against. Not bad."

"Nup." Russ shook his head. He shut his mouth hard on the garbled word. "Better than I expected."

"Well," Aaron nodded at him, "there's *my* part. Signed, sealed, and *dee*livered."

"Aaron—" Russ looked up at him coldly, glad to have something concrete to vent his feelings on. "You want to be careful. Anyone hearin you would likely come to the conclusion you and I had made a bargain of some kind. I wouldn't want anyone to get afoul of any wrong ideas."

"They won't from me," Aaron said hastily. "I just thought I'd mention it."

"Okay," Russ said. He looked thoughtfully at Aaron's face, not letting any of the things he was thinking get through. "Just so's we understand each other."

"You fellers talkin over anythin private?" Bill Martin said. He had come up and was standing slightly behind them, waiting for Aaron. Russ turned and looked at him sharply, but Bill's smooth brown face told him nothing.

"Aaron was just sayin the vote was surprisin," Russ said. "Seein how so many of you boys have been against buildin that breakwater for so long."

"Guess that storm we had was the last straw," Bill suggested.

"I'm not surprised." Russ's lack of interest was so clear in his voice that Bill, after a hasty glance at Aaron, retreated swiftly.

"See you outside, Aaron?" he said over his shoulder.

"Just a minute," Aaron called after him. He stayed where he was, just waiting almost as if he felt there was something more Russ had to say to him. He even made Russ feel it.

"There's nothin more to say," Russ answered the unspoken request impatiently. "Submit your bid with the others. You've got my word it'll be considered favorably. It'll stand every bit as good a chance as any of em. I can't say any more than that."

"That's good enough," Aaron told him. He turned as if to follow Bill, then turned back again, grinning vacuously, his eyes dull to hide the intensity of his interest. "Oh, Russ, d'you make it a practice of lockin your kids out if they don't come home early?"

Russ looked at him steadily.

"Why, what d'you mean, Aaron?"

"Oh, Gene turned up at twelve, one o'clock last night, lookin for a place to bed down. Got Annie up and generally woke the house."

"Godsake," Russ said, keeping his face clear of expression with an effort, "I musta locked the door by mistake. We're all heavy sleepers. He probably couldn't raise anyone. Hope he didn't make too much of a nuisance of himself."

"Heck, no. I'm always glad to have him around." Aaron looked thoughtful. "Them kids said anythin to you yet?"

"You mean about their gettin married?" Russ heard his own voice going on steadily and he was amazed that it sounded so natural when it should have been shaking with the force of the anger that was boiling thickly inside him.

"Yeah," he said smoothly. "Gene was sayin just the other night he thought it was about time he settled down."

"Got anythin against it?"

"Not if you haven't. I guess they're both old enough to pick out who they're goin to marry."

Aaron said nothing for a minute. When he looked at Russ there was, in spite of him, a spark of amusement in his eyes. He gave the visor of his cap a flick, shoving it far back on his head.

"Funny, ain't it," he said, "the way things work out?"

Russ was still thinking that over when he went looking for Gene.

If Gene had gone to anyone but Aaron Billings, Russ would have let him go his merry way until he found out for himself how difficult life could be. When he'd learned his lesson, Gene would come crawling back.

But by going to Aaron Billings, Gene had pulled a new factor into the situation. Now Aaron knew what it was all about; Aaron was laughing up his sleeve about the whole thing. Russ had read that much into the almost invisible gleam of amusement in Aaron's face. Now the first heat of his anger had gone, leaving a cold flame burning behind his eyes, a flame that showed through this time.

He found Gene at the wharf, hard at work. He walked over to stand beside him and he knew Gene had seen him coming, though his eyes didn't lift from the barrels he was heading with crocus.

"Gene, I want you," Russ said. He didn't wait. He walked back to the old Buick at the same even pace he'd come down the wharf. He got in and waited. Gene was slow enough, but Russ knew he'd come. He did, finally, and stood beside the car, his head bent a little to look in at his father.

"Get in," Russ jerked his head at the other door.

"I can't leave the wharf. I'm workin."

Russ started the engine. Gene went around the car and got into the front seat. Russ swung the Buick around and headed for home. Gene, after one silent glance of useless protest, settled sullenly into his corner.

The old car lumbered up the Ridge Road at her top speed, swirled into the drive, and out into the barnyard. Instead of stopping her there, Russ sent her down over the little slope to the pasture and stopped behind the barn where the brown grass made a wide level space well out of sight of the house.

"Get out," he said.

Seeing suddenly what was coming, Gene felt an icy ball dissolve in the pit of his stomach, leaving him weak and momentarily unable to move.

"I can't."

"By god, you get out," Russ said. "I'm not goin to have it said all over town you made a fool of me goin to Aaron Billings like that."

"No."

"Come out here." Russ got out and came around to open the door. He got hold of Gene's arm and hauled him out of the car. His long face was red and his eyes were beginning to look blind. He was breathing hard, deep even breathing. "Now you're goin to get the lickin of your life," he said. "I can't take a club to you any more, but I can give it to you this way."

"I can't fight *you*." Gene's voice was a horrified croak. Standing there, his eyes were barely an inch below his father's, but he was beginning to feel again like a misbehaving six-year-old.

"Scared?" Russ said. He reached out and slapped Gene, the

red marks of his fingers springing out startlingly on the fair skin.

Gene took a step away and every trace of emotion had gone out of his voice.

"Don't touch me again," he said. "If you do, I go. An this time you won't come haulin me back."

Russ slapped him again, harder.

For a second they stood there eyeing each other, neither of them quite sure what was going to happen—then Gene turned away and went up the slope to the house, trying not to stumble. The red shimmering haze behind his eyes made everything he looked at uncertain and fading.

GRACE thought she'd got to know the sound of Russ's old engine so well she couldn't make a mistake about it; so when she heard the Buick lumber into the yard, she glanced unconsciously at the clock.

Only two, she thought. I must've been wrong.

But when the front door opened and shut five minutes later and heavy steps pounded up the stairs, she stood frowning in the middle of the kitchen, listening to the steps moving about overhead. She heard feet go quickly along the hall and then a bedroom door opened.

There, she thought, feeling the heat of foreboding warm along her cheeks. That's Gene and something's wrong. He's never been home in the middle of the day. And I'll swear that was the Buick.

Hastily she set the kettle she'd been holding down on the back of the stove and went quietly in through the hall to the foot of the stairs to stand there listening.

She could hear Gene moving quickly around his room and finally curiosity got the better of her and she started upstairs.

She began talking casually, before she reached his open door, to make him think she'd just happened up there by chance.

"Gene, that you? I never had a chance yet to make your bed. What brings you home this time of day?"

Then she reached the door and stood there staring. Her eyes went quickly from the smooth counterpane with the yawning suitcase spread out on it to Gene's stiff back. He'd heard her coming and had had time to go over to the window so he could be standing back to her when she came in.

"Gene, weren't you home last night?"

"No, Ma."

"Well, I don't know. Is there somethin wrong?"

"Ayep."

"Well, don't stand there like a gawp. What is it? I think you better tell me about it when you kids take to stayin out all night. All I hope is you were under cover somewhere an didn't get your death." Grace didn't want to keep on talking —she wanted to stop so he could have a chance to tell her what was wrong, but there was something about his broad stiff back, so inflexibly turned to her, that made her know she wasn't going to like whatever he might tell her.

"You weren't out roistin around, were you, somewhere? If you got too drunk to come home, Gene, I'll be mad. You know I don't think much of you boys drinkin."

"Ma," Gene turned on her, "for pete sake, can't you think of anythin else happenin but one of us gettin too drunk to come home?"

"Don't use that tone to me, Gene. I won't stand for it."

"I'm sorry," he said. "But I've got something to ask you. When are you goin to think we're grown up? When are you goin to stop treatin us all like two-year-olds?"

He turned his back on her again and looked down into the yard, seeing the pattern of sunlight through bare limbs on brown grass, seeing the hens picking their bobbing way across the brown packed earth of the barnyard. But his ears were tensed to catch any sound she might make.

For a second she made none. Then, moving like a much older woman, she came slowly into the room and crossed it to look into the suitcase Gene had opened on the bed. She sat down heavily and Gene, hearing the bed springs creak, knew what she was doing. Automatically she reached out and smoothed the two white shirts he'd tossed into the gaping bag.

"What is it, Genie," she said softly. "What's wrong?"

For a moment the old familiar name made the muscles of his throat jerk spasmodically, then when he remembered that she used to say the same thing to him when he'd come to her with a cut finger or a scraped knee, his resentment returned more strongly.

"Well, tell me where you're goin?" Grace said finally when she saw he wasn't going to answer her.

"I'm leavin for good," Gene said tightly, not looking at her. "I'm goin for good and all."

In the middle of her silence, he did turn finally and the sight of the four red marks across his pale face drove whatever else she'd been thinking right out of her mind.

"What's that on your face?"

"That's one of the reasons I'm goin," Gene said. He was fighting hard to keep his voice level, but it got away from him. "I'm just a little bit too old to be slapped around like a kid who isn't behavin just right."

"Who?" she said, feeling her lips stiffen on the word because she knew the answer.

"My father." For a second Grace almost thought he was smiling, then she saw that it was a grimace of pure unreasoning rage.

"I won't have it," she said stiffly. "I will not have you fightin with your own father. I won't stand for it."

"In the first place, I didn't fight," Gene said, his nostrils flaring slightly with the effort it took to keep his voice down.

"I stood there and let him get away with it. I should've killed him. I had to come away or I would of."

"What *are* you?" Her own voice was a thing neither of them were familiar with. It was low and ragged as if the words strangled her. "What kind of kids have I got that act like savages, that talk about killin their own father?"

"Maybe we're all a little too much like him," Gene said and turned his back on her again. "Look at Stanny," he said. "He's got that kid scared of his own shadow. Look at Mary. Look at Jake. Ma, for pete sake, what's he tryin to do to us all?"

"Gene," she said easily, regaining her own composure when his threatened to break. She got up and went over to the window so that she was standing close enough to look up into his face. "I want you to stay here till you settle down. You've had some sort of a misunderstandin with him and you're all tore out and you aren't in any shape to make up your mind over anythin as important as this."

"Misunderstanding! Well, I guess you could call it that, but it's been goin on the past ten years an more."

"Now," she said soothingly, crooning the word out. "You're all rucked up. You have to understand your father. He's a man with a quick temper. He gets upset over little things sometimes."

"You call my life a little thing?"

"Now, that's not what I meant. I don't know what you two have been huffin about now an I don't want to hear it till you get settled down again. It's always blown over before and it will this time—just give it a chance."

"That's what I'm not going to do," Gene said. "I don't want to give it a chance."

He moved around her, turning away instead of toward her, and went over to the chest of drawers. He fumbled in one of the open drawers and came back with an armful of shirts and socks and spread them carefully in the suitcase.

Grace knew without surprise that this time it wasn't going to work—no matter what she said to him or how she tried to persuade him, it wasn't going to touch Gene. And because she had never stopped to think about her kids being really grown up, she had never prepared any other means of reaching through to them—she had only the way she had just used on Gene—and it had failed.

His face, as he bent over the suitcase, was so like Russ's that, as she stood there in the door, the illusion was so strong—she was so sure it was Russ—that she felt as young as he looked. She wouldn't have been surprised to look in the mirror and find herself twenty years younger. She actually did look down at herself, but the sight of her own hands, large and a little mishapen, brought her back sharply to the realization that this was her son; this was the first of her children to leave her and she had no way to stop him.

But because she couldn't help herself, she tried once more. "Gene."

He said nothing, but the way his back stiffened told her he was listening at least.

"Gene, don't go. I don't want you to go."

Gene did nothing—he just stood there, his back to her, waiting. To save them both the embarrassment of his not answering, Grace turned and went out of the room, leaving behind her a silence so definite that she felt as if she didn't have to shut the door; there was already a door shut between them and now she stopped to think, she realized that it must have been shut for a long time.

There was no way left for them to understand each other; there was no common ground, because she would always be aligned with Russ against her own kids. For a second she resented Russ, thinking: He's drivin my own children away from me. But the habit of years was stronger than a momentary impulse toward understanding and by the time she reached the foot of the stairs she was angry with Gene.

I certainly never thought I'd ever be called on to stand and listen to one of my own children tell me I've made a failure of bringing up my family, she thought bitterly. It's a fine thing when a mother who's tried as hard as I have has to listen to anything like that.

Here I always thought it'd be a pleasure to grow old, having my own kids around—

She came into the kitchen to find Mary at the sink washing, and her thoughts had become so real to her that she started talking immediately and as if Mary, instead of Gene, were responsible for the resentful anger that made her say the things she was thinking.

"I looked forward to growin old—when you get along so far and have so little, that's about all you *can* look forward to. And I thought it'd be a happy time, gettin old, with my kids beside me. I never thought I'd live to see the day they tried to kill me. You're all settin out to break my heart—you'd all like to see me in my grave before my time."

Mary had turned at the first sound of her mother's voice, but when she realized what Grace was saying, her face closed back into its habitually heavy, uncaring look. Carefully she started drying her hands on the roller towel beside the sink, taking great pains with it as if it were the most important thing in her life.

"What's wrong now?" She threw the words over her shoulder.

"I'll tell you what's wrong." Grace was almost panting with anger. "It's that brother of yours. Gene's leavin."

"Oh."

"Well, is that all you've got to say about it? I suppose you think it's a fine thing, too. I suppose you'd like to see me get old here alone with nobody to care whether I live or die."

"I don't think it'll come to that. You've got Pa. And Jake and Stanny and me."

"My own son," Grace said. She hadn't even heard Mary,

probably nothing but the sound of her voice had penetrated.

"I knew about it." Mary turned to face her. Her expression was a strange mixture of defiance and embarrassment. "He came and asked me last night what I'd do. I told him I'd get out and just as soon as I could."

That got through the haze of self-pity Grace had evoked for herself and stopped her in mid-word. She stood staring, her eyes wide, her mouth moving soundlessly.

"All right," Mary said. She went over to the table and dropped wearily into one of the straight chairs. She looked listless and uncaring, sitting there, her face hardened—not youthfully—into a mask of inertia. "Don't say it, Ma. I've heard it all before. We're ungrateful."

"Yes," Grace said tightly. "You are. *All* you kids are. You never stop to think of all me and your father've done for you when it comes to satisfyin your own selfish ways. You always think of yourself first."

"Yes, I guess we do," Mary agreed. "But you've made us. You've always done everything for us. You've always given us everything. That's what's wrong with us."

"Well, I certainly would like to know what parents are for if they can't do things for their own children."

"You've done too much for us." Mary put her elbows on the table and propped her head heavily in her hands. "And maybe not enough. Did you ever stop to think of that? You've kept us being babies. Look at me. Just take a look at me."

"Mary—"

"You better listen. I've been wanting to get this off my chest for a long time now and you better listen. You've done so much for me all my life I never could do anything for myself. If I wanted to pick up and go the way Gene's doing I couldn't—not now. I'd be scared to. I'd be afraid because I'm twenty-one and I don't know how to take care of myself. Without my father and mother to watch out for me and take care of me, I'd starve."

"Mary, I—" Grace tried to say something—she didn't know what it would have been because her whole mind seemed to have turned black, her head felt as if it were stuffed with cotton batting.

"Did you ever stop to think how hard it is to live in this house?" Mary's voice went on with a steady unplanned hammering of monotonous distaste. "You've done a lot for us, but still we all come second. He's first. He's over this house like a tent. Nobody ever uses the best chair in the livin room because it's his chair; even when he isn't here, nobody sits in that chair. Nobody touches the morning paper till he comes home at night to read it first. Why, we wouldn't know if the world had come to an end till he came home to read it in the paper and tell us all about it."

"Mary—you listen. You don't know what you're sayin. He's your father and he's my husband. This is his house. And while you're livin in it, I will not have you feelin that way about him."

"You can stop me talkin," Mary said. "But you can't do much about the way I feel, can you?"

"I don't know what to make of you. I think you've all gone crazy."

"It wouldn't surprise me," Mary said. "Sometimes I wonder myself. After a while, livin here, you get to feel as if you really weren't there at all—you want to pinch yourself to see if you can still hurt and you wouldn't be surprised sometime if you didn't."

"Mary Walls!"

"It isn't much help to have you standin there just sayin 'Mary' over and over. Why don't you try sometime to see how it must be?"

"I—I guess I didn't know." Grace's whole face felt stiff and as if it didn't belong to her. "I thought all these years I was doin the right thing. I didn't know any other way." She stopped and then said wearily, "I tried my best."

Mary sat for a moment watching her, not sure whether or not to be sorry; then she got up and came slowly over to her mother. Hesitatingly she put her arm around Grace's solid shoulder.

"Please," she said softly. "I didn't mean to make you feel bad. I didn't mean to hurt you. I just wanted you to see how it was."

For a moment, remembering the things Mary had just said, Grace tried to resist the comfort offered by those arms strongly around her; but she couldn't do it. That strength was something she needed and had found again. Something of the strength she had known a long time ago with Russ was here in Mary where it was closer to what she'd wanted all her life, where it came closer to being what she needed because it was a strength of her own kind. She put her forehead down for a moment against Mary's hard shoulder, then stood away, shaking her head.

"There, I don't know what gets into people times like this. We all say what we don't mean."

"That's right." Mary looked straight over her mother's head. "We do. You see, it's like this, Ma. You've held the family together so far. But you can't any more. You've got to let those who want to go."

"I suppose so." Grace put her hand wearily to her forehead. "I know I'm behavin like a foolish old woman. My kids'll have to leave me sometime and I've got to get used to it, that's all."

"That's right." Mary's old embarrassment at any show of personal feeling had come back as far as her tongue, but her eyes on her mother were questioning, as if Grace knew something she needed to know and might tell her if she waited long enough.

"But why can't they go peaceably? Why does everyone have to get all rucked up?" she started again, her voice rising.

When Mary said nothing, Grace's rebirth of anger faded, leaving her tired.

"You'll help me, won't you?" she said softly.

Mary nodded, unable to say the word. They were standing there in the middle of the kitchen staring at each other when Gene came down the front stairs and went out the door without coming into the kitchen. They both turned their heads with identical listening looks, and then glanced at each other again.

"He never even came out to say good-by," Grace said.

"He's not going far if I know him. It isn't as if you'd never see him again. Let him go now."

"I guess I better. I guess we all need a chance to settle down before we say any more to each other. I guess I said the wrong things, too."

MARY had trained herself to walk, when she left the house, as if she had no particular objective in mind. She went slowly, almost dawdling, down under the apple trees and along the edge of the woods to the old County Road that went parallel with the main road up along the side of the Ridge. The old County Road was nothing now but two rutted tracks that meandered aimlessly along through the woods. In the early spring it was a morass of water which had washed all the soil from around boulders and under the roots of cedars, so that in a dry season it looked like the naked flesh-stripped backbone of some great animal.

Once it had been the main road out of Christian Ridge. Then, after the other roads had been improved, this one was abandoned. But even then it had been the one road by which an automobile could bypass the Ridge village. The village had been the last one on the Freehold road to permit automobiles in its main street. It clung for years to the questionable distinction. Never had one of the noisy, indigestion-ridden machines sullied its main street. They went bumping in and out over the old County Road, their drivers hanging on and swearing, until one night a rash traveling salesman had rebelled and put his machine through the main street at full speed, bringing sound sleepers upright in their beds. Once the ice had been broken, it was pretty hard to let it freeze again, and the old County Road fell into complete disuse.

It was seldom used now and never for anything but a wood road. Occasionally when he'd been cutting wood down that way, Jake would wait for a good fall of snow and take the wood sled in through it; but the snow had to be deep, otherwise the road was completely impassable by anything but foot.

Just before she left the orchard, Mary stood at the entrance of the old road for a moment, sighting up along it thoughtfully. If only the color of a shadow would stay one thing long enough for you to decide what it was, she thought. But it shifted and changed even while she was thinking, and was something else in an instant, as mobile and fluid as water and just as hard to pin down.

The cold fall light made everything look to her as if it had an edge—everything but the old cedars themselves. Even the rounded granite boulders thrusting their way up through what had once been leaf mold and rich black dirt, had an edged look, making them as thin and inconstant as their own shadows. Light fell in sharp lines, hard as the blade of a knife, acute angles through the trees, giving illusory and fleeting importance to a rock or a root.

Looking at it and feeling what it made her feel gave Mary a deep sense of a lack somewhere in herself, an incompetence, a not-knowing-how.

"I just don't know enough," she said thinly. "I don't know enough about it."

She glanced back over her shoulder at the house, saw her

mother coming out the shed door, and plunged into the shelter of the cedars in case Grace might see her and call her back for some reason. Once out of sight of the house, she went faster, picking the familiar way along the rough old road, feeling almost two-dimensional herself, because the light made everything else so flat.

When she'd gone half a mile, she turned sharp left along a narrow path she'd swamped out three years ago, went up through the alders into a fringe of young spruces, and came out in her Aunt Hat's back pasture. Her lack of confidence was gone and she was beginning to have that I-know-just-how-to-begin feeling, but she greeted it with a certain amount of diffidence, remembering how many times before it had betrayed her and gone out from under her fingers like sand, leaving her more completely discouraged with each departure. She had an idea that she'd be all right if she could only recapture the feeling as well as the look of things—perhaps if she could remember how it had made her feel. She went frowning up across the pasture, trying to concentrate on her own emotions when she'd looked at the two-dimensional road.

"Hello." Her Aunt Hat met her at the door. "I had more'n half a suspicion you'd be along today and when I looked up and see you comin out of the woods, I thought, there!"

"Well—" Mary looked at her with a sheepish grin. "I didn't know but what I'd have another stab at it."

"You get discouraged," Hat said thoughtfully. "Anythin like that, when it don't come out just the way you wanted it, you get awful discouraged. But I notice it never lasts very long."

"I wanted to find out, too, if Pa came up to see you a week or so ago," Mary said quickly.

Hat nodded and her wide mouth tightened a little.

"He was here."

Mary followed her into the kitchen and sat down by the

table. Hat went over to the stove and felt the side of the coffee pot.

"Plenty here," she said. "You better have a cup with me."

Seeing that she wanted to talk, Mary tried to hide her own impatience to get started with what she'd come for. She wanted to hear what Hat had to say but at the moment it didn't seem to her she could bear wasting the time, sitting here talking.

"I don't know," she began.

"Well, in a way it concerns you, too, so you might's well hear about it," Hat said.

"Okay." Mary settled herself into the chair and waited while Hat poured the coffee for her. It came out of the pot as black as pitch and hardly less fluid in consistency.

"There." Hat settled down in the other chair. "That's certainly the way to make coffee. You make it in the mornin, good an strong, and leave it settin. Then, by this time in the afternoon, why you got somethin worth drinkin. Just the way I like it." She took a sip of the coffee and looked pleased. A little less Spartan, Mary dosed hers plentifully with sugar and evaporated milk before venturing to taste it.

"Yes," Hat began comfortably, "he come up here a week ago Monday night, it was, all set to do me good."

"That so?" In spite of herself, Mary's mouth quirked into an unwilling smile. She could see so plainly the way Russ must have come in, big and expansive, looking as if he were in every corner of the room, though he sat in only one.

"Why, he give the impression this place would be harder for me to handle now I'm alone than it was when Ma was alive, just as if she was ever able to help out around. Yes, an he got real put out when I said it would be just that much easier, because now I wouldn't have to fetch and carry for her so much." She hesitated and then, in case she'd sounded too harsh about her own mother, added,

"Poor old mother. She had sort of a hard time of it the

last few years, I'm afraid. It always was hard for her to sit by an watch other people doin all the work. Her fingers must've been itchin to get into things."

"They must have," Mary said, clutching at her slipping memory of the feeling she'd been trying to capture, knowing that decency alone kept her here listening to Hat have over her troubles. "Well," she said, knowing that Hat might as well get the whole thing out of her system now, "I take it you told him you didn't want to come down and live with us."

"Yessiree, bob," Hat nodded emphatically. "That's just what I told him. And I also told him about all the plans I had for ways of makin enough to keep me here. It made him kind of mad, I'm afraid, and I'm sorry for that, seein how much he's done for me and Ma. But I just couldn't stand it, not havin my own place."

"That must have been what got him so upset," Mary said thoughtfully. "When I got home that night, he was there in the kitchen and acting just like a bear with a sore head."

"That's what it was, all right," Hat said. "I guess if there's anythin he can't bear, it's havin anyone stand up to him in anythin."

Suddenly reminded of her own troubles, Mary nodded.

"Yes, I guess you know that's well as anyone." Hat looked thoughtfully at her niece. "I don't know. Watchin you kids grow up, I've wondered a lot which one of you'd bust out first."

"It won't be me."

"You scared of him, too?"

Mary stared levelly at her for a moment, but it wasn't an angry stare, merely thoughtful.

"Probly," she said. "But I won't be the first because Gene has already."

"'N there!" Hat said, her eyes bugged out a little and she hunkered up on her chair until she was sitting on the edge of it.

Mary couldn't help grinning at Hat's expression of pleasurably titillated anticipation.

"Yes, I know," Hat said. "But I simply do not care. I've always been willin to admit I got a nose for gossip as good as the next one. Now stop settin there like a graven image and tell me what happened. Why, lord god amighty, I could sit up here from one year's end to the next and not know what went on in my own family, it if warn't for you."

"Nothing happened," Mary said. "Not what you could really call anything. Gene and Jake had some sort of a ruckus and then Pa duffed in and got Gene so mad he just packed up and went."

"Lord," Hat said, her agile mind rapidly pinning together the various possible combinations of events that might be hiding behind this skeleton of news. "Now I won't say I'm surprised—I woulda been, though, if it hadn't happened soon. I will say I thought it'd be you."

"Me?" Mary glanced away. "I guess I'm not a very good rebel."

"Hunh," her aunt snorted. "There'll probly be a bigger explosion when you do finally break out. Well, that Gene," she said wonderingly. "I always thought he was sort of pusillanimous."

"I guess he fooled us all."

"My lord in the windswept heaven," Hat said; she let herself go back into her chair with a deflating-balloon sort of motion. "I bet Grace is some old tore out over this."

"Not very," Mary refused to meet Hat's eyes. "She's takin it all right."

"Well, maybe." Hat was unconvinced. "But it ain't the sort of thing she would. However, maybe she's changed."

"Probly."

Hat, seeing that she'd already said enough about Grace, shifted her point of attack rapidly.

"I've wished," she said, "that lady who was around so much

123

last summer, I sort of wished for your sake she didn't have to go away when she did."

"Lucy Simmons?" Mary said, not because she wasn't sure who Hat meant, but because she wanted to say the name and Hat was about the only person she could say it to and have her know who it meant.

"You was different while she was around," Hat said. "It seemed to do you good to have somebody around who could talk to you about things you both liked. Now me, I talk a lot, but I can't say anythin to you about that." She jerked her head toward the woodshed. "Mainly because I don't know the first thing about it."

"Nemmind," Mary said. She got up, smiled at Hat, and turned toward the shed door. "Well, I don't know but what I'll go see what I can do."

"Yes, go along with you," Hat said and sat watching the door close slowly.

When she shut the shed door behind her, Mary shut everything else on the other side of it away from her. Sometimes it even seemed as if she shut herself outside, the self that spent its time groping vaguely around wondering what was going to become of it. She still had a lack of sureness; uncertainty was stronger in her here than it ever was anywhere else, but it was an uncertainty that took none of her identity away from her; it wasn't a degradation of her personality, but a building up.

The little shed room was bare enough. In the middle of one wall there was a round zinc-lined hole that had been cut to take the stove pipe from the small air-tight stove Hat had given her the first winter she'd used this little room. The wide boards of the floor were painted deep blue and were bare except for the small square of old rug that lay under the easel by the north window.

Mary went over and peered into the stove, thinking Hat must have meant it when she'd said she expected her. There was a bed of coals glowing warmly there and Mary put another stick of wood in on top of them before shutting it up again.

There was one other thing in the small room, the thing you noticed first when you came into it. In the far corner, partly in shadow, stood a huge silvered tree root they'd found on the shore last summer. Looking at it, Mary smiled a little, remembering the way Lucy had walked slowly around it, her eyes thoughtful.

"Now that would be a good thing to have," she'd said, smiling. "You could do surprising things with that."

Together, they'd loaded the great rounded nub of silvered wood into the rumble seat of Lucy's rattling roadster and hauled it up to the Ridge. Hat, seeing them coming from the window, had come rushing out to the shed door, her eyes wide with amazement.

"For the land sake, what've you two hauled home now?" she'd said.

"Well, we don't quite know yet," Lucy'd said. "But if you've got a hatchet, or maybe an old chisel and a hammer, we'll find out."

Speechless, Hat went and got the old carpenter's hatchet she kept in her tool drawer and handed it to Lucy. Then she and Mary had waited while Lucy did some more thoughtful walking. Her sharp foxy features, under her short mop of iron-colored hair had been concentrated on what she was thinking, but when she looked at the two of them, Hat astounded, Mary beginning to be amused, she'd laughed.

"This is really more in my husband's line," she'd said. "I'm just going it blind. But I'll bet you anything we can get a woman out of that."

She had, too. In a chunky rounded-off sort of way, she'd evolved a woman.

"Well, there." Hat had sounded a little shocked. "I don't

know's I ever see anyone sit just like that, but if I ever had, that would look somethin like it."

It had been sitting there in the corner ever since, a great mournful, prehistoric-looking chunk of cedar, a crude woman, the forehead down on the huge drawn-up knees. Every time she looked at it, Mary started thinking about that summer and what it had meant to her, knowing Lucy even for the short time she had.

At least now she knew there were people somewhere doing the things they wanted to do, doing the things she wanted to do.

Sometimes she wasn't sure, though, but that made it worse —it was like getting a glimpse of something fascinating and desirable through an open door and then having the door slammed in your face.

If only Russ were different; if only he thought what she wanted to do was as important as what people thought she should do.

She picked up a piece of charcoal and started blocking out the fresh canvas and in five minutes had forgotten them all.

"FOR chrissake, Aaron," Russ said. He grabbed his pipe up off the desk and sat looking at it as if he'd never seen it before. Then because he couldn't find anything to say and because the situation was completely new, he just sat staring angrily at Aaron.

The stillness in the office after his own voice had echoed and faded out left Russ wondering just what was going on behind the implacable look on Aaron's face. There he sat, his cap for once perched on his knee instead of on his head—there he sat, apparently completely at his ease, his legs crossed, one toe swinging. But he seemed to be inordinately interested in the gyrations of that toe.

"You might at least give me credit for a little horse sense," Russ said.

Aaron looked up at him, a quick reserved glance. There was no flicker of change in the expression on his brown face. It looked closed and much too quiet. Suddenly Russ got up and went over to the window where he wouldn't have to sit and look at Aaron and where Aaron couldn't see his face.

He clasped his hands loosely behind his back and stood staring down into the street two stories below him. He saw, without noticing, the two women meet on the sidewalk outside the Red Front. They stood talking for a minute and turned and went into the store together. He saw the school kids start coming, in trickles and bunches, down past the store fronts. He took out his big watch, glanced at it, and stuffed it back into his pants pocket before he realized he really hadn't seen what time it was.

"Will you tell me," he began carefully against Aaron's silence, "will you tell me what the hell you mean by comin up here and practically accusin me of not carrying through on some deal you say I've cooked up with you?"

He stopped and heard Aaron clear his throat, the way a man will just before he says something. After that Aaron was silent for so long a moment that Russ thought he wasn't even going to say anything then. But when he'd nearly given up, Aaron moved slightly in his chair.

"I didn't say just that, did I?" he began. "What I did say was, I thought you said you'd consider that bid favorably. Them was your exact words, if I remember rightly. You also said you'd be pleased to see that job go to somebody right here in town instead of an outsider."

"Now, look," Russ said. "Maybe I did say that, I don't remember exactly. But what if I did? This is a business deal from the word go, Aaron. Your bid was put in an considered right along with the others and it was rejected because there was another one that give us a better price."

"You said—" Aaron began stubbornly.

"For pete sake," Russ said bitterly, "what are you, a sixteen-year-old? Look, you're a business man, you know how these things're done. I'm not going to stand up and hold out for any one bid against a better one, not if my own brother submitted it, I wouldn't. Get that straight."

"I can't see how this here out-of-town company's bid was so much better than mine. You don't even know what the final cost'll be."

"I'll tell you," Russ said, holding his patience roughly. "I thought the whole thing over pretty careful. And what I decided wasn't easy, see? You're right enough when you say we can't be sure of the exact expense, but we came close enough to the final figure to let me see it was lower'n yourn. Then, too, this company's got all the equipment, and first-class equipment, too, right at hand, where you'd have to lease it. I thought it all over and I figured the best thing to do was give them the job. That's how it is and that's how it's goin to stand."

"By god," Aaron said. He got up to face Russ. "Next time I submit a bid on a job, you can bet your life it'll be on a cost-plus basis. Cost-plus! Sounds to me like a damn good way to get rich quick."

Russ turned on him like a wounded tiger. He even snarled. Unconsciously Aaron backed away.

"I'll tell you somethin," Russ said clearly. "My job means a lot to me. I've had it a long time and there's never been a word against my honesty or the way I've done that job. I'm proud of that record, see? I got a right to be. And when I do anything that ain't straight, you'll see elephants dance."

"That sounds good from you after what we talked over."

"Talked over," Russ said and his voice sounded as if his loose collar had suddenly become too tight for him. "You've got a hell of a nerve to stand there and say that to me. What did we talk over? Not a cussed thing."

"Not in so many words. I didn't think it was necessary. I've done business with you before. You never were a one to put everythin out in the open. You know it, too. I've made many a deal with you without havin it down in black and white."

"That was personal business," Russ said. As abruptly as he'd lost control of his temper, he found it again. Out of some well of composure, he'd dragged an icy calm. "I've never made a deal on town business with anyone, and I never will."

"That warn't the way I understood it."

"I don't know what you need. A blueprint, maybe. I said it plain enough and often enough." Russ smiled tightly, but he was beginning to wonder just what was behind all this. "And I've said it in so many words. There never was a deal."

Ostentatiously he turned his back and started fiddling with the papers on his desk. He filled his pipe carefully and stuck it into the corner of his mouth.

"Hadn't been for me," Aaron said, "they'd never of voted for it. You know that, don't you?"

"Maybe not when they did," Russ said easily. "They would have eventually. Don't misunderstand me, Aaron. I realize you had a lot to do with the way that vote went. It was a help and I'm grateful."

"You've got a darn funny way of showin it."

"Listen," Russ said. He started talking in even paced syllables. "This is the way it is. Evidently you expected somethin I never was willin to give you. I'd give you a hand, yes. Any time. But I wouldn't do anythin that'd make people think I was tryin to influence them for a personal reason. Not for God Himself, I wouldn't. And you're a long way from bein God."

"Since when've you been afraid of havin people think you had personal reasons for anythin?"

"I can see it isn't doin me any good to talk to you now."

climbing a tree and looking straight out over the tops of shorter trees instead of down to the ground.

The car that had floundered in through the old tote road to the orchard soon after dark was parked inconspicuously on the grass under the first apple tree. The two boys had been sitting there for nearly an hour, alert, in absolute silence. One was perched on the front fender, a rifle lying loosely across his knees and the other sat farther back with one hand on the spotlight switch.

At a slight sound farther down the orchard, they both jerked to immediate attention, still in silence. The sound came closer until it turned into the separate leisurely thud of hoofs. Then it stopped.

The boy at the light aimed the spot carefully in the direction he'd marked and snapped it on. The deer, a big doe, had just lowered her head to get the few bitter windfalls under the tree, and now she lifted it again with a startled snort and stood facing them. Her front legs were wide apart and her eyes glowed milkily green at them.

"Shoot, why don't you? Shoot, you darn fool."

"I c-c-can't."

"Well, gimme the gun." He took his hand off the light just as the doe lifted one fore foot and pawed at the ground. Her eyes faded slightly as she turned her head a little away, but the light fascinated her and brought her head on again. He grabbed the rifle with a low growl of impatience, but it was loud enough for the doe to hear, loud enough to break the queer thread of enchantment that held her eyes on the glare of the spot. She rose on her hind legs, whirled and, just as the rifle shot whipped the darkness into jagged splinters, went for the timber, her white flag flickering. The boy with the rifle took another snap-shot at the vanishing tail before he flung the gun down. Then, watching with startled eyes, they saw the white flag falter and sink and vanish.

"By god, we got her."

"Yeah, that's all right. But you be careful how you handle that gun. Throwing it around like that. My old man ever finds out I took it, he'll skin me alive. That's his best rifle."

"Well," the heavier, slower voice stiffened them. "I guess he's gonna find out all right, just as soon's he pays your fine, young feller. Turn on them lights now, and I'll jest take that gun for safe-keepin myownself."

Freeman Ford was an immensely fat man and he groaned slightly as he stooped to pick up the rifle. The dim lights from the car glittered momentarily on the shining badge pinned to his overall straps. He had been standing in the edge of the woods twenty feet away for the last fifteen minutes, waiting to see if they'd get the deer.

"I should think you boys would get wise," he said complacently. "Every fall I pick up four or five of you jackers in this orchard—I should think you'd begin to get onto it that this's one of my best huntin grounds." He laughed, a deep-bellied, lardy chuckle, at his own humor. "Yessir, one of my best huntin grounds, only what I get's fair game."

The boys hadn't said a word and he figured rightly it was horror that kept them still.

"Got any rope in there?" Freeman gestured toward the car.

"Maybe a piece under the seat," the bigger boy said. He walked stiffly over to the car, fumbled under the front seat, clanked metal together, and came up with a short length of clothesline.

"Ain't much," Freeman said disparagingly, "but I guess it'll haf to do. Come along, now, I've got to have a hand."

The boy who'd got the rope for him followed him down under the trees to where the deer lay, a great shadowy mass, on the dark ground.

"Come along, you," Freeman yelled back to the shadowy figure still standing beside the car. "I want you both where I can keep an eye on you."

The dim shape started reluctantly toward them and stopped

far enough away so he couldn't possibly see what was going on in the circle of light from Freeman's flash. Together, Freeman and the bigger boy lashed the doe's hind legs together and hung her from a stub of a limb. Her forelegs trailed brokenly on the ground. Freeman took out his big pocketknife, whetted it a couple of times against the sole of his shoe, and competently cut her throat.

"That'll take care of her," he said. "Now, I'll tend to you. Here." He thrust the flash into the boy's hand. "Hold that for me."

He took out his notebook importantly, wet the tip of his pencil on his tongue, and stepped over to hold the book against a tree trunk.

"Well, now, I'll just have your names," he said easily, "an make it snappy. I ain't got all night, I got a regular beat to cover. Don't doubt but what I'll get a couple more bucks before the night's out." Once more his own sense of humor seemed to choke him. "Come on," he said, recovering. "Names."

"M-mine's Fod Davis," the boy who'd worked the spotlight said, his voice sounding weak and scared. Freeman wrote it down carefully, bearing hard on the pencil and making the letters big and round.

"Fod Davis," he said slowly, spelling it out. "Your old man Milt Davis from over the back side of town?"

"Ayuh." Fod's answer was a desperate gulp.

"Hope you got dough to pay your own fine, then," Freeman said, "cause if I know Milt, he ain't goin to waste any money on you. Just as soon see you work it out, wouldn't he?"

The boy didn't answer and Freeman turned to the other one, a mere shadowy form in the darkness.

"What's yourn?" he asked.

Instead of answering him, the boy began to cry, gulping harsh sobs that left him breathless.

"Please, Mr. Ford, I never shot her. It was Fod shot the

gun. I never had nothin to do with it. I was shakin so I couldn't. Don't tell my father please. He'll—you don't have to say you caught us. We'll never do it again, honest, Mr. Ford."

Freeman heard him out, but his face was disgusted.

"What you blubberin about?" he said harshly. "You're in jest as deep as this kid is. You're here an it's your old man's gun. Now cut out the cry-babyin an take your medicine like a man, pete sake. You're old enough to break the law, you got to expect to take what's comin to you. Trouble is, you young brats never stop to figure out laws're made to protect people instead of punishin em—till you go around breakin em." Freeman had a theory about laws and he was well on the way to airing it when he remembered where he was and what he was doing.

"Come on, come on." He drew himself up. "Name."

"Stanley Walls."

Freeman wet his pencil again and wrote the name down slowly, saying nothing this time, just watching the letters forming themselves on the white paper almost as if he himself had nothing to do with putting them there. He could feel himself begin to get a little sick deep in his stomach.

Goddammit, he was thinking, why couldn't I of seen who they was before I went shootin my mouth off? Why couldn't I of kept my big mouth shut till I found out who he was?

He knew perfectly well, now, what he had to do and he wasn't liking it much. He shoved the notebook and pencil back into his pocket. In the dim light, his big face gleamed slightly where he was sweating in spite of the chilly nip of the still air.

"Come on down here an help me haul that deer up here," he said. The three of them hauled the heavy carcass up to the car and piled it roughly over the fender.

"Get in," Freeman said then. "My truck's out to the end of the road." He climbed to the running board, feeling the light chassis give with the weight of his body. Young Davis took the wheel, turned the car, and headed slowly out toward the main road. Freeman was kept too busy dodging low sweeping branches to think much about what he was going to do.

Just inside the entrance to the tote road, the lights picked up the glint of metal from the radiator of his truck and they stopped while he made the two boys shift the doe into the closed van.

"Where you want us to go?" Fod said sullenly when it was done.

"Down to his house," Freeman said and they both knew he meant Stanny. "An don't try any funny business. It won't do you a mite of good because I ain't that forgetful."

He watched the lights fade out down the hill before he went back slowly to his truck. He still had the rifle and he stopped to look at it before he started after them. It was a lovely thing and felt as light as wood and steel possibly could in his big hand. It balanced perfectly to carry and he could feel his palm slide smoothly over the oiled stock. The blued steel of the barrel must have reflected starlight because there was a faint sheen along it that turned from blue to chestnut where it hit the wood. He snapped it to his shoulder and stood for a long moment peering along the sights, caressing the trigger lightly with his forefinger. He lowered it finally and then, unable to let it go at that, brought it back quickly to his shoulder, feeling the wood slide against his cheek. The motion he used was lithe and smooth and practiced and not at all like his usually short-breathed and jerkily uneven movements.

"I'll bet that set him back plenty," he thought.

Reluctantly he let the gun go, stood it in the front seat and climbed laboriously in. He wasn't thinking anything as he let off the brake and the rackety little Ford started down the hill.

At the bottom, when she'd lost momentum, he switched the ignition on and slipped her into gear.

When he pulled to a stop in front of the Walls house, the other car was already parked there and the two boys were sitting on the running board waiting for him. Evidently it had occurred to neither of them to go in until they found out what he was going to do. They still looked scared, but they weren't as scared as they had been, their attitudes told him that.

"Stay there," he said, "till I go in an have a talk with your father."

And again they all knew that he was talking only to Stanny. The entire situation revolved around Stanny and had ever since he'd jerked out his name in the darkness of the old orchard. Fod realized that he had suddenly become incidental and he wasn't going to push himself forward any more than necessary. He stayed where he was, but Stanny got up and came over to Freeman.

"What you gonna tell him, Mr. Ford?" he said softly. "Ain't there any way we can fix it so's he don't have to know?"

"If they is," Freeman looked at him, seeing the boy's white face dimly, "I don't know of it."

He shook off the detaining hand Stanny had laid on his sleeve and went up to the big front door. He never failed to be awed at the Walls house and the idea of going into it made him nervous, but he couldn't let that bother him at the moment. He gave the knocker a lusty slam so that it bounced twice of its own momentum.

He heard steps faintly, but not so faintly that he couldn't recognize with relief that Russ himself was home. The light snapped on and Freeman, caught like a fly in the middle of a butter dish, could feel himself trying to shrink.

Russ opened the door and stood for a moment blinking owlishly at him. He looked out of place in the gracious old hall, but what kept Freeman tongue-tied for a second was the fact that Russ had on a pair of heavy horn-rimmed glasses and he'd never known that Russ had to use them. He had been reading because he held a big crumpled sheet of newspaper in one hand.

"See you a minute, Russ?"

"Oh, it's you, Freem." Russ took off his glasses and stuck them into the pocket of his shirt. "Sure. Out here, or you want to come in?"

"Don't matter."

"Well, come along in, then." Russ turned and started away down the hall, taking it for granted that Freeman would shut the door and follow him. Freeman did. They went along the hall past the front room door and Freeman, snatching a quick look in, could see Grace sitting by the round table sewing. She glanced up as they went past and he looked quickly away.

Watching Russ's back, Freeman kept thinking, you forgot what a big man he was if you didn't see him every day—then when you did see him again, you were always surprised.

Russ must stand a good six foot three or four, Freeman thought. And he was straight. The heavy wool shirt, loose on his shoulders, made them look even wider than they were. His huge back blocked out everything else and Freeman kept his eyes glued on it.

You got to forget you don't like him, Freeman kept telling himself. You got to forget about that an remember you want to keep your job. Just forget you hate his guts, that's all. That's easy enough.

Russ showed him into the small office and Freeman stood looking around at the room. There were papers everywhere, piled on everything, and the top of the big roll-top desk was so inundated with them that there was nothing to see but paper.

"Well, Freem, what can I do for you?" Russ said easily.

Do for me! Freeman thought. That's a laugh. It's what I'm doin for you. But he knew that wasn't true. He knew he wouldn't be doing what he was doing right now unless he expected something for it. All Russ had to do was drop a word in the right place and Freeman knew he'd be looking for another job.

"Picked up your youngest boy tonight." Freeman came directly to the point.

"So? What's he up to?" Russ didn't look surprised or mad, just raised one eyebrow.

"Jackin deer."

"Whereabouts?"

"Up in that old orchard off back of the old Bailey Place."

For a second there was a change of expression on the brown face confronting him. The brows seemed to grow heavier and the pale blue eyes darkened slightly.

"Cussed young fool," Russ said coldly. "He mighta known there've been more jackers picked up there than there ever was deer."

"Well, I thought I better come an see you before I done anythin about it."

"You did just right, Freem. I'm glad you came to me," Russ said. He sat chewing his lip, evidently deep in thought. When he looked up, Freeman thought he caught a glimpse of a twinkle deep in the frosty eyes. "Well, I tell you, my inclinations would be to let him take his medicine." He stopped, waited.

"Oh." Freeman looked away. "I don't know's that's—well, he's young."

"Yeah," Russ nodded. "I was hopin you'd say somethin like that, Freem, just to let me know how your mind was runnin. As I say, I'd be inclined to let him take his medicine, but there's his Ma."

"Ayeh."

"She's not awful well an that boy's the apple of her eye. I'm afraid it'd be too much of a shock to her if he was to get into a mess like this. What you think?"

"Well, I thought of that, too." Freeman swallowed valiantly, remembering the way the light had shone on Grace's firm pink cheeks as she'd looked up. "The—the law's all right in some cases, but it seems to me there's circumstances sometimes that, well—that ought to be outside the law." Damn him, he thought. He's makin me say it all so's there won't be any chance of it ever comin home to roost. That's how to get things done, all right.

Russ had heard Freeman hold forth on his theory of law often enough to know that this was a bald-faced lie, but there was nothing but gratification in his face when he leaned forward.

"Well, Freem, it's nice to know you agree with me. I guess, seein how his Ma ain't very well, an he's young, we better overlook it this time. You know, it's not what I hold with, but I can see you feel pretty strongly that's what we should do. So I'll let it go."

You'll let it go, Freeman thought.

"Was there anyone with him?"

"Milt Davis's kid from the back side of the island."

"Well, just so's there won't be any echoes comin back to get you in dutch, Freem, we better let him off, too, hadn't we?"

"I spose so," Freeman said grudgingly.

"Don't you think we should?" Russ caught his tone and leaned forward a little farther—his face sharpened out somehow until it made Freeman think of a great hawk sitting there waiting to pounce.

"Yes," he said hastily. "Yes, I do."

"You see, if we didn't," Russ said patiently, "he'd be sure to make talk about nothin happenin to Stanny and it'd come back on you pretty hard."

"I see it would," Freeman said drily. He got up quickly and picked up his hat. "They're both out front. By the way, I got your rifle, too. It's out in the truck."

"I'll come out with you an get it," Russ said. They started

their parade down the hall again. Just inside the door, Russ stopped.

"Just a minute, Freem," he said, taking one hand out of his pocket. "Just because I like to see a man doin a job good, I want you to take this an get yourself a good cigar on me."

Freeman took the bill without looking at it.

"I'll do that," he said and followed Russ down across the dead grass, stiff with frost, to the cars.

The boys were still waiting and they stood up as the men came toward them, but Russ went by them as if they weren't there. He went over to Freeman's truck and took the rifle from the front seat. He snapped on the headlights and went around front to examine the gun carefully.

"That's a good gun," Freeman said.

"Yeah," Russ straightened up. "Quite a scar there on the stock," he said levelly, but he was angry.

"I didn't notice it," Freeman said. "One of them give it a toss when they heard me comin. Must've hit a rock or somethin."

"Probably," Russ said. "Well, good night, Freem."

"Sure you got everythin you want," Freeman said, knowing it was the wrong thing to say, but finding it necessary to make some sort of backhanded sop to his manhood.

Russ straightened up and came around to the door, the rifle in the crook of his arm.

"Look, Freem," he said. "I don't know's I want you to go off feelin like that. I don't like it, somehow. If you think you've done anythin you shouldn't have, why you fix it up right now while you've got the chance. I don't want you to go off feelin as if I'd made you do anythin that you didn't want to."

"I don't know what you mean, Russ," Freeman said softly, knowing he'd gone a little too far.

"Well, I'm glad of that," Russ said, still in that same patient tone. "You sayin that makes me sure you don't feel as if I *made* you do anythin. You're an officer, Freem, if you feel as if you hadn't done your duty, why you better do somethin about it."

"I'm satisfied," Freeman said numbly, staring straight before him at the lighted dash, feeling the warm wet feel of the bill in the palm of his hand.

"Good," Russ said. "I like everyone to be satisfied—and if you are, Freem, I am, too."

"Well, I am," Freeman said. "Good night, Russ."

He started up the old truck and put it down the drive. He was well out of Russ's sight before he slowed down enough to look at the bill; it was folded so he could see the big white twenty in the corner.

Twenty dollars, Freeman thought, that ain't much of a value to put on a man's conscience. But just one kid jacking deer ain't worth a man's job, neither—besides, he might just as well have been one of the ones that never get caught.

It was a long time before he remembered the deer. And that made him feel a little better. At least, they hadn't got that. He could use it himself.

RUSS waited until Freeman was gone before he went over to stand before the two boys. He towered over them and he seemed to sway with anger, but he didn't let it get into his voice.

"I don't want to hear any more about this," he said. "It's all over and no thanks to either of you. But if I hear anythin said about it ever, I'll hobble your feet together an hang you head down over the stern of my dory. Hear?"

"Yes, Pa," Stanny said.

"How about you?" Russ turned on Fod when he said nothing.

"I ain't said nothin yet," Fod said, "an I don't aim to."

"Good. I just want you to know I'm not foolin," Russ said. "You needn't think it's because of you you aren't over in court right now. You young fools, you oughta picked some place farther off. You know's well's I do, he's got that orchard marked."

"We'll remember next time," Fod said.

"You better."

Russ started to turn away from them and Stanny had just begun to get the all-gone feeling of relief in his stomach when his father seemed to change his mind. He turned back and jerked his head toward the house.

"Better come in now, Stan, I want to see you."

He tucked the rifle under his arm, carrying it loosely and as if he was accustomed to its feel. He went back up across the lawn without waiting to see if Stanny followed him. Stanny glanced at Fod, gulped slightly, and without a word of farewell, started for the house. Fod stood where he was, watching, until the wide front door closed behind Stanny's narrow shoulders, and the porch light went out. Then he climbed thoughtfully into his old sedan and drove away.

Russ treated his youngest son much as he had treated Freeman Ford. Stanny turned from the door to see his father's big shoulders silhouetted against the light in the office. Then he vanished, leaving the door open. When Stanny stepped into the room a moment later, Russ was already sitting in the swivel chair behind the desk. The rifle lay across the piled papers before him, light gleaming richly from its oiled stock and sleek barrel.

"Shut the door," Russ said.

Wordlessly, Stanny did, taking great care to make no noise, letting the knob go slowly that the latch wouldn't click. Then he just stood there, waiting, feeling like a kid called into the principal's office for some infraction of the rules.

"What happened tonight, anyhow?"

"I guess you know most of it," Stanny said. "Freeman told you, didn't he? He caught us jackin deer in that orchard back of the old Bailey Farm."

"He told me that." Russ jerked his head impatiently. "What I want to know is howcome you kids were foolish enough to try anythin there. You ought to know he's got that place docketed."

"I never thought."

"You never thought!" Russ mocked him angrily, moving his big head forward with each word. "Well, it's high time you did." He stopped, hesitated, and said, "You see any deer?"

"Just one, a doe."

"Get a shot at her?"

"Yeah. He come along right afterward."

"What'd you do with her?"

"Well, gee, he took her." Stanny looked startled. "I never thought. He had her in his truck."

"Oh, he did, did he?" Russ grinned slightly. Then he narrowed his eyes and looked with ill-concealed distaste at Stanny's worried red face.

"You know that's Park property, don't you?"

"Ayeh. I know. But I never shot her. Fod did."

"With this gun?" Russ put his hand on the beautiful stock, his heavy brows drawing sharply into a frown. "You let that young hooligan use this gun?"

"I—I had it first," Stanny mumbled. "I guess I got buck fever or somethin. I couldn't shoot an he grabbed it."

"Honest to god," Russ exploded. "I don't know where the blue blazes I ever got a kid like you! I taught you how to shoot, didn' I? You ever see me with buck fever?"

"Yes. No." Completely miserable, Stanny backed slightly away from the desk, his thin face growing rapidly paler. Here he'd expected to catch it for jacking deer on Park land and it sounded to him as if he were catching it for not being able to shoot the deer.

"Well, I hope you see what he done to it." Russ flipped the gun over violently and the dent on the stock stood out in the light.

"I never noticed that," Stanny said breathlessly, leaning forward.

"Well, you do now." Russ snatched up the gun and stood it in the corner beside his chair. "Now get up to bed."

"Pete sake," Stanny said, stirred to momentary rebellion. "It's only ten-thirty."

"Get to bed just the same," his father snapped.

Stanny went out through the hall and when he passed the open front room door, Grace called to him.

"Where you goin, Stanny?"

"Bed," Stanny said grumpily, watching her fingers move surely over the square of cloth in her hands. Every time she put the needle through the tightly drawn surface inside the embroidery rings, it made a distinct popping sound in the still room. Surprised enough to look up at him, Grace put down her sewing, and glanced from him to the big Seth Thomas over the fireplace.

"Pretty early for you."

"I'm tired," Stanny said and slid out the door without explaining. He'd be darned if he'd tell her the old man had sent him to bed like a baby for not being a good boy. It was going some when you could get away with treating a guy fourteen years old like a blasted baby. At the foot of the stairs he hesitated and, glancing back along the hall, saw that his father had been standing silently in the office door listening. He grinned sardonically at Stanny who, without speaking, went up the stairs three at a time, dashed into his bedroom, and slammed the door.

Once inside the room, he took off his leather jacket, stripped his sweat-shirt over his head, and went over to look at himself in the mirror. He examined his thin smooth arms and shoulders dispassionately, but with deep concentration.

Sighing, he went over to the big chair under the window and took a thick paper backed book out from under the thin cushion. Holding it under the light, he looked closely at the before and after photographs, read again the exultant balloons of words issuing from the smiling mouths. "In ten weeks Joe Adonis did this for me." "Six months ago I was a weakling." "I found out why Marge was so cold to me."

Well, he shrugged and stuffed the book back under the seat. No chance to do any of the exercises tonight. It'd be just like the old man to come up to see if he'd really gone to bed. He undressed hastily and crawled into the bed and fell asleep quickly.

In his office, directly beneath Stanny's room, Russ waited until he heard the springs creak overhead. Then he got up, turned off the light, and taking the rifle with him, went back to the front room where Grace was sitting.

When he came in, she looked up, spotted the gun, and made a clicking sound of disapproval with her tongue. Russ grinned.

"Somethin the matter?" he asked politely.

"Russ, I should think there'd be one room in this whole house you could keep your guns out of."

"What's the matter with guns in the livin room?"

"Well, it's not the place for em."

"Anythin as pretty as this is good enough for any room," Russ said, stroking the rifle lovingly, as if it were alive.

He stood it in the corner by the fireplace, sat down with his paper, and groped around for his glasses. Finally remembering he'd put them in his shirt pocket, he fished them out and settled back comfortably to read. He'd just begun to be interested in what he was reading when he became uncomfortably aware that Grace intended to talk to him. He didn't enjoy being talked to when he was trying to read the paper, but there was that peculiar waiting atmosphere in her silence that made him know she had every intention of talking.

She cleared her throat in preliminary action and Russ rattled his paper warningly. He even interrupted his story to turn a page ostentatiously, but it was useless.

"Wasn't that Freeman Ford came to see you?" Grace began.

"It was." Russ turned another page.

"I don't remember ever seein him here before," she said thoughtfully. "No, I don't believe I have."

"Probly not," Russ said. "He never came before."

"I should think," Grace said, bending her head more closely over the embroidery frame, "you could do your business at the office durin the day without havin it tail over to nighttime, too."

"I do except when there's an emergency."

That ought to get her, he thought pleasurably.

"Emergency!" The word brought her head up sharply and she stared at him, her eyes getting wide.

"Ayup."

"Russ—what's wrong?"

"Oh—" He started to laugh, satisfied that she was roused and not wanting to tell her. "Nothin really. Freem just wanted to ask me about somethin, that's all."

Grace, glancing at him sharply, saw that he wasn't going to tell her what had happened and decided it couldn't be too bad if he didn't look any madder than that.

"Well," she said, "you men. You always have to have secrets."

"That's right," Russ said.

Grace sighed with exasperation, but let it go. It made her mad, though; it made her so mad she had to go to bed because if she hadn't she would have asked more questions and she didn't want to give him the satisfaction.

"I'm goin to bed, Russ," she said. When she got over to the door, she stopped and looked back at him. "If you're up when the kids come in, you be sure they lock the doors."

"Sure, I always do."

"Well, I know, but I'm scared you'll forget sometime."

"Twon't do any harm if I do," he said easily. "There ain't anybody going to crawl under your bed."

"Well," Grace said. This isn't the time to say anything to him about anything that bothered her. They'd had it out before. But she was still put out enough to say it. "I've always been nervous since you started keepin all that money in the house."

"It's in the safe, ain't it?"

"Yes, but what good's a safe with a broken lock?"

"Lord, Grace, if you can't find one thing to worry about, you find another. Nobody even knows that safe's there, let alone the lock bein broken. Go on to bed. I'll take care of everything before I come up."

He watched her go with amusement. Ever since she'd found out about the amounts of money he kept in the wall safe in his office, she'd been after him about it and he always knew when he'd beaten her in an argument because she brought up the matter of the safe. Well, he'd let her stew about it. He liked the idea of keeping money in the house where he could get it if he ever needed it in a hurry—and more money than he'd once made in months.

About an hour after she'd gone up, Jake came in and Russ heard him, too, go up the stairs to bed. He waited until the house settled into silence—except for the creaking of timber and the first tentative sound of a cricket from the kitchen—before he got up and took the rifle out to the door.

He went quietly up the stairs and stood listening outside Stanny's room. When he opened the door, Stanny's breathing, steady and slow, almost but not quite a snore, filled the room. Russ went over to the bed and hit Stanny lightly on the shoulder, bring him up gasping and stammering.

"Get dressed warm," he said shortly, "and go get in the car. Hurry up. I'll be by the side door waitin."

He didn't give Stanny a chance to ask any questions; by the time he might have Russ was halfway down the stairs again.

Five minutes later, Stanny, dressed in heavy pants, lumberjack, and larrigans, came downstairs and went out through the shed to the barn.

Shivering with cold and apprehension, he climbed into the front seat of the old Buick. Beside him the shining chrome of the new car gleamed and he would have preferred to take her, but Russ had never let the kids touch her. He never used her himself unless he had to. The old car started easily, her well-oiled engine, in perfect condition as everything of Russ's was, purred under the high square hood.

The smell in the barn was cold, the old scent of grease and metal, acrid in the still air, made Stanny's head feel heavy. He drove the car out to the shed door and sat there wondering what the old man was up to now. Whatever it was, Stanny knew he wasn't going to like it. Sometimes he even wished he were dead and well out of Russ's way.

Russ came out as soon as the car stopped moving, stuffed something into the back seat, and climbed in beside Stanny.

"We're goin over to the Cape," he said. "Take her as far as that old road that goes up over the hill."

Stanny shoved the car into gear and swung her out into the main road. For the next ten minutes, neither he nor his father said a word. The only sound Russ made was a disgusted grunt when they hit the turn into the Cape Road, going a little too fast, and the tires splattered gravel and the Buick rocked like a fifteen-footer in a heavy sea. Her differential complained slightly over a ledge and Stanny could feel his father stiffen beside him, but he was too tight with nervousness himself to worry about the car.

The headlights picked out the slight break in the wall of alders beside the road and Russ sighed with relief.

"I taught you to shoot an you get buck fever," he growled. "I taught you to drive and you can't even judge a turn."

"Put her in there now and get out."

Wordlessly Stanny did as he was told. Once out of the car,

he felt the circling cold from off the water go through him as if he weren't there at all. He stood shivering like a whipped puppy as Russ groped around in the darkness of the car. Somewhere, off to the eastward, Stanny could hear the waves coming up the shore and they made a sound like wind through heavy spruces.

Russ turned and thrust a bundle at Stanny who took it because there was nothing else he could do. It was fabric of some kind, he felt through his thick gloves, and then he recognized the fusty odor of old burlap.

"Take them crocus sacks," Russ said, "an walk ahead. We got about an hour's hike an three hours before it starts gettin light."

"What're we goin to do?" Stanny heard his voice crack and shoot up with fright.

"I'll show you," Russ said. "Only go quiet now."

Above their heads the sky looked pale and the stars that had been so bright just a few hours before were beginning to look pale and far away, too; the spruces were black against the faint light. And as they went up over the grown-up ruts of the old road, the silence settled over them like a sack over their heads. Stanny knew that his feet stumbled uncertainly in the frozen ruts, but he didn't seem to feel anything. There was nothing but stillness and the dead chill of still fall air under the trees.

About three miles in from the Cape Road, the path started uphill and came out on a barren that had been cut over several years ago and was growing up now in brambles and fireweed. They crossed it at a slow walk, the boy forced into cautiousness by the absolute silence from his father. Even when Stanny made a point of listening, he couldn't seem to hear the faintest rustle from Russ's feet as they moved through the dead sweet fern.

Suddenly Stanny stopped in his tracks.

"I don't want to go no further," he said. "I don't want to go."

Somewhere off to their left, his voice started up a flurry of sounds and he stood aghast, hearing the crackle of brush as whatever it was faded off across the barren.

"There!" Russ said as if he'd been expecting this all along. He evidently sat down on the nearest stump because when he put a shielded match to his pipe a moment later, the light was only three feet above the ground instead of six.

"Sit down," he said. "Might's well wait till things quieten down a little."

He said nothing whatever about the noise and his voice was low and evenly monotonous, almost like a whisper; but Stanny knew him well enough to know that he was almost too angry to speak any louder. And now Stanny knew something else; he knew what they were doing up here on the barren before sunrise. Russ was showing him how to take a deer on Park land without being caught. The shaking that had made him unable to shoot last night was back in him now. Not violent yet, but promising to work up to something. He sat down, clasping his hands together nervously, trying to stop their quiver.

Nervousness and fear of his father, combined with a painful desire to show Russ that he was as good as any man, kept him silent. He realized that Russ hadn't been angry because he'd got caught jacking deer on Park land; Russ had been mad because he hadn't got the deer. Now he was being given a chance to exonerate himself and he had to keep calm.

He had to. He felt a great tide of relief and pride flooding through him. His hands, when he held them out, weren't shaking now. He could do it now; he knew he'd be able to do it. Then Russ got up.

"Come on," he said, in a mere whisper. "I'll go first. I've got the torch. There's some old apple trees about half a mile along. Ought to be somethin there. When I say 'Hst,' you stop and get your gun up. I'll get down with the light and you shoot, see?"

Stanny felt the smooth butt of the rifle as his father thrust it at him and took the crocus sacks. With the actual gun in his hands, he felt even more confident. He felt himself ghosting along through the scrub, knowing that he was moving now as silently as his father ever could. Ahead of him, the man went a few steps, stopped, half-turned, and stood there, listening.

Stanny could sense each move, almost as if there were some current of air like an actual tie between them that made him aware of the slightest motion Russ made. With the gun in his hands, he was the hunter. And somewhere ahead of him was the hunted—ahead of him with Russ.

Suddenly everything stopped and Stanny stood motionless in his tracks, the rifle poised, ready to snap to his shoulder. Ahead of him Russ had stopped walking again and stood listening once more. Stanny listened, too, trying to sift some suggestion of a sound out of the stillness. He was beginning to shake a little now; he could feel the tremors in his legs.

Trying to steady himself, he started bringing the rifle up. He had it halfway to his shoulder, when Russ said, "Hst."

Stanny heard the noise Russ made getting down and it was so much closer than he'd expected it to be that it made him jump. The powerful torch flashed on, pinning the young buck unerringly to the background of spruces. Stanny wasn't looking at the deer. He was looking at Russ's silhouette against the beam of the light.

Russ was so close to him that if he had moved the rifle barrel two inches, it would have touched the back of his father's head.

"Shoot," Russ said.

Stanny could feel his finger on the trigger start to tremble. He snatched his hand away as if the guard were a trap that would tighten to hold him, dropped the rifle, hearing it crash into the dry brush, turned, and ran. Behind him, Russ yelled once and let him go.

Stanny pounded down across the barren and into the old

road without stopping, his heart booming in this chest. The ruts nearly threw him, but he kept going—running when he had the breath, walking when he hadn't, until he crashed against the bumper of the parked car.

Whimpering with pain, he circled it and went on down across the road to the shore. The sky over the water was an even pale gray and the water itself like gun metal. He was still standing there, his lip tight between his teeth, trying not to howl, when Russ came down the road and got into the car. Without looking in Stanny's direction, without speaking, he started the Buick and drove away, leaving Stanny behind.

THE ONLY restaurant in Christian Ridge was Joe's Place and it occupied the entire first floor of a two-story, false-front business block across from the high school building. The black-lettered wooden sign that creaked in the thin November wind above the door, read: Joe's Place. Good Food. Joe Lampher, Owner & Prop.

During the rush hours, Joe did a good business; most of the town's business men ate lunch there. The linemen for the telephone company ate there when they were in town. And anyone who was just passing through usually dropped in for coffee or a meal depending on the time of day. But during the off hours, Joe had plenty of time on his hands and he spent it behind a copy of the *Bangor Daily News*, sitting in a straight kitchen chair just inside the barrier of plants he kept in what had once been the show window of a men's furnishings store.

It was a good vantage point. From it, Joe, who had a natural interest in the comings and goings of his neighbors, could see quite a good distance both up and down the main street without craning his neck unduly.

He was sitting there at nine-thirty, deeply engrossed in the

153

funnies, and he had just discovered with a good deal of pleasure that the *News* had added a new strip to its repertoire. A slight movement outside the steamy window, caught in a half-seen flash from the corner of his eye, made Joe look up to see Stanny Walls come slowly down the street from the direction of the Ridge Road and start in toward the school house.

"For pete sake," Joe said aloud, glancing at the battered wall clock that hung over the empty cashier's cage. "Kids nowadays."

Bob Flynn, the fish-buyer from Portland, who was sitting at the counter having his third cup of black coffee of the morning, glanced up.

"Smatter with em?" he said, not because he wanted to know but because he was a convivial man and it would have bothered him all day if he hadn't asked Joe the expected question.

"Well, judast," Joe said. "There's Russ Walls's kid just gittin to school and it's nine-thirty. Fine thing."

Bob got up from his stool and, carrying his coffee cup, came languidly over to peer out the window.

"Can't see anythin," he said bitterly. "Why the hell don't you clean them windows, Joe?"

"Ain't nothin but steam," Joe said aimiably. "If you could manage to lift your head you could see out over it. Or is that too much of an effort?"

"When your head feels like mine does," Bob stretched his neck tenderly, "anythin's too much of an effort. Boy, I thought I could hold my own at a bottle with any man, but you fellers down here take your drinkin serious, don't you? I like to died last night and here I am shakiern' a baby this mornin, and the fellers I was drinkin with, they lit out for the outside before sun-up."

He managed to get his head up far enough to peer blearily out over the fog of steam that rose halfway up the window.

"That little runt?" he said unbelievingly.

"That's him."

"Good lord," Bob said, really shocked. "How old is he?"

"Why, how the devil should I know? He goes to high school. Must be thirteen, fourteen. I don't know."

"Well, I be damned," Bob said. He stood watching until Stanny, by slow and deliberate walking, had managed to inch his way up over the steps and in through the wide door. "It's certainly hard to believe that boy's any of Russ's get," Bob said. "I thought all his kids was big like him."

"All are, but that one."

"Three hits, one error." Bob laughed, winced, and immediately sobered again.

"Well," Joe reverted to his grievance, "if I'd ever got to school an hour late, I'd a got my tail warmed good, I can tell you. But I bet he won't, bein Russ Walls's kid."

"Russ just about runs this town's far as I can see," Bob said softly. "They ain't much he ain't got a say in, is they?"

"I wouldn't know," Joe turned suddenly cautious. "He ain't offered to buy an interest in my place yet."

"Man like that," Bob grinned, "he wouldn't go wastin time with a rat trap like this joint of yourn."

"I notice you," Joe said, without animus, "always come around when you git hungry."

"Simply because they ain't any other place in town." Bob angled slowly back to the counter and sat down again. "Russ is a good man to do business with. You know where you are with him."

"That so?" Joe said, and something in his voice made Bob turn his head, slowly, and look at Joe for a long moment.

"You don't think so?"

"I wouldn't know," Joe shrugged to show his disinterest. "I never done any business with him an I wouldn't be in a position to know."

"Well, you certainly talk a lot for a man who don't know nothin," Bob said. "Guess maybe you've heard somethin or other makes you think he ain't."

"No, I don't hear nothin," Joe said. He picked up his paper and flipped it decisively. "I just stay here an mind my own g.d. business an don't hear nothin."

"Okay," Bob grinned. "Okay. I was just wonderin."

"You got a right to wonder." Joe's voice was strained through sheets of newsprint. "It's a free country, ain't it?"

"Guess it is, if you say so." Bob finished his coffee and stood up, putting his dime on the counter. "Well, I gotta be gettin along."

"See you next trip," Joe said, without looking up from the paper. But when the door closed behind the buyer, Joe looked up to stare after his lanky figure as it went dimly down past the window and out of sight. God amighty, Joe thought, I better watch my tongue. Sooner or later it'll get me in dutch.

WHEN Stanny went in through the school-house door, he stood for a moment at the foot of the wide stairs trying to make up his mind just what course of action to pursue. When Russ had driven off and left him alone there on the shore, he'd still been too scared at what he had almost done to get his thoughts straightened out. Whenever he got himself calmed down enough to stop shaking, he'd think, What if I *had* shot him; and then the shaking would begin all over again.

Finally he'd begun to realize that he was going to have to walk the eight miles home and he started to get mad. That warmed him up enough to make him forget how close Russ had come to getting a bullet in the back of his head. The long walk back through the thin windy cold of the November morning Stanny spent trying to decide whether to go home and go to bed or go to school. He was sleepy, so sleepy it was hard for him to think at first; but when the wind came up soon after sunrise, it woke him up and he decided it would be simpler all round if he went to school. That wouldn't involve the long explanation Grace would demand if he went home. Any story would do for old Bailey, the principal; but Grace would have a lot of embarrassing questions.

Yes, all in all, Stanny decided, it would be easier if he went to school.

He hitched a ride the last half mile with Fernald's milk truck and when the driver let him off at the Ridge turn, Stanny stood in the gutter blinking sleepily after the pursy-looking back of the truck as it drew away from him, up the long grind to the Ridge. The half mile of sitting still after his long walk in the chilly wind had nearly done him in. Twice he'd caught himself nodding and now he felt good and ready to crawl right into bed and stay there. For a minute he began to think it wasn't worth it, going to school. If he hadn't been such a cussed coward, he'd have kept right on up to the Ridge with the truck and gone home. He could have thought of a story to tell to keep his mother quiet.

He was standing there rubbing sleep from his eyes when he saw the two women coming down the opposite side of the road from town.

Aw hell, he thought, now they've seen me an it'll be all over town. Wonder what time it is, anyhow.

Their advance decided him, though, and he turned right and started hastily up the road toward school and duty. He kept his head down and his eyes on the yellow gravel in the gutter, but he knew they were watching him because their voices stopped as he neared them.

"Ain't you kind of late for school?" one of them called across to him and Stanny had to look up at them.

"Oh, hello, Mrs. Peters," he said politely. "Yeah. I missed the bus this mornin."

After he had gone by them, their voices floated back to him again and Stanny realized with a groan that they might easily have seen him get out of the truck and know that he hadn't come down from the Ridge at all. Oh gosh, he thought, why do I bother?

The center of town at nine-thirty on a November morning was usually deserted. It was today except for One Arm Billy Harper. One Arm Billy came out of the drugstore just before Stanny reached it and he had evidently been under the impression that there was nobody in sight, because he jumped and half turned as if to go back in when he saw Stanny. He didn't though; he kept on coming and when he passed the boy, he glanced at him out of the corners of his small red eyes and broke into a shambling run that lasted until he was a safe distance beyond him. Stanny didn't even have the heart to turn and yell after him as he might have if he hadn't been feeling lower than a caterpillar's belly. He said the rhyme they yelled, though, over to himself; but he couldn't find the ambition to make it come out loud.

> "One Arm Billy,
> Can't do no harm;
> Silly old Billy,
> Only got one arm."

He turned to stare after the old man and Billy, who had stopped running, was still making pretty good time, but he had his head swiveled around to stare back at Stanny and when he saw Stanny looking, he began to trot again, still keeping his head twisted back so far it looked as if he had it on backward. Stanny watched until One Arm Billy stumbled and almost fell, then, feeling considerably better, he himself lit out for school at a run.

He'd slowed down by the time he reached the duck-board walk and he went very slowly up the stairs and into the building. Once inside he wasn't quite sure what he'd better do. The second period was just starting and if luck was with him, he might sneak into his homeroom, get his book from his desk, and be waiting in the lab when Old Bailey came in to start algebra. There was no class in his room that period and he got the book without difficulty.

When he went into the lab, Jay Blake the janitor was giving the big bottles on the shelves a cursory dusting. He glanced at Stanny, made a grimace with his lips, but said nothing. Stanny went over to the long bench that stood along the wall, lay down on it at full length and for a moment tried to deceive himself into thinking he might study. But it wasn't much use; he could feel his eyelids getting heavy and the clinking noises Jay made got farther and farther away.

"Mr. Walls." The acidulous voice brought Stanny erect with a jerk. He dropped his book and stooped to fumble after it sleepily. He looked up at Old Bailey's thin face, seeing the glint of his rimless glasses, and grinned in hopes Bailey might be made to see the joke. That didn't work either.

"Mr. Walls, if you must sleep, will you do it at home in the future."

"I wasn't sleepin," Stanny protested eagerly. "I was lyin there thinkin when you came in."

"Oh, really?" Bailey looked interested. "Well, if you snore while you're studying as loudly as you do when you're thinking, I can understand why your ranks aren't any more inspiring than they are."

In the barrage of laughter, Stanny turned and slunk into the corner seat beside Fod who was awaiting him eagerly.

"Ol bayster," Stanny mumbled out of the corner of his mouth. "Anyone'd think he *was* somethin."

"If you have anything further to say, Mr. Walls, will you kindly say it to me?" Bailey's voice was sharp in the room.

"I was jest askin where the place was."

"I assigned the lesson yesterday. It is customary to know where it is before the beginning of class, I think. And I will expect you in my office at three-thirty to explain why you find it necessary to arrive at school an hour late."

Blazes, Stanny thought, that'll mean I'll miss the bus and

have to walk home. But he subsided and the class came slowly to order. After the recitation started, Fod wrote on a slip of paper and slid it cautiously across to the shelter of Stanny's book.

What'd your old man do last nite, it read.

Tell you at recess, Stanny scribbled under it and slipped it back.

For Stanny the class passed like a dream and the clang of the recess bell caught him unaware and made him jump, dropping his book again and lettin a spilth of papers fan out across the floor.

He said "Hell," and scrambled after them.

When he finally went out the door, Fod was waiting for him.

"Well," he said, his face twisted into a gloating grin, "what happened? You git a whalin?"

"Whalin?" Stanny said. "You crazy?"

"Bet you did. He certainly looked mad when he come out last night. I'd a been scared."

"You don't know my old man." Stanny surveyed Fod loftily. "Whalin, for pete sake. Maybe that's what happened to you. Maybe that's why you're so sure I got one."

"Judast," Fod grinned. "My father don't care *what* I do, long as it don't bother him. I never even thought to mention to him what happened."

"You shoulda hung around last night, though." Stanny put his hands in his pockets and rose slightly on his toes. "You missed all the fun."

"Hung around!" Fod said. "Fat chance."

"Well," Stanny shrugged. "You sure missed all the shootin."

"Come down off your high horse an tell me what happened, will you?"

"Me an my old man went out an got us a deer."

Fod's mouth dropped open and his eyes bugged out. Satisfied with his effect, Stanny started away, but Fod wasn't letting it go at that. He grabbed the elbow of Stanny's sweater and brought him around.

"Hey, listen, tell me more."

"That's all there was to it," Stanny said. "We just went up on that barren over near the Cape and got us a deer, that's all."

"Well," Fod said. "We-ell."

"Ayup."

"You mean, you actually shot a deer?"

"Callin me a liar?" Stanny said. He drew himself up haughtily.

"Heck, no," Fod said hastily. "You say you and him went an got a deer, I'll believe it. He certainly is a hum-dinger, ain't he?"

"That's no lie," Stanny said expansively. "I guess there ain't anythin he don't dare to do."

"Gosh." Fod was temporarily reduced to a state of mono-syllabic envy. "I sure wish my old man was more like him. I probly *woulda* got lambasted good if he'd found out what happened."

"Pa's quite a guy," Stanny said. "He ain't ascared of nothin."

The bell rang, ending the recess, and they separated. Feeling twice as tall as he really was, Stanny strutted off down the hall. But he was deflated again that night when, after his session in the principal's office, he missed the bus and had to walk home, alone.

School teachers, he thought. He kicked viciously at a frozen clunk of gravel and shivered in the wind that still blew thinly over the land. It was like a flood of thinness, a flood of winter, and it found the gaps in his jacket more unerringly than a blustier wind would have. He thrust his red hands deep into his pockets, clutching his history book tight against his side.

Most of them teachers only taught school anyhow because they weren't good enough to do anythin else. Look at old spindle-shank Bailey; how long'd *he* last doing a man's job?

He tried to picture Mr. Bailey aboard a dragger and the resulting image made him choke with laughter.

Wouldn't *that* be something, now. Probably he'd be sick when he got his first whiff of a ripe bait bucket. Probably he'd upchuck before they even got outside the harbor. You take a guy like that, he wasn't man enough to hold down a man's job; he had to go teaching school where he could boss a lot of kids around like a dictator. That's all he was, nothing but a cussed dictator.

Stanny looked up hopefully as the small truck pulled by him, slowed, and stopped. He broke into a run, came alongside, and got in breathlessly.

"Gee, this is swell," he was saying. "Thought I'd have to walk the whole way. Oh, Gene!"

"What's the matter?" Gene glanced at him. "Don't you want to ride with me?"

"Ayeh, sure. But I just thought it was Aaron. This's his truck, ain't it?"

"Well, what of it?"

"Jeepers," Stanny said. "You're touchy. I was just wonderin. I heard you was stayin there to Billings's, but I never seen any signs of you before now."

"I'm stayin there," Gene said flatly. "You can tell that to anyone that's interested."

"Okay, okay," Stanny said. He slumped down on his spine and stared out the window. Finally Gene twisted a little in the seat.

"Er—I was—" he began. "How's Ma?"

"Same as she was when you left."

"She ever say anythin to you about it?"

"Nobody ever says anythin about it." Stanny looked at him. "'S far's I can see, they're jest actin like you never lived there at all."

"Isn't she even mad?"

"Well, you know how Ma is. It's pretty hard to tell what

162

she's thinkin. I guess she probly would say somethin if it warn't for the old man."

"She usually says right out," Gene said. He looked a little hurt. "If she ever has anythin to say about anythin, she always says it."

"Well, I don't know, pete sake," Stanny said uncomfortably. "You know they never say anythin to me. If that's all you give me a ride for, just to find out what they're thinkin, why don't you come an see for yourself?"

"If I have to do that to find out, I'll never know," Gene said heavily. "By the lord, I'm out of it and I'm not goin back."

"Well, then," Stanny said, as if that settled it. "How, er—" he began, trying to sound as if he weren't prying, "what made you go down to Aaron's?"

"Where else was there to go?" Gene glared. "There warn't any other place."

"What's Annie think of it?"

"Listen," Gene said, "if you'd like to know any more about my business, why don't you write me a letter?"

Stanny shrank into his seat, completely cowed out of his momentary confidence of being on the inside.

"I never meant nothin," he said. "I was just wonderin."

"Well, wonderin won't do any harm. Keep it up."

He stopped the truck at Aaron's driveway and sat waiting for Stanny to climb out.

"I won't take you any farther," he said. "Be simpler."

Gene put the truck in the lean-to and started for the house, thinking it was queer that these two houses should be so much alike and yet so basically different. He had to cover up, in his own mind, the fact that it was still hard for him to go into the house where he himself was living and not find Russ and his mother there. So he started talking as soon as he opened the kitchen door.

"Well," he said. "Brr. Gettin cold out, you know it?"

Annie, who was alone in the kitchen, turned to look at him.

"My lord, do you always come into the house like a flock of hens?"

Gene laughed unnecessarily hard. He went over and kissed the back of her neck lightly, in the place just below the clipped line of her hair.

"Mmmm," she said.

"Like that, do you?"

"I wouldn't tell *you*."

"Got a new job today," he exploded suddenly, unable to keep it quiet longer.

"Why, I didn't know you were plannin on changing your job."

"I wasn't." Gene grinned. "I got fired. Art said business was gettin bad and he didn't see how he could keep so many men on. He said I was the last one hired, so I was the first fired. God, it was all of five years ago he hired me, too. Well, anyway, he kicked me out this noon, so I went and got me a job down to Willard Simmons's boat yard."

"For heaven sake," Annie said, properly impressed. In a town where a boy started work on one job as soon as he got out of high school and usually worked at it all his life, a man's changing his job was a step that was considered for weeks and perhaps longer. It wasn't a thing he went out and did in the course of an afternoon.

"That's right," Gene said. "Old-Off-Again-On-Again-Walls, they call me."

"I should think so. This one pay any more?"

"All you think about is money," Gene started, the twinkle getting deeper in his eye. But when she started to bridle, he added hastily, "Five a week more."

"Well, there," Annie said. "I'm just as glad you got fired. Why, you'd probly be working for Art Ferguson two more years before you'd get a five dollar raise."

"That's just about the way I figured it," Gene told her. "I

164

figured it was all to the good. But I still think Art's a liar. Business gettin bad, he tells me. Judast, there hasn't been enough of a change in the amount of business he does in the last twenty years to let him say business was getting bad *or* good."

"Oh, he probly had some reason. Maybe someone canceled an order and he started getting scared."

"Probly. Well, heck with him. Here I am, practically a millionaire. Know what I'm goin to do?"

"What?"

"As soon as I hit my first ten thousand, I'm going to buy you a diamond ring for each finger. Then when I get to be a millionaire, why I'll start on your toes. But I've got to be at least a millionaire first because you have to be that rich anyway before you can afford to wear diamonds where people can't see them."

"You fool," she said fondly. "That doesn't sound quite decent. Imagine me with diamonds on my toes."

"I bet it'd be cute." Gene grinned. "You could wear those open toe shoes and then at least folks could see the diamond on the big one."

"Stop it," Annie said. "I don't know what there is in that to make me blush but I am. Now stop."

"Won't." Gene came closer to her. Standing behind her, he put his arms around her waist and he knew from the quickened sound her breath made that she was as conscious as he was of his fingers just touching the soft underside of her breasts. "You smell good." He sniffed deeply the fresh smell of her hair; the clean soap and water way her skin smelled made him feel as if he wanted to bite her. She stood quietly, leaning against him.

"I missed you today," she said, her voice low.

"Oh, darlin." Gene leaned forward just enough to touch her cheek with his mouth. "I wish I *was* a millionaire. You know what I'd do. I'd build me a great big house right on top of the Ridge. And on top of the house, I'd build a big glass room, glass on all sides, way up where nobody could see us. And then one day a week, we'd go up there and, by judast, all day long we'd—"

"Gene Walls!" she turned on him, half-angry, half-laughing.

"We would, too," he insisted, laughing himself, backing away from her. "All day long and you'd like it."

"I don't know how you can tell whether I would or not. Besides, that's no way to talk. A glass room, for heaven sake!"

"Be nice, wouldn't it."

"Gene, you stop."

She stamped her foot and he was so pleased he had to kiss her. It was nice, he thought, the way she sort of let herself go against him, as if she trusted him, as if she knew without his having to tell her that he'd never harm her.

"I love you, I love you," he said.

"Mmmm," Annie said again.

"Look." Gene leaned back a little, keeping his arms around her, so he could look down into her face. "In the meantime, we got to have a house without a glass room, I guess. So I been sort of looking around. If you could stand it, we could get the old Freeman Place, down at the corner."

"Oh," Annie looked startled. "You mean, live off the Ridge?"

"Well, it's better than no house at all. It's just till we get started. As soon as we can, why we'll have a place of our own, anywhere you want it. By judast, I'd even build it right in the middle of the harbor, you say the word."

"I know it." She tried to move away from him, but he wouldn't let her go and she gave up without much of a struggle. "Well, that's not a bad old place. We could get along there."

"Good. I was talkin to Jay about it today. He says he could put it in shape by the first of December. So we better do somethin about it, hadn't we?"

166

"I suppose so."

"You don't sound very eager."

"I'm scared," she said. "I'm sort of scared, but it'll be all right."

"It's all right now. I called that preacher in Freehold, I was tellin you about him. I told him we wanted to get married on the twenty-eighth. That'll give you a few days to get used to the idea, old girl."

He kissed her again, hard, and just as he let her go, Aaron said, "And in my own house, too. It ain't decent."

Gene jumped and moved away hastily, trying to look as if he hadn't been within ten feet of her.

"It's all right," Aaron said. "Don't get scared. I left my shotgun out in the shed. Just got to wonderin where my supper was is all. See now Annie's got somethin else on her mind."

"Well," Annie said. "you go on in the other room and sit down and wait. I'll call you when it's ready."

"All right." Aaron started obediently for the door. He hesitated in the doorway and turned. "But I'm hungry so maybe I better take Gene with me, just to be sure I'll get fed sometime."

Feeling his ears go suddenly hot, Gene followed him into the dining room. Aaron picked up the morning paper, glanced thoughtfully over the top of it at Gene, and settled down to read. But he looked up again almost at once.

"You want part of the paper, Gene?"

Gene shook his head, tongue-tied before the amused glance. When Aaron went back to his reading, Gene sat looking at his straight brown face. The way this man lived and acted was strange to Gene, the way his children talked to him and the way he answered them. Gene simply couldn't understand the relationship among these three because it was so totally new in his experience. And then to have him sit down to his paper and offer part of it to somebody else before he himself had finished it. It was as simple an action as that that brought

Gene's thoughts to a head and made him stare as if he tried to get some explanation from the closed planes of Aaron's thin face.

I'd like to know what it is, Gene thought, that makes a man the way he is; or makes him so much different from another man. Maybe he doesn't have anything to do with it himself; maybe he just keeps on the way he is from the very beginning and couldn't change if he wanted to.

Since he'd been a kid, he'd had a habit of comparing other men with his own father—and usually the other men came off bad seconds. It was that way with Aaron. Gene's common sense told him that Aaron wasn't two hoots and a holler beside Russ; but he saw too that any man, given the choice of the two with whom to associate, would have chosen Aaron every time.

Sitting at the table with them that night, he started thinking what little things made a big difference, what small family customs could bring out so sharply the different ways people lived who were so narrowly separated as next-door neighbors were. There was never any feeling of strain here, none of the old familiar feeling of rush, hurry-let's-eat-and-get-it-over-with silence he had grown so accustomed to in his own home. They ate here leisurely, with a good deal of talk and not necessary talk either. At first Gene had found it hard to fit in with them. When Ralph or Annie had said anything, he'd always looked first at Aaron to see what he was going to do. Now he didn't. He had begun to feel himself relax, to let go, to feel as if he belonged and he knew it was a feeling his own family could never give to anyone.

"You had enough to eat, Ralph?" Annie said suddenly, looking up as Ralph shoved his chair back and got up.

"D'ever you know him to go away from the table hungry?" Aaron grinned. "Honest, sometimes, before he started workin, I used to think I'd have to scrap him just to make ends meet.

Was a time when I surely thought he was goin to bust me, just eatin."

"Begrudge me the very food I put in my mouth," Ralph said.

"Well, I don't do any more'n break even on you." Aaron winked at Gene. "Goin out tonight?"

"Didn't know but I might." Ralph hesitated before the mirror over the sewing machine by the window. He ran his hand hopefully along his chin and shook his head. "Anythin I get tired of doin, it's shavin."

He took a dipperful of water from the teakettle and started up the back stairs.

"Oh, Gene," his voice floated back to them, "you an Annie like to come? Didn't know but we might go to Freehold to a show."

Gene glanced questioningly at Annie who shook her head.

"Guess not tonight," Gene shouted and they could hear Ralph go on up the stairs and the sound of his feet moving about overhead.

"Howcome you never want to go out with them any more?" Gene looked curiously at Annie who pursed her lips and raised an eyebrow knowingly.

"I think it's high time we left em more to themselves, that's all. With us along all the time, it can't be so very nice for Ralph."

"He wouldn't ask us if he didn't want to."

When she looked at him Annie made him feel as if he didn't know what it was all about.

"I know that," she said. "I just think he'd like to be alone with her, but he doesn't realize it himself yet."

"Well, good gosh." Gene's eyes opened wide. "If he doesn't, I'd like to know who does."

"Maybe they ain't all as impetuous as you, Gene," Aaron said. "Annie says a thing like that an I don't know what she means either. But they's something behind it."

"What I mean is"— Annie looked them both over with the scorn of an understanding woman—"it'll do both Ralph and Mary good to be alone together more often. It'll help them make up their minds about each other, that's all."

"I wouldn't say there was much doubt about Ralph's mind," Gene said.

"I know that, too." Annie left him with the distinct impression that what she'd meant wasn't that Ralph needed to be alone with Mary, but that Mary needed to be alone with Ralph.

"This matchmaking," Aaron shook his head. "Well, go to it. Only you two want to go anywhere by *your*selves, you can use my truck."

Aaron was gone and they were sitting there at the table alone when Ralph came down. He was dressed in his best gray suit and his heavy overcoat, and his sleek head and face looked fresh and scrubbed.

"Sure you won't change your minds?" He hesitated momentarily in the door.

"Thanks just the same," Gene said.

"Oh, that's okay."

A little relieved, Ralph went out and got into his car. For a moment he sat looking at the gleaming dashboard and the spotless windshield. He liked things new and shiny and clean-looking and he was that way himself. There was a new look about his head, almost too new, almost unfinished.

He saw what appeared to be an infinitesimal spot of dust on the dash and wiped it off with the rag he kept in the glove compartment before he turned off the overhead light and started the car. The clean sound of the engine pleased him too; he'd spent so many years listening to the coughing rattle of his asthmatic old Ford that he never failed to get that particular proud thrill of ownership when he touched this car. He put it in gear gently, seeming almost to feel with his hand the way the gears meshed just beyond his sight. Sometimes he wished there weren't anything between him and the engine so he could have the pleasure of seeing as well as hearing.

It had been habit more than anything else that had made him ask Gene and Annie if they wanted to go with him and he was relieved when they refused. The four of them had always gone and done together, but now, quite suddenly, their whole status had changed. It was uncomfortable for him now to be with Gene and Annie, and when they were with him, he found it hard not to listen to them, not to think that those two in the back seat were close together in the way he wanted to be close to Mary but never could be. He would keep straining to see in the rear-view mirror what was going on behind him, straining his ears to hear what their low voices were saying, and he didn't like to do it but couldn't help himself.

Ralph had been up to the Walls house twice since Gene left, but he was still nervous about it. Things seemed different. He hadn't seen Russ, but Grace was always there and although she always seemed the same, there was a change somewhere.

There was another thing that added to his nervousness, but that had always existed. Whenever Ralph went into the Walls house, he felt as if he were coming home and finding strangers. He himself had been too young when they'd left the house to remember what life had been like there. But he had heard Aaron's stories of himself and his own father. Through the stories, the old place lived for Ralph as it had been years ago —and he was always surprised to see the changes strangers had made there.

Outside the door he hesitated, looking at the flood of light from the window, wondering if maybe it wouldn't be better to refuse when she asked him in to wait. To say, "Oh, no, thanks, I'll wait out here in the car," and say it as easily as if it were the thing he'd always said. But it wasn't and he knew he could never make it sound as if it had been.

Grace let him in and he sat down, letting his overcoat fall open over his knees so he wouldn't be chilly when he went out again. I've got to get that heater hitched up, he thought. A fine thing, here I got a car with a heater after all this time and I haven't even a chance to hitch it up.

"Mary's upstairs, Ralph, dressin," Grace said, her warm voice sounding like a river of comfort. "She'll be down in a minute."

"Fine," Ralph said loudly, knowing that it was going to be too loud, and when it came out the way he'd expected it would, he subsided into embarrassed silence until the snapping of the fire in the stove got to sounding too loud, too, and he had to say something more to drown it out.

"Well," he began heartily on the first thing that came into his head, "how've you been?"

"Fine, just fine," Grace said, just as heartily as he'd asked.

"Been a cold fall," Ralph said hastily against the threatened return of the silence.

"Oh, I don't know," Grace said. "Along about this time of year, you get to expect it, don't you?"

"That's true." Ralph nodded as if a truth he had never before considered had been laid suddenly bare before him.

Driving away from the house with Mary, Ralph could feel himself begin to breathe more easily, as if he had escaped from an atmosphere too thick to be livable.

"I'd like to know," he said, remembering the relief with which both he and Grace had turned to Mary as she came into the kitchen, "just what your mother thinks of me, anyhow?"

"Why, you *do* know. She thinks you're nice. She always has."

"Maybe she always has," Ralph insisted stubbornly, "but she's changed her mind now."

"I don't see—"

"Oh, I mean since Gene left. It's almost like she thought I'd been the one to make him go. I feel as if she was blamin me for something and I didn't have a thing to do with it."

"I know what you mean." Mary swiveled around in the seat so she could see his face. "But it's not you, Ralph."

"I wish I knew what it was, then," he said. "I always used to like to talk to her. I always thought she was swell. Oh, I still do," he added hastily. "But it's pretty hard to like anyone when you're sure they aren't likin you very much."

"I wish I could make you see how she is," Mary said. "You see, all her life she's been wrapped up in her own family, her own kids. And now the time's come when naturally they start to go away from her. She just can't understand how that is, Ralph. She just can't see why they should want to."

"That's not very good is it?" Ralph fumbled for what he was thinking. "It wouldn't be good for anyone to feel like that."

"It's not good for her. It's doin what you're talking about to her. See? She thinks it must be something outside that makes them go. She just can't see it's natural for kids to leave home. And now hers are doin it, why she's decided it's some outside influence on them. In Gene's case, it's Annie and you and your father."

"Oh," Ralph said flatly. "I guess I didn't understand about it."

"Well, I didn't myself until I stopped to figure it out. You see, she's been actin the same way with me—. She found out, or rather I told her, that I thought Gene was right. I told him the best thing for him to do would be get out."

"My god," Ralph said. "You did?"

"Well, wasn't it good for him?"

"How should *I* know?" Ralph said. "I'd never of done it."

"You mean you think I meddled?"

"No," he said hastily. "No, I never meant that. What I meant was, I never would have known enough to do it. I wouldn't of dared, that's all."

"Oh," she said a little flatly. "Well, skip it. I was just trying to tell you how it was with Ma."

"Yeah, I see." Ralph moved his hands uneasily on the wheel. He felt as if he'd let her down somewhere, but he couldn't put his finger on the place. He felt suddenly as if she'd expected him to say more than he had.

"I always thought a lot of your mother," he tried heavily. "I always used to think my mother might of looked like her."

"You can't remember what she *did* look like, can you, Ralph?" She fell in with him as if she were relieved at the change the course of talk had taken.

"Nope," he shook his head. "Gosh, I was only two when she died."

"I don't know," Mary said bitterly. "Sometimes I think most kids would be a lot better off if they got taken away from their parents when they were one or two. Maybe put in some sort of a home until they were old enough to take care of themselves. After that let em go and make their own messes of their own lives. At least they'd have the satisfaction of knowing the mess was their own personal business. They'd know nobody else had anythin to do with it."

"Good god," Ralph said, shocked.

"There," she soothed him, "I didn't mean to scare you, Ralph."

"I didn't have any idea you felt like that."

"I don't. Not really."

He strained to see her face and could make out only a dim pale blur.

"You're just sayin that now." He knew she was sorry already that she'd said as much as she had to him. Never since he'd known her had they ever progressed to this particular level of communication and he didn't want to do or say anything now that would scare her off. He wanted them to be able to go on from here.

This night would be a landmark, he thought. This night was important because for the first time she had tried to let him see just a little how she felt. It warmed him to sit there and listen to her. If we can only keep on from here, he thought, it won't be so hard.

"You must know an awful lot about people, how they work, I mean," he said.

"No." The word sounded so fierce that he felt his nerves go taut with surprise. "I don't know a darn thing. Not even how I work myself."

"I wish I could help," Ralph said suddenly, surprising himself as well as Mary. He sat tautly, staring straight at the road, not daring to move his eyes from the cone of light. "I wish there was somethin I could do for you. If there ever is, Mary—"

"I talk a lot," Mary said. She put her hand on his arm and Ralph thought he could feel the warmth of it through the heavy sleeve of his coat. "I don't mean anything much by it."

"Well, I meant what I said."

"I know you did. I didn't mean that. Oh, I guess I'm just trying to say I know you're decent, Ralph."

"It ain't that at all. I'm no decenter than the next guy," Ralph said, daring. "I wouldn't want to help just anybody. It's because I love you, I guess. I always will."

Her hand tightened for a moment on his arm as if she were trying to make him see something without saying it. Then the hand moved and when he felt its pressure lift, Ralph glanced over at her, wishing he could see her face. It was hard saying something like that to somebody you couldn't see. Made you feel as if you were talking to the wind.

"Ralph," she said softly, "if it wasn't for you, I think I'd go crazy."

So pleased he couldn't find another thing to say, Ralph just sat there, hoping she'd want to put her hand on his arm again, and when she didn't, he didn't even seem to mind that.

But the silence lasted long enough for him to lose his elation and begin to be uncomfortable. He was glad when at last they turned the corner by the traffic light at Freehold and started down the wide elm-lined main street. Already the town had been decorated for Christmas and although it was a week night and most of the stores were closed, the high strings of colored bulbs stretched across the street gave the place a festive look. He parked the car across from the big movie house and as they went into the lobby together, he turned to look at her face, expecting after this to find something new and different about it. When he saw that it looked as it always had, brown and closed and a little disdainful, he felt himself slip back into his own old despondency.

He found himself looking at everything as she might be looking at it and trying to think as she might be thinking about it; and doing that made him lose all his own pleasure in being places where people were, in being with people he didn't know personally, but knew were a good deal like him. He lost it all, thinking that she might be finding it shoddy and dull and uninteresting, and not being able to tell from her face whether she did or not.

For a second, when she saw him looking at her, Mary smiled, and it was all right. But it didn't last long. Lost in the anonymity of the dark, surrounded by other people, Ralph couldn't find his own self-confidence.

Being with her in a place like this, he could never take any pleasure from what was going on. He spent all his time wondering how she was feeling; and he made them both miserable by keeping after her about it.

"You comfortable?" he mumbled in her ear and, not satisfied with her half-seen nod, moved her coat slightly behind her shoulders, or leaned across her to see that whoever was sitting in the next seat wasn't crowding her.

"You like the movie?" he kept asking.

"You want me to go up and get some candy?"

"You okay?"

And in spite of her constant reassurance, he was positive that she wasn't enjoying herself and was merely sitting here beside him waiting for it to be over because she knew he enjoyed going and didn't want to spoil his fun.

The way he felt did something to his self-respect and, sitting so close to him, Mary could feel it happening. It was as if he were turning from flesh and blood to something soft and inhuman like sand. And she couldn't stop it. There was nothing she could say that was strong enough to reassure him. It seemed to her sometimes that he didn't really want reassurance; he wanted to think that nothing he could give her or do for her was good enough.

As he sat there growing more and more aware of her, she sat getting tenser until she felt as if her nerves were stretched taut between two poles of feeling and someone was using a sledge hammer against filaments that should have broken under a touch.

It's not decent, she thought, for one person to be able to do that to another. I've got to do something about Ralph. But it's not decent the way we make each other feel. And she couldn't think of anything to do. All she could use to tell him what she meant was what she said and what she did, and he couldn't find the confidence in himself to make him believe she meant it.

There was only one ground on which they could meet where Ralph could regain or keep his identity. There was only one experience they had in common which gave him back anything of himself; and that wasn't satisfactory, because what he gained, it seemed to Mary, had been taken from her.

It grew up in them both like a tide and was completely necessary to them both, but for reasons so different as to defeat the necessity.

She sat there knowing that somewhere on the way home, Ralph would pull the car off to the side of the road and turn to her there, waiting, in the dark. She wanted him to, but not because he needed the reassurance he could get from finding her when he put his hand out. She could feel herself getting her mind set to meet him as he wanted her to, and that wasn't right. She shouldn't have to make herself be there.

When he did, at first it was all right. The way he felt was good and he didn't maul and she liked that. But their eagerness to make it stay all right defeated its own purpose. It was as if they handled gently out of fear something that should have been handled strongly and so it slipped through their fingers, leaving them more alone than they had been before, and wondering what had gone wrong with something that just a minute ago had been so perfect and right.

When he let her out under the big chestnut tree by Russ's back door, Ralph stooped to kiss her lightly and it wasn't the way he wanted to kiss her. But he couldn't make himself do any more. It was as if the effort it would have taken was completely beyond him.

Mary stood watching the lights of his car fading down the Ridge Road toward home. She stood watching the way the sharp blades of light scythed along the roadside. And when she turned away, after the lights had vanished, and put her hand on the latch of the door, she was suddenly so weary that she could hardly close her fingers around the metal with enough force to lift the latch; she was so completely done that it seemed to her she couldn't possibly climb the stairs to her own room. And when she found herself, somehow, standing beside her bed, safe and enclosed and away from him, she wasn't sure how she'd managed to get there.

IT STARTED to snow on the night of Gene's wedding and Gene and Annie came back to the Ridge together through an almost deafening thickness of swirling white, damp heavy snow that comes early in the year and won't last. When it hit the ground it melted, but in the air it was almost solid.

The leather seats of Aaron's truck were cold, but they sat far apart and looked straight ahead as if they couldn't bear the thought of touching each other or of saying anything. Gene drove slowly, feeling rather than seeing his way, thankful for the storm that made it necessary for him to give every atom of his attention to the road.

He hadn't turned to look at Annie since they'd left the drab brown house in Freehold and started home. He didn't know what she was thinking about, she was so still it scared him a little; but he himself couldn't forget the awful room where they'd stood together while the minister married them.

Gene had been excited, almost to the bursting point, when they'd gone up the concrete walk to the door of the house. He'd reached out to touch her hand, not daring to take it because he'd have had to kiss her right there if he'd done that. The gray low racing clouds pouring in from the east, hanging low over the land, hadn't looked gray to him then.

"It doesn't seem possible," he'd said to her before the door opened—but then it swung in before she had a chance to answer him and he felt as if he'd lost something important and would never find out what it was because she hadn't had time to say the words that had started to shape in her mouth. She'd never say them now, whatever they'd been.

He wanted to turn to her quickly and say something, anything to make it easier for her, to make her forget the room with its cold white paneling, its stiff brushed fireplace with the turkey wing beside it, the icy gleam of the hard golden floor. But he couldn't because it was so clear in his own mind. It seemed to him that he could still feel the stinging in his nostrils when he breathed; that harsh dry smell of disuse and dust in a seldom-opened room. The air itself in that parlor had been rarefied and like another element—even the minister's lardy voice had sounded as if he were talking through water. He'd cleared his throat experimentally before beginning, as if there were two or three small pebbles far back in his throat. And his eyes had looked moist—damp and happy.

Gene wanted to say, It wasn't the way I meant it to be. But when he glanced at her quickly, all he could see was a blurred shadow and that wasn't a thing you could say to someone who was nothing but a shadow.

"You see," he started, as if he'd been talking steadily all along, "I figured it was the only thing to do. If I hadn't done it now, I probably never would have. D'you see that?"

Annie moved slightly, but he couldn't tell whether it was agreement or protest; and he couldn't take his eyes off the road again.

"I don't know what there is about him," he said. "All he has to do is look at me and I feel like a kid, like a two-year-old. I had to get away from him and you had to help me. You've still got to." He knew it wasn't necessary for him to put a name to the pronoun. And it wasn't hard for him to say this now; not being able to see her made him able to say what he was thinking about his father and for the first time he found words for a feeling.

"He's got us all buffaloed. We do what he wants us to before he even says he wants it."

"Didn't he want you to marry me?" Annie said in a barely audible voice. "You never told me that before."

"Hell," Gene said violently. "He didn't care who I married. It didn't matter who it was. But I had to live there. He knew he could manage whoever it was once he got us under that roof, under *his* roof."

"Well," Annie said loudly, "he'll find it a little harder to do by remote control. He can't touch us now, Gene. He can't do a thing to us."

"Yeah," Gene said heavily. But when he turned the truck into the Billings drive, he still felt strange, as if he had no right to turn in here knowing that he didn't intend to go any farther tonight. He was glad that the snow was so thick he couldn't see the lights of his father's house across the wide fields.

As if he had been waiting for them just inside the door the minute they set foot on the doorstep, Aaron flung the door open and stood peering out at them through the whirling snow. He held a big kerosene lamp in one hand slightly over his head so that he could see against the glare. Over his shoulder, Gene caught a glimpse of Ralph's grinning face.

He hesitated, knowing from their smiles that he and Annie had never succeeded in fooling either of them and feeling a little foolish when he thought of the elaborate way they had announced quite casually that afternoon that they thought they might run up to Freehold to a show.

Looking back, he had a brilliant picture of the tableau they must have made. He and Annie standing together by the door, Aaron still at the table, looking at his paper. He couldn't remember Ralph being in the room, but now, in retrospect, he saw Ralph standing by the water bucket, glancing at them over the poised tin dipper. Aaron's face had looked unsuspicious and quite calm as if he fully believed they were going to do just what they'd said they were. But now Gene knew he hadn't fooled them for a minute.

"Well," he said to Annie, "looks like we better face the music."

"You might's well come in, now you're here." Aaron's voice sounded pleased and self-satisfied. "I said to Ralph, the minute you went out, 'Those kids ain't going to any movie, not on a night like this with a good storm brewing.'"

"You old fox," Annie said. She went past Gene like a shadow, flung herself at her father and made Ralph yell something and grab the lamp as it tipped. "I might have known we couldn't put anything over on you."

"Gene, you better come in, too," Aaron grinned down at him. "Don't look so mad. Hell, if I hadn't wanted you two to get married, I could jest as well put my foot down sooner, couldn't I?"

Blushing like a school kid, Gene went past him into the warmth of the kitchen which made his face even more fiery. Ralph grabbed him and slapped his back enthusiastically.

"Congratulations, old son," he said. "You got a darned good cook."

"I could tell that by the way you been puttin on weight," Gene grinned.

"Hah." Aaron turned on them, beaming over Annie's head. "I'm some glad to have somebody in the family can out-talk you, Ralph. You been makin us all miserable—now we got somebody can out-talk you and I mighta known it'd have to be a Walls."

He held out his hand and Gene, taking it, tried to picture the way his own family would have acted under these circumstances. It would have been an occasion of angry silences and the silence of each of them would have had a different quality. Grace would have been hurt and angry; Russ just mad because they'd gone off like that without saying anything to any of them; Jake, knowing what they had come home for, would have been sullen. It would have been pretty impossible and now that the whole thing was over and had been done this way, he saw it was the only way it could have been done.

"Well," Aaron said suddenly, "I guess Ralph and me better show you what we been doin while you were gone."

He took the lamp and led them in through the front room and up the stairs.

"We spent the whole evenin clearin up in here." Aaron looked with relish around the big front bedroom. "Yes. It's cleaner now than it's been for the last five years, I wouldn't be surprised. We figured you two had better have it."

"What would you have done if we hadn't gone off to get married?" Annie said, her eyes amused.

"Why, I wouldn't have mentioned it, but there wasn't much

doubt in my mind where you were goin. I've seen that look before and it just means one thing."

Annie went over to the bedside table and stood looking down at the orange flowers.

"Why, you even took them from downstairs."

"Well, we thought it'd be only right to have some flowers around," Aaron said. "I don't know what gettin married'd be without flowers. Too bad they ain't real ones."

"They're beautiful, Pa." Annie looked at him and then glanced at Gene meaningly. He left the doorway where he'd been hovering, looking in, almost as if he didn't dare come into the room.

"It certainly looks good, Aaron," he said thickly, smelling the scent of water and strong soap that hung over them like a cloud. "You certainly must of worked hard."

"He sat on the bed most of the time," Ralph protested, "just telling me what to do next."

"That's the way it goes," Aaron nodded. "Maybe I did, but that's how it is. The fellers with the brains get to sit around and them that just has bull strength, they get to do most of the hard work."

His joviality broke down suddenly under the strain and they all stood staring at each other in silent embarrassment. Neither Aaron nor Ralph could think of anything to say to get themselves out of the room now they'd got into it and Gene and Annie weren't helping much. She just kept going from the bureau to the table, touching things and Gene, unable to look at anyone, stood in the middle of the room glaring with concentration at the first inanimate thing he'd happened to set eyes on.

"Well—" Aaron cleared his throat uncomfortably. "Well, guess that's all, ain't it, Ralph? I hope, er—you'll be as comfortable here as I was—" He blushed and went out the door as if it had been the only gateway of escape and he a man with a hungry tiger at his heels.

Ralph grinned and jerked his head after him.

"Nervous sort of fellow, ain't he?"

When the door had closed behind Ralph, they stood there, one on each side of the huge bed, staring across it at each other. For a moment Gene didn't know whether she was going to laugh or cry; but she decided to laugh—even then he stood and watched her before his relief bubbled up in laughter too.

THE SKY was the color of goose feathers and looked as if it would be just as soft to touch when Jake came out of the house and crossed the frozen yard to the barn door. He could smell snow in the air, that fresh clean smell the wind has before snow and as he shoved the door open, a few hard flakes came whirling in a little eddy around the corner of the building.

He stood in the open door to watch the curtain of the squall sweep in across the water until it blotted out all trace of the town; then it came striding up across the sidehill until the first flakes were stinging against his face. The flakes were small and hard and dry like sand and they hurt, but the pain was grateful to him—he felt as if he'd like to make it worse somehow—he wanted to feel pain that would be so great he wouldn't be able to keep from yelling. He ground his fists into his eyes and stood swaying, wondering what was wrong with him, wondering if he was going crazy.

Jake had always looked forward to winter. Summer was all right, but it was only the cream on the bottle—it was only the time when you began to see the results of a whole·winter's work. The foundations of his days had interested him more than the results. Winter was a time for putting in order, for getting things in shape, for planning a year's work. But he

184

couldn't seem to feel the same interest in getting things done any more, not even in planning how to do them.

With a lot of men inertia is an inborn thing, something so indigenous and familiar they don't even notice it. They spend their days doing their ordinary work with an economy of motion and trouble, taking so much time they don't have any left to feel inert. Jake was like that. His days went past now, though, with heavy feet. Sometimes, while he stood empty-handed and idle, watching them go by him, he thought he might be sick; he worried for fear there might be something wrong with him. He had taken to spending a longer time in front of his shaving mirror examining his own face with puzzled eyes, looking for some trace of disease or dissolution in his red healthy features. He could find no change or sign and would go away reassured, only to be back before the mirror again inside an hour.

Since Gene had gone, Jake lay abed longer and longer in the mornings. This morning he had stayed in bed long after Stanny went rushing down to gobble his breakfast and race for the school bus. He'd stayed there until Russ, in a sudden flash of anger, had come bounding up the stairs to stand in the door, hands on his hips, glaring.

"You goin to get up today?"

Jake turned over on his back so he could see his father. He even took his cigaret out of his mouth before he answered.

"I was just gonna get up."

"Well, your majesty," Russ began. "Just what gives you the idea you can loll around in bed all morning smokin cigarets while the rest of us are up and workin hard? Who d'you think you are, the star boarder?"

"Nope." Jake's voice had sounded sleepy and it enraged Russ.

"Well, in god's name, get out of there now. I don't keep you around to spend your time in bed. I sh'd think you'd grow callouses on your backside. If there isn't enough work around here to keep you busy, I'll find some more. There's that wood you got to cut this winter. How about that?"

As if he had to tell me when to cut wood, Jake thought bitterly. As if there was anything on this place I didn't know inside out—and know it better than he does.

"By the lord," Russ had said, "I'm not runnin a poor farm here and you kids think I am, I'll have a for sale sign up on this place so fast you won't know what hit you before you're out in the street. Think that over."

Jake had lain, listening to his heavy steps go firmly down the stairs again. When he heard the Buick creak out of the yard, he got up and came down to the kitchen where his mother, silently, took a plate of dried bacon and eggs out of the warming oven and set it in front of him.

"Where's Gramp?" Jake looked blearily around the room. He'd been hoping his grandfather would be there to act as a sort of safety valve on his mother's wrath.

"He was up and out an hour ago," Grace said. "He's gone up to Hat's. He's not a lay-abed."

Jake sat there, his legs sprawled as far across the floor as he could sprawl them. He sat there watching her, knowing that she was mad at him, knowing that every puff he took on his cigaret made her madder. Grace had never been able to hide her temper and as she grew older it got away from her more obviously.

Finally when she had stepped over his left foot twice on her trips to and from the table, she turned on him.

"Jake, what's wrong with you, anyhow? Lately you've been enough to drive anyone insane. First you lay abed till you get your father mad at you, then you come down and hang around here in the kitchen till I'm almost out of my mind."

"Well, I got a right to eat my breakfast, ain't I?"

"Not at nine o'clock in the mornin, you haven't. Why, my Lord, if I waited breakfast till now for you every morning, I'd never get my work done. Anyone'd think all I had to do was wait around till you decided to get up. I certainly hope I've got better things to do with my time."

Jake looked at her somberly, one heavy eyebrow, reddish in the morning light, higher than the other.

"Any time you want me to go somewheres else," he said, "I'm of age. I can take care of myself. All you have to do is say the word."

"Now, look." She spun on him, her face red with suppressed anger, "I've taken all that kind of talk from you young ones I'm goin to. Your place is right here with your father and mother, where you belong. You've got a good home and we give you everything you could ever dream of needin. More, too. It's all pure foolishness and I am not going to put up with it from any more of you."

Having built up to his moment, Jake prepared to enjoy it. He got up and took a doughnut from the plate. Then he went over to the door, grabbing his cap and jacket from the hook as he passed.

"That reminds me," he said, his hand already on the latch. "About Gene."

"Gene," Grace echoed. She stopped in midstride and stood glaring at him, her eyes clouded and her face getting even redder. Jake saw that everything he'd said this morning, except those last two words, had gone out of her head as completely as if he'd never said them.

"Yeah. I wondered if you'd heard. You never said anythin."

"You know perfectly well I haven't heard a word from him since he left. If there's anything I ought to know, you come out with it and don't stand there like a ninny."

"He's married," Jake blurted, startled by the look on her face. "Got married a week or so ago. They're movin into the old Freeman Place."

Very carefully Grace went back to the table and put down the plate of food he'd scarcely touched. She stood making ineffectual swipes at the worn oilcloth she'd wiped carefully three minutes earlier. She was too stunned to think it strange Russ hadn't mentioned this to her, and when she thought of it, she'd realize he hadn't because as far as Russ was concerned, Gene was nothing but a casual acquaintance now. At the moment she felt as if somebody had pulled a sack down over her head and tied it; her voice sounded as if it came out of a void and was in no way alive.

"I don't see why he couldn't have told me."

"Maybe he thought you wouldn't be interested," Jake said, watching her. "Maybe he thought you'd see it in the paper and if you was interested, you'd get in touch with him."

"I don't believe it," Grace said, wanting the fullest measure of pain. "I will always believe he just forgot about me, his own mother and he forgot about me. When he went out of this house, he just put us all behind him like we'd never been his own flesh and blood."

"He married Annie Billings," Jake said, because there was no answer he could make to her and he had to say something into the silence.

Perfectly willing to have her wrath turned against the outsider, Grace seized on Annie's name with relief.

"From the time she was knee-high, I never trusted that girl. She's sly. Sly, you hear me? All you have to do to know that is look at her face. I never trusted anyone couldn't look me right in the eye and she never could. She's a sly deceitful girl and now I hope she's satisfied, she's come between my boy and his own family."

"Well," Jake began, struggling to put his unusual moment of perception into words, "you could of said that same thing no matter who he married." He waited a minute and then when she didn't answer, said, "Couldn't you?"

"I don't want to talk about it with anyone. I just want to be let alone. I want you to go away, Jake, and leave me alone."

The minute he'd got outside the door, Jake started to be

sorry he'd told her about it the way he had. Then he'd been mad at the old man and had taken it out on his mother and he was a little sorry. But he was still mad enough at Russ to forget how much he must have hurt Grace.

Standing there in the barn door, he started thinking about what he wanted to do. There was so cussed much to be done and he couldn't seem to get started. He put his hand on the smooth haft of his double-bitted ax, stuck into its rack just to the left of the door. He stood hefting it, feeling its perfect balance, watching fascinated, the reflection of gathered light off its blade.

In his mind's eye he could see the thick growth, the sixteen acres of it that stood between Russ's north field and the beginning of Hat's kitchen garden. All summer Jake had been looking forward to the time when he'd start cutting that wood —even now he could see the way the clean big chips would fly under the steady chunking of his ax, could see the smooth V-shaped scarf of the cut low down in the smooth brown trunk.

Years ago, one winter, he had cut over the old wood lot with his father. After the snow came they'd built a thick brush half-shelter and kept a big fire going in front of it all day. Jake could remember sitting there, his face hot from the fire, the thin-fingered wind creeping up and down his spine. They had eaten their lunches there in the shelter, not talking much to each other because it hadn't been necessary to talk. There had always been a pleasant sort of amused understanding between them that hadn't called for words.

But once, just as they'd started to cut over the lot, Russ had said something that Jake would always remember—and not because it was unforgettable, but because it was actually the last time he could remember Russ speaking to him as if he were an understanding human unit, as if he were a thinking person who understood that when a man like Russ said a thing like that, it wasn't laughable or soft.

Russ had just taken his first cut and suddenly he straightened up and let his ax hang from his hand to stand staring down the long lines of the trees. Jake, following his father's stare, saw the quick smoky blue flash of a screaming jay cut across the duller smoky blue of the straight up-and-down trunks. Suddenly everything had sharpened for him momentarily. The whole country lay spread out before him, though he couldn't see it. It was merely a consciousness of what lay beyond his sight—acre after acre of tall trees like these; hill after hill with the straight old spruces marching up their hard-ribbed sides; the earth itself, rich with rotten wood and leaf mold, lying, still warm, under the snow as if it stored up the heat of the summer sun and held it against the cracking cold. The land was hard and clear with no shadow, with nothing to blur its edges. It was gemlike and because that was a peculiar word for him to think of, a strange description for him to give to country, he stood staring, his eyes stunned with the suddenness of insight. It seemed to him he could feel, coming up to him through the frost and snow, some sense of what land meant to men. He knew why a man held his land to him and kept his hands on it to the last gasp of life left in him. He could see why a man would fight all his life just to get a piece of land to leave to his sons—why he was satisfied only in that, knowing that through his sons it would go on, be realized in a way he'd never had time to do. A man's life was incidental, but he was a good man, a successful one, if he could leave land, free and clear, to his son.

"Look at those trees," Russ had said, his voice quite low with none of its harsh overtones, almost a dreaming voice. "Think how many years it took to grow a big tree as straight and tall as they are.

"Lord, a man's life ain't anythin compared to the time it takes a tree to live. And then we come along an cut em down and chop em up just to keep us warm. I don't know whether it's worth it." He stopped suddenly and looked at Jake, his thin wide lips slightly curled as if to say, It's all right for you to laugh, but if you do I won't say any more. Jake's face was sober and tight and young-looking, turned on his father with a sort of unsurprised understanding.

"Yes," Russ said, "it must be pretty hard on a thing like a tree to think that someday some little louse of a man, any man, can come along with an ax and cut it down.

"By god, it'd take a pretty big man to be worth it.

"Sometimes I even get wonderin if maybe trees have some sort of society. You know, like men do. Here a bunch of men livin in a town, they have to have what they call a social system to get along under, they just can't go on livin so close to each other without makin rules and pickin a head man. If they tried bullin it along without ever askin their neighbors if they agreed, why, there wouldn't be one man in town speakin to another.

"But you take trees, they just go along, growin straight like these, gettin along all right without one being any better than another. They feel peaceful, too.

"Of course," he said softly. He took a swing at a small dead cat spruce with the back of his big ax and a thin showering of dry brown needles spilled down over him and some of them stuck to the rough wool of his lumberjack.

"That's how they solve it, I guess. They just choke out the trouble makers and the ones that obviously ain't goin to amount to anythin. They just kill them off. That's the way to do it, I guess. Just go ahead in a businesslike way, and kill out the unfit ones."

He snorted loudly, amused by something.

"They say the Chinks used to do that with their girl babies because they never wanted anythin but sons. They just went ahead and threw them off a high rock somewheres."

He glanced at Jake who was standing with his mouth open now.

"Well," he said suddenly. "Well, we aren't gettin much done, are we?"

From time to time all through that first day, Jake would look up to catch Russ watching him with a peculiar, half-ashamed look on his wind-reddened face.

He's wishing to God he never said all that, Jake thought. He's trying to tell me not to mention it to anyone. And he couldn't think of a way to make Russ see that he never would. It wasn't a thing a man would tell to anyone else. Sometimes it got to be necessary to say something like that, it welled up until finally it just sort of boiled over. And if you happened to be around when it boiled, you just listened and didn't say anything and never mentioned it again, either to the man who'd said it or to anyone else.

He tried to make his father see that by the way he acted —he just acted as if it hadn't happened and by the time they'd finished work that afternoon and were ready to go home, Jake could sense that Russ was easy in his mind about the whole thing, that he had almost forgotten it.

They went down the tote road in the early winter dusk, side by side, their axes over their shoulders. It was still-cold and the wind had died. Jake could hear the squeaking of the hard dry snow under his larrigans. Each time he took a deep breath he felt the small hairs inside his nostrils freeze together and let go again. He strode along watching the blue shadows growing up from the ground, feeling like a man walking on his own land.

That's the way I've felt ever since, he thought now—wondering a little why he remembered so clearly the one time he and his father had reached any sort of understanding, the time when he had really liked his father, now that he suddenly hated him. That's the way I've felt up till now and he's taken that away from me and I ain't worth anythin without it.

I could get out, he thought. I'd like to clear out and let the whole thing go, put it down to profit and loss.

But his mind stopped there abruptly. He couldn't seem to drive it on to think of alternatives. He just stopped short as if he'd come up against a stone wall when he thought of leaving his own place and starting out again in another and a stranger place.

Well, he thought, I've put all of me there was into this place and I've let it get a strangle holt on me and now I can't even think about leavin it. He knew what he was doin when he started me out and he just went ahead. He knew I'd be a good hired man all my life, and save him money, too.

I don't believe, he thought with a rare flash of insight, he ever forgive me for hearin him say what he did that day. Russ didn't feel like that now either. Now the place was just a place to make money for him—just a place he was smart enough to take away from another man and turn to making dough for him.

It seemed to Jake, standing there looking down over the harbor, that his father was spread out over the town like a tree. He had sent out branches here and roots there and you could never grub him out, root and branch, not now. He was too deeply implanted. There'd always be a little piece you'd miss and when your back was turned, that little piece would take root and come up until you began to feel its shade and looked to find it a full grown tree again.

He thrust the ax back into its niche and started out across the yard to his car. He didn't feel like working, he wanted to do something unusual for a change and it was so unusual for him to get into his car and drive away from the place at ten o'clock in the morning that he felt rare excitement taut in his muscles.

Halfway down the Ridge Road to the village, Jake remembered that his mother had said something about her grain man not coming this week. She'd said she needed a bag of grain for the hens and the man hadn't turned up. Well, that was excuse enough for him to be going somewhere. He'd go to

Freehold and pick up a couple of sacks for her and then he wouldn't have to do any explaining.

Russ's Buick was parked in front of the Masonic Hall and when Jake went by it, he turned his face away as if by not looking at it he could keep his father from coming out of the building, or noticing him if he did.

The tail end of the dry squall was whipping by him as he left the village and started the long slow grind up the hill to the Freehold Road. He liked the way the wind spread the thin dry snow out fanlike before him over the tar.

When he hit the outskirts of Freehold, he thought for the first time of the way he was dressed. Respectability to Jake meant putting on a good suit of clothes before going to town. He glanced down at his ragged jacket and greasy pants and shrugged. What the heck, he thought. It's nobody's business what I look like. As long as I'm covered that's all I got to worry about.

But he felt uneasy when he parked in front of the feed store and got out. Once out he felt exposed and as if people stared at him. Well, let them stare. He was wearing an old hunting cap of Russ's and he thrust it back until its peak pointed straight up and his heavy forelock stuck up so thickly the cap was almost invisible from the front.

He got the two sacks of grain, loaded them into the rumble seat and then stood teetering on the curb. He thrust his hands into his pockets and glanced casually up and down the street before crossing over to the Green Front.

He knew what he was going to do, and he really didn't want to. Certain early experiments Jake had made with more innocuous stimulants had taught him he had no head for liquor and he hated feeling the way he did the next morning. But he went into the store, bought two fifths of cheap whisky, and came out to put them carefully in the front seat where he could glance down every now and then to be sure they were all right.

Slowly he backed away from the curb and headed down toward the river road. Once down where he could see the wide cold brown arm of the river above the dam, he pulled the old Ford in under a big pine on the wrong side of the road and sat watching the gray light shifting across the water. The day seemed warmer now, or perhaps it was because he'd found a natural lee from the easterly wind; but he began to feel warmth creeping back into his fingers that had got cramped on the wheel. He took off his heavy gloves and rubbed his hands together, the dry sound of his hard palms the only noise in his personal vacuum.

He felt starey; the water seemed to have a pull for his eyes, its silent eddying made him feel sleepy. He reached out for one of the bottles, without looking, and tore the wrapping off it, letting it go on the oily bare floor boards. He unscrewed the cap and took a long pull at the bottle, trying not to smell the stuff because it made his stomach lurch. He sat reswallowing until the discomfort ceased and he began to feel warm in his throat. It spread too slowly for him, so he took another long gulp before screwing the top back on and giving it a smack with his palm as if it were a cork.

He sat there all afternoon and finished off one fifth before he roused himself. The whisky, for some reason, didn't seem to have much effect on his brain. He knew what he wanted to do, he just couldn't seem to do it fast. He handled the car like a man dreaming and his hands and feet were so heavy he couldn't move them as quickly as he could think about it. He was conscious of every bone in his body, severally, and could feel each one of them weighing him down a little more.

In Freehold he made one stop, at a drugstore, and spent five cents for a package of breath sweeteners. They made it necessary for him to take a long time getting home. He thought it would be a good idea to finish the whole package, just to make sure. And since he couldn't do two things at once, each time he wanted one, he had to pull the car off the road and sit there until he'd finished it.

IN THE morning, coming down early to build the fire, Grace found the two sacks of chicken feed piled in the middle of her spotless kitchen floor and stood, open mouthed, staring at them before she hastily dragged them out into the shed and stood them up against the wall.

Jake was the first one down and he came in shakily, his hair on end and his eyes bleary. Grace looked at him once, quickly, and looked away. She didn't glance up as she got him his breakfast and Jake, after gulping two cups of black coffee, went out through the shed door, slamming it behind him.

Hearing his feet go at a stumbling run through the shed, Grace went to the door and got it open just in time to see Jake doubled over the railing on the back stoop.

"What's all the excitement?" Mary said, behind her. Grace shut the door quickly.

"He was drunk last night, that Jake. He's out there now, sicker'n a dog. I only hope his Pa don't come downstairs till it's over."

"Jake!" Mary knit her heavy brows.

Grace only nodded.

"But I never knew him to touch the stuff."

"He never has since the first time he tried it," Grace said. "It made him sick then, too. He had sense enough to let it alone after that."

Somewhere out behind the barn the crows suddenly started holding a congress and the raucousness of their yelling made both women turn to stare out the window. They had evidently caught an owl in the old dead hackmatack and they were whirling around it like insane black leaves, each one screaming.

"I don't know—what d'you suppose makes them do that?" Grace looked pleadingly at her daughter. "It almost seems as if they go crazy."

"I don't know," Mary said blankly.

For a moment they stood staring at each other, their faces almost identically puzzled, as if they each expected a revelation, as if there were some important question each of them had asked the other.

Mary's glance dropped first. She looked hastily at the coffee cup, empty in her hand, put it down on the table and started for the door.

"I guess I just don't understand any of you," Grace called after her. "It's almost like you weren't my own flesh and blood at all."

IT WAS like flying, it was like freedom after slavery, it was like being dead. It was like nothing that had ever happened to him before and Stanny never wanted it to stop.

The wind whipped tears from his eyes and he could see, only blearily, the way the hardwood shores slid by, the bare leaflessness of the trees straight up and down against the snow and each trunk melting into the next one with the speed of his passing.

Waiting for the first chance to use the ice boat had made Stanny think of the way he used to wait for the first good kite-flying day in the spring. And being in her now was like being aboard a kite. He remembered watching the angular soaring of his kite and wondering what it would be like to be up there if the kite had only been big enough to hold him. Now he knew—it would have been like this.

197

Lying flat on his stomach, he worked his head around until he could look back at his grandfather. Nat, with both hands busy with ropes, bared his few brown teeth in a grin of pure delight. He shouted something that Stanny couldn't hear, but he nodded and grinned back before turning away.

The ice, that early that year had been a smooth green-black, had thawed and refrozen and was now milky and faintly blue and opaque. Along the shores of the lake snow had drifted, dry and fine, to obscure the rocks.

Stanny couldn't remember ever having waited for anything with the same anticipation he had felt looking forward to this. The things he'd waited for, like Christmas and the last day of school, they weren't important, they couldn't compare with this. He would probably feel differently when it came time to look forward to them again, but at the moment the ice boat was all he could think about.

Every trace of ice in the cow's bucket set him to wondering when the lake would be thick enough to hold. Whenever the mud puddle that gathered in one of the ruts under the chestnuts froze solid enough so that he could pick up a sheet of ice and stare at the splintered sun through its bubbled iridescence, he would drop it immediately and go wandering out to stand under the big old Spy tree examining the ice boat.

Nat, scarcely less eager himself, would watch him, grinning, and then proceed to drive him crazy with stories of the unusual open winters he could recall.

"Why, hell," Nat said, "you wouldn't believe it maybe, seein as you're only fourteen, but I can remember winters around here, you'd swear it was March or April all winter long. Not so much as a smidgin of snow or ice. Some winters, I can remember, it was all you could do to find frost in the ground."

"Aw." Stanny made an unbelieving sound. "Seems to me if there ever was a winter like that, I'd of seen some signs of one in fourteen years."

"Well, I ain't sayin things now is the way they was in the old days." His grandfather would stare off at the horizon, thoughtfully puffing his pipe. The narrow harbor had already taken on its gun-metal wintry look and that morning the clear cold air made the islands loom until you weren't sure they weren't floating in the air instead of in the water, but according to Nat, it might have been midsummer.

"Things was always a lot worse or a lot better," he said. "By the lord, as I get older, I can see that. Nothin's the same.

"Why, we've hed winters here when that harbor's been closed up tighter'n a bull's—" He glanced at Stanny thoughtfully, and finished, "tighter'n a drum. I've seen times when they hed to take the mail out to Hardacre Island on a sled, two men haulin, over the ice. The next year, why they'd be open water, nothin but open water. Not even the mud puddles'd freeze. It all depends. You take one year has a hard winter, the next one's bound to be easy.

"We hed a pretty hard time jest last year, so if I was you, I wouldn't go countin too much on bein able to use that ice boat."

Stanny looked at him skeptically.

"Well, I don't believe it. I can't remember anythin specially hard about last winter. There warn't a day it was so bad the bus couldn't get through to school. An I can't remember neither any winter the lake didn't freeze over hard enough to go on."

"Sall right." Nat shook his head. "I'm jest tryin to get you so's you won't be disappointed out of all proportion. All we can do is wait an see. But the signs is wrong. The signs is all bad. They was buds on the lilac a week ago. Did you know that? I never said anythin about it at the time."

"Well, if they were there a week ago, where are they now?"

"They was only a couple," Nat said. "And I took em off. Thing like that's so unusual it really ain't fittin for a man to see it. I just took em off."

"If they'd a been any," Stanny said, "you'd a had the whole family out to see em. I know you."

"It hurts me," Nat said loudly, trying to put a note of pathos into his voice. "When a man gets to be my age an still livin, he begins to think he deserves a little of them good things he always hears is comin to him in the after life. He gets livin so long, he begins to think maybe he'll get a little of the good of them still on earth. Now, me, I ain't particularly desirous of havin the pie they say's comin in the sky—I don't even want the harps an wings. I don't want nothin but a little christian civility an goddam little of that. From my own family."

"I heard you startin," Grace said. She had come suddenly around the corner of the house and stood there now, her hands on her hips, staring down at Stanny and her father. "I could hear you shootin off way around the other side of the house."

"Can't even talk out loud," Nat said. "My lord, if I didn't pay my board, I'd go down an live with Will Hutchins."

"Humph." Grace wasn't impressed. "Seems to me you've changed your tune since the time Will fobbed off that rifle on you."

"And they say elephants don't never forget anythin," Nat said.

Stanny turned his back on them both and stared longingly at the ice boat. That was always the way it was. Just when his grandfather started talking to him as if they were two men together, then another one of the grown-ups always had to turn up and take the conversation away from him as if he weren't even there. They just talked to each other right over his head and he might as well have been a fence post.

Well, gosh, he thought, and kicked viciously at a frozen clump of grass. He could talk all he wanted to about it being an open winter. It wasn't going to be and Stanny knew it. Probably the old man was just tired of the whole idea and was going to let the ice boat sit out there under the apple tree all winter and just rot away. That's what was wrong, he realized it now. Nat had tired of the idea or thought it would be too much effort, and he just wasn't going to bother.

IN LATE November, winter closed down over the land, sealing it in, choking all the traces of warmth and ease from it with thin icy chains of frost and sleet. The ground, before lasting snow fell, rang like iron and cold was the only reality.

The fire of fall had burned out and winter, before snow, was the ashes of the year. The few hardwood trees were skeletons of trees, maple, chestnut, elm, birch. Their limbs looked bony and cold and dark against the sky. There was almost an indecency in that bareness, as if the land between the coming of winter and the first lasting snow had been caught unaware and with more of itself exposed than anyone should have seen.

Only the spruces gave dignity and an illusion of comfort to a country that needed a lot of it. Their heavy green-black silhouettes along the Ridge were like a barrier, something to stand between the town and whatever extreme of weather that might have come upon it out of the west. But there was no protection at all from the east—to the east there was nothing but a waste of water, heaving and cold and green, and the wind from the east blew without hindrance.

The lake froze hard enough to hold and Stanny had just started to be hopeful again when the thaw hit and after it the snow. But the snow was dry and the cold came back and finally he saw, one day, that the lake had frozen thick enough and hard enough to crack and there were people skating far out on it one Saturday morning in early December.

"All right," Nat said. "Guess I was wrong. Even the signs don't work the same as they used to."

"Well, that's all right," Stanny said impatiently. "But when do we start gettin the ice boat goin?"

His grandfather sighed involuntarily and glanced down at Stanny's eager face. Recently the whole project had started to look pretty impossible to Nat. Somehow the effort involved seemed almost too much for him to contemplate.

Along about the first of December, every year now, he went through a period of depression so great that physical motion was almost too much for him, so deep that the contemplation of anything more distant than the next moment seemed a piece of foolishness for a man of his age. The period usually lasted a week or so and, he knew, was all in his mind. Physically he had seldom felt better than he had these last few years, but the idea of anybody living to be as old as he was got him down. And the possibility of his not lasting out the winter just coming up bothered him too. So his mental lassitude carried over to his physical condition and while the depression lasted, he simply couldn't face any unusual undertaking. It was just too much of an effort.

"We got to be careful," he said. "It's all very well for people to skate on thin ice, but when you got anythin as heavy as this ice boat, why you got to be sure your ice is good and solid."

"It's solid," Stanny said bitterly. "I guess I can tell when a lake's froze hard enough to stand that much weight."

"Maybe you think you can," Nat said. "I tell you. I ain't quite sure in my own mind yet an till I am, why, I wouldn't get a mite of pleasure out of it. Now what you do, you keep your ears peeled, an when you hear somebody's been out on it in a car or they've started to cut, why you tell me an we'll get that ice boat up there if I have to haul it myself."

"Okay." Stanny wasn't impressed with his grandfather's cautiousness and Nat himself realized that he hadn't put forth a very good argument. It was the best he could do, though, at the moment. He just didn't have the resilience to do or say any more about it. It would have to be good enough.

The short December days dragged slowly by and Stanny, frantic with worry, got up early each morning to scan the sky. If it had snowed or if there had been the gray feathery clouds that meant thaw, he thought it would be too much to bear. But each morning was clear and cold, with the rime of frost heavily over the barn roof and the thick furry crust on his window seldom melted down during the day. He began to feel as if he were holding his breath and if he should let it go, the weather would change.

Nat's spell that year was about the worst he could remember. He spent his days bundled into the rocker beside the stove where he could shove his feet into the oven when he began to feel the creeping chill from the floor, or thought he could. He took to lying abed until Stanny had left the house so he wouldn't have to look at his accusing and disappointed face. Nat would lie there, feeling himself pull together, as if the cold of his own age were as strong upon him as the chill of the outer edges of his sheets where the sparse warmth of his thin old body had failed to do anything but emphasize their cold. Even his bones felt cold and it was all he could do to lie there and wait until he heard the door slam and knew that Stanny was racing down the drive to catch his bus.

After that, he'd get up and dress quickly, because it was lonesome here in the upstairs part of the house for an old man, alone and cold beyond words.

Each morning he would come down and take a hasty look out the door, hoping the weather might have changed enough to offer him respite. But it never had. Feeling guilty, he would go in to huddle over the stove with his breakfast coffee in his hand until the circling chill had been driven out of him. And he would stay there all day in case it should come back.

Then, one Friday morning, along toward the middle of the month, he woke knowing instantly and with such great relief that for a moment he felt weak, that the depression had gone and he was himself again.

Out of habit he waited until Stanny had gone before he went downstairs; but once down, he went out to the door and stood there just breathing. It seemed to him that it had been quite a long time since he'd had so much fresh air in his lungs and the lifting of his ribs made him feel young again.

"Pa." Grace came to the kitchen door. "You'll get your death of foolishness standin there like that. Come on in, now, an have your breakfast."

"Ha," Nat said. He grabbed her around the waist and did a spry wing-ding across the kitchen floor. "By god, the way it smells out makes you glad you're alive."

Panting with laughter, Grace shoved him into his chair.

"Well, I'm glad to hear you say that. Way you've been mopin around here, I didn't know but what you were ready to give up."

She had watched with sympathetic amusement his annual descent into silence, knowing it well from years past, and knowing that it would pass, too.

"Yessir," Nat shook his head. "Dunno but what I'll give old Stanny a surprise an break out that ice boat. Think Jake'd haul it up to the lake for me today?"

"You can ask him," Grace said as Jake came in through the dining room. "He's right here."

"Ask me what?" Jake rumpled his hair violently, yawned, and stretched. "What is it now?"

"Want you to haul that ice boat up to the Lake for me today."

"Oh, for pete sake," Jake said. "I thought you'd forgot all about that. Why don't you be sensible? Like as not you'll kill yourself with that contraption."

"That's up to me, ain't it?" Nat said tartly. "If you don't want to oblige me, say so. I can afford to hire Cy Bailey. He'll take it up for me for a couple of dollars. I ain't a beggar."

"Jake," Grace said. "You can do it. It won't take you fifteen minutes. I guess you can spare that much time from all the work *you* been doin lately."

"Oh lord," Jake said. "Yammer! I'll do it. I never said I wouldn't."

"Well, you don't have to be so grudgin about it. I guess there's little enough any of us ever ask you to do." His mother looked at him, but in spite of the words, her voice wasn't angry. It sounded puzzled and a little uncertain and it got through to Jake who flushed heavily.

"Do we have to have a fight the minute I put in an appearance in the mornin?" He sat down and started eating fast. "I'll do it. Just give me a chance to get my breakfast down, is all."

"Well," Grace said, but she let it go there and Nat hadn't said anything more, preferring to let it rest now that he'd got what he wanted.

That night, Stanny, with a face of alarm appeared in the kitchen.

"It's gone," he said loudly, looking accusingly at Nat. "She ain't out there."

"Gone? What?" Nat looked innocent.

"That ice boat. She's gone. She ain't in the barn, neither, because I looked."

"Oh," Nat said. "Why didn't you say what you was talkin about? Well, I tell you, I figured we'd never git very far with her settin out there under the apple tree, so I gut Jake to haul her up to the lake for us today. Didn't know but what we might try her out tomorrow."

Stanny subsided into a mutter of "gee's" and "why didn't you tell me's" and "tomorrow's?"

"If it's a good day," Nat said cautiously, remembering the week he'd just put in. "If the weather's fair, we'll try her out."

It was a good day, clear and cold, with a nice wind blowing from the northwest. It was a wind, Nat felt, that might lead to almost anything before the day was out. They got Grace to put them up a lunch of thick sandwiches and great slabs of cake, and started off to the village, both of them wrapped in layers of wool sweaters and jackets. At the post office, they managed to hitch a ride with the mail truck on its eight o'clock trip to Freehold. And they spent their entire day on the lake, whizzing rapidly down its length before the wind, and hauling, tacking, and tugging up it again. After the third trip, Nat said a little wistfully, "Makes me think of the old Chinaman ridin the toboggan. He said all it was, was, 'Whizz. Walk a mile.'"

It was worth it, though, he thought, watching Stanny. It was worth every minute of it, just to see the kid's face.

Stanny couldn't quite believe the day was gone, and he wasn't sure what had happened to it. But the sun was below the top of the mountain when he looked and the crew of men who'd been cutting ice all day at the northern end of the lake were getting their tools together to go home, when Nat said finally, "Well, guess we better make this the last trip."

"Aw," Stanny said protestingly, but not very hopefully. He tried to make the trip down the lake last a long time. It made him feel the way he did when he ate an ice cream soda, taking little sips.

Together they hauled the ice boat up on the shore alongside the Appalachian Club landing, took down the mast, and stowed it carefully under the float.

"There," Nat said. "I guess she'll ride out any rough weather there all right."

He'd been almost right about the ice boat. She worked just enough like a catboat to make him homesick for salt water. And he'd got thinking today about the times he'd gone out with his Great Uncle Miles, when he'd been a boy.

"D I ever tell you about my Great Uncle Miles?" he said to Stanny, as they started up through the dark tunnel of the old wood road. "He was a man had the kind of a life any

206

man'd like to have. He hed hisself a little farm and he raised everythin he needed almost, an what he couldn't raise, he traded for. Hell, they warn't a man in the Ridge could beat Uncle Miles to a trade. He was what they call a sharp dealer. Fond of a bet, too, he was.

"They's a story they tell about Uncle Miles. I never knew whether they was any truth in it or not. He wouldn't never say when I ast him. Just grinned. Said he couldn't quite remember.

"Well, anyhow, before he come home here an settled down. he was first mate aboard an old four-sticker used to run between Boston an Eastport. Good man aboard a ship, too. They warn't a patch of bottom big as my hand anywheres along the coast he didn't know an know by heart.

"S I was sayin, one night they put into Portland harbor. Uncle Miles, he'd been aboard for a week, an he was just about ready to break loose. He ups an bets he can go into any house in Portland, take a feather bed outn' the best room, an, what's more, get the feller that owns it to help him take it out of the house.

"I ever told you this one before?"

"Unh-unh." Stanny shook his head, already engrossed.

"Well, they went ashore an started up the street. About five of them in the bunch, I guess, with Uncle Miles leadin. They come abreast of this house looked pretty fine, looked like the kind of a house'd have a feather bed.

" 'How about this here one, Miles?' one of em said. Uncle Miles give his cap a shove, the way he had; many's the time I seen him do it myself. He marches up to the front door, which is open. Since it's just about suppertime, they ain't nobody in the front part of the house. He could hear em all out in the other room, eatin away. He goes up the stairs, real quiet, an into the front room an there, sure enough, there's this big old feather bed.

"I dunno how he done it without gettin the whole house

down on him, but he gut it off the bed an out into the hall an over to the top of the stairs. Then he give it a heave off into the downstairs front hall, an then he jumps down on top of it.

"You can see how that might make a little racket, a man like him. He'd go near two hundred pounds, solid bone an muscle. Then he started haulin the feather bed around an makin the cussedist noise you ever heard.

"Out comes the feller owns the house. He stands there sort of flabbergasted for a minute. Then he says, 'What the screamin blue blazes you think you're doin?'

" 'Why,' says Uncle Miles, cool as a cucumber, 'I'm tryin to make my bed an I'm havin a devil of a time doin it. Give us a hand, will you?'

" 'Well, for pete sake,' says the poor guy who only owns the house. For a minute, I guess, he was too darn surprised to say anythin else. But when he gut his voice back, so I've heard tell, he said enough to make Uncle Miles raise an eyebrow an he warn't never any slouch at slingin the English language around.

" 'They ain't no need to take on,' Uncle Miles says calmly.

" 'Take on!' howls the poor feller. 'You take· your christ-less, blue-whiskered bed out of here an do it fast.'

"Uncle Miles never made a move. He just stood there sort of starin an it made the feller so mad, he muckled onto the feather bed and threw it out through the door Uncle Miles had thoughtfully left open. Then he turns around to Uncle Miles, triumphantlike, an says, 'An you, too.'

" 'All right,' says Uncle Miles, lookin offended. 'If that's the way you feel, then I'll be damned if I'll make my bed in your hall.'

"He outs the door an picks up the feather bed, slings it over his shoulder, an marches off down the street with it. When he gets out of sight of the house, where the feller is still standin in the doorway starin after him, he stops to collect the bets.

"Well, he was quite a feller, Uncle Miles."

Stanny, choked with laughter, had already forgotten about leaving the ice boat.

"Yessir," Nat said. "He was. What made me think of him, when he come back here to settle down, he gut hisself a little sloop. Warn't much to her. But she'd go like a scairt rabbit. Warn't nothin in the whole harbor could touch her, an, by judast, he put her through places where it looked like he oughta took the paint off both gunnels.

"I remember once I was out with him. I warn't any more'n a kid, but I can remember it. Good breeze, they was, due northwest. Anyone else wouldn't a took her out in a chop like they was that day, let alone with a kid aboard. But he warn't scared of man nor devil.

"We come up alongside Hardacre Island, on the offshore side, an they's a big bar there that's out of water come low tide. It warn't any more'n half-tide then, an the waves was breakin over that bar, looked like whipped cream.

"They was a feller on shore, gunnin; Joe Stacy, it was. He said afterward when he see Miles Fernald bearin down on that bar in his sloop, he shut his eyes tight because he knew what was goin to happen an he didn't want to have to see it. It did, too. By judast, he put her right into it. There was a sort of bump an a hell of a scrapin an then we was over. I was never so scairt in my life. He looked down at me an grinned.

" 'Scrape the barnacles off her arse,' he says.

"But I never said nothin till we gut ashore an I felt solid ground under my feet. I was too scairt to."

"Well—" Nat started to say something more, but they came around a curve in the old road, their feet on the smooth-packed snowy rut making no noise, and when he saw the two deer ahead of them, a little off to the side of the road, he stopped, the words he'd been going to say choked in his throat. Stanny, following his grandfather's stare, didn't spot them at first, they were so still; but when he did, he could feel his own breath starting to come hard.

The two were standing, their heads nearly touching; the big buck was moving his head a little, from side to side, but the doe was so still she might have been carved out of a blue-brown wood, and not real at all.

As Nat and Stanny stood watching, the doe moved slightly. She lifted one forefoot and pawed a little at the ground, and her head began to move, too, as if there were a string between it and the buck's. When he moved, she did. Suddenly the buck reared, bringing both forefeet off the ground. He went up until he seemed to tower over the doe before she rose to meet him. For a second they looked like two boxers, sparring lightly at each other, as if they were feeling out their opponent. The doe came back to earth first. She dropped her feet and put her head down, feigning indifference, looking for some trace of grass left under the snow. When the buck lowered himself, he got one hoof across her shoulders. At the touch of him, she whirled and snapped, almost like a dog. He moved away from her, snorting, pawing the ground, but watching her. He was in the blue and his coat made him hard to see in the growing shadows. But when he moved forward again, toward the doe, he seemed to grow out of the beginning dark. She kept her head down, pretending to graze, pretending not to see him. But when he reached out and nipped at her, she didn't move. Once more he rose, towered over her, but this time she didn't. She lifted her head a little to look at him, then let it drop, but she wasn't grazing now, or making any pretense of it.

She shivered a little as the full weight of the buck came down on her and then began again the slow steady side to side motion of her head. The great muscles in the buck's haunches bunched and the doe's forelegs stiffened against his thrusting force. His huge shoulders seemed to rise and subside above her regularly, like waves. Then suddenly they were both still, so still they might have been one animal instead of two.

They were apart again so quickly that Stanny wasn't sure

how it had happened. The doe, whirling, let fly with her hooves and the drumming sound they made against the hard barrel of the buck was loud. She spun around, crossed the road in a flurry of leaves and snow, and disappeared into the woods on the other side. The buck stared after her for a moment and moved with great dignity up onto the crown of the road. He lifted his head, sniffed deeply, and rose again on his hind legs, pawing the air. He turned in a complete circle before he lowered himself and, with a snuffling sound, vaulted into the underbrush after her.

Stanny stood listening to the sound of his hooves fading down the wind, feeling the sweat drying on his forehead.

"By god," Nat said, his voice low.

"Wha—" Stanny began and had to stop to get his breath. "What made him do that on the road like that?"

"He felt good." Nat glanced down at him. "He was feelin good and had to do somethin to let off steam."

"Did she—was she feelin like that? What'd she kick him for?"

"Oh, she felt like it, all right, but she's a woman," Nat said disgustedly. "She was just tryin to make him think she didn't. But he warn't fooled for a minute."

"I—I never seen anythin like that," Stanny said. "Never before." He looked up at the old man, trying to hide the quick breathing that he couldn't seem to help.

"They ain't many people have," Nat said. He started briskly down the road. "It's somethin you see once an never expect to again. As a matter of fact, that makes twice I've seen it. It's somethin to remember."

"Yeah," Stanny said. While he'd been watching the deer, he'd been thinking what a story it would make to tell Fod, but something about his grandfather's voice made him change his mind. He guessed he wouldn't tell Fod. Fod would only have something dirty to say about it and Stanny thought suddenly it hadn't been like that at all—it hadn't been something to snicker over. He felt as if he'd seen something important and good and if he'd thought of the word "beautiful" he would have used that too.

They came out of the wood road into the comparative light of the tar and started in silence down the long hill to the village. In some of the houses people had already decorated their Christmas trees and now that dusk was closing in, they were lighted. The small colored lights pointed up the windows all along the way.

"If I was you," Nat said finally, "I wouldn't mention to your Ma about what we seen. She might not understand how it was."

"I guess I won't tell anyone," Stanny muttered, not looking at his grandfather.

"Well, maybe it's just as well. You was lucky to see it, though, this late. Their matin season is in November, maybe a little in December. But this is kind of late."

"Yeah," Stanny said, and then, quickly, "Gee, don't the town look nice, all lighted up?"

"Hmmm," Nat said thoughtfully. "Yeah. It sure does."

He glanced away from Stanny's closed-looking embarrassed face, sighing a little. He was beginning to get the reaction from the long day in the cold and he was tired. He didn't think he was going to be able to make the long haul up the Ridge and he was wondering what to do about it. Maybe they'd find Jake or Russ downtown and be able to get a ride up with them.

Russ's Buick was still parked in front of the Masonic Block and Nat sent Stanny up to see how long before Russ planned to go home. He himself sat wearily on the running board staring at the big community tree in the parking space across the street. He was thinking maybe he shouldn't have let Stanny watch those deer, maybe he should have yelled or something. But he'd thought at the time it would be a good thing for him to see, a thing like that. A lot of times anything plain and out in the open like that did a kid like Stanny a lot of good.

He sighed a little, tiredly, and sat watching the bright blobs of color the big bulbs made against the heavy, almost green black of the tall tree.

THIS is my place, Russ thought; and the thought was an immense satisfaction to him. It was so great that he could feel it in his stomach like a tightening anticipation, the way a kid feels on Christmas Eve when he's just old enough to know with his mind there isn't any Santa Claus, yet still young enough to wonder if maybe the people who told him there wasn't might not be wrong.

Russ was standing on the point of built land just below the Coast Guard Station looking off along the line of the new breakwater and he could see it as clearly as if it had been there in its actuality. He stood easily, his rubber-booted feet spraddled on a couple of weedy rocks, his taut big body almost leaning on the northeast wind that whistled in over the ocean behind him.

Turning until he faced into the wind, Russ stood looking up the sweep of the Eastern Way toward Hardacre Island. Between the snugged-down look of the island spruces—the trees looking as if they grew out of the water—and the bluff beginnings of red granite headlands, the water had a black-green look, shot with silver and white.

Russ could remember when the small white coastal steamers that met the Boston boat out of Rockland had tooted their side-and-a-half way down the stretch of shoaly water between the Island and the mainland to tie up at the Steamboat Wharf —long since wrecked and the timbers used for something else. He'd heard people, the summer people mostly, bemoaning the

213

fact that the steamer no longer ran. They said that one of the most picturesque things about the Ridge had gone when the steamer stopped running and the motor busses took over the traffic. In a way, Russ could agree with them. He loved the look and feel of accustomed things; but in another way he was just as glad they'd gone. They'd been old-fashioned and there was one thing a town could do without. It needed modern transportation. He doubted very much if any of the summer people themselves would have used the boat if she still ran. They mostly came and went in their automobiles, and those who didn't used the Flying Yankee which came from Boston to Bangor in five hours.

The trip from Boston via the Boston boat and the old *J. T. Mace* had taken a night and a day and nobody it seemed had that much time to frittle away on just traveling nowadays. He'd heard somewhere that the *Mace* had ended her days as an excursion boat on the Hudson and his one glimpse of the Palisades made him think it was quite a come-down for the old girl. It had probably been safer for her passengers, he admitted with a grin. If there'd ever been anything in the way, the *Mace* had always run it down, and she probably never had a chance to chase moose in the Hudson.

In the old days it had been all right; people liked traveling, they liked getting places in a leisurely way. But now it was different and Russ put most of the blame on the young kids. They wanted to get from where they were to where they were going as soon as they thought of it.

It was funny, the attitude people had toward time. You could tell pretty much how important a man was by the time he saw fit to waste. There were men he could name who wouldn't have been able to find time to stand here the way he was standing, not doing anything, just looking up the Way. They'd call it wasting time, and go hurrying off without a backward glance, as if a world might come to an end without them there to keep it from total disruption.

He figured that was why he'd got along so well. It took a big man to be able to waste a little time now and then without busting a gusset about what was happening to his business in the meantime. A big man knew he could afford to take it easy once in a while; it almost seemed as if wasting a little time let him work harder when he had to.

Russ turned his back on the wind again, his eyes watering from the unaccustomed bite of it. There had been a day when he could have stood behind a spray hood facing into a wind like that for hours at a time without blinking, but that was something a man got out of the way of.

The wind was strong enough to prevent any work being done out here today, but Russ knew that beneath the heaving surface of the harbor mouth the foundations of his breakwater lay, sturdy and tough as the bluff headlands at his back, deep in the black water. Well, he thought, why shouldn't I say "mine"? God knows I had more to do with its being there than anyone else in this town.

He watched for a moment the pitching boats at their moorings in the harbor, their high white bows pointing into the eye of the wind. It wouldn't be much longer now that they'd roll like that to every little capful of wind out of the northeast. He tried to picture how it would be once the breakwater was there to stop the long uneven storm swells, to break the whining sweep of that devilish wind. He even thought he could see a difference now.

Pride was like a taste in his mouth, a sound in his ears.

By god, he thought, looking down at his unaccustomed rubber boots, Russ, old boy, you've come a hell of a long ways since you started out.

There'd been one while there, when he'd been nothing but another fisherman butting his way through day after day of mean weather out of Christian Ridge, he'd thought he wasn't going to make it. But he had. He'd done everything he wanted to, he had had everything he'd ever wanted and more.

And he dated the turn of his luck from the year he'd taken over the old house on the Ridge. From that day on, it seemed as if things had broken right for him. He'd just had to turn his hand to anything to have it succeed.

This is my place, he thought, looking up along the harbor, noting each familiar wharf-head; seeing the row of buildings along the main road; feeling the location of each house on the Ridge itself. I've made it and it made me.

He wished they'd been working today when he happened by. He liked to see men working, something going on no matter what it was. Somehow a project of any kind that involved labor on the part of men gave a place an air of prosperity. He resented each day of bad weather as if it had been an affront offered to him by a personal and highly inconvenient God.

There was only one thing to mar his complete satisfaction. Somewhere there, under the concealing surface of the Harbor, between the shore and the shoal was a deep-hole. Nobody had known it was there and nobody could have foreseen it. What Russ couldn't understand was how the company's surveyor had missed it the first time. He had explained lamely that there had been very little time allowed to make the survey and perhaps he'd been too cursory. At any rate, it hadn't been discovered until after the contract was signed and there was nothing that could be done about it then.

But he was smiling tightly as he did when something pleased him when he turned and picked his way up the forsaken shore past the pile-driver that lay helplessly on the flats waiting for the flood.

The old Buick was poking her nose over the edge of the built land and her blind headlights, peering through the thin dry grass, looked curiously like eyes. Russ grinned up at her with a good deal of affection.

"You worried, old girl?" He spoke to her as he might have to a cow or a horse. "Keeping an eye on me, ay?"

On the edge of the parking space he turned for one more look out across the harbor before he climbed into the car and sent her waddling up along the shore road. When he went by Willard Simmons's boat yard, he peered into the yard, went on by, and fifty yards farther up the road, suddenly swung the car into a driveway, made a quick turn, and came back to pull to a stop in front of the yard.

He got out and went down along the road to the shop, his feet feeling clumsy and almost as if they didn't belong to him, clumping along in the rubber boots. That was another thing a man got out of the habit of, wearing boots. Once he'd worn them all the time—they'd been his ordinary footwear—but that had been years ago and now he found them heavy and too clumsy. They made him feel off-balance because the easy torsions of his lithe body had long ago become accustomed to lighter footgear.

He shoved the wide shed door open, his arm prepared for the pull of the window weight on a cord that held it shut, and peered into the dusty interior. He stood there in the door, his nostrils widening to take in the smell of clean wood and paint.

Letting the door swing shut behind him, Russ went on down the long shed, his eyes not missing a thing, to the big dragger that stood on the ways just inside the shed. When she was done, the big rolling door could be opened and the ways deposit her in the water. Already, above her, the forms were laid down for another just as large as she was, and he judged she must go a good forty feet or more overall. He stood for a moment admiring her lines, noticing the sheer of her bow caught against the dusky light from a cob-webbed window.

"Russ."

He turned to face Willard who had come up behind him.

"Hi, Willard," he said easily. "Don't know how you get a line like that." He nodded at the big white hull.

"Oh, figurin close," Willard shrugged.

"Yeah, but how do you do it every time?"

"Luck."

"I believe you," Russ said. He turned his back to look once more at the dragger's lines.

"See you got another one on the way." He jerked his head at the new keel.

"Ayup." Willard turned to look at it with the judging eye of one seeing a thing for the first time. "Two more on order too. Got all I can do, about."

"That so? I dunno's I like to see so many draggers bein built." Russ shook his head.

"Oh, I don't know." Willard bristled a little. "Nothin wrong with draggin."

"Maybe—maybe not. Lot of the fellers say a dragger'll ruin a piece of bottom for anythin else for the next five years."

"Oh, god, you know how people are. Somethin they ain't got theirselves, or don't quite trust, why, it can't possibly be no good. You take it from me, Russ, from now on they's goin to be more an more boats like her an less an less of these little pea-pods you see hootin around out there in the harbor. Why, if I was a young man myself, now, I'd get me one of these just as quick as I could spit. So'd you. That's where the worth-while money is."

"Everything's expandin," Russ said sadly. "Everything's gettin too big. I like to see a man doin a little business an doin it well without all this waste than see him make ten thousand a year an waste five more."

Willard went through a series of motions intended to express scorn. He shoved his cap far back on his shining bald head, scratched his pate thoughtfully with one little finger, sucked his right upper canine.

"Sounds funny comin from you, Russ. You was always a feller could see the right chance."

"Maybe I'm gettin old."

"Somethin in that," Willard agreed. "None of us gettin any younger. That's the way it is."

"Ah," Russ said vaguely. He wasn't too pleased having Willard agree with him so easily on a thing like that. It made him think maybe he really was getting old and didn't know it. He certainly didn't feel any older than he ever had, but having anyone agree without question that he was ageing didn't go down too well with him.

"Willard, there was somethin—"

Willard didn't say anything, but the quick jerk of his head told Russ he'd been expecting just what he knew was coming. Russ grinned a little to himself, not letting it show, at the way word traveled in the Ridge. If I was to cough, he thought, they'd have a hurricane the next day.

"I heard Gene was workin for you," he said easily, as if it didn't matter.

Willard nodded.

"Ayup, that's right. Been here near a month."

"Good worker?"

"All right," Willard said. "Anyone's good right now, the way I'm rushed."

Russ, watching him, noticed again the curious mannerism he always developed when he was nervous. He kept jerking his head to one side as he talked and it gave a confidential appearance to his conversation if it were only about the weather or the price of potatoes.

"Hmm." Russ sounded thoughtful. He made his face blank. "Art Ferguson said he had to fire Gene because he warn't very handy. Don't know how you make out so well with him."

"Now, look, Russ," Willard began hotly. "You ain't got no right to come around here tellin me who I can hire to work for me an who I can't. This is a free country, by god; an this is my boat yard an you ain't got any say whatsoever in what I do or who works for me."

Russ looked surprised.

"Why, Willard, I don't know what I did to get you so steamed up. Just mentioned Gene workin here is all."

"I don't know what call you got to mention it," Willard snapped.

"Maybe not." Russ stuck out his under lip and looked judicious.

There was a long silence and he could sense Willard boiling up beside him and trying not to spill over.

"Perley Stanley was tellin me the other day," Russ began with apparent unconcern. "He said he was thinkin of havin a couple of draggers built."

"Thinkin of it!" Willard yelled. "Thunder, he's doin more than thinkin of it. Them's the two I got on order."

"That so?" Russ's eyebrows shot up. "Why, I got the impression, the way Perley talked, he wasn't sure whether to have you build them or have em built up the Bay to Jonas Rae's yard. He even ast me which I thought was best."

"Whatta you want to do," Willard said, "see me bankrupt?"

"Good god, Willard, I never thought."

"You certainly take good care to see to it," Willard said carefully, "that the scales are weighted, but always on your side."

Russ shook his head.

"I'm sure sorry if I've said anythin to disturb you, Willard. Maybe I better go along till you cool off."

"Maybe you better," Willard said. "An if it's any satisfaction to you, he'll get his pink slip next pay day."

"You mean you're goin to fire Gene? Well, now, it's your doin if it's anybody's. I certainly don't want to see the kid's way made hard for him, but of course if he isn't a good worker you want to get rid of him whether he's my kid or whose he is."

"Yeah." Willard looked as if he'd swallowed a green gooseberry. "That's just what I figured. He really ain't a very steady man to have on a job."

"I'm sure sorry to hear that," Russ said. He turned away

slowly and started toward the door, noting out of the corner of his eye that Willard was keeping pace with him.

"You, if Perley says anythin more to you, you might tell him I understood that was a straight order about them draggers." Willard's words were pulled unwillingly out of him.

"Well, I did say I thought you'd be the man to do the work, all right," Russ said. "I'll just make a point of seein Perley to make sure he understood me."

"You might do that," Willard said bitterly. Then he stopped walking, letting Russ go on alone, but he watched the wide back steadily until the swinging shed door cut it out of his sight.

Russ had put the whole thing out of his mind as soon as he got out of sight of the shop. As he went back to the car he was thinking, Suppose I ought to do some shopping—Christmas day after tomorrow.

The winter was going fast and now he was surprised to think it was Christmas. He stopped in at the drugstore and spent twenty dollars on shaving lotion, powder, and perfume and candy. Everything, except the candy, were things his family would put away in a drawer and forget until Grace cleaned house in the spring and decided they were old enough to throw away without feeling guilty.

ON Christmas Eve, Pansy Galley was in the drugstore doing a little last-minute shopping for the kids' stockings. Somehow she never managed to come out right in her figuring. Each year she decided it was because the kids had grown so much since the Christmas before and she never allowed for that difference in the size of the stockings they'd hang up. Every year she found she didn't have enough and had to make this last minute trip for candy and some little ten-cent things to fill out the gaps in that row of stockings.

As she leaned thoughtfully over the glass case of candy, the door opened and closed again with force enough to start the big panes of plate glass in the show windows rattling. Pansy looked around, interested, saw that it was only Aurora Ellis, the telephone operator, and started to turn away again. But there was a new look to the habitual amazement of Aurora's plump face, a sort of titillated amazement mixed with enjoyable horror. Aurora caught her eye and came panting over to her.

"My lord, Pansy," she said, "somethin jest happened to me that ain't happened since I was knee-high."

"That so?" Pansy was noncommittal. Sometimes when Aurora got started it was pretty hard to turn her off. Sometimes Pansy wondered if the sitting there day in and day out listening to other folks talk had done something to Aurora's sense of fitness. Once she got started talking on her own, it seemed as if she just couldn't bear to stop.

"Yessir," Aurora said. "Was Jake Walls outside when you come in?"

"Why, I didn't see him," Pansy said. "I guess I'd of noticed if he had been."

"Well—" Aurora drew in her breath and held it a moment. "Well, when I come out of the house and started down to the store here, I see this car parked out in front and I noticed there was somebody leanin against the fender. I never thought anythin of it till I got right up with him. Thought it was maybe just some man waitin for his wife to do a little shoppin. When I come up to him, I see it was Jake Walls."

"Well," Pansy said, disappointed as she'd known she would be when she let Aurora start in. "I guess he's got as much right on the public streets as anyone, hasn't he?"

"I'm not sayin he ain't." Aurora reached up a little self-consciously and patted her wave back into perfect place. "It was what he said to me that give me much a start. I was going by him and he said, 'Hiya, Babe, what you doin tonight?' "

Pansy gasped and stared.

"That's the god's truth," Aurora said. "And I don't know's it's very flatterin to have you look as if you'd seen a ghost."

"But, Aurora," Pansy said protestingly. "He's young enough to be—er."

"I know it," Aurora said honestly. "That's why I was so surprised. You could of knocked me over with a feather. You could."

"But Jake Walls. He's always so tight-mouthed. I always thought he was real bashful. Never could get more than a hello out of him."

"I was wonderin," Aurora said. "I thought he was probably drunk, so I come right by in a hurry. I didn't even speak to him."

"Drunk?" Pansy said.

"They say he's been carryin on somethin fierce lately." Aurora looked thoughtful. "They say he's tight's a billy goat half the time."

"Well—" Pansy shook her head. "That certainly don't sound much like Jake Walls to me. The way Grace talks about them kids you'd think they was God's chosen people. Guess she's findin out now it's not all the way she thought."

"Well—" Aurora shook her head. "I guess anyone sets theirselves up to be so high and mighty has a fall every now an then. The talk is, she was real cut up when Gene left home."

"Left home," Pansy echoed. "Why, I thought he got married."

"Well, he did. But that was afterward. My lord, Pansy, here you are livin practically next door to them an you don't know half that goes on."

"Course I don't have your advantages," Pansy said.

"I spose you mean I sit up there all day just listenin in to other folks business," Aurora said snappishly. "Well, there's a lot more to runnin a telephone office than that, I can tell you. I just happen, sometimes, to hear things."

She stopped, looked thoughtful. She was a little put out at Pansy for saying a thing like that, but she wanted to tell what she had to tell and she didn't let her momentary anger stand in her way.

"Sometimes you can't help hearin a lot of things," she said. "Interestin, too."

"Like what?" Pansy, not without satisfaction, resigned herself.

"Well, there's a lot of talk goin the rounds about the Wallses right now. There's talk about Russ."

"Russ!"

"That's right," Aurora nodded. "The foreman of that company's building the breakwater lives there to Mrs. Parsons's house. The other night Aaron Billings was in to see him."

"Well, I don't see anythin in that," Pansy said tartly.

"You mean you ain't heard? Why, it's all over town how Aaron Billings was sayin he was goin to get that job. He was so sure he'd even started orderin the stuff."

"Well, he just didn't put in a low enough bid," Pansy said. "I heard about that. His bid wasn't as good as the one Mr. Frisbie's company made, that's all."

"Well, that's as may be." Aurora threw her head back skittishly. "But they's folks that say Russ Walls told Aaron that job was as good as his."

"Maybe he did," Pansy said. "But Aaron didn't get it, did he? Maybe they's a lot of people would rather see Aaron get it, but if he wanted more money than the other feller, the town would naturally give it to someone else."

"Well, I don't know," Aurora said. "All I know is, Aaron Billings was some old hot under the collar about it when he was in to see Mr. Frisbie. I could hear him yellin way down the hall."

"Yes," Pansy said. "And I'll bet you never shut your door, neither."

"Honestly, Pansy, you *are* mean! You know how cold she keeps that house. If I shut my door I don't get a bit of heat from the downstairs and then I have to sit there and freeze all evening."

"Hum," Pansy said, and turned back to her contemplation of the candy display.

"Well," Aurora said, in an offended voice, "I certainly don't want to bother you, but is Andy comin to pick you up?"

"Yes, he is."

"Do you mind if I wait an go along with you? I don't want to have to go past that Jake Walls again, if he's still there."

"You can if you want to," Pansy said. "I'm sure he wouldn't do anythin to you, but you can wait and go along with Andy and me."

Ten minutes later when they came out of the store, Andy was waiting. They went slowly up the road and let Aurora off under the lighted tourist sign in front of Mrs. Parsons's house. Neither Jake nor his car were anywhere to be seen.

"Well." Aurora got out. "Merry Christmas to both of you, I'm sure."

"Same to you," Andy said heartily.

Later when Pansy told him the story, he laughed uproariously.

"Good lord," he said. "Jake must be pretty hard put to it."

"Yes, but what I want to know," Pansy said, "is there any truth in that story about Russ and Aaron?"

"Oh, I've heard somethin," Andy said. "Nothin definite. And I don't believe there's a mite of truth in it. You know how this town is, a yarn like that gets started from almost anythin."

"That's what I thought myself," Pansy said. "But sometimes you can't be sure."

225

"I'd forget it if I was you. No sense lookin for trouble. An besides, that ain't like Russ."

"I know it." Pansy went to finish filling the stockings, but the story stuck in the back of her mind and was there when she went to the next meeting of the Ladies Aid.

I REMEMBER when you kids were all little," Grace said at the breakfast table that morning. Her eyes, apparently on the swirling snow that sheeted past the window, weren't really seeing it. They were looking down a long hall of years, a long corridor marked out with Christmas trees, to the time when the kids had been little. Her voice had that musing remembering sound that doesn't mean the actual remembering of incidents, merely the mental recollection of another time, a time that had been happier—a time that seemed to have been happier because of the faultiness of human memory and the imperfection of the present.

"Well," Russ remarked staring mazed at the snow, "this Christmas certainly ought to remind you of it if any would. Look at that snow."

He felt a deep sense of gratification, almost as if the snow had been called up at his personal behest.

"Yes, it's certainly a good old-fashioned Christmas this year."

Grace looked at him as if she hadn't heard the words, only the voice.

"You remember how the kids used to get us out of bed at three or four o'clock in the mornin? Why, I remember one year when Jake was, let me see, he couldn't have been more than ten."

"Pete sake, Ma, that old yarn," Jake said protestingly, looking up from his plate.

The rest of them, though, let her go on, knowing that she'd

get the story out sooner or later and wanting her to enjoy it.

"Yes, that," she said imperturbably. "You wanted a sled and wasn't sure you were going to get it. I woke up about one o'clock in the mornin and it sounded as if a pack of rats were crawlin around the tree. I got up and went out in the livin room." She looked at Mary who was watching her with a patient, prepared-to-be-amused look. "I couldn't see a thing," she said. "Quiet as the grave. Then, all of a sudden, I noticed a long white thing down under the tree and I couldn't remember puttin anything like that there."

"I said, 'That you, Jake?' " Grace twisted her head, listening for an answer from the voiceless years. "Not a sound. I went over and put my hand down and there he was. I tell you, I houted him out of there some old quick and back to bed again."

They all looked at Jake with an excess of good feeling as if the story made him more personally beloved. Then Stanley laughed and Jake made a half-swipe at him across the table.

"Here, now," Russ said, without sharpness.

Momentarily the story had drawn them together, made them into a family entity with its joint feelings and shared little private jokes.

"Those were the days," Grace said heavily. "Those days I never thought we'd ever see a Christmas when we weren't all under the same roof."

Her eyes met Russ's suddenly angry ones defiantly.

"Christmas is the time, if there ever was one, for makin up quarrels," she said. "It's not decent for families to have to split up so children aren't welcome in their own homes."

"Anyone," Russ said with level intensity, "who comes to this house is welcome."

He got up to go into the other room where the Christmas tree was waiting, but he didn't get through the door in time to miss Grace's retort.

"You have to make them want to come first," she said.

When Russ disappeared there was an uncomfortable minute of silence, then Stanny started precipitously, "I certainly wish the rest of this family was as young as me. It's certainly a strain on me, havin to wait till the rest of you sit around an eat. My gosh, I can't understand anyone who could eat breakfast before havin the tree."

"You *ain't* et what you could call a lot, have you?" His grandfather leaned forward and looked at Stanny's cereal bowl which was still well over half full. "Don't you know oatmeal's good for you? My god, when I stop to think of the vitamins and things like that they've found in oatmeal since I first started eatin it, I think to myself, it's a wonder I ever lived to grow up, not knowin."

"You got em just the same whether you knew or not," Stanny protested.

"That so?" Nat lifted a white eyebrow. "Well, I never figured they did me much good. Thing like that, why a man has to have knowledge of it before he gets any of the benefits out of it."

"Pa," Grace said protestingly. "I never knew a grown man could talk the foolishness you do. What on earth difference does it make whether you knew they were there or not? They were, and they must have done you just as much good as they did after you found out about it."

"Well," Nat said doubtfully, "I'm not so sure of that. Nowadays you never can tell when some new vitamin's goin to come along an stab you in the back. Them days, not knowin, I bet we jest went around sheddin vitamins like a duck does water. I won't never believe one of em stuck."

"For pity sake," Grace said helplessly against the laughter of the three kids. Immediately restored to good humor, she got up and started for the door.

"Well, you can all sit there an talk as long's you want to. Me, I'm goin in an open my presents. I ain't even goin to wash the dishes."

Stanny let out a whoop and was past her almost before she'd finished speaking. She said, "Mercy," good naturedly, and let him go. Jake and Nat got up, glancing at each other with amused eyes, and followed Grace into the other room. For a moment Mary sat poised on the edge of her chair, wanting desperately to go after them, to get back into that protective shell of friendliness and good fellowship that had been around them momentarily when Grace was telling the story about Jake. She wanted to call Jake back and say something to him, something that would make him see what she felt and how badly she wanted to belong to them. But something in herself stopped her, kept her from saying the word that would bring him back, something compounded from the memory of unconscious rebuffs.

Shy people use such devious means to give themselves the sense of belonging to at least one other person—slight things have a deeper significance. A touch or an accidental glance has a hidden meaning that nobody else can see in it. They sense more, sometimes things that don't exist. They pour more of themselves into slight contacts, but in such an ungraceful way that they seem almost sullen and the result is repulsion instead of attraction. And she was so familiar with that repulsion in others that she shrank from making the attempt again.

Her inability brought back the sense of deep loneliness, the desperate feeling of being outside, the horrible crawling desire to get in that had become so strong in her lately as to be almost a physical sickness.

She got up and went over to the window, letting her eyes grow dazzled with the ghostly whirl of the blizzard past the glass. She had been out in it last night when the snow started. At ten o'clock it had begun to snow—thinly at first—small flakes with pauses between them, as if the weather couldn't quite make up its mind. By ten-thirty it was snowing heavily, still small flakes, but thick. Snow curled and lapped around the houses like fog. Up on the Ridge, it fell straight down through the spruces, sifting through the needles with small sibilant sounds. In the open where there was no interference to explain the constant hissing noise of the snow, the flakes were so hard that the sound of their striking together in mid-air was clear.

When Mary came down the road there was nothing but darkness overhead and the strange pallidity of the snow, already beginning to be heavy underfoot. She could tell from the dry small flakes, falling straight down through the windless air, that this snow was going to last, this was going to be a real one, softening the Ridge, leveling the wide sloping fields. The snow didn't soak through her wool jacket and when she brushed it off, the cloth underneath wasn't wet. She stood still in the middle of the road and put her face up —her face felt hot and the flakes were like small icy fingers against her skin.

It seemed to her that the receding circling hissing sound of the snow was tenable enough to be something inside her head. Flakes caught in her hair and she brushed at them, feeling with a little chill of pleasure the iciness of them, going down the back of her collar.

Suddenly, and unexpectedly, as it always did, the familiar feeling of self-confidence, of absolute certainty, took possession of her so completely that she found herself wondering how she'd ever been able to doubt that she could do whatever she wanted to. It was wonderful. It was like being born if you could have known what was happening, not completely blissful, but with a hangover of discomfort like a pain.

She found the turning of the driveway and went confidently up toward the house, a dim mass, untouched by light. She went through the unlocked kitchen door, shutting it and locking it behind her. And when she turned the key, her confidence was gone—it was like coming alone and naked into a place of strangers and as if nobody you had ever known or could ever know had been there before.

She stared abstractedly at the snow, trying unconsciously to make out the ragged line of the Ridge, knowing she couldn't. She found herself wondering if anyone, seeing what she saw from that window and never having seen it before, would be as conscious as she was of the invisible beetling presence of land behind the snow, and she decided they would. The Ridge could make itself felt even when it was most invisible.

"Mary." Russ's voice behind her made her start and turn defensively. He was standing in the door watching her with curious cold blue eyes. "D'you think you could tear yourself away long enough to come in the other room? Your mother wants all you kids in there and everybody else is sittin around waitin for you."

"Sorry, Pa," she said hastily and started in by him. When she passed him, Russ, looking at her, thought suddenly that she didn't look well.

"You all right?" he said and the unaccustomed solicitude startled her almost more than his unexpected voice had. She looked at him, an oblique glance that left him baffled and feeling angry.

"Sure," she said. "Of course."

Relieved that he let her go with that, she went quickly into the front room and sat down. The others were there, waiting patiently. Only Stanny seemed to have imbibed any suggestion of excitement and he was standing tensely in the middle of the room, his eyes on the door. As soon as Russ came in, Stanny made a dive for the big tree that stood in the corner by the front window.

Grace always liked to have it there because the lights looked so pretty from outside the house. Just before Christmas, every year, she made Russ drive her around town after dark so she could see and compare the lights of other houses with those of her own. She had never yet found a tree or the front of any house that looked as pleasant to her as her own did. Now, in spite of the luminous light coming in from the snow outside, she went over to the tree and turned on the strings of tiny bulbs.

"There." She looked down at Stanny. "You can give out the presents."

Mary, watching her young brother with amusement, saw that he at least hadn't become too detached from his childhood not to have done a little looking around. He made instinctively for the packages that were his and carried at least four to his own chair before he managed to find one for anyone else. Well, why not, she thought with pity. After all, he's only a kid yet and the rest of us forget it and expect him to act like a grown-up. It must be tough for a fourteen-year-old in this house—it must be like a pigmy living with the giants. The taut excited look of Stanny's thin back as he burrowed in the pile of bundles under the tree made her think of an eager puppy, excited to the point where he forgets all his training.

Although she had been sitting there thinking what a child he was, Mary herself waited until he'd cleaned everything out from under the tree before she started opening the batch he'd doled out to her.

"Well," Grace said, as she usually did, looking up from her own treasures, "every year I keep thinkin there'll be less packages, but it always seems as if there never is."

Russ, tearing tissue paper impatiently off his socks and ties, glanced over at her with a friendly grin.

"Old Santa," he said. "He usually manages to do himself proud."

In the general rustling excitement, none of them noticed Mary's frozen silence. She was sitting as if transfixed in her chair, staring with eyes that refused to believe what they saw, at the large flat package Stanny had handed her last of all.

She wet her lips and moved them slightly, trying over the sound of the name written in the upper lefthand corner of the stiff brown envelope. Then, suddenly, a reassured happiness that was almost too acute for her to bear in silence made her slump back in the chair. Instinctively, wanting to keep this wonderful thing that had happened all to herself, she thrust the flat package behind her, hoping nobody had seen it and turned hastily to the others still in her lap.

Annie was wrong, she was thinking. Lucy wasn't like the rest of them. Mary didn't care what was in the package; it could be anything at all and still not make a difference. What mattered to her was the name Simmons printed in the return address corner. It made her feel as if there was someone, somewhere, to whom she meant something as a person and not as an appendage to her family, not as a sister or a daughter, but as herself. But whatever it was, it was too wonderful to share; she had to get it upstairs somehow, take it away like a magpie with a spoon, to pore over in secret and alone.

But she looked up and caught her father's eye with a distinct feeling of dismay.

Oh lord, she thought, I might have known that wouldn't get by him.

"What's so private?" Russ said, not unkindly. "Wouldn't be that package from New York, would it?"

"New York?" Grace looked up. "Who's got anythin from New York? Who on earth's sendin you presents from New York?" Her curiosity picked Mary out accurately.

"Well," Mary mumbled, feeling as if her hands and feet had grown suddenly to twice their normal size. "I don't know yet. I haven't opened it."

"Go ahead an do it," Russ said with the encouraging nod you give to a child who is trying vainly to speak a company piece. "You know anyone named Simmons?"

"Simmons, ha? That the name?" Grace said. "Well, for

the lord sake, Mary, open it, why don't you, before we all die of curiosity. Wonder who it could be?"

"Well, I know who it is," Mary said loudly, knowing her voice was too loud. "It's a friend of mine, that's all."

She fumbled blindly with the bright red ribbon on the package she had in her hand, keeping her head well down, hoping they'd forget about it and let her alone.

"Why *don't* you open it?" Stanny said impatiently. "It ain't a time bomb, is it?"

"Looks like a picture to me," Russ said judiciously, eyeing the thin edge of the brown paper he could see from where he sat.

"When d'it come?" Grace looked at Russ.

"Yesterday's mail," he said. "I brought it up with me at noon and put it in here. I set out to say somethin about it then, but I thought it was probably a Christmas present all right and the place for it was in here."

Mary, seizing on any possible out, said quickly, "Well, it's not a present. It's something for me, not a present. I'm not going to open it."

They stared at her for a moment in amazed silence, then Jake got his voice back.

"I know," he said loudly. "She's got herself a boy friend and that's his picture. She wants to go off by herself to open it."

Relieved and a little pleased at the possible explanation, Grace smiled over at Mary.

"Well, there," she said. "Doesn't matter what it is. It's her present. Let her open it wherever she wants to. Lord knows we got enough to keep us busy with our own."

Mary kept her head down, refusing to meet their eyes, knowing that the bare anger in her own would lead to a showdown and willing to hide behind any pretense to keep what was rapidly becoming an important secret.

Stanny glanced at her once, carelessly, and then, noting

with the peculiarly horrible instinct boys sometimes have for the worst possible thing they can say, started half-chanting. "Mary's got a boy friend. I'm gonna tell Ra-alph. Mary's—"

"Stanley," Grace said sharply. The use of his full name brought him up short. He looked questioningly at her and then at his father.

"That's enough out of you," Grace told him. Mary, listening, resented her mother's interference almost as much as she did her brothers' inference; but she kept still, knowing that it needed only the slightest protest from her to turn them all on her again like a hungry pack.

She sat there in their midst as long as she could stand it and until she thought their curiosity had cooled down a little. Then she got up, casually gathering together the opened bundles and their wrappings, and managing to stick the big flat unopened parcel under her arm.

"Well." She glanced at her mother with a weak smile. "I've got so much stuff here I guess I better take some of it up and put it away."

Grace looked a little surprised and started to say something. She liked them all to leave their presents spread out on the big table for a few days after Christmas so she could look at them herself and maybe show them to anyone who happened to come in. But she could see, and interpreted rightly, the look on Mary's face and let her go without protest.

"I'd give a good deal," she said thoughtfully, after Mary was out of hearing, "if I knew exactly what was in that package. Musta been something she didn't want anyone to see."

"You want to know and I'll speak to her," Russ said. "No reason for her to go off like that without showin you if you think it's somethin you ought to know about."

"Oh, no." Grace shook her head. "It's not that. It's just my nosiness. Nemmind saying anything else to her. I'll find out sooner or later, soon's she calms down."

Mary's departure had broken up the ceremonious sanctity

of the circle and, one after the other, the men disappeared. As each one went, Grace would look up and say, "Now, one o'clock's dinnertime and I want you all here right on the dot. This is Christmas and it's the one day in the year I won't have no waiting around for you all to get here whenever you want to."

Mary, after she had gone upstairs, closed her door carefully behind her, settled down on the bed and proceeded methodically to fold up loose paper and coil string and ribbon into neat little circles. She tied the whole thing together in a firm square package, taking great pains with the knot. She did everything she could think of to put off opening the package that lay beside her on the bed.

Finally there was nothing else left to do and she took the package up in both hands, feeling lightly around its edges. Whatever it was, it had been carefully stiffened with cardboard and was unyielding.

Even now, when there was nothing to keep her from opening it, she wanted to keep the pleasure of anticipation a little longer. It was good to know that Lucy hadn't forgotten about her.

At last she untied the string, laid back the outer wrappings and sat looking down at the contents of the package. Her first reaction was one of dismayed relief.

"My lord," she said softly. "What if I'd opened this downstairs."

She sat for a moment staring at the two water colors, imagining too clearly what Grace would say if she could set eyes on them. Then she forgot about what Grace would have said, and sat looking at them with pleasure. Technically she knew very little about water colors; just enough, in fact, to know that these were. One was a reproduction. In the background the faintest suggestion of stormy ocean, in the foreground a looming bare tree, a couple of houses, a wet-looking snowy dirt road. The name in the lower righthand corner

236

was one she'd never heard before, John Whorf. The other was altogether different. It was an original and the colors were in complete contrast to the dark, distant-looking tones of the first. It was the picture of a woman, lying on sand in a little cove between high overhanging ridges of red rock. The colors were brilliant, summery, warm; and the flesh tones of the woman herself were almost tropical. She looked as if she'd been lying there soaking sun until her skin itself would have burned if you'd touched it. But the two great arms of rock were forbidding, harsh, jarring against the peace of the quiet water and the still figure—they looked ominous. In the lower corner of this one there were only initials—LAS.

Getting up, Mary went over and stood the stiff-backed pictures on the little mantel that was the only thing left to show where the fireplace had been walled in years ago. Then she went back and sat down on her bed to look at them. Propped up there, they caught the brilliant snow-light from outside and each, in its way, was as warming as a fire would have been. For a long time she sat looking at them, her head on one side, her hands propped against the bed.

Damn, she thought. I wish I could do that.

Then, for fear Grace would think it queer if she didn't come back downstairs, she went over and took them down and stowed them carefully in the bottom drawer of the bureau, packing sheets and pillowcases back over them smoothly, so they looked as if they hadn't been disturbed.

This was her room and she knew that nobody came into it, least of all her mother. Yet somehow she felt safer with something material and opaque between the precious pictures and any possible examination.

When she went downstairs, she found Grace in the kitchen competently getting dinner. She had apparently forgotten all about the mysterious package and neither of them mentioned it.

Somehow the day dragged on. Christmas was a day that

meant a good deal to Grace and she had always insisted on having her family spend it together. But her family, confined between the same walls, found so little to say to each other and so little to do, that the hours pressed in on them heavily. Stanny spent his time mooning around the kitchen until Grace turned on him and drove him into the other room like an enraged hen with an excitable chicken. After that, Jake went off out to the barn and didn't show again until Mary went to call him to dinner. Russ and Nat, apparently the only two who could find something to keep them reasonably out of the way, sat in the front room reading, Russ, as usual, deeply engrossed in the paper; Nat rediscovering an interest in the old western stories that had been untouched for years in the glass-fronted bookcase.

They sat around the table in the unaccustomed splendor of the dining room itself, eating the inspired meal Grace set before them. And eating it in complete silence. Watching them, Mary wondered if they could feel as clearly as she did the silent tension that always seemed to build up among them when they were forced into each other's company for any length of time. It was almost as articulate as sound to her—but, looking at their quiet faces, she decided it was apparent only to her for what it actually was. If any of the others had been able to recognize it, she knew they would have been as uncomfortable as she was, and that was a thing that showed through.

Jake finished eating first, pushed back his chair, and got up, his eyes defiantly on his mother's face.

"Ma, I'm goin downtown," he said quickly, his young voice sounding heavy and stiff. "Thought I'd just take a look downtown to see what's goin on."

Surprisingly enough Grace only nodded at him instead of protesting.

"Can I go, Ma?" Stanny said eagerly, having waited the outcome of Jake's proposal with interest.

"No, you can't," Jake said before Grace had the chance. "If I want company, I'll ask for it. Till then, you wait."

"Oh, gosh." Stanny frowned and settled back in his chair. "Anyone'd think none of you had ever been fourteen. I spose I'm too young to go anywheres with you. Where you goin, anyhow?" he shouted suddenly. "Somewhere you don't want nobody to know about?"

Jake turned at the door and glared at his younger brother.

"You shut up," he said. "It's none of your business where I'm goin, or why, see?"

"Oh, boys," Grace said—suddenly her bone weariness was there in her voice. "I wish you wouldn't argue. It does seem as if this one day in the whole year, you don't have to argue."

"There ain't any argument," Jake said flatly. "I'm just sayin he can't go, that's all."

"All right, Stanny," Russ said easily. "You just settle down now and spend your afternoon here to home. I guess it won't kill you one day out of the year."

"Pete sake," Stanny said, goaded into bravery by the obvious unfairness of it all. "I shd think he might, too. You never see him stayin home when he don't have to."

"Well, he don't have to," Russ said sharply, as Jake went up the front stairs. "And you do. That's the difference. See?"

"I see all right," Stanny said.

"Stanley," Grace said again and her tone restored Stanny's sanity. He glanced once at his father who was staring at him narrowly, his big hand holding one of Grace's best real linen napkins, arrested halfway to his mouth. For a moment they sat there, eyeing each other across the table, before Stanny's eyes fell and he mumbled something Russ couldn't hear. He got up and started for the door.

"What was that you said?" Russ turned a little in his chair, but Stanny had gone. Russ half rose, as if to go after him, but Grace stopped him.

"Oh, let him go, Russ," she said tiredly. "Let him go. It's all right."

"I'm not going to stand for that kid sarsing back whenever he feels like it." Russ stared at her.

"You don't," she said. "I've never seen you. Let him go this time."

"There's no reason why I should," he said and got up from the table, but to her relief, instead of going in to the front hall after Stanny, he turned through the living room door and she heard him settling down in his chair once more.

For a flash Grace's eyes met Mary's—and both their faces were eloquent with relief.

"Lord," Grace sighed. "I'd like to see us spend just one day together in this house without having it end in a fight."

Mary realized then that she hadn't been alone in feeling the tension that held them all stiffly inside their own little globes of solitude. Grace felt it too—perhaps they all did. Maybe that was what made it so bad. Maybe they all felt it.

Jake came downstairs again, wearing his best overcoat and a soft gray felt hat, pulled low over his broad red forehead. He went through the kitchen without speaking, but his mother followed him to the door and stopped him there where nobody could hear what she said to him.

"Look, Jake." She put her hand on his arm just above the elbow and he could feel her fingers moving nervously. "You goin downtown, you say?"

"Ayeh," he nodded, not looking at her.

"Look, you think you might see Gene?"

"I might."

"Here." She whipped her other hand out from under her apron and handed him a package done up in plain white tissue and tied with a silky looking white ribbon. It looked neat and efficient, but somehow festive. "If you do, you might give him this. I—It's nothin much, but give it to him. And say I said Merry Christmas."

Jake took the package clumsily, his red face looking redder. "Okay."

"And Jake—"

"Yeah?"

"You don't need to mention it to your Pa."

"Don't worry." Jake gave her an unhumorous grin; there was almost too much comprehension in his face and Grace, who hadn't expected it, found herself sheering off from the moment when they might have understood each other. "I ain't any too anxious to talk to him myself," Jake said.

He thrust the package into the big pocket of his coat and went heavily, squarely, out across the bare-looking snowy desolation of the yard to his car. Grace stood in the open door watching him take the stiff old horse blanket off the radiator. Jake knew she was standing there looking after him, but he didn't glance back again. He climbed into the car and went hurtling down the drive. As soon as he'd got out of sight of the house, he pulled the car off to the side of the road and reached into his other pocket for the bottle. The first taste and smell always made him feel nauseated and he sat waiting for the feeling to pass before he took another deep swallow and felt warmth begin to sift through his chilled body.

When he drove on he was feeling almost human again because he had started to forget about his father and when that happened Jake *did* feel almost human. He stopped in front of the old Freeman house, knowing before he went up to knock on the door that nobody was home. It had the deserted look houses get when people go away even for the day. He was just as glad. He hadn't seen Gene to speak to since the night he'd found out how things were shaping up for him and he wouldn't have bothered to look for him now if it hadn't been for Grace. He pulled open the storm door, put the package inside so they couldn't miss it when they came back, and went back down the walk to his car.

His chief sensation, now that he knew he wasn't going to have to see Gene, was one of relief. It was pretty difficult for him to forget how Gene's face had looked that night in the little upstairs room when he'd leaned over and said, "You're nothing but a hired man around here, see?"

He had thought, if he stayed out late enough, nobody'd be up when he got home—but he had forgotten all about the present Grace had given him for Gene. If he'd remembered that, he might have known she'd be there waiting for him to see what Gene had said, how he was looking, what he'd done.

But he forgot about it and when he parked the car and went uncertainly up to the back door, he thought the light in the kitchen was the small one she usually left on until the last of them were in at night and the door locked.

He had a hard time making his fingers contract enough to lift the latch, but he managed it at last and went on in hitting his shoulder heavily against the jamb as he passed.

Momentarily, looking at his mother, Jake couldn't seem to make his mind understand that she was really there, sitting beside the table. But she was; she was, and if he'd known it, he wouldn't have come into the house at all.

Instantly his mind was clear, transparent in its clarity, and it told him that his tongue and his body were completely out of his control and if he could once get by her and into the safe obscurity of the other room everything would be all right. So he said nothing; he concentrated on crossing the kitchen floor to the darkness of the doorway of escape. But it was hot there in the kitchen and she was saying something to him and he knew he was going to have to answer her somehow. It was an effort for him to stop and turn to face her, but he couldn't understand what she was saying unless he looked at her.

"What?" he said stupidly.

"Did you see Gene? What did he say?" Grace said eagerly.

"Did he look all right? I been waitin since suppertime to hear what he said."

"He lo-ooked fi-ine." Jake strung the words out, trying to make them sound normal and his own voice sounded to him as if he were trying to talk around a mouthful of hot potato. "He sa-aid Mer-ry—" Jake started again and suddenly stumbled to a chair and sat down, because if he hadn't, he would have had to sit down on the floor and then she'd know what was wrong with him. "Christ-mas," he finished heavily.

Drunk as he was, Jake could see her face too clearly. There was little change in her expression; it still was the look of exasperated but pleased anticipation—that didn't change. It just looked suddenly as if it had set and would be that expression for the rest of her life; as if never again would she be able to change the look on her face.

Jake looked at her, horror struck, trying to tell her it was all right—but he couldn't move his tongue, it lay in his mouth like a swollen piece of flannel and he couldn't get a word out around it.

Grace leaned forward a little, not much; but it seemed to Jake as if her face grew bigger and bigger as she got closer, until she might have been almost touching him.

"Go to bed, Jake," she said clearly. "I'll talk to you in the mornin."

He couldn't remember going upstairs and she must have helped him because he knew he couldn't have done it alone. But he remembered lying in his bed feeling as if each of its legs, one after the other, lifted six inches off the floor, kicked twice, and settled back down again with a jar.

TRYING to talk to Jake was like trying to talk to a stone or a piece of wood. There was something wrong with him, Grace knew, but her knowledge went no further than that. She knew only that there was something wrong.

He sat at the breakfast table with his head in his hands, not looking at her, not even bothering to drink the black coffee she put in front of him. Even when she sat down opposite him and leaned forward to talk directly to him, she might have been alone in the room for all the response she got out of Jake.

At first she'd been mad, so mad she knew she wouldn't be able to say a thing to him without making him mad, too. But something in the defenseless misery of his bowed head changed her anger to compassion. And that was strange, too, because if there was one thing Grace could not abide, it was what she called "drink."

"Jake, listen," she tried again. "It's so foolish. If only you'd believe me an see what you're doin to yourself. That makes twice now you've come home like that, so drunk you couldn't hardly walk—and I don't know how many other times I didn't know about."

She stopped and waited a minute to see if he'd say something, but he didn't move. Defenseless was a queer word to think about Jake, but that was the way he looked to her, what she could see of him. Tufts of his stiff bristly hair stood straight up between his big fingers and all she could see of his face was his heavy chin and his full-lipped mouth. The loose look of the mouth made her remember suddenly how he'd tried to talk to her last night and how he hadn't been able to make the words come out.

"If there's any reason for you actin like this," she began, "why won't you tell me what it is? Maybe if I knew, too, it'd make it easier for you. We might be able to do something about it."

Jake lifted his head from his hands and looked at her dully, his eyes half-shut with the effort it took to make them focus.

"You always have to know," he said heavily. "You have to know, don't you?"

"Of course I have to know when there's somethin wrong with one of my kids. It's only natural a mother would want to know," Grace said quickly. "Especially when I see you tryin to kill yourself. I ought to know why. That's what a mother's for, to help her kids, Jake."

"You ought to of begun a little sooner," Jake said. He got up and started for the door.

"Well," Grace said, seeing she wasn't going to get any satisfaction out of him. "All I hope is, you were sober when you saw Gene and Annie yesterday. I only hope nobody else saw you in the condition you were when you got home here. I've always been able to hold my head up in this town, specially when it came to my kids; but it doesn't look like I was going to much longer."

In all her tirade only one sentence seemed to mean anything to Jake.

"Gene?" He stared at her blankly. "I never saw Gene."

"You sat right there last night and told me you'd seen him," Grace said, disappointment and hurt making her sound harsh. "You said he told you to tell me Merry Christmas."

"Well, it ain't so," Jake said. "No matter what I said last night. I never see him. I left the package right inside the door because there warn't anyone to home. I must of been dreamin last night."

"No," Grace said tightly. "You weren't dreamin, Jake. But I want to tell you this. You better stop. Apparently, when you get drunk, you don't know what you're doin or sayin, and sometime, if a stop isn't put to it, you're goin to do somethin that'll get us all in a mess. And I won't stand for it.

"Understand me, Jake," she said after his retreating back. "I will not stand for it. I'd rather see you dead."

When he'd gone out, she went flying up the stairs to his bedroom. Ordinarily, she never went into the kids' rooms to do anything besides clean them, but this time she felt justified in what she was going to do. She had a vague idea that he couldn't have bought liquor anywhere on Christmas Day, so he must have had it in his room and if there was any more there, she knew the right place for it.

She went over the room with a fine-tooth comb. All she found were three empty pint bottles in the closet, stuffed in behind a pile of dirty shirts and shoes. She took them downstairs and out to the edge of the woods where she threw them as far as she could into the alders.

Jake was standing in the barn door when she came back to the house, but he didn't speak to her and after a quick glance at him, Grace went on into the house.

GENE stood for a minute on the sidewalk looking at the house, before he started up the walk that led to the front door. He'd passed the corner lot house at least twice a day ever since he'd lived on the Ridge, but he never thought he'd live to see the day when he'd be going up the path to its door knowing that he lived there and that his wife was waiting inside for him. It was a small house, set far back on the triangular lot of land formed by the acute angle of the junction of the Ridge branch-off with the main road. He knew it was old—it looked it; besides, Gene could remember somebody telling him that old Jonas Freeman, grandfather of Jay Freeman who was Russ's age, had built the house for his first wife back in the early eighteen hundreds. It had been called the Old Freeman House ever since, down through decades of degeneration from a new house to what it was now. No matter who lived in it, it was always the Old Freeman House. The intervening occupants had never stayed there long enough to make any impression on its name.

But somehow you expected more from an old house than this one had to give you, Gene thought. It wasn't much more than a square, unimaginative, high-sided box. It had needed paint and shingles for years and still did. And still would, he added mentally, if it was going to be up to him to do anything about it. Age, even in houses, ought to have some grace to recommend it. And he thought of his father's house, up there on the whaleback of the Ridge, and turned to glance, scowling, up at the glooming spruces. No matter where he went in this town, there was no getting away from the Ridge, nor from Russ, because the two were so mixed up in his mind that one was merely the symbol of the other.

He turned and went quickly up the walk, hearing the crunching of the frozen snow underfoot, noticing with moody eyes the shaggy burdocks thrusting up barely through the snow crust along the gap-picketed fence. Just before he reached the door, he glanced up to see the front curtains swaying slightly. He scowled again, wondering how long she'd been standing there watching him.

But he forgot his momentary irritation when she opened the door and stood aside to let him in.

"Hello, darling," she said, smiling at him.

Just looking at her was enough to make him feel suddenly overwhelmed with the remarkability of the fact that she was his wife and had been for over a month now.

"For heaven sake," Annie said. "What'll the neighbors think?" She got away from him and shut the door.

"They'd probably think it was mighty funny if it only took a month for me to get tired of hugging you," Gene said, purposely to see her blush. She did, so he had to kiss her again.

"Now, stop." She escaped in the direction of the kitchen this time and he followed her. Once out there, she took pains to put the table between them. "Go on and wash and then come eat your dinner. You'll be late to work if you keep lally-gagging around like this."

Gene's mood burst like a balloon when it's touched with a cigaret. He remembered what it was he'd been trying to think how to tell her when he came up the road. And because he couldn't think how to do it yet, he sat down to eat silently, so deep in thought he didn't even notice what he was eating.

"Don't you like your dinner?" she asked finally, watching him.

"Yes, sure." He looked to make sure what it was before looking up at her. "It's fine."

"Something's wrong with you, then."

"Nothing's wrong. Guess I was just feeling thoughtful."

"I saw you lookin at the house." She glanced down, moving her knife idly along a crease in the oilcloth table cover. "When you came up the path. You were thinking how awful it looked, werent' you?"

"Well." Anxious to make her think that was it, he grinned. "It isn't exactly the palace I promised you when we got married, is it?"

"Oh, that!" She shrugged, her eyes twinkling. "I discounted about fifty per cent of that."

"Guess it was a good thing you did." In spite of himself, a wave of discouragement made his voice dull.

"It's not that bad," she protested. "I've done some looking at it myself the last few days. It's really a good house. We could fix it up and make it look nice as any. It's just been let run down."

"Oh, I don't know. I never could get very enthusiastic about fixing up a place someone else'd have the use of sooner or later."

"We might even buy it," Annie said, watching his face.

"Before you make the down payment," Gene said harshly, "I'd better tell you, I lost my job this morning."

There, he thought, now I've gone and blurted it out just the way I didn't want to. He started to get up to go around the table, but when he looked at her face, he saw it wasn't going to be necessary to comfort her. She didn't need it.

"You don't look very concerned about it," he said, his voice going sharp.

"Well, I'm not as concerned as I might be if I didn't know how smart you were. What's a job? My lord, Gene, don't look like it was the end of the world."

"A job's a hell of a lot here. There's so many jobs and so many men to fill them. After that—nothing." He started to get angry. After all, she's all right, he thought. She won't have to get out and scrounge around to find another job. All she has to do is sit here and wait for me to do something.

"Well, you haven't exhausted all the possibilities yet," she said.

"Two jobs in one month," Gene raised an eyebrow.

"You don't want to forget you'd had one of em for six years."

"Oh, I know," he said wearily. "It was a good thing, Art firing me. Well, I suppose it was a good thing Willard fired me, too."

"You may be surprised at how it'll turn out," Annie said resolutely. "You might have gone on doing the same thing the rest of your life."

"Well, it would be nice to go on doing the same thing for more than three weeks. What I'd like to know is why I couldn't keep that job. The work warn't hard."

"Didn't he give you any reason for letting you go?"

"Just said he couldn't use me any longer."

"That's funny." Annie knit her brows and sat staring at the table cloth. "Well," she said brightly, at last, "maybe you just aren't suited to that particular job."

"Hunh," Gene said.

Suddenly she got up and came around the table to him and put her hand lightly on his shoulder, but he wouldn't look up at her.

"Don't be mad, darling," she said. "I'm scared, too."

"I'm not mad. Not really. It's just that I wanted—well, hell, nothing's gone right from the beginning. Nothing's the way I wanted it to be for you. I had such big ideas. Everything was going to be lovely. I was going to build a house for you that'd look as if it'd last forever. What do you get? This old shack. You were goin to have such a nice wedding. What did you have? That old tomb up there in Freehold with its corpse for a minister."

"Shut up," Annie said harshly. "Shut up."

She got both hands deep in his hair and pulled hard, bringing tears of pain and surprise. She pulled his head back until he looked directly up at her.

"I got what I wanted most," she said fiercely. "I got you, didn't I?"

It was all very well, he thought. For a while she could make things seem all right for him again, but it didn't last. Even while he was sitting there drinking reassurance from her, he began to think of Willard and the way Willard had told him that morning.

Things had looked pretty good to Gene that morning. When he and Annie had come down from Aaron's house the night before and found the small package waiting for them, shut carefully inside the storm door, Gene had realized how much his estrangement from his own family had been bothering him.

The few weeks since he'd walked out of the house, now when he stopped to look back over them, seemed very long, out of all proportion to the rest of his life. And he did miss the folks. It was queer, in a town the size of this one, how seldom you saw people. You'd think you'd always be running into one or the other of them, but he never did. Russ he had seen occasionally, but only at a distance. Stanny, once or twice, had gone up by the house on foot, turning to look curiously in at the blank windows and Gene had seen him then and thought he looked frightened and almost as if he were looking at the house against his will. Mary, Jake, and Grace he hadn't seen at all. And when he stooped to pick up the small bundle and saw the neat way it was wrapped, he knew instantly who had wrapped and tied it, even before he saw the familiar writing. What he wondered more about was who had brought it down. Which one of them had come up the walk and knocked at the door and stood there waiting. And what had he been thinking about? And had he been relieved or sorry when it had occurred to him irrevocably that there was nobody home and that he must go away without a word?

"What is it?" Annie had said, behind him, when he made no move to unlock the door, but stood there looking down at the package.

"Why it's a present," Gene remembered saying. "Ma sent us down something."

"From your mother?" she'd said, almost as if she couldn't believe him.

He had turned and handed her the package while he got out his door key and he remembered the way she'd stood, turning it over and over in her hands, as if there were some reassurance, some charm hidden in the fact of its existence.

"Come inside," he'd said. "We'll open it by the tree."

They had opened the small bundle there beside the tree and for a moment everything had been all right again. The fact that Grace had thought of them—that somebody had come down from the house on the Ridge on Christmas Day and left the package at their door to let them know she hadn't forgotten them. For a moment it made a little spot of warmth around them that took in everything, the tiny tree, the old ungracious house, the scared unhappiness that young people have when they're estranged from anything as solid and meaningful as parents.

There had still been a flicker of that feeling, a mere echo of it, along his senses when Gene went off to work the next morning. Walking down to the shop through the thin early bitter cold, it had warmed him, it had given him a pale flame of confidence to warm the corners of his mind. The morning was suddenly very beautiful to him. Everything, in the clear brittle light just after sunrise, had a new significance, an importance of black and white. The world looked as if it were encased in a thin skin of ice and the sun had drawn all color out of it, leaving only black and white and the faint memory of color.

There was the black shadow and the white light; there were the black spruces lining out their scalp-lock along the Ridge between the white sky and the white fields; there were the black islands snugged in between the pale water and the pale sky; and Gene himself was a small black figure on white, but belonging.

As he went down the winding path from the road to the door of the shop, he was aware of the man standing there idly, but he didn't notice who it was until he was nearly up with him and Willard turned around.

"Nice day, Willard," Gene said.

"Yes, yes," Willard said and then he just stood there jerking his head quickly to one side.

"What's up?" Gene grinned, recognizing Willard's nervousness.

"Gene, before you go in, I wanted to talk to you."

"Well, here I am."

"Yes," Willard said again. "Yes."

"Er—" Gene caught a little of the nervousness from him. "Well, was it somethin important, Willard?"

"Yes, yes, it was."

Gene stood waiting, confident, with no inkling of what it was Willard was trying to say to him.

"Hells bells," Willard exploded. "I thought it'd be easier if I waited till after Christmas. Thing like this, seems too bad to do it just before. Now, by god, I wisht I had. It ain't a mite easier."

Gene's eyes narrowed a little, but he still didn't say anything. He couldn't now.

"You better go get your check, Gene," Willard said. "I won't be needin you any longer."

"My check?" Gene echoed stupidly.

"Yeah. Go along up to the office an collect your time. I'm layin you off."

"Any reason for it? Haven't I been doin all right?"

"Sure, sure. It's just I don't need any extra men just now, that's all. You better go get your check."

Willard turned his back on Gene and stood waiting for the sound of Gene's steps going away. For a minute Gene stood there wanting to tell him what he could do with the check. But he didn't do it, because suddenly that check had come to be pretty important. He was going to need it and he couldn't tell Willard what to do with it.

"Okay," he said and started numbly up the path to the office.

<hr/>

AS HE grew older, Nat Hanna began to notice that he withdrew more. It was a sort of retreat into memory. The only thing that remained the same for him was the country he lived in. The land itself was the only thing that had a lasting quality and that only because it was hard, unyielding, resistant land. This particular strip of country that lay like a bulwark between the ocean and the continent had captured him long ago by its loveliness. It had for him a strange quality of old enchantment, though in his mind he put none of those words to it. It was a nice place to live, he thought. It was a good place where a man had to work hard to make any impression on the land and even then, ten or fifteen years after he was gone, there was nothing left to make anyone know he had ever been there, except maybe an old house where his kids lived; or if they hadn't had his feeling for the land, an old house deserted, or where strangers had come in and taken over and changed, putting their own few weak scratches on the earth.

He liked that. He liked country that could keep itself to itself, that didn't let the few things a man could do in his lifetime make any difference to it. It just lay there, quietly, taking whatever a man wanted to put into it; and then, after the man had gone, it lay there quietly covering up the things he'd done.

In Nat's own lifetime he'd seen it happen time and time again. He'd seen the time when houses stood, strong and four-square, in wide fields where now there wasn't even an indentation in the earth to show where the cellar had been. He had seen the spruces grow in an apple orchard, closing in on the tamer trees with a sort of implacable gentleness like a tide of wilderness, choking out the domesticated trees until, in the spring, where there had once been acres of bloom, maybe a man would find one or two high insistent branches with a few niggardly blossoms. All the rest would be deep-breathing spruces.

Somehow, knowing how the land closed in behind a man, comforted him now that he was getting old enough to think about death as a probability instead of a possibility. It made him feel as if maybe it really didn't matter how hard a man worked to get things—he saw that the land treated them all the same, the men who got things and the men who didn't.

And when he thought of the words "And man goeth to his long home," somehow it made him have the feel of this country, with the seasons rolling over it and the years—the long years and the weather, always the weather because that was the big thing that made the land what it was.

He thought more often now of the people he had known

and always they were young when he remembered them. He was young himself. And when he looked at Grace, sometimes she seemed to be a stranger to him and not his own daughter, because when he thought of his daughter, he thought of a young girl. Sometimes they all seemed old to him and Stanny was the only one he could meet as an equal; they all seemed so much older because they were always wanting something, or working for something, or trying to get something, and he had passed beyond understanding about that.

The things he saw with his eyes had gradually come to be the dream and what he remembered closer to the reality.

Often he found himself playing a game, something like the one children do, of peopling the houses they pass with families, complete down to the smallest child. He did that. But he could go back further, he could put a house in a place where no house stood, he could bring back people whose very names had died off the land. And all his houses and all his people had been real at sometime or other—that house had stood where he placed it now in his mind and those people had lived in it at sometime.

"You see that little clearin right down there," he said to Stanny. They were standing on the back step looking down over the slope of Russ's fields toward the harbor. "That little tiny clearin there about two points to the south of south of Pete Jennins's barn?"

Stanny, straining his eyes along the direction indicated by his grandfather's arm, cast about to find some indication of a clearing in the thick green of the spruces.

"There," Nat said impatiently. "Boy, what's wrong with your sense of direction? My god, anyone'd think you could tell south by now."

"I see it," Stanny said hastily, not quite sure he did.

"Well, you can blieve it or not, but oncet," Nat began, "that clearin was all of a three acre piece. Good land, too. You can tell it's good land by the way them trees have come up there.

That's about the thickest stand of hardwood I ever see. You see the way they look heavy in a kind of off-square piece there?"

"Ayeh," Stanny agreed eagerly. "I can make it out now. Sort of a square with a little jog taken out of one end of it."

"That's it," Nat said. "Well, that whole piece of woodland there belonged to Josiah Jennins. He's dead now. And his great-granddad had it on a deed from the Commonwealth of Massachusetts. Place about a hundred and twenty acres, it was then. Think of that, will you?

"Then, lemme see, 1882 it was, old Billy Saylor and his old lady bought up them three acres right in the middle of it. I never could see why Jose'd go an sell three acres right outn the middle of a piece of land, like that. But he done it.

"I uset to set up there on my back porch, when I hed time to set, watchin Billy eat his way into that spruce woods. Why, lord, it was jest exactly like a rat eatin hisself into a great big cheese. Billy et in, an then he started eatin round and round til he hed that whole three acres stripped jest as clip an clean as a regular lawn. Each year he'd cut out a little farther.

"He was sort of a queer old duck. Nobody knew where in the devil he come from. He an his old lady jest sort of turned up oncet an wanted that piece of land. They was lots said Billy was runnin away from somethin, but I never put much stock in that. Why, hell, they said that about anyone went around mindin his own business with any sort of steadiness.

"Was queer, though, that Bill. Claimed he couldn't neither read nor write an even made his old lady sign the title deed an Jose said afterward, Bill, he put 'X' after the name. But Jose said one day he went in to see em. They used to be weeks at a time neither one of em'd show an people uset to git worried. Well, Jose he went in to see was everythin all right an there, by god, set Bill as big as Billy-be-damn, areadin away in an old book with the craziest letters in it. Jose, he always was a one to bust right out with what he was thinkin.

" 'Bill,' he says, lookin at the letters, 'I be condemned if I ever would of knew you was a foreigner. What kind of printin is that?'

"Bill, he up an threw the book clearn acrost the room."

" 'Why don't you mind your own business?' he says. 'You never see me comin into a man's house an callin him dirty names.'

"Jose, he admitted afterwards, he was sort of mad, askin a man a decent question an havin him lose his temper like that. But he was still curious, so he stands for a second watchin Bill take off acrost the clearin. Then he picks up the book to see was they anythin on the outside to say what it was. He said afterward it was some sort of a book about frogs and the guy who wrote it had a long name beginnin with 'A' but he couldn't remember it. Jose never did find out what kind of language that was, but he said it was a godawful lookin mess an anyone could read that certainly ought to be able to read English.

"Well, what I set out to tell you was about Bill's sister Kate. By the lord, there was a woman to make any man set up an take notice. When Bill's old lady died, he buried her an took to his bed, an a week or so later his sister Kate turns up to take care of him. And by the judast, she was the one could do it. Why, that woman had a pair of shoulders on her that was all of three feet across. She was a good six feet four inches high and there warn't an ounce of fat on her a man could see. And voice! Why, when Kate warn't even tryin, provided the wind was fair, you could hear her laugh a mile away.

"Bill, he warn't a very large man an Kate could of picked him up in one hand if she'd been a mind to. Why, I myself once see her reach down an take aholt of their little punt they had an flip it over like it warn't anythin but a stick of cord wood."

Nat stopped talking and stood staring down on the slow

heavy drift of the spruces with the little off-square patch of hard wood growing up in it.

"Well, you never told me about them before," Stanny said. "What ever happened to them? They move away?"

"Nope," Nat shook his head. "It was pretty bad. You better take a tip from this yarn, Stanny, an don't never do any smokin in bed.

"Bill, he always did. Him an his old TD darn near burnt that place down many a time an he finally succeeded. Jose said one night he thought he heard Kate ayellin. He took a look out his bedroom window, musta been near two o'clock in the mornin, and there was flames coming up over the tops of the trees jest as if they was comin out of a blowtorch. Well, Jose, he went arunnin, but it was too late.

"They was tracks in the snow to show Kate got out all right, but Bill didn't; so everyone figured she'd went back in after him an couldn't get him. Alls they ever found was a few teeth and some flaky lookin ashes might of been bones. Leastwise—" He sucked a tooth thoughtfully. "They buried them for bones."

Stanny said "Ugh" in a satisfactory tone and Nat grinned.

"Judast," he said. "You don't want to go lettin a little thing like that bother you. Why, when I stop to think, I don't know's they's any much cleaner way a man could die. Fire, like that, don't leave nothin unpleasant."

"Well, I wouldn't like it." Stanny shivered his thin shoulders distastefully.

"All right, like I said," Nat told him. "Don't go smokin in bed, that's all." He glanced off, thoughtfully, at the Ridge, his blue eyes misty and a little faded but not missing anything he looked at. "Nor I wouldn't go smokin anywheres else, neither, till I was a lot older'n fourteen."

"Oh, gee," Stanny said. He let his breath out in a relieved long whistle of air. For the last three days now, he'd been worried. Nobody had said anything to him and he hadn't been able to see any particular difference in the way people acted, but he'd been expecting the blow to fall from some quarter sooner or later.

"If it was you," he said carefully, "took that package of cigarets out of the place there in the barn, I wisht you'd said somethin about it earlier. I been thinkin it might of been Ma."

"Well, it warn't your Ma," Nat said. "And you know right well it warn't. If it'd been her, you'd a heard somethin about it long before this. As it was, I thought I'd let you stew a little. Give you some time to think it over. Maybe get a little scared."

"Well, if it's any satisfaction to you, I have been," Stanny said.

"Good. That was my intention. An besides, it's a tom-fool trick to smoke in a haymow, too." Nat shoved his hand into the pocket of his black suit coat and brought out a half-empty package of cigarets. "What'll I do with em? I never use the cussed things."

"You could throw em away," Stanny suggested, looking with interest at the package.

"Well, you're sprier'n I am," Nat said. He handed the cigarets to Stanny. "Spose you do it."

"All right." Stanny stuffed the package into his jumper pocket and started down toward the edge of alders. Once there he hauled it out again, bringing a nearly full pack with it. For a second he looked, with a grin, at the two packs of cigarets before he took the one his grandfather had handed him and gave it a heave. He stood watching it soar over the alders, thinking, I'll bet that's why he started telling that story. Just to get around to smoking.

He thrust the full pack quickly back into his pocket and turned to see if Nat was watching him. His grandfather was still standing on the back step but he didn't seem to be looking Stanny's way.

Stanny'd been wrong about Nat's reason for telling the

story about Bill and his sister Kate. When he had seen where it was heading, he'd decided it would be a good chance to say something to Stanny about the cigarets he'd found in the little hollowed-out space in the haymow. He'd noticed several times that Stanny seemed to have something of interest cached in the barn. He'd seen him head out that way twice now, stop just outside the door to look around casually, and then disappear into the barn.

Remembering his own youth, it hadn't been very hard for Nat to ferret out Stanny's reason. At first he'd thought he'd just take the cigarets and not say anything about them, let the kid worry for a while, maybe that would be enough. But his own up-bringing was too strong in him. He'd been whaled too many times himself for smoking in the haymow to let Stanny get away with it.

He was just as glad it had turned out that he could find some reason for the story. He couldn't seem to help telling those yarns, none of them with much point, just rambling on about people. Sometimes he thought Stanny must get kind of sick of hearing them. But it seemed necessary for him to bring them back, all the people he had known.

When a man gets so old, Nat thought, that he can walk along the street in his own home town where he was born and raised and not know half the people he meets, why, then, he just naturally has to think about the ones he *did* know.

I DON'T know why I've bothered," Ralph said, in a low curiously defeated voice. He leaned back in his seat and stared at his hands locked on the wheel. Mary, glancing quickly at what she could see of his profile, looked away again as quickly. She could feel apprehension starting to be stifling in her throat. She'd had a feeling as a kid in school when it got near her turn to recite—a mental clamminess and a physical shortness of breath—and she had the same feeling now.

The evening had started out all right, the way their evenings always did, but something had gone wrong with it.

It's hard to say when an atmosphere changes, when something happens to make an easiness go taut and uncomfortable. You don't know whether it was a word that did it, or maybe the lack of a word. You might have said something at just the right moment, or refrained from saying something. Only there's no way of knowing what it would have been or when you could have spoken or not spoken.

And now this, she thought. Ralph hadn't been saying much. Then, when he parked the car in front of the house and turned off the ignition, he put his hands on the wheel, stared at them steadily, and said the unforgivable.

"You'd think I'd have the sense to let you alone, wouldn't you?" He glanced at her with a half-smile. She could see the way his cheek filled out and knew what the expression on his face would have been if she could have seen it.

"I—I don't—"

"Don't. For godsake, Mary, don't say you don't know what I'm talkin about. Give yourself credit for a little sense."

His voice brought her up sharply, made her start to feel angry. But he kept on talking. If he knew he'd started to make her mad, he didn't care.

"Most people look at a guy like me," he said. "And what do they think? They think, There's a nice steady boy. Good old Ralph. Is that what you think? What *do* you think? Tell me that much, anyhow."

"I think I like you more than anyone else, Ralph. We've always had good times together. We get along. I don't see why you can't let it go at that."

"Well, we can't," Ralph said sharply. "It was good enough in the beginning. For a while it was all right. It's not now. Maybe I give you credit for more sense than you've got really.

I do, if you honestly mean you can't see why we can't keep on the way we've been doin. You see, good old Ralph has turned. I want more than that now."

Mary sighed. She felt immensely tired and heavy, sitting there listening to him and not knowing how to answer or what to tell him.

"You must have known I'd say this sooner or later," Ralph said, protesting against the sigh. "Most girls would wonder why the devil I'd waited so long. You don't wonder, do you, Mary? You know perfectly well why I haven't, don't you?"

He waited a minute and when she didn't answer, he began slowly, "It wouldn't be so bad for you. I'm no bargain, but I'm not so bad. I'm gettin along all right. I've got a good job and I'll have the place when Dad goes. I'm not rich, but I won't be penniless."

"My lord, Ralph, you sound like something out of the Sears and Roebuck. What do I care how much you'll have?"

"You would if we were married."

"Ralph—"

"No, wait. You see what you're doin, don't you? You're tryin to make me stop. I've loved you since I was knee-high. Seems like I have now, anyhow. Sometimes I've thought I'd give up, get me another girl. But I never saw one meant two cents to me when I thought of you. I'll always be that way, I guess. But you never let me ask you to marry me before. You know why I haven't, too, don't you?"

He waited for her answer and when it didn't come, said, "Don't you?"

"Yes." Her voice jerked out of her as if she had no voluntary connection with it and she said quickly, "No."

"You're lyin," Ralph said coldly. "There've been a lot of times when I could have said what I'm sayin now. You knew it, too. And each time you've stopped me. No," he said quickly when she started to speak. "I know it hasn't been as clear as that. But that's what it's amounted to. You've stopped me just as if you said: Don't say it yet.

"Well, I never did. But I'm goin to now. I'm goin to have it out of you if I have to beat you up to get it. I want to know why."

"What're you trying to do to me?" Mary said and he could tell from the sound of the words that her teeth were clenched hard. "What d'you think you're doing?"

"I'm goin to get some definite word out of you if we sit here all night. That's not a heck of a lot to ask, is it? Just tell me what it is about me that you don't like. And if it's there, why do you keep on goin with me? Don't you know that as far's everyone in town's concerned, you and I are engaged? Don't you know we're goin together? You know what that means, don't you? What it means to everyone but you apparently."

"I didn't think. I never thought about it."

"Well, do it now. This is your chance. Do a lot of thinkin. While you're at it, you might think over the fact that I've got to the stage where I want you so much I can't be around you unless you—unless we—unless I know."

"I want to get out," Mary said. "I don't feel good."

"It's like that, is it?" Ralph said. He still wasn't looking at her and he made no motion to touch her. "As bad as that. I—" He sounded as heavy and tired as Mary felt. "I didn't realize I made you sick."

"Ralph," she turned to him desperately. "You've got to help me. I don't know what it is. I don't know what's wrong. You've got to help."

"I can't help you unless you let me."

"But I don't know what to do."

"Look." He was able to forget his own trouble, sensing a desperation in her. "Just calm down. Just try to tell me what's the matter. You know I'd do anythin in the world to help you. You don't seem to understand, I've been askin you to marry me. I'm in love with you. All you have to do is tell me what I can do an I'll do it."

"No," Mary said heavily. "You've got to tell me. I can't tell you. I don't know what I want."

Ralph put his forehead down on his hands. He could feel the cool smooth rubber of the wheel against his face. For a moment so blank it was relief, he wasn't thinking anything; there was nothing at all. He felt blessedly empty and uncomplicated and for that moment everything was all right, before he started to think again. He didn't know what she was trying to make him say. Whatever it was, he didn't want to know. He wanted her to get out of the car and go away and leave him—but that was just for a moment.

"Look, dear," he said. He lifted his head and looked at her sitting there. Her face was turned toward him; he could see its faint lightness. He could see the dark blur of her mouth and, somewhere behind his eyes, he knew how it looked. He saw the heavy underlip, the thin, almost invisible line of the upper, the way they came together firmly, turning slighly down at the corners. And thinking of it was enough to make him feel suffocated. She was sitting there, implacable and silent, waiting for him to tell her something and he didn't know what it was. This was the first time she'd ever asked him for anything and now she wanted help and he didn't know what to do.

"If you're tryin to tell me somethin," he started again, trying to keep his voice calm, "go ahead. If you're in some kind of a mess, tell me. I'm not particularly *good*." He had to grope for the word and couldn't find the right one so the wrong one came out emphasized. "You won't shock me. I don't care what it is. If that's it, you don't even have to tell me at all."

He stopped suddenly because she made a queer noise, a stifled sort of sound, and he was afraid for a second that she was crying. His momentary relief when he discovered it was laughter faded when she didn't stop. She kept it up, a low steady sound that made his hackles rise. He reached out and touched her shoulder. It was shaking and she didn't seem to know he'd touched her.

"Stop it," he said loudly. "Stop it, will you?"

She didn't hear him and Ralph grabbed her firmly by the shoulders and shook her until her breath was coming brokenly and she couldn't laugh any more.

"Cut that out," he said. "You'll have us *both* crazy. Start it again an, so help me, I'll slap you good."

Then, because he had her there and could think of nothing else to do, he kissed her. For a moment he thought it was going to be all right, everything was all right—she didn't try to push him away as he'd thought she might—and then he realized with horror that she wasn't doing anything at all, she was just sitting there waiting for him to get through.

"Well." He straightened up, keeping his hands on her shoulders. "There's not even that now, is there?"

"Ralph, look," she said. "I don't know what's happened. It's something I can't understand. But you wouldn't want me. I'd drive you crazy inside of a month. I couldn't ever make anyone happy."

"It'd be different once we were married," he said desperately. "You'd see what a difference it would make. Why, you'd have somethin to do with your time. You'd have an interest in life. The way it is now, I don't believe it does you much good, livin the way you do."

"What d'you mean, living the way I do?" She stiffened, trying to see his face.

"Well, I just meant here, with your family. There can't be much for you to do with yourself. Anyone gets tired and rubbed the wrong way, livin like that. It's not good for anyone and it's doin somethin to you. It's gettin you so you don't know whether you're on your head or your feet."

Because there wasn't anything she could say to him and

because he sounded so deeply worried, Mary pulled his head down to her, letting him kiss her the way he'd wanted to before. It wasn't hard to do; even now, she liked it herself, and when she felt Ralph's arm around her shoulder begin to shake, it set up an answering tremor somewhere deep inside her. His voice was unsteady, too, when he said, "What made you do that? How can you do that and then not let me say anythin —not give me a chance?"

"Because you're so decent," she said—her unhappiness making her voice sound old. "You're so decent, Ralph."

"My lord." He shoved himself upright in the seat, taking his hand off her shoulder. "Is that it? My lord, Mary, can't you see what you're doin to me? Can't you see what it does to anyone to tell him you let him kiss you like that because he's decent? Christ," he said. "My good christ."

She heard him hit the wheel with his clenched fist and the little humming sound it gave off, vibrating under the blow, made her head swim.

"You make me so I can't kiss you," he said desperately. "You make it so I can't even *want* to do anythin to you any more."

TOWARD the middle of the afternoon, Annie went for the eighth time to the front window to see if the car was still there in front of the house. It was. There it stood, drawn well in from the road, its fender driven into the heaped windrow of snow the plow had left along the gutter. She could make out Jake's profile, and see that he had pulled some sort of a robe up around him. It made her nervous, knowing that he was sitting out there, wondering what was wrong with him.

Jake was the one in Gene's family Annie liked least of all, and there certainly wasn't any love lost between her and the rest of them. She'd never been able to bear Russ and she knew pretty well what Grace thought of her and the knowledge made it difficult for her to think very kindly of Grace. Grace was the sort of woman, Annie told herself, trying to justify her dislike, who'd commit murder to keep up appearances. Even the tentative overture Grace had made at Christmas hadn't gone down with Annie the way it had with Gene. He'd wanted to think it meant his mother had forgiven him for whatever it was he was supposed to have done to her. He had been prepared to hope she'd make some sign at Christmas, knowing what that particular season had always meant to her, and when she had, niggardly as it had been, Gene was ready for it. Since then Annie hadn't been able to mention his family to him without bringing on the beginnings of a quarrel. Although she was pretty sure the making-up hadn't gone any further than that. If Gene had been up to the house on the Ridge, she was sure he'd have told her about it, and he hadn't mentioned going.

As for Stanny and Mary, Annie shrugged mentally, moving back from the window cautiously so Jake wouldn't look up and see her staring out at him. That Stanny was certainly no better than he should be. She knew what high school kids were and Stanny Walls, from some of the stories, was better than average as far as deviltry went. She couldn't recall just at the time any specific story she'd heard about Stanny, but there'd been some, she was sure of that.

And Mary—she'd always thought Mary was her friend, but she hadn't seen her to speak to since that tiff they'd had last fall. It certainly wasn't *my* fault, Annie thought. When I see anyone getting big ideas that don't suit them, I'm certainly going to speak my mind about it whether they like it or not. I didn't think much of the way she was acting, seeing Ralph was so interested in her. And then she went off the handle like a wet hen. It's always the truth that hurts, she thought virtuously, and I guess it hurt her, all right.

But when it came right down to it, Jake had always been the one of the Wallses she simply couldn't abide. She glanced out the window again, but he showed no signs of having moved or intending to. He was no better than an animal, big and dumb and kind of scary. Gene himself had said Jake made him think of an animal and Annie drew no line of distinction between the two descriptions.

After Gene had gone out that noon, she sat down at the dinner table to have another cup of coffee in peace and quiet. He was still looking for work and was beginning to show signs of cracking and it was all Annie could do to keep from screaming while he was moping around. She thought it was the Walls coming out in him, and she walked easy when he was there, and it was a relief to her now when he went out of the house.

After Willard had fired him, Gene had worked two weeks for John Garvey who had a gravel pit in on the old Brown's Pond Road. Then, after the two weeks were up, John had laid him off, saying he'd only been hired temporarily and now there wasn't any need for an extra man.

She'd been sitting there thinking about their slender bank balance and the way it was dwindling, when she heard somebody come around the house and up to the back door. She'd thought at first it must be Gene coming back for something and started quickly for the door to let him in. But when she looked out through the tiny pane of glass in the storm door, she saw Jake's heavy red face instead and for a moment had considered not opening the door at all, just pretending she wasn't home.

She put one foot behind her, starting a cautious withdrawal, keeping her eyes fixed on Jake's oblivious face. But her concentration worked the wrong way and he glanced in and saw her there so it was too late to do anything. For a second she stood still, hoping against hope he hadn't seen her and would go away. She didn't know what he wanted, but whatever it was, she knew she didn't want to see him.

Jake jerked his head impatiently and rattled the latch. She went slowly over and opened the door and then just stood there, letting the cold air flood past her into the kitchen, but preferring that to the possibility of his accepting her invitation if she asked him in.

"Gene in?" Jake said, not bothering to notice that she kept him standing.

"No."

Jake looked surprised.

"Ain't workin, is he?"

"What do you want?" Annie said. "If you've got anything to say to Gene, you'll have to come back later. He's out."

"Pete sake." Jake leered at her heavily. "You certainly ain't what you could call hospitable, are you. An me your brother-in-law."

"There's no reason why I should be," she said tightly. "Not after the way you've treated me."

"How d'you mean?" For some reason her words seemed to startle him. He looked at her sharply, trying to find her exact meaning.

"Well, none of you've been near us since we got married. For all of you, we might have starved to death down here. That's what I mean. And if you ask me, it's a pretty small way to act. You Walises think you're God, every one of you."

"Oh, that's what's botherin you, hanh?" Jake grinned and leaned comfortably against the door, making it impossible for her to shut it. "Baby, if you only knew. I thought maybe you'd got wind of somethin that might give you the right to be mad."

"I don't know what you're talking about," she told him harshly. "And I don't want to. There was a time when we'd have been glad to see you coming, any one of you. But that's over. Now we aren't. And I don't know how I can say it any plainer."

"My," Jake said. "I always wondered what Gene see in you. He musta fell for you when you was mad. You're real cute when you look like that."

"You get out of here," Annie said. She made a move to reach past him for the door latch, but she couldn't quite make it without stepping from the doorway itself and she didn't want to give him the chance to get by her and into the house.

"Now, now," Jake said soothingly, still grinning. "That's no way. I come down here peaceable to see Gene, an what happens? You try to kick me out. That's no way."

"It's my way," Annie said. "I'll thank you all to stay away. You've managed it so far and we've got along all right. You might's well keep it up and that goes for the rest of your family, too."

"Lord," Jake said. He stood out of the way. "You got any objections to my waitin to see my own brother?"

"Not if you want to wait outside," Annie told him shortly. To her relief, he stood away from the door, just stood there squarely, looking at her until she came a step or two outside, grasped the latch of the storm door, and slammed it viciously. There, she thought, let's see what you make of that.

Shaking and a little ashamed of herself, she went back into the kitchen and stood there waiting to see what he intended to do. She didn't know quite what she'd expected when she'd opened the door to him, but it couldn't have been pleasant, because her heart was pounding wildly and her hands when she held them out and looked down on them were shaking visibly.

Her relief was almost strong enough to be ridiculous when she heard him going back around the house to the front walk. She went quickly in through the front room to the window to watch him. Her first thought had been that he must be drunk, but his progress down the walk was steady enough to make her see he wasn't. She stood just inside the curtain so he couldn't see her if he turned, but he didn't turn. He went down to the road, climbed into his car and then, instead of driving away, he sat there and lighted a cigaret.

That had been three hours ago. He was still sitting there. Occasionally he lit another cigaret, but as far as she could see, that was all he did. As the short winter afternoon wore on, she got more nervous, until by the time it started to get dark, she was ready to scream at the thought of him sitting out there in the cold like a graven image. There was something so implacably patient about him that the thought horrified her.

She was in the kitchen starting supper when she heard the car engine and she was standing there stiffly listening, hoping it was Jake's car when Gene came in the front door and through the hall. The sight of his face was enough to make her forget about Jake—she had never seen his pleasant light features look so dark before, she couldn't remember ever having seen that particularly blank look in his eyes, the blankness of anger strong enough to be blinding.

He looked at her, not as if he didn't see her but more as if she were unimportant.

"I should have had the sense to see it before," he said.

"What're you talking about?"

"I should have had the sense," Gene shouted. His face had turned a dark red and his eyes, staring at her, were the eyes of a stranger and then, she thought, not a complete stranger because he had for a moment the look of his father.

"I been wonderin why it was." His voice had turned to a mumbling monotone. "I thought it was funny. Here I was, workin my heart out, trampin the streets like a cussed begger, wondering why it was I couldn't get anywheres. Well, now I know."

"Gene, for the love of god," Annie said, her eyes wide and frightened.

"Yes," Gene said bitterly. "You wouldn't believe it, would

you? You wouldn't think a man could do that to his own son. Well, he did. We might as well give up. We might as well stop tryin."

"Did Jake do something to you? What did he want?"

"He wanted to tell me why I couldn't get a job here or hold one when I did get it," Gene said, still not looking as if he knew her. "It's my father. My own father! I didn't think he'd do a thing like that."

Suddenly the pieces fell into place for her and her hatred was as strong as his. She started to say something, to tell him that she hated as much as he did, but before she got the words out, Gene turned and a moment later she heard him going upstairs. When the door closed behind him, she knew he didn't want her and there was nothing she could possibly have said to him to make it any easier.

When she went to look out the front window again, Jake's car was gone and she thought numbly, That must have been his engine I heard.

JAKE felt suddenly as if the top of his head had caught fire and the blaze was threatening to spread downward. He sat straight up in bed, feeling cautiously along his scalp and it seemed to him the skin was sensitive, both on his fingertips and over the hard boniness of his skull.

He got up and padded silently over to the window, inserted his fingers in the two-inch opening and eased it up until he could thrust his head and shoulders out into the air. The night poured over him and along his bare shoulders like black ice water, but it made no impression on the heat that pulsed inside his body.

He went back to the bed and fumbled for a moment behind the headboard, finding with the ease of familiarity, the neck of the flat bottle he had cached between the head of the bed and the wall.

It didn't seem to help much this time. The heat grew inside him until he began to feel as if his body were visibly pulsing with each audible beat of his heart. He was afraid of something and it made it worse because he wasn't quite sure what it was. Fear was unbearable cold that stirred the hair on the back of his neck, cold that seemed to burn him by contrast.

Not quite sure what he was going to do, Jake climbed slowly out of bed again, moving awkwardly as if he weren't confident that his arms and legs would do what he wanted them to. He started dressing, still using great care so that nobody would hear him moving around in the still house. Occasionally he took another swig from the bottle, holding it up after each one to try and see how much he had left. He stopped once just to listen and the sense of aloneness and silence made a light sweat spring out on his forehead. Knowing that there were other people in the house, but that they were shut away from him by dark and sleep, made him feel all the more alone. He needed someone, he needed to hear another voice, but there was nobody to talk to and he wouldn't have known what to say if there had been.

He went out into the hall and quietly down over the stairs, his eyes, accustomed to the dark, seeing everything in a sort of pale gray haze. Once he got outside, it seemed lighter as if more space around him gave him a greater range of vision. The bitter black cold was almost liquid, but he didn't notice it although he wore only his dungarees and a thin white shirt.

The lack of reality of the night and the cumbersome solidity of his own movements made him begin to think that this was all a dream and he really wasn't standing here in the barnyard staring about him as if he'd never seen the place before. He began to be sure that he was either lying in his bed imagining all this or that he was asleep and dreaming. He began

273

to think if he tried to touch anything, forgetting that he'd already touched the door when he came out, he'd wake up and find he hadn't moved from his own bedroom.

To prove it, he went slowly over to the barn door and put his hand on it, feeling with an acute sense of shock the wood, rough and cold, beneath the heat of his palm. He pushed the door open wide so that he could stand peering into the darkness, smelling the congealed odor of motor oil and rubber and the faint dry smell of hay. The two big cars, when he finally made them out, were like shadowy monsters waiting beneath dark cold water.

I'll show him, Jake thought suddenly. He eased the door back on its rollers until there was space enough for the big old Buick to go out. He thinks more of that car than he does of me. I'll show him.

He fumbled his way slowly over to the Buick, feeling his hand slip easily along her polished fender. When he got into the driver's seat, he began to be afraid again, because he had never so much as touched this car before and knew that Russ would half-kill him if he could see him now. The strangeness of the thick wooden wheel under his hands swung him back into that dream feeling he'd had in the yard. He was shaking, but not with cold, as he felt for the starter and heard the old engine turn over smoothly.

Like a watch, he thought, reluctant admiration for well-treated machinery making him feel what Russ himself must feel for this car. He put her into low and, without lights, swung her into the barnyard and around the corner of the house toward the road. When he hit the tar, he turned the lights on and clashed her into high without bothering to use second. The old car bucked a little, almost stalled, and settled down into her regular waddling.

Upstairs in his bedroom, Russ stirred, half woke up, thinking he'd heard a car go out. Then, hearing through curtains of sleep, the fading sound of the motor, he decided it had only been a late passing car on the road and settled back to sleep again.

RUSS had just sat down at the breakfast table, glanced at Jake's empty chair and said, "Jake not out of bed yet?" when the phone rang in the front room. They sat counting the rings and when it stopped Grace pushed back her chair.

"Nemmind," Russ beat her to it. "It's probably for me, anyhow."

He went into the front room and they could hear his voice say "Hello," when he took the receiver off the hook. The rest of them sat around the table, listening unconsciously, the way you do, trying to hear what's going on but not really caring whether you do or not.

Grace though was frankly inquisitive. A phone call this early in the morning was unusual and if anything were happening, she wanted to know about it.

She got up finally and went in to the living room door. She was just in time to hear Russ say in a strange breathy-sounding voice, "Found him just now? I'll be right down."

He hung up the receiver and went by her as if he hadn't seen her. She caught at his sleeve.

"Russ, somethin's happened."

He kept on going.

"Is it Gene?" Grace said, having a hard time getting the words out.

"Jake," Russ said over his shoulder. "He smashed up the Buick sometime last night. That's all I know, Grace."

"I'm coming with you," she said.

"No, you stay here."

She knew then that he had lied to her.

Russ hauled the car in to the side of the road, got out, and went stiffly up along the snowy shoulder to the remains of the old Buick. With a chill of horror, he looked quickly at the car, and then at the three men who stood there in silence, watching him.

"Lord," he said. "What a mess."

"Ayeh." Pete Willey, the constable, came over to stand beside him, looking down at the Buick. She was well across the gutter, and she'd hit the tree so hard that the engine had been shoved right up into the front seat. When she left the road, she'd plowed deep into gravel and dirt, scattering it in sheets to both sides. Russ turned his back quickly.

"What—where's the kid?"

Pete jerked his head and Russ, following the direction of the movement, saw that there was something lying on the ground under the old car robe he kept in the Buick's back seat. Walking slowly, as if he had a weight on each foot, he went over and lifted the corner of the robe. His eyebrows twitched slightly and for a moment he wanted to shut his eyes.

"I found it," Pete said. "He—his head was right out through the windshield. We had a devil of a time gettin him out. God, Russ, I'm sorry."

"Except for that," Russ said, "he looks like he was asleep. You'd think his face'd be more cut up, wouldn't you."

He let go of the robe and, when it covered what was left of Jake, it was hard for him to believe that it was his own son lying there.

"Pete," he said, "call Joe Ballard for me, will you? I'll stay here till he comes. Tell him to hurry."

"Yeah, I'll do that," Pete said. He got into his own car and started her so fast that his tires dug through the snow and left a little scattering of gravel behind them.

When the sound of his engine died, Russ went back to stand looking at the Buick. He had forgotten the other two men and when he didn't speak, they went on down the road, talking together, their voices low until they were out of his hearing.

She really *had* been trying to work, Mary told herself. She'd been trying. She put the brush down carefully, and walked backward away from the easel, trying to get the painting on it to look as if it were an entity. Even to her it looked diffused, as if the various parts of it had identities of their own and were all straining to get as far away from each other as they possibly could.

"Well, I *did* try," she said aloud, looking with distaste at the painting. "And that's all the good it did me."

It just didn't seem to matter. It wasn't important enough to bother about. It never would be and she knew that now with a certainty that took away all her old confident power of concentration. It was just a mess of paint blobbed on a canvas and it wouldn't ever be anything else, not if it was up to her to change it.

Well, she thought, you might as well forget about the whole thing—now. And it was a relief to have made up her mind at last. Now she knew what she had to do. After dithering around the way she had all these years, it was like putting down a physical load to make up her mind.

I could never go away, she thought, looking at the canvas. I was a fool to think I'd ever be able to.

But by this time the thought was so familiar that it had stopped giving her that thick, choked, walled-in feeling it had at first. Now it was old and like a deep aching something wrong with her. She was conscious of it, but it never really bothered, it never got to be pain. She could remember distinctly the moment when she had changed from thinking, Someday I'll go away and never see them again; to thinking, I could never go away, not now.

You wouldn't think the way a woman looked when something happened to her would be enough to make you change the whole pattern of your life. It hadn't really been so much the way she looked as the way she failed to look. Mary saw it the first time that morning after Russ had left the house. Grace had come back out into the kitchen, sat down, picked up her fork as if she weren't quite sure what it was.

She looked across at her father who was staring at her queerly.

"Jake's been killed," she said heavily, and put the fork down again with such care that none of them heard it touch the table. "Jake was killed last night," she said.

And then, in the moment while they were trying to take in what she'd said, her face had had that queer lack of expression that Mary had grown to know so well in the last week. Her face seemed to settle, almost to sag, as if the bones under the flesh had grown too tired to be solid.

Mary had sat staring, feeling her own bones turn to fluid sympathetically, not quite realizing what Grace was saying. Nat had shoved back his chair to stand up, but he'd settled back again helplessly. Stanny, still eating, had started to cry; but he kept on eating desperately, as if it were important that he shouldn't stop, as if something would happen to him if he stopped for an instant what he was doing.

"He'll choke himself," Mary said, turning her head with an effort to look at Stanny and she saw Nat reach out gently and take his fork away from him. Even after it was gone, Stanny's hand kept on moving, as if he had no control over it, then it stopped.

Mary had spread her own hands out on the edge of the table and she looked down at the fingers thinking they looked detached, disembodied, as if they didn't belong to anyone,

278

but had just been put down there for a moment and forgotten.

Now I can't go, she thought. Now I can never possibly go away and leave her. It would kill her.

Looking up again, she dragged her eyes back to Grace's face and the expression was gone. But it had come back. It hadn't gone for good. Since then, it seemed to Mary, whenever Grace stopped thinking, or whenever she was tired, that lack of expression, that hopeless inability to understand, had come back. It was now the familiar look of her face in repose and it made her unfamiliar.

Mary went slowly over to the easel, picked up the brush, and smeared it across the face of the canvas from one corner to the other; and then to make it diametrical, crossed it with another stroke. She stuck the brush in a jar of turpentine, thinking, It won't matter if I don't wash it out. As she turned away, she glanced once at the crouching wooden woman in the corner.

"That goes for you, too, sister," she said and opened the kitchen door.

Her Aunt Hat was sitting at the sewing machine, her heavy leg working the treadle busily and the clacking hum of the machine filled the room, but when she heard the shed door open, she twisted around in her chair.

"That you?" she said. "For the lord sake, I thought you'd be another good hour yet. It ain't even started to get dark."

"Oh," Mary shrugged. "I couldn't seem to get interested."

"D'you do anythin I can see?" Hat said eagerly. "Sometimes when you git really started, it seems as if I couldn't wait to see what you're doin."

"Sure, go ahead." Mary went over to the stove and spread her fingers widely over the heat. "Go take a look at the masterpiece. It's right there."

She stood watching the door after Hat had gone out into the shed. It was open and she could hear her aunt's heavy feet go eagerly along the little passage to the shed room. Then the

279

steps stopped suddenly and Mary thought she heard the surprised intake of breath. There was a long silence and the feet started back again, but they came slowly now and hesitated outside the door, almost as if Hat didn't want to come back into her own kitchen.

"Well," Mary said, her eyes on the unmoving door. "Tell me what you think of it. I wouldn't be surprised if it was the best one I've ever done."

She was a little ashamed of herself when Hat did come in. The look on her ruddy face was like that of a child that's been slapped without reason and her wide eyes looked puzzled.

"Well?" Mary said again.

"I—you never done that before," Hat said and Mary saw with surprise that her lips were trembling.

"I never felt the way I do now before," she said harshly, defending herself against something that hadn't even been said.

"It was a real nice picture before you did that," Hat said. "I wish you hadn't of. I'd of been proud to have it in my parlor."

"Ahh," Mary said. She turned her back deliberately and stood staring down at the stove. She could see her own face distorted in the gleaming side of Hat's teakettle and the sight of it fascinated her; she could feel her eyes widen and the face blurred until she was staring at nothing, thinking nothing, feeling empty.

"Well, I would of," Hat said. "I've always wanted one of em, ever since you started in. I never had the nerve to say so to you. Now you've went an ruined that one, by all that's good an holy, I will. An you can git just as stiff as you want to."

She eyed Mary's straight back with regret.

"They's little enough that's pretty around without you goin and ruinin pictures like that. Look at all that paint wasted, too."

She came over and put her big hand on Mary's arm.

"Look dear," she said. "I know it's been an awful hard time for you. But it's been hard for everyone."

"It hasn't been hard the way *you* mean," Mary said harshly. "That's part what's wrong with me. You mean about Jake, don't you? Well, that's how it is. You see, I never loved Jake."

"Jake was your brother," Hat said, her eyes puzzled.

"He might's well have been a perfect stranger," Mary said. "I never knew anything about him. All I ever did was say Hello to him in the morning and good night at night—when he was there. I'd do that to anyone."

"You're all wrought up," Hat said. "I'll make a nice cup of coffee and that'll make you feel better."

"My lord." Mary started to laugh helplessly. "I believe if I came and told you I was sick to death, you'd say a cup of coffee would fix it right up."

"You'd be surprised," Hat said with unruffled calm. "Just how many things you *can* fix up with a cup of my coffee."

"Oh, lord, I'm an ungrateful brat," Mary said suddenly. She went over and sat down carefully in a chair by the table, looking at Hat's broad back. "Here you've let me come up here whenever I wanted to and make a mess of your shed and this is the thanks you get."

"Not another word out of you, Mary Walls, till you get this inside you. Then you'll be more sensible. You're talkin through your hat anyway." Hat came over and set the full cup down in front of her with a bang nicely calculated to impress while it wasn't quite enough to slop the coffee. "Drink it," she said and stood there, her hands on her hips, until Mary picked up the cup and took a good swallow.

"More like it," Hat said. She took her own coffee over to the plain rocker by the window and sat down, spreading her big legs comfortably. "Now you listen to me. You're actin foolish. You are."

281

"Well?"

"Sometimes I ain't quite sure," Hat said. "Maybe you ain't got the sense I give you credit for. I spose you think it's been a hardship to me, havin you around. Well, it ain't. I was being purely selfish when I said you could come up here. I wanted company and you're the only one in the family I could ever stand havin around. Now what d'you think of that?"

Mary's jaw had dropped a little.

"Yes, well you might look surprised. I spose you thought I figured you was a misunderstood genius or somethin. Well, maybe you are, but I wouldn't have the sense to see it. All I know is, I've got a good deal of pleasure out of them pictures you been paintin out there an the next time you set out to mess one up like that, by the lord, you come in an ask me first if I want it. You hear?"

"There won't be any next time," Mary said. "I'm sorry but that was the last one."

"Mary Walls, you *have* gone crazy."

"I've come back from being," Mary said. "I was crazy to think I'd ever amount to anything. I was crazy as a loon ever to think I'd get away from this place and maybe get a chance to do something on my own."

"*Now* what?"

"It's no good. I'm stuck here the rest of my life and what good's it going to do me to mess around with anything like that? Look at me. I haven't got a friend to my name. The only one I did have, I lost because we argued about my painting."

"A pretty poor friend," Hat said.

"I'm beginning to think she was a better friend than I knew. I'm beginning to see she had the right idea."

"Well, look," Hat said. "Will you tell me why, all of a sudden, you've made up your mind to this, when all these years you've just been waiting for the chance to go away?"

"I couldn't leave her, not now." Mary looked down at the table, unable to meet her aunt's bright inquisitive eyes.

"You mean your Ma, I spose."

"Look at her," Mary said. "I'm just like her. She's kept to herself all her life, minding her own business, bringing up her family. She's given us her whole life, an now there's two of us gone. If I went, too, she'd go crazy."

"I have known your Ma a good many years," Hat said judiciously. "And I would say that that's the last thing she'd ever do. But I ain't so sure about you. And for your information, you ain't the least like her. I don't know who you take after, but it certainly ain't Grace."

"Yes," Mary said. "It's easy enough for you to talk. You don't give two hoots what happens to her. I tell you, you didn't see her face when she heard about Jake. You weren't with her when Gene walked out."

"Takin it pretty hard about Jake, is she?" Hat said.

"Well, why wouldn't she?"

"It's a thing that has to happen to everyone," Hat said. "And you probly think I sound heartless."

"Not that way and not at twenty-three."

"That makes it worse," Hat said. "But people are queer. Sooner or later they find out they can get over most anythin even if they think at first it's goin to kill them."

"She felt it, too, you not coming to the funeral." Mary stared accusingly at Hat, feeling her face getting hot, wondering if she was going to be sick.

"Well, I tell you how I felt," Hat said. "I jest could not *face* goin into that house after the way your Pa talked that night he come up here."

Suddenly Mary put her face down in her hands and started to cry, knowing that this was what she'd thought was going to be sickness.

"Oh, poor Jake," she said heavily. "Poor old Jake."

Hat sat watching her for a moment wondering whether to

let her keep on crying or not. Some unrecognized instinct made her see that this wasn't the sort of crying that did anyone any good. There *were* two kinds and Hat knew it because she'd done both in her time. There was a time in anyone's life when they just had to sit down and have a good cry, and that was the kind that worked just like a tonic. After it was over, you knew it was over, and whatever'd made you do it in the first place was just sort of washed away in the flood. Then you felt better. But the other kind never did you any good because then, more often than not, you were just crying because you couldn't think of anything else to do.

Looking at Mary she could feel a sort of sympathetic despair washing up over her. It sounded to her as if Mary had suddenly let go; it was as if something that had been holding her up all her life had just broken. There'd be a long silence when Mary's thin stiff shoulders under the heavy blue sweater would look rigid, and then, all at once, as if the sound were torn out of her against her will, she'd make a noise that sounded as if somebody had taken a piece of heavy cloth and ripped it across quickly.

Hat shook her head. Getting up she went over to stand looking down on Mary's bent head. The very defenselessness of that head made her mad.

"Stop it," she said and anger made the words harsher than she'd meant them to be. "You stop it this minute. I won't stand for it. If you really was cryin about Jake or about your Ma, I'd say go ahead. But you ain't. You're just sittin there bawlin because you've decided to do somethin you don't want to and bawlin ain't goin to get you anywheres."

There, she thought. I've done it now. Her anger vanished and a sort of hard pity took its place. Here's this kid, she thought; here she is, sittin here cryin because she's scared and if I tell her so any more outspoken than that, she'll never come back. And thinking that, Hat realized suddenly that she, too was lonely; that she needed whatever it was Mary could give her and was going to lose it.

"Well, I don't care," she said aloud. "I don't care. If that's the way it's goin to be, that's the way it's goin to be.

"You're nothin but a coward," she said. She started to touch the dark head that had grown so still, but she let her hand drop back to her side before the motion was completed. "I thought you was different, but you're just like the rest of em. You ain't got a mite of backbone left.

"I spose," her voice turned a little musing. "It ain't really your fault. At least, that's what you could tell yourself. You could say it was all Russ's fault, his and your Ma's. For takin such good care of you, I mean; an not ever lettin any of you make up your own minds about anythin.

"Well, I thought once you'd get away from it, but you ain't goin to."

She turned and went over to the window so she wouldn't have to see what she was doing to Mary. She knew, before she started talking again, she wouldn't be able to say what she was going to, not seeing what it did to Mary.

"You been sayin ever since you started comin up here, sooner or later you'd go away. I always said, yes, you would. I believed it at first. But you ain't never done a thing. You've just set, hopin sometime somebody'd make you a present—hopin somebody'd come along and say, 'Here, here's enough money to go away.' Well, they ain't goin to do it an you might's well stop believin in fairies.

"You ain't never so much as turned your hand over to do anythin about it. You've just set and waited all your life. An I guess that's what you're goin to do from now on."

She stopped to listen without turning her head. She thought she'd heard some sound behind her, and she stopped to listen, trying to decide what Mary was doing, without turning to look at her face.

She was shaking too much to say anything else, though she

285

had more to say. So she kept still. In the utter silence, she could hear the tick of the grandfather's clock, way off in the front room. She could hear a scuttling sound in the chamber over the kitchen, and thought, Them squirrels, I wish I knew how they get in.

Behind her, Mary got up and went slowly across to the door. Hat heard it open and shut again, but she didn't turn her head to look until Mary had to rattle the loose old catch to make it fasten. Then Hat swiveled her eyes around just enough to see the black thumb latch lift and fall again. This time it caught and the outer door closed quietly.

By putting her forehead against the cold glass and peering hard, Hat could see Mary going off down the path to the road. She was walking slowly, but she had her head up.

"Well, there," Hat said. She stood watching until Mary turned left and went slowly down the road toward home. Then she went over and sat down in the chair Mary had been sitting in and stared at the round foolish face of the alarm clock on the shelf of the stove.

I ought not to keep it there, she thought, it's too hot.

"Oh, dear," she said, recognizing her own symptoms suddenly. She wobbled up the corner of her apron and caught the first tear, but didn't stop them. Finally, feeling considerably better and smiling a little at her own foolishness, she leaned back, sighing, blew her nose heartily, and wiped away the last traces of dampness.

She sat there for a moment trying to remember what it was she'd saved to do the next time she felt bad and remembered she'd been going to give the pantry a good hoeing out. The clock said four-thirty and for a second she felt a flood of disappointment, thinking, There won't be time to start before supper; but she remembered there wasn't any need to have supper right on the dot any more. I can do anything I want to, she thought.

She went briskly to the catch-all drawer and fished out two

or three big clean cloths, poured herself a pail half full of water from the teakettle and grabbed the can of cleanser off the sideboard as she went by.

"High time this pantry got a good cleaning," she said, standing in the door and looking around to decide where she'd start in.

MARY'S mind felt empty as a water bucket somebody had turned bottom up. She felt washed-out, as if when she looked in the mirror she'd see nothing but a whiteness; she felt the way she once had, a long time ago, when she'd eaten too much fudge one Christmas and had been sick to her stomach. Emptied out and weak.

In these short winter days, all afternoon long you were aware of night coming. As soon as the sun started down again at noon, you began to notice a new chilliness that grew until it reached a peak with the dark greens and deep purples of night. All afternoon night was a shadow over the day, a shadow that grew longer and longer until it closed in over the land like water.

Just before dark on a winter afternoon was the loneliest time; it was a time to make you cower and run for shelter; it made you feel as if the world were nothing but a knife edge between the winds and you were walking along it with no shelter except what you could get by running to find people, to find someone, anyone who could talk to you.

Ever since she could remember, Mary had thought of winter as a big hill. You climbed steadily up one side of it and then, suddenly, you were going down the other. Thinking back, she figured it was probably because Grace always said she never felt the winter was really done with until they got over March hill. But the peak of the hill Mary thought of always came earlier, along about Christmas. Until then the long slow grind was all uphill; but afterward you slid down, going faster and faster, until March was nothing but the long slow gliding stop to winter.

I wish it was over, she thought, and then felt old because she could never remember having wished away time before. She had never seemed to have enough of it, but now she felt old because she was walking down the road alone in the gathering winter dusk and wishing the winter were over.

When she reached the familiar drive, she stood hesitating on the corner, not wanting to go into the house but unable to think of any other place to go. There was one other place, but her pride kept her away from that, though now she could feel herself yearning for the domesticity Annie always surrounded herself with. After all, why should I? Mary thought. Pride, hell, I might's well forget about that. Besides, Gene's my brother—I've got a perfect right to go and see him.

Turning quickly, before she could change her mind again, she went quickly down the road toward the village. The street lights were on now and she waded in and out of the circles of light, watching the thin branches of the trees spraddling darkly across the snow, growing bigger nearer the center of each circle, fading out tenuously as she reached the diameter and plunged off into the blue unlighted road. It was getting colder and the hard snow of the road, packed and smoothed by sled runners and the tires of cars, squeaked under her moccasins, the thin sound of cold in the lonely dark.

The last house on the Ridge, just before the road turned and went precipitously down the hill to the village, belonged to Andy Galley and he had built it out nearer the road than the other houses were. It was so near that when Mary went past, she could look in through the lighted front windows and see Andy sitting beside his radio. Beyond him, around a big table, his three kids were sitting. She couldn't make out what they were doing, but it was something that took all their attention. She stopped in midstride and stood there watching them, her hands thrust into her pockets and her shoulders hunched against the cold. There was a relaxed comfortable look about the room and the people in it that made her more conscious of the nagging unpleasant little wind that had come up as the sun set.

Pansy Galley was in a hurry to get home. She'd been down to the weekly meeting of the Ladies Aid and after the meeting a few of them had got together and got started talking about one thing and another and before she realized it, it was nearly four-thirty.

"My lord in heavens," Pansy'd said. "Here it is nearly suppertime and Andy and the kids'll be worse than wild Indians if I don't get home to feed em."

She was a little ball of a woman and her best speed, although her short legs twinkled, wasn't really fast. She always counted on it taking her a good half hour to get up the hill. She walked a little bent over against the wind with her hands clasped in front of her to keep them warm. When she finally breasted the hill, she stopped for a breather and, looking up, saw the still figure standing in the road ahead of her apparently staring in through her own front windows.

Pity sake, she thought, and since her curiosity was a good deal stronger than her discretion, she started along the shoulder of the road, keeping as well as she could in the shadow, and trying to make no noise. She was nearly up to her front walk when the figure turned and came plunging down the road toward her. Determined not to be cheated out of her satisfaction, Pansy stepped out of the shadows directly into the path of the peeper.

Mary, confronted suddenly by the apparition of Pansy in her fur coat, jumped like a startled colt and came to a dead stop. Pansy, seeing who it was, was surprised at her own lack of surprise.

"Why, hello, Mary," she said. "I been hopin I'd see one of

you soon. I been meanin to tell you how sorry I was about Jake. It was a cussed shame."

"Thanks," Mary said. "Thanks very much." She made a careful detour around the determined little figure and went on down the snowy road, knowing that Pansy stood staring after her before she turned in at the gate. Glancing up at her windows, Pansy thought with a great deal of satisfaction, Well, you certainly didn't see anythin *I* have to be ashamed of, Miss.

She went in through the front door nearly exploding with what she had to say and the minute Andy glanced up at her, she began.

"Well, I'm certainly some glad I keep this house lookin good an clean."

"Hunh?" Andy stared. "What brought that up?"

"Well, I was comin up the road just now an what do you think? I see somebody standin out there in the middle of the road starin in the window—just standin there starin, an you'll never believe it when I tell you who it was."

"Well, pete sake," Andy grinned. "Warn't Jack the Ripper, was it?"

"It was Mary Walls." Pansy stopped for breath. "That's who it was. I've always said that girl was strange, an now I'm sure of it. Can you imagine anythin so brazen? Goin around lookin into other people's windows!"

"Oh, she probably was jest goin by," Andy said soothingly. "You don't know."

"Well, she certainly was standin still when *I* saw her," Pansy said decisively. "An when she saw me, she started walkin again. I said how sorry I was about Jake, an she never even stopped. She just said thank you."

"They ain't much more anyone can say is they?" Andy said. "What'd you expect her to say?"

"Well, she might at least have stopped to say something. There warn't no need to go by me as if I was a perfect stranger. Them Wallses have always been like that. Grace is just exactly the same. Never has a word to say. Why, times we've had her down to the club an gone out of our way to make things pleasant for her, she's set there just like a bump on a log all afternoon. Much as ever she could manage to say she'd had a nice time when it was over.

"An that's another thing."

"What's that?" Andy looked at his wife with affection tempered with amusement. "You brought me home some nice juicy tidbit?"

"Well, you don't have to talk like I was always draggin gossip in to the house." Pansy bridled a little but was unable to forego her triumph. "They say you ought not to speak anythin but good of the dead, but somebody in a position to know told me young Jake Walls was drunk as a lord when he hit that tree. Think of that and they've always set up to be so much."

"Maybe he was." Andy shrugged. "I wouldn't know. But better men than Jake Walls have got drunk before."

"Well, there." Pansy started taking off her hat. "Poor young fellow. I spose so. I never thought Jake was so much, but it's a shame it had to happen."

She disappeared into her bedroom and when she came out a moment later, Andy saw that she'd forgotten about both Mary and Jake.

"Well," she said comfortably, "I spose I'd better get your supper, hadn't I?"

"If you don't get it pretty sudden, I'll divorce you," Andy said, grinning.

MARY'S ears were still tingling when she reached the corner and turned up the walk that led to Gene's front door. She knew perfectly well that Pansy Galley had caught her staring into windows like a peeping tom and could feel her hands going hot and cold in quick succession with embarrassment.

Lord, she was thinking when she reached to knock on the door, I hope she never says anything about it.

Her embarrassment over the actual happening had swallowed any trepidation she might have felt about coming down here to see Gene and Annie and she was still thinking of Pansy Galley and the kind of story she might start, when Gene opened the door. He stood straining his eyes to make out who she was. Mary, who could see his face clearly, saw his expression change. He looked blanked out with surprise and then the flood of happiness made his whole face light up.

"Mary," he said. "Well, for pete sake, what're you doin down here? Well, come on in. We were just sittin down to supper. You're just in time."

My lord, Mary thought, trying to remember how long it had been since anyone had been that glad to see her. Gene didn't give her a chance to answer him. He grabbed her arm and hauled her after him through the dark little hall to the kitchen.

"Hey, Annie," he said. "Guess who's here."

Annie turned to look before she committed herself. For a moment the two girls stood staring at each other past Gene, then Annie smiled.

"Heaven sake," she said. "You certainly are a stranger. Gene, go in an get another chair from the front room while I put an extra plate on."

Happily, Gene went, leaving them alone.

"Look, Annie," Mary said quickly. "I want you to know I'm sorry about the way I acted last fall."

Annie looked at her and smiled easily.

"I don't know what you mean," she said. "Was there something wrong?"

"Don't you remember that last night I was up to your house?" Mary said, numbly.

"Oh, heavens." Annie started to laugh lightly. "You mean you've been remembering that all this time and thinkin I was mad? Oh, Mary, you never did!"

She was still laughing when Gene came back.

"Well," he looked from one to the other. "It certainly looks like old times to see you two fooling around again."

It may look like it to you, Mary thought drearily. But it wasn't the same and she knew it as well as Annie did. It wouldn't ever be the same because Annie wasn't going to let it. If it weren't for Gene, she told herself, she'd get up now and go before they came out into the open; but she couldn't leave him. He sat looking at her as if she'd given him a present just by her being there.

They sat around the table eating and Gene seemed determined that they shouldn't stop talking. Whenever silence threatened them, he had another question ready for her. He wanted to know what she was doing, what they were all doing, what had happened since he'd left.

But behind his feverish talk, there was something Mary couldn't put her finger on—it was almost a dread of silence, as if he were afraid of what he might think about if he stopped talking long enough to give himself the chance.

When they'd finished eating, Gene got up and went into the front room. Hesitating by her chair, Mary looked over at Annie.

"Come on," she said. "I'll help you wash up."

"I guess you won't do anything of the kind," Annie's heartiness was almost good enough. "You go right in there and talk to Gene. It won't take me a minute to get this stuff out of the way."

If she had sounded the way she used to sound, Mary would have overridden her protests, recognizing them for the usual polite refusal. But this time there wasn't any doubt about it. Annie didn't want help.

"Well, all right," Mary said slowly. "But I feel mean, leaving you with all this mess to clean up."

"It's all right," Annie said. "I don't mind a bit. Go on, now." She made shooing motions with her hands and Mary, summoning a weak laugh to match the atmosphere Annie evidently wanted to create, turned toward the front room.

Gene was standing looking out the dark window when she came in and for a minute she could look at him without having him aware of her. He was thinner than he had been, and he looked tight and nervous. Gene, who hadn't had a nervous bone in his body. Because it made her feel as if she were spying on him, Mary moved quickly and he heard her.

He turned on her swiftly.

"What about Jake?" he said.

"What?"

"What really happened?"

"Oh, lord, Gene," she stared. "You know as much as I do."

"How'd he happen to have the old man's car? Stanny's the only one ever drives that car. I don't believe he ever let Jake touch her."

"I don't know," Mary said. "I don't know a thing you don't. All I know is they called up that morning saying they'd found him. Pa didn't know anything about it either."

"I'll always think there was more to it than anyone saw," Gene said savagely. "Was he tight? There's been a lot of talk."

Mary looked at him thoughtfully.

"Well, since you had that brush-up with him, he'd been doing a lot of drinking. I don't know how much. But too much for Jake."

"He never had the head for it." Gene pushed his hand wearily back through his hair. "Lord, I spose I've got that to

294

wonder about now. All my life I spose I've got to wonder if what I said to him that night started him off."

"If that's keeping you awake nights, you might as well forget about it," Mary said, trying not to look at him. "Nothing you said made him do whatever it was he did that night."

"I might have started it."

"You sound almost as if you wanted to think you had." Mary lifted her head until she could look him in the face. "What's wrong, anyhow? What's the matter with you?"

Instead of answering her, Gene said, "Jake was down here a couple of weeks before he—before it happened."

"Well, what's strange about that?"

"You know I'm out of a job, don't you?"

"No, I didn't. But I don't see—"

"You will." Gene slumped down in the rocker by the window and spread his feet out as far as he could. "Since Christmas I been piddling around with a job here and a job there, none of em for more than two weeks. Then I couldn't get one at all, see? So I was out lookin one day an Jake comes down. Around noon, it was. He come to the back door and asked for me. I wasn't home an Annie wouldn't let him in. She said his eyes looked funny, or somethin. Anyhow, it scared her and she wouldn't let him. So what does he do? He sits out there in front in his car all afternoon till I came home. Ten below zero it was, darned near. And there sits Jake like it was midsummer.

"Along about dark, I came home and found him there. He yelled to me and when I saw it was him, I went over to the car.

" 'You ain't workin, are you?' Jake says.

"I said no, but I didn't see what it had to do with him.

" 'Well,' Jake says, 'I thought, seein's how you did me a favor once, I'd come down and tell you why you can't get a job.'

"I don't know what I said then. I guess I just stared at him.

He started to laugh and I swear to God I never heard anything like it. It was enough to give you duck-bumps.

" 'Well,' he said, 'you might's well give up an leave town.'

"I said what the devil was he talkin about, or somethin like
that.

" 'Well,' Jake says, 'I've found out why you can't get a job.
It's Pa,' he says. 'He's been going around droppin a word here
an there. You know how he does. You've seen him do it.
Well, that's what he's been doin to you. And that's why nobody'll give you a job.'

" 'See, Gene?' he says.

"Then before I could say anything more to him, he started
up that old car and went off up the road as if the devil hisself
was camping on his tail."

"I don't believe it," Mary said. She stood staring at him,
her face twisted with surprise. "I don't believe he'd do a thing
like that."

"Well, if it's not true——" Gene looked up at her and she
saw suddenly what there was about his face that was different.
He had begun to look hopeless. "If it's not true, why can't I
get a job? What's he tryin to do, Mary? Does he want to
see me starve?"

"I don't know." She put her hand up to her face and the
skin of her cheek felt hot. "I don't know what he's trying to
do."

She didn't want to believe what he'd just told her, but she
shut her eyes and could see her father's face, the way it looked
when he got mad, and she knew it was true.

"It's all right," Gene said suddenly. "Pete sake, don't look
like that. I'll make out." He grinned at her with a sudden
flash of his old carefree expression and that glimpse of it
showed her exactly how he had changed.

"It doesn't do much good to get away from him, does it?"
she said.

"It's because you can't," Gene said. He spread his fingers

296

wide and looked at them. "There's no way to get away from him, not really."

"You'd been better off if you'd never listened to me," Mary said harshly. "You never should have listened to me."

"Oh, well," Gene shrugged. "I'm not thinkin about that. That's over. I wouldn't have listened if you hadn't been tellin me what I wanted to hear. That hasn't got anything to do with it."

"We-ell," Mary said.

Gene looked up.

"Did Ma say anything when I didn't come to the funeral?"

"She thought you might," Mary said. "I think she thought up to the last minute you might come."

"You can see how I couldn't, can't you?"

"I can see all right," Mary nodded. She realized suddenly that standing there listening to Gene and watching him was making her sick to her stomach. She felt as if he had begun to come apart before her eyes and she couldn't even say good-by to him. It took all the power she had left to turn and get out of the room.

When he looked up and found her gone, he went quickly after her and caught her at the door.

"Hey," he said. "You can't go off like that. What'll Annie think?"

"Tell her I had a headache," Mary said, over her shoulder. "Tell her I didn't feel good. Oh, and say thank you for me, will you."

"Okay," Gene said. "Okay."

He stood watching until he could no longer differentiate between her dark figure and the night itself. He felt almost as if, if he kept looking at her, she might turn and come back; but if he took his eyes off her, he knew she wouldn't. When he couldn't see her any longer, he went in and closed the door.

Gene had once heard or read somewhere that fear was like a poison and not nearly so slow as you might think. Why it had stuck in his mind to be dredged up now, he didn't know. When he'd heard it, it hadn't meant much to him, but now that he was afraid, he seized on it, thinking, Now I know what it means. It wasn't a subtle fear the guy had been talking about; it was nothing but downright, pervading penetrating fear of physical harm, of what was going to happen.

He knew what it meant because now he was afraid, and being afraid, realized that he had never known an emotion like this one. It met him in the morning when he woke up and lay halfway between sleep and waking, feeling his muscles going taut with a foggy beginning of that feeling. It meant remembering suddenly that he was afraid, that he didn't know what was going to happen to him, and he didn't know what he was going to do about it. It sat at table with him and made it impossible for him to eat. His food stuck in his throat and had no taste. Fear walked down the road beside him like a dog or a shadow. It meant that he sat in the kitchen at night like a bump on a log, completely incapable of talking, not hearing what Annie said to him, making her repeat her words before he could string them together into any sequence of sounds that made sense.

He had begun to hate Russ, not with the young hatred of scorn and rebellion, but with the abject hatred of fear and blame. Yet Russ's physical existence exerted a peculiar strong pull on him. He found himself hanging around town, going the places he'd go if he were hunting for his father, trying to see him. He had nothing he wanted to say to Russ and made no effort to speak to him, but he felt satisfied if he could see him at a distance; maybe catch a glimpse of the old man going into the Masonic Hall.

Once he saw Russ get out of his car and go into the post office. He crossed the street quickly and went in, too, to find Russ at the stamp window. Gene went up and stood behind him, nonchalantly, apparently just waiting his turn.

Russ had turned away from the window quickly and almost hit him. When he looked up and saw that it was Gene, Gene recognized with pleasure the sudden startled look in his father's eyes. But Russ won. After the first moment he was completely self-possessed and somehow he managed to give Gene the impression that he knew what Gene was thinking.

Russ nodded and grinned.

"H'ya," he said.

The sound of his voice struck Gene dumb. He stood staring until Russ raised an eyebrow slightly, nodded, and walked away. Only after the door had shut behind him, could Gene move.

"Well, Gene." Larry Phillips, the postmaster, stared out at him through the bars of his window. "You want somethin or you just in here to get warm?"

Gene turned and lunged out through the door. He was just in time to see the big new Buick haul away from the curb. He stood there staring until it vanished up the road.

There, he thought, that's the first word I've had out of him since it happened. That's what I've been waiting for. And it's not worth it.

He had needed that meeting to show him that it was all over; he could never go back to them. There wasn't any room for him any more, he had been cast out.

But I'm your *son*, he thought. I'm your own son.

And his mind furnished the answer to that so quickly that it might almost have been a mental echo.

So was Jake, his mind said coldly. So was Jake his son.

It was only midmorning, but he couldn't think of anything to do but go home. And he thought of that as the lesser of two evils. As the winter had worn on, he had exhausted, patiently and slowly, every possible source of work. It was just the way he had told Annie. There were so many jobs and so many men to fill them. And now he knew that even if there had been a job, a man would think twice about giving it to him. There just wasn't any other place to look.

The last two weeks he'd been hard put to it to find something to do after he left the house in the morning. Once he had even taken his skates with him, sneaking them out so Annie wouldn't see them and know what he was going to do. Instead of telling her he'd be home for dinner, he'd said he'd grab a sandwich uptown. She hadn't questioned that and for a moment he'd thought she even looked relieved.

He had stopped in at the restaurant and had Joe Lampher make him a roast beef sandwich to stuff into his pocket. Then he'd gone on, up the road, to where the path cut over through, past the old Brown's Pond Road, to the river. It was just light as he went and he began to feel like a kid suddenly let out of school. He hadn't been skating on the river since he was a boy and he was beginning to lose his first feeling of guilt in anticipation.

The path angled across the old road and up over China Hill and the thick growth of spruces, on top of the hill, thinned out into an old blueberry clearing. Through the bare thin-limbed wild cherries he could see the beginning-to-be-steely glint of the river ice. He went down the hill and came out of the thicket of bushes into a narrow water meadow that followed along the river. In the spring, in the wet season, this ground was impassable; the sturdy clumps of thick grass hid morass and swamp and muck and the tortuous arms of deep brown water. But now the water had frozen and, as he stepped from one grass clump to another, he could feel the crisp edges of the thin ice crunch under his feet and the frosty sound of it made him feel young, very young, because it was a sound he could remember out of his childhood.

He could remember one night, years ago, when he had come along this same path and down this same hill to skate. He'd been twelve or thirteen, still young enough to have that cold curling ball of apprehension in his stomach at the idea of being out so late at night and alone and far from home. The ice had frozen that year before the snow came and, at night, was black and the path of the moon across it was like moonlight across calm black water. For a moment he'd hesitated, trying to make up his mind whether it really *was* ice; even feeling its hard slippery surface under his feet, he still hadn't been sure. It wasn't water, but it might have been something else, some substance he'd never heard of; it wasn't ice. Maybe it was black glass, he thought. But as soon as he'd started to skate, the long silver lines of curled shavings behind him made it ice again. The fear of aloneness had gone then, and exhilaration had taken its place. He had never been so free, he had never been so alive. But when he started home along the path over China Hill, the ball of apprehension was back in his stomach and he was glad when he saw the first glimmer of a street light through the trees and knew he had come back to safety and company.

He had never seen the ice that clear black, like water, again and today it was pale and shimmering and gray-white with twisting little furrows of snow blown into windrows along the shore.

He sat on a frosty hummock of grass to put on his skates, hid his larrigans and went out for a few practice turns. At first he felt clumsy, but that passed quickly, and when he struck off upstream, with long steady strokes, the skates felt like another part of his body.

The air was so clear and cold it burned his lungs and now that the sun was full up, he could see the gleaming frost crystals, fading and shifting ahead of him. There was no wind and the river was deserted and by noon, even with frequent stops to rest, he was twenty miles up country.

This back country had always fascinated Gene, but he had forgotten a little what it really looked like. That was the way it was: when he was there, each detail of it was so clear that he thought, I'll never forget what it's like. Then, after he had gone again, or even while he stopped looking at it, it grew faint and faded.

He had nearly forgotten it.

The wide land of marshes that went miles to the moss-hung spruces, marshes sketched over with silver trickles of ice; here the trees seemed shorter and the land itself drained of emotion. It was a land for moose and the wild geese with north in their screaming throats. He had covered its roads on foot and he knew the narrow double-rutted tracks and the few forlorn houses where people still lived. He knew better the old houses, long deserted, whose ridge poles slumped tiredly against the sky. On spring nights he had slept in them, waking in the night to see stars through the bare timbers. He had gone out into the apple orchards in the early damp mornings and found the deer to lower their heads and stare at him under the heavy gnarled blossomy boughs, before they whirled, snorting, and plunged away into the oblivion of tangled underbrush and swamp cedars.

Looking from the river across the frosty marshes, he thought that this would be no place for a man to live. He needed the harsh aggressiveness of the Ridge, not this faint, simply-colored land that lay beyond it, but it fascinated him and the feeling was old and sad and like something half remembered.

He ate his sandwich, chewing slowly, standing there on his skates looking at the shield-like countryside, the deserted watery wilderness of forgotten land.

Afterward he went a short way into the marsh, kicked a hole in the shell ice with the toe of his skate and lay on his stomach sucking up the icy brown water. The taste of it, peaty, smoky, swampy, made him feel the way he did when he looked at this country. Now it is in me again, he thought, and getting up, he skated quickly back the way he had come with the taste and the feeling still strong to see if he could keep them this time. When he came back to the Ridge, he had forgotten, but it seemed as if the swamp water was still faintly bitter in his mouth.

But Annie had taken even that away from him. She'd stood stock still in the middle of the kitchen floor, staring at the skates under his arm, at his smoothed-out contented-looking face, and she'd started to laugh, helplessly and without humor.

"My lord," she said finally. "So that's where you were all day, so that's what you were doing while I was sitting here hoping and praying you'd get a job. You never stayed away a whole day before and I thought maybe you'd started working."

"I can't look for work all the time," he'd said defensively.

"No." She glanced away from him. "Well, get ready for supper. It's nearly ready and I imagine you're good and hungry, all that fresh air and exercise."

She was shaking with rage and she had to stop talking then or say something worse.

She put his supper on the table and stood waiting for him to start eating. When he sat down and looked around expectantly, she said, "There's no meat. The money goes farther when you don't buy it."

"It's all right," he mumbled. "I had a roast beef sandwich this noon."

"Was it good?" Annie turned her back on him deliberately. "How'd it taste? I had bread and milk, myself."

Suddenly the fried potatoes he'd been eating choked him and he couldn't swallow. When he did and started to tell her how it had been, he found that she'd gone. He could hear her moving around upstairs and then even that stopped.

He sat for a moment, staring straight before him, wondering what had happened to them. It was like living in the house with a total stranger, but worse because she hadn't always been a stranger. Only months ago she had been the girl he loved and then his wife. And now she was a stranger and that made it worse. There was no longer anything he could say to her, there was nothing for him to say to anyone, and the fear he had forgotten through the day came back and sprawled itself beside his chair.

NOW he started home in the middle of the morning, draggingly, not wanting to go, but not knowing anything else to do, not having any other place to go. He never knew now what her mood would be. She might meet him at the door, hopefully, and then he would have to see the flicker of hope in her eyes fade out before his words. She might be upstairs when he came in and then he would know that she had seen him coming from the window and hadn't been able to summon up even that faint response for him.

She had seen him coming; she must have been in the front room. When he came in the door, he saw the quick splash of color her skirt made as she vanished up the front stairs and knew that today she hadn't been able to face him. For a moment he stood there stupidly, his mouth a little open, staring after her.

He was sitting beside the stove in the kitchen, his feet up on the ledge, when she came down at noon to get his dinner. When she came into the room, she looked at him startled, as if she hadn't known he was there.

"For heaven sake," she said heartily. "When did you come in?"

"Oh," Gene could feel his voice drag heavily over the words. "Quite a while ago."

He didn't have the heart to say to her: You know when I came in. You know because you saw me coming and went upstairs so you wouldn't have to talk to me. He couldn't face the possibility of a fight; it just wasn't worth the trouble.

But as he watched her moving around the kitchen, studiously keeping whatever she happened to be doing at the moment between them, he got back enough of his resilience to say, "Something's happened to us, hasn't it?"

He knew by the quick eager way she turned to face him that she'd been waiting a long time for him to say something like that.

"Whatever it is, it's not my doing," she said, staring at him, her thick brows slightly drawn down, not quite into a frown.

"I suppose you mean it's mine," Gene said, stung. "I suppose you think I have any influence on my father. My lord, Annie, I can't stop him from doin anything. I told you when you married me, you'd have to help me. Now I need you to."

"All right. All right. I'm not saying you *can* do anything about him. Don't think I don't see how it is, Gene. But it makes me sick to my stomach to see you knuckle under the way you're doing."

"What else do you expect me to do? The only other thing I can see is go out and shoot him."

"Oh, for pity sake, Gene," she said angrily. "Don't be so foolish. Anyone'd think this was the only place in the world to live. I see what he's doing. But he can't do it to us if we go away. I admit maybe it's impossible for us to live here. He's made it impossible. And it's an awful thing to do to your own son."

"Now it's out, isn't it?" Gene said heavily. "That's what you've been wanting to say for a long time, isn't it?"

"Well, why not?" She put down the kettle she was holding and turned on him defiantly. "Is it a crime to say the truth? You know it's so. I do, too. There's nothing here for us and there never can be as long's he's here. He's seen to that."

"And he's done a damn good job," Gene said bitterly. "I can't even get to talking about work to anyone now."

"Well, what're you going to do? Sit around and starve to death? Because if you are, Gene, I'm not." Annie took the kettle off the sideboard and put it down on the stove with a crash that made him jump. "I love you, Gene, and you're my husband. But I'm not going to sit around twiddlin my thumbs while you make up your mind what you're going to do. I just cannot stand it."

"I don't know what to do," he said desperately. "I feel like my insides had been hauled right out. I can't think what to do."

"Go away."

He stared at her blankly, thinking, Away!

"Well?" she said.

"But, Annie, it's a hard thing to decide. Look, here we are. This place means a lot to me. It's my *home*, can't you see that. I've always planned to go on living here, because here a man can have a decent life. Why, I'd die in a city. I'd go crazy."

He sat stricken into silence, thinking what it would mean to him to leave this place. When he said "my home" to mean no longer this certain piece of ground, the Ridge, the islands, the harbor, the thick spruce woods, the water. It was simply that the word "home" would never mean any place but this to him and he couldn't conceive of a life worth living in any other place. His entire childhood, everything that went into his growing up, had been to the end that he'd be ready to make a life for himself here, in this little town, where there wasn't a man he met on the street he couldn't call by name.

"I could go fishing," he said desperately. "I haven't tried that yet."

"Oh, Gene, stop kidding yourself."

"No," he said. "I could."

"Look, where're you going to get the money to start? What're you going to do for a boat? And what d'you know about fishing?"

"My father went lobstering in a skiff," he said. "He didn't start with much and look at him now."

"I don't want to," Annie said. "It makes me sick to look at him. And it makes me just as sick to see what he's done to you. Look at you, for a change. For godsake, for godsake, can't you see you'll never amount to anything till you get away from him?"

She waited for a long minute, staring at him hopefully, and when he said nothing, she tried once more.

"It's my home, too," she said. "It means just as much to me as it does to you. But it's not worth losing my self-respect over. The only thing left for you to do is go crawling back to him saying you're sorry. Well, I won't do it. If you do it, you'll do it alone."

Gene shut his eyes suddenly. He could feel himself cringing as if he'd been battered beyond endurance.

"You can't leave me," he said. "I can't do without you."

"I couldn't have left you the way you used to be. Honest, Gene, you aren't the same person you were four months ago. You wouldn't have stood this then, no more than I would. Now, look. He's worn you down till you're half crazy."

"Yes, I guess I am." He shoved his fists hard against his closed eyes, seeing against his lids the explosion of yellow wheels that changed to red and faded. "I think sometimes that's what's wrong with me."

"It's not what's wrong with you," Annie said harshly. "I think it *is* what's wrong with *him*. There's only one person he thinks about ever, and that's him. Not one of you mean anything at all to him. Look at the lot of you. It didn't do Jake any good, being his son, did it?" She stood leaning above him. "Did it?" she repeated tightly.

"All right." Gene opened his eyes and stared up at her. "You win. Where do we go from here?"

For a moment he thought she really was going to lose her temper.

"No."

"Whatta you mean 'no'? I said I'd go, didn't I?"

"That's not good enough and you know it. If we go away with you feeling like that, it won't mean a thing. We'll be back just as quick from anywhere else as we went away from here."

"Well, how do you expect me to feel? Want me to cheer or something? My god, Annie, I've been trying to tell you how I feel about this place, leaving here. It isn't easy."

"No, I don't expect you to cheer. But you've got to hold your head up. If you go sneaking away like a licked puppy, what's the good in that?"

"Oh," he said. "I see what you mean."

Suddenly he *did* see what she meant and she was right. He got up slowly and went over to the window to stand looking out at the bleak backyard.

"I saw him this morning," he began slowly, not turning to look at her. "I met him in the post office and he spoke to me. I can't ever go back, Annie. Even if it wasn't for you, I couldn't ever go back. So you're right. We've got to get out and get out fast. And we will."

Exhilaration at having made up his mind swept over him, clearing away the sludge of inertia he'd been bedded in for a month now. All at once he felt light and free and as if he had suddenly come back to life and found it well worth the effort. When he did turn to face her, he looked like himself again for the first time in weeks; and he realized, seeing the change of expression in her eyes, how much of a strain those weeks had been for her, too.

"Wait," he said. "You wait, old girl, we'll show em."

He went over and lifted the cover from the steaming kettle, sniffing deeply.

"Hm," he said appreciatively. "Coffee, too. I want coffee with my dinner."

Annie grabbed the coffeepot and shoved it quickly onto the front of the stove.

"My lord, if you want anything enough to ask for it like that, you're going to get it before you change your mind," she said.

Gene, seeing her arm tensed under the weight of the tea-kettle, thought suddenly that there'd been something else bothering him lately. He stood looking down at her bent head and the little short curls at the back of her neck caught the light and shone. He reached out and touched one of them, lightly, so lightly that she didn't seem to feel it. But when he moved his hands down to lay it against the smooth skin just under the curls, he could feel the tension his touch had built in her. He leaned forward, just far enough to reach her ear with his lips. For a moment he just stood there, feeling with exultation the quickening of his own breath. It was all right. It was all right now.

"Never mind the coffee," he said.

Annie didn't look up from what she was doing, she didn't turn her head.

"It's broad daylight." Her voice sounded hurried and a little scared.

"Then I can see you. That'll be nice."

"It's warm in the bedroom," Annie said. "I had the radiator open all morning almost."

Gene reached out and took the teakettle out of her hand and set it on the back of the stove. Then he shoved the coffee-pot off the cover and away from the heat. When he looked up Annie was standing in the door. She disappeared immediately and he could hear her feet going quickly up the front stairs. He went after her as quickly, turning the key in the lock of the front door as he passed it.

WELL," Fod said. "I dunno what happened. All's I know's what people are sayin. And they're sayin he was drunk."

"You're a dirty liar." Stanny turned on him with a snarl.

"Who d'you think you're callin a liar?" Fod's fists, still at his side, bunched hard. His jaw stuck out a little and his face began to get hot.

"You heard me." Stanny looked with dismay at Fod's hands. He didn't like fights and he didn't want to fight with Fod and he didn't even know why he was saying the things he was now. He knew only that he couldn't let Fod get away with saying anything like that about Jake, now that Jake was dead.

"You goin to make that stick?"

"I said it," Stanny blurted. He felt as if he was going to cry and he couldn't—he couldn't with Fod looking at him. "You're a dirty liar."

Then, before Fod could get set for him and because he couldn't wait any longer to let out what he was feeling, Stanny jumped and the two boys rolled wildly in the snow in the gutter.

"I'll show you who was drunk," Stanny kept saying, clenching his teeth on the words, hammering wildly at Fod's distorted brown face.

"Call me a liar," Fod growled. One of his fists exploded against Stanny's cheek bone and for a minute there was nothing in the world but stars. When they faded, Fod was bending over him, panting.

"You had enough?"

"No, by god," Stanny said. "I'll show you."

He got cautiously to his feet, watching Fod.

"I ain't goin to jump you before you're ready. Not the way you done me." Fod bared his teeth. "You dirty little so and so, you jumped me before I was ready."

They circled each other cautiously, their fists up. Stanny's nose was running and he kept sniffing, not daring to wipe it. Then, before he knew how it had happened, Fod had him down again and they were whirling in the snow like two tomcats. Neither of them could do much harm to the other, until Stanny started to tire. After that Fod got home a couple of blows that nearly winded him.

Stanny went limp and Fod, sensing his victory, pinned Stanny's narrow shoulders to the ground.

"Take it back. Who's a liar?"

He had reached across so that his sweater-clad arm pressed hard against Stanny's mouth. Stanny twisted just enough to get his teeth apart and brought them to, grindingly, against the mouthful of wool. The resultant explosion made him know, for the moment before he was too busy to know anything, that he'd managed to get some of Fod, too.

Five minutes later, Fod got up and walked away, leaving Stanny behind on the ground, his face in the snow. He was sobbing convulsively and there was a salty taste of blood in his mouth. When the sound of Fod's steps faded, he sat up and stared after him, cautiously exploring with his tongue the place where one of his big front teeth had gone into his lip. It stung and felt raw and his nose hurt and his whole body felt as if he'd been put through a concrete mixer.

He got up slowly and started getting himself back into one piece. The whole front of his shirt was torn away and as he zipped his windbreaker over it he was thinking how he could get into the house past his mother and get the shirt changed before she spotted it.

By god, Stanny thought, if I was only big the way Jake was, he couldn't have done that to me. I woulda been able to lick him. I got to get some muscle, that's all. I got to take those exercises and get big enough to lick the whole bunch of them.

He was thinking, too, that if he got that big, if he could only grow, his father would like him the way he'd liked Gene and Jake. Suddenly he saw that he was the only man left. Now it was going to be up to him.

When he went slowly up the drive to the house, he was looking at it with the feeling that it came closer now to being his than it ever had before. Because now it would be his in reality someday. He'd have to study about the things anyone ought to know to run a place like this, too, now that he was the only one left.

As he came up the drive, his grandfather appeared around the corner of the house, saw him, and stopped dead.

"Good land of the livin," he said. "What in god's name you been doin? Buttin against a few stone walls?"

"Got in a fight," Stanny said, moving his lips stiffly. "Had a fight."

"D'you win?"

Stanny shook his head.

"But, by god, I will next time," he said.

Surprised, Nat didn't say anything about the swearing. He stood for a moment looking over the wreckage of Stanny's face.

"Well," he said at last, "you better come in the front way. We'll go upstairs an see what we can do about that mess before your Ma sees it. Maybe we can get it fixed up so she won't notice too much."

"I don't care if she does," Stanny said. "Everybody gets in fights once in a while."

"That's true," Nat said soberly. "Only I don't think this is just the time to go makin issues of it with your Ma. You better let me see what I can do."

"I can take care of myself," Stanny said.

"Nobody said you couldn't." Nat, after a surprised moment, took in the situation. "But you can let a feller help you, can't you? As a favor to me?"

"Oh, sure," Stanny nodded painfully. "I guess that's okay. You can help."

Stanny led the way to the door and Nat followed.

FEBRUARY was no time to start spring housecleaning; but what Grace wouldn't admit to herself was the fact that she couldn't feel comfortable in the house again until she'd cleaned it thoroughly. Ever since Jake's funeral it seemed to her there was always that faint funereal odor of carnations; the smell of damp clothes and people crowded into a warm room in cold wet weather. It was the smell of death in winter and it nearly drove her crazy.

She'd started in early in the week at the very top of the house, spending the first day in the attic with the front dormer windows thrown wide open. She'd had to wrap herself up in her old gray sweater and her hands got cold, so she went down, early that first morning, and got a pair of white work gloves from the shed.

For a moment, before putting them on, she stood with them limply in her hands, looking at them as if there'd be some special message for her in the way the fingers looked full and bent, almost as if her son's thick young hands had left a permanent record in anything as easily moved as cotton.

If only I'd been able to talk to him, she thought. When I saw how he was beginning to act, if I could have talked to him somehow to make him see I wasn't mad, just that I wanted to help him. But even now, when it was too late, she couldn't think what would have been the right things to say to him. That was some slight comfort. If she'd thought of the proper thing now, it would have made her weak attempts to get at Jake less than nothing. But they were still the best things she could think of and so her regret was impersonal and intangible instead of being pointed and something that hurt. Those last few weeks before Christmas it had been as if Jake had been shut off from the rest of them, as if he'd been going around in a dazed, complete, glassed-in world of his own, from which he couldn't escape, to which nobody else could penetrate.

I tried, she thought, shoving her hands hastily into the

gloves, working the fingers to get the shape of his hands out of them. It wasn't as if I didn't try. I did everything I could for that boy: I talked to him, I tried to tell him what he was doing. But talking had never had any effect on any of them.

And then he went and did a thing like that, she thought, and stopped, her eyes wide and dazed with the thought because it was the first time it had occurred to her. For a second she had an almost intuitive insight into the loneliness he must have known before she told herself harshly that she was being a silly old fool. Not Jake, maybe any other one of the kids, but not Jake. She didn't even think the word "suicide." Her thoughts skirted out around it as if it had been a gap in her mind. She shook herself, physically, pulled open the shed door and went hastily in through the house.

It was so still now. With two of them gone for good and not coming back, somehow it made a difference in the quality of the silence that settled down over the house when the others had gone out. Stanny was off to school, Russ downtown, her father had headed up the road early that morning, saying he was going to see Hat. As for Mary, Grace didn't know where she'd gone, but she'd vanished soon after breakfast and Grace figured she'd probably gone on one of the walks that took up most of her time lately. She'd wished, more often than once, that there was something a girl could do, short of a job. Sometimes she even wished that Mary would settle down once and for all, marry Ralph, and put an end to the long solitary days she spent.

She went on up the narrow attic stairs and stood looking, with a momentary sinking of dismay, at the mess she'd let herself in for. Outside the open window, the high golden-looking sky was clean and cold and the sharp edge of the Ridge, in the rarefied winter air, razored its way across the world. She went over to the window and stood looking up the side of the Ridge, trying to envision what the view from the top down the other side must be with winter thick over the woods and snow stretching for miles under the spruces, but it was impossible. Beyond the top of the Ridge there was nothing, nothing at all.

Permitting herself a wry smile for having fancies like that at her age, Grace turned her back resolutely on the Ridge and pitched into the long undisturbed, heterogeneous piles of culch that the careful sifting of years had permitted to accumulate in the attic.

Now she turned it out thoroughly, shoving the growing piles of old letters, magazines, rags, broken furniture, ahead of her toward the stairs like a snowplow breaking out a road. She cleaned with a ruthlessness that surprised her. Ordinarily she was a saving woman. In her kitchen there was a bag on the back of the pantry door into which went every rag-tag of string and paper that came into the house. In her cellar were jars and bottles she would never use but couldn't bear to throw away in case one of them might come in handy sometime when she ran short.

There were trunks of her things up here now and she dusted and swept around them, but left them unopened, knowing their contents by heart. She knew too that she'd never use any of the outmoded dresses or the old suits belonging to Russ and the boys, but she was completely and congenitally incapable of throwing any of them away. So she left the big old curve-top trunks alone and when she got the pile of junk to the top of the stairs, she had a sudden change of heart and went over it carefully, picking out everything that anyone would conceivably want someday and putting it carefully back where it had come from in the first place.

It took her one whole day to clean the attic to her satisfaction, but when it was done and she went downstairs feeling as if she'd been run over by a steam roller, she had the dubious satisfaction of knowing that the attic, for the first time since they'd taken over the house, was clean as she had always intended it to be someday.

315

There, she said to herself, moving logily around the big kitchen getting supper ready, I wouldn't be ashamed to have the King of England go up in my attic, now, or even Annie Blaisdell, she added, thinking of the most particular house-keeper she could lay her tongue to.

When she started on the upstairs rooms the next day, she began with a little less zest, but the results would be the same although they took longer to accomplish. It took her just a little longer to clean a window than it had the day before, just a little longer to sweep a floor. It was an accumulating weari-ness that she knew well from previous house-cleaning sprees; it would get worse as she went along, until on the last day when she would be sweeping up chip-dirt in the wood cellar, she would feel like putting the broom in the fire and throwing the dustpan just as far as she could heave.

Jake's room was still and quiet. Right after the funeral she'd given it a good turn-out and put away all his things so there was little to do to it now, but an unused room gathered dust, so she went over it and over Gene's as carefully as if they were going to come back into them that night. She even started to put sheets on the beds until she thought what a waste and what a piece of foolishness it would be. So she merely cleaned the rooms and spread up the bedspreads and shut the doors be-hind her resolutely.

Stanny's room, no matter how she tried, always looked clut-tered and it seemed to her when she got through cleaning, it was every bit as messy as it had been when she started; but she had the satisfaction of knowing there wasn't a particle of dust anywhere in it and that the windows were so clean there might have been no glass there at all. She even went over the tiny black model planes, handling them carefully, feeling the delicacy of the light wood and the fine wire struts, putting them back, clean, in the spot she'd found them. Stanny always made such a fuss after she'd cleaned his room, claiming she moved things around so he never knew where he was when he went back into it, she took pains to see that nothing was changed. And she did it with pleasure, seeing momentarily, how seldom any of them went out of their way to humor Stanny.

She even found the physical culture magazine he kept under the cushion of the big chair and put it back again with a sigh. She didn't quite approve of some of the pictures in it, but she understood why it was there and knew, although she would forget again quickly, how it must be for Stanny, being small, and trying to hold his own in a world of big people.

In the door, she stood glancing back over the room. She looked thoughtfully at the model airplanes, remembering how fragile they'd felt in her own careful hands and wondering how Stanny, whose bony young fingers were clumsy enough with anything else, could manage to put together those miracles of delicacy.

Mary's room, when she came to it, made her sigh a little, a half-exasperated half-relieved sigh. It *was* a relief, she had to admit, to come into a room that one of her family used commonly and find it as neat and as bare as this one. The exasperation was because it wasn't what Grace would have called a fit bedroom for a young lady. From what she could see, from the door, there was little or no way of knowing whose room it was. It might have been any room in any boarding house and its look of cool impersonality made her just a little mad. She went out of her way to make their home nice for her kids and then one of them refused to acknowledge the hominess of it, refused to the extent that she made her own bedroom look like any room in any boarding house, and there was nothing worse Grace could think of to say about any room.

Grace liked a room to have character, and she resented it because from this one she could learn nothing of her own daughter, who was beginning to be a stranger, too, as her two eldest sons had been, but in her own way.

It was only at house-cleaning time, twice a year, that Grace came into this room. The rest of the time Mary took care of it herself. And that made Grace feel resentful at finding so little to do; there just wasn't anything to catch the dirt. A table, a chair, a bed, and a chest of drawers, that was all. But she cleaned it as savagely as if it had been piled high with dirt in every corner. Finished, she glanced back casually, and saw that the bottom drawer of the chest wasn't quite shut, something white had jammed in it and held it open a little at one corner.

Going back, Grace found that whatever it was made the drawer stick so that she had to pull it all the way out before she could get the obstruction out of the way. There was nothing in it that she could see but the sheets and pillowcases Mary used on her bed, but they weren't quite straight; one of them had been so badly rumpled by the edge of the drawer that she had to take it out and shake it smooth again. When she'd taken the first one out, she decided she might as well straighten out the whole thing. One by one she lifted out the heavy sheets, piling them neatly and squarely on the bed so she could put them all back into the drawer at one lick.

When she reached the bottom of the drawer and found there what looked like two thick sheets of cardboard, she took them out, too. There was no question in her mind about her right to look at whatever she found in the bedroom of her own daughter. The fact that they might have been put there to keep them out of her sight never entered her head. Automatically, she turned the top one over, found it a picture of a big old tree, and held it off to look at it.

"Now that's real nice," she said softly. "A real pretty picture. What on earth she wanted to go burying it in a drawer for I can't see."

She even turned to glance thoughtfully around the bare walls, trying to think where the picture would show up to the best advantage before she glanced down at the other one, gasped, and dropped it as if it had come suddenly alive in her hand. It landed face up and she stood looking down at it, feeling the shocked heat of her own blush. She touched it with the toe of her shoe before she could believe it was really there. And she knew why the pictures had been so carefully hidden.

It was plain, downright indecent, a thing like that. And her own daughter. Stooping to pick it up, Grace felt as if she were handling a snake. It made her slightly sick to look at the woman, spread out there in all her shamelessness. In the first place, her nakedness was indecent, and in the second place, it wasn't decent, either, even in a picture, for anyone to look as if they were enjoying anything as much as that naked woman was enjoying the sun.

To Grace there was nothing lovely about the painting; she didn't even see the colors. She could see nothing but that mishapen nude woman and the only parts of her you could really see were the parts that should have been covered up anyhow, she thought.

She put the sheets carefully back in the drawer and then, taking the pictures, one in each hand as if the touch of them contaminated her, she went downstairs and along the hall to Russ's office. There she laid the pictures on his desk, the woman underneath where she couldn't see her and the one of the big tree on top.

Mary didn't come home to dinner that noon and Grace was just as glad of it. She wanted to see Russ before she spoke to Mary and when he came in she was waiting for him, her firm cheeks bright with anger and a sort of shame that had been growing in her ever since she found the pictures. She felt as if she'd uncovered something indecent. The way they'd been so slyly hidden added to her feeling. Grace was a woman who believed firmly that nothing gave tone to a room like a good picture, but she had also been taught that nakedness was a sin and that the corporal existence of the human body was nasty and something to be hidden.

"Russ, I want to see you," she said abruptly as he came in the door.

Russ stared and lifted one eyebrow.

"Well, here I am," he said. "You can see me."

"Come in here, will you?" Grace turned and headed for the office and Russ, after a puzzled moment, followed her. He'd seen her mad before, but this time there was something more than anger and he couldn't figure out what it was.

When he came into the office she was standing by the desk and she pointed wordlessly at the uppermost picture. Russ went over and glanced at it curiously.

"Kind of nice, isn't it?" he said. "Where'd it come from?"

"Look at what's under it," Grace said, without answering his question.

Russ picked up the picture of the big tree and glanced at the one beneath it, did a double take, and whistled softly.

"Now there's a right nice piece," he said crudely.

"Well," Grace said on an explosive exhalation. "I guess it's plain enough where your children get their dirtiness."

"Wait a minute," Russ said soothingly, seeing that he hadn't taken the right course. "Settle down a little and tell me what this is all about. Where'd you get that, anyhow?"

"That, as you call it, was hidden in your daughter's bottom bureau drawer."

"Pete sake," Russ looked a little startled. "Mary?"

Unable to answer him, Grace merely nodded.

"Well—" Russ picked up the picture and carried it over to the window to get a better look at it. He glanced once, hastily, at Grace and brought it back again. "What you making all the fuss about?"

"Fuss? Look, Russ, I am not going to have indecency in this house. I don't know where it came from or what it's all about, but I want you to speak to Mary. It's high time one of us did. I don't know where she goes or what she does and it's high time we found out, if she's going to bring stuff like this into the house. I've always tried to make my kids be decent and I've always had trouble with them. Now they're too much for me and it's up to you. I want you to talk to her."

"We-ell." Russ drew the word out. "I don't know but what you're going at it a little strong, Grace. After all, it ain't a crime to have a picture, is it?"

"Like that one? Yes," she said firmly. "I won't have it. Bringing stuff like that into a perfectly respectable house. She knew how I'd feel, too, because she hid it so nobody could see it. She must have thought it was pretty bad to go hiding it."

IT WAS always easy to tell, with Grace, just how she was feeling. Her temper stuck out all over her and the various degrees of it were just as clear. So Mary knew the instant she set foot in the kitchen, light and warm and like a center of life in the quick death of the winter night, that her mother was angry. A few moments later she knew that Grace was mad at her and that it was a personal and direct anger.

"Your father wants to see you," Grace said without turning her head when she heard Mary come in.

If the reason for Russ's wanting to see Mary had been something that Grace didn't know about or something of which she hadn't been the instigator, she would have accompanied her announcement with a wry, barely sympathetic smile. Since she didn't and didn't even bother to turn her head, Mary decided correctly that Russ wanted to speak to her about something that had disturbed Grace.

She stared at her mother's back, resenting its firmness, its indisputable air of rightness. There was something about the set of Grace's shoulders when she thought she had a righteous cause of anger that had always set her children's teeth on edge.

She could make her back look stiffer and more displeased than most woman could their faces.

Risking making her even angrier, Mary hesitated.

"Is it anything important?" she asked. "I'm pretty tired."

"Maybe if you'd spend your time doin something useful instead of out rantin around the roads all day, an gettin into god knows what, you wouldn't be tired," Grace said tightly. "And I never knew him to want to say somethin to any of you that wasn't important."

"You don't know what it is, do you?"

"You know I'm not in the habit of mixin in, when he wants to see one of you," Grace said, evasively.

"Well, I spose I'd better go see what I've done now," Mary said bitterly, her eyes on her mother's broad back.

Grace turned to face her and Mary saw with amazement that she was blushing with an embarrassment that made it almost impossible for her to meet her daughter's eyes.

"Yes, I think you better," she said. "He's waitin for you now."

Mary turned and went into the hall and along it to the open door of the office, racking her brain to try and figure out what it was she'd done. Whatever it was, it had been enough to get Grace rucked up to the point where she couldn't think straight. She poked her head abruptly around the corner of the door and Russ looked up and saw her.

"Oh, yeah," he said. "I've been waiting for you to come in."

"Ma said there was something you wanted to see me about." Mary eyed him warily, wondering why he didn't look mad, too. Usually when there was something that got Grace that upset, Russ would be even more so; but now he just looked amused. He waved his hand, beckoning her over to the desk. Mary moved slowly across to him and saw for the first time what it was he had spread out on the desk-top.

"Oh," she said.

322

"Yeah." Russ glanced up at her curiously. "Seen these before?"

"I guess you know I have."

She had stiffened and stood glaring down at him as if their positions were reversed and he had been the one who should have been standing where she was. The look was enough to set Russ's hackles on end and he could feel his amusement fading out and a little ember of anger, caught from Grace, beginning to flame.

"What's the idea," he said evenly, "having pictures like this hidden around your room? Is that any kind of a picture to find in a girl's bedroom, I ask you?" He held up the water color of the sun bather and looked at it. Luckily it took all his attention, leaving him none to spare for the expression on Mary's face.

Staring down at her father's oblivious head, Mary felt—not for the first time, but for the first time strongly enough to feel it in words—that she would like to see him dead. The knowledge that he thought he was doing nothing wrong, that he felt he had a perfect right to invade her privacy like this, was physically painful to her and her face showed it for a second before she could control it, and after that it was as closed and as impersonal as ice.

When she didn't answer him, Russ looked up at her.

"Your mother's pretty upset about this," he said, trying hard to keep his irritation out of his voice. He might have succeeded if Mary had had the sense to keep quiet.

"I suppose neither of you ever thought I had the right to a little privacy," she said.

Russ's complete amazement showed. He opened his mouth, shut it again; and seeing his eyes begin to bulge a little, Mary knew she'd said the one thing she shouldn't have.

"Privacy, for the love of pete," Russ said loudly. "Whose house is this, anyhow? I'll tell you, my girl, there isn't a room in this house me nor your mother haven't got a right in and don't you go forgettin it. Anything that comes into this house is our business and I intend to see it stays that way, see?"

"I see all right." Mary turned and started for the door, but the tone of his voice was enough to stop her.

"Come back here," he said. "I haven't finished yet."

She stopped and turned around, but she didn't go back.

"I want to know what you mean by havin anything like this around."

"I don't see anything wrong with it."

"Well, if you don't, why was it hid way down in the bottom of a drawer? Why didn't you have it up on the wall if you never see anything wrong with it?"

"I knew if I did something like this would happen," Mary said. "It seemed easier to hide it."

"I should think so," Russ said, lifting his voice a little. "My lord, what kind of kids have I got, bringin indecency into their own home?"

Because there was no answer, Mary said nothing. But she was beginning to see what a fool she'd been to stand up to him as much as she had. If she hadn't, he'd been prepared to be amused and, because she couldn't keep her mouth shut, she'd precipitated his anger.

"I want an explanation and I want it mighty quick," Russ said. He tapped the offending picture with a long forefinger. "Where'd you get this piece of filth, anyhow?"

"That was the package that came Christmas," she told him stiffly.

"You mean somebody *sent* you a thing like this?"

She didn't answer until he leaned forward a little over the desk and glared up at her. Then she nodded dumbly.

"Who and why?" Russ said.

Mary clenched her jaw slightly, feeling her whole face take on a look of heavy sullenness and knowing that the look only infuriated him the more.

"A friend of mine sent it to me," she said. "A friend of mine who knew what I wanted to do."

For a second he didn't seem to understand what she'd just said and then his whole face sharpened suddenly. It was a change of expression that fascinated her into staring.

"What you wanted to do," he repeated. "Now I guess we're coming to it. Spose you tell me what it's all about."

She didn't know why she was saying all this. She'd given the whole thing up for good. But here she stood, her hands clenched, feeling as if this were the most important thing she'd ever said to him.

"I want to go away and study," she blurted suddenly. "I want to learn how to paint."

Russ went back in his chair with a crash that made her jump.

"For the love of a just god, you want to do what?"

"Paint. Paint."

He looked at her as blankly as if he'd never heard the word before and wouldn't recognize it if he heard it again.

"Well," he said, sitting up again, "I will be eternally condemned. Of all the cussed fool things I *ever* heard of, that's the cussedest. Are you standing there telling me I should give you my hard earned money just so you can go fiddle around with paints? Is that it?"

"Well, I don't know where I'll get it if you don't."

"I should like to know—" His voice went up a tone and Mary knew he hadn't even heard her. "If you can tell me, I should like to know just what sort of ideas you kids get into your heads about what money's for. Do you think I spent as much as I did seeing you get a high school education—and that's all you need for what you're good for—just so's I could put out more while you set around messing with paints?"

Mary shut her eyes for a second, holding back the words she might have said.

"Answer me," Russ roared.

"I don't know what you expect me to say to that."

She could feel her fingernails cutting into her palms and the sensation was the only thing that kept her from yelling back at him.

"Well, I should think not. It'd be a pretty thing, wouldn't it! Russ Walls's daughter going away to the city to learn to paint. Now, look," he said, suddenly softening his voice. "I've never said much to you, Mary, because you're a girl and I figured it was up to your Ma to keep you straightened out. But I guess I got to come to it. Here you are, twenty-one years old and you got a good boy interested in you." He hesitated a moment, wondering about Ralph. But he decided Ralph was the lesser of two evils. "That is, I guess he still is, ain't he? Well, I've got no objection to Ralph. Now, 1 just want you to get this foolishness out of your head and settle down like any girl would.

"See," he said reasonably. "You think it over and see if I'm not right. Once you got married and settled down, why you'd have plenty to keep you busy and you'd forget all about this silliness.

"Now, you go trotting off to the city and god know's what'll become of you. You couldn't support yourself. You don't know how."

"I won't do it," Mary said, her voice as cold as his had been a moment ago. "It's not foolishness and I won't do it."

She reached out suddenly to snatch the two pictures off his desk, but Russ saw what she was going to do and beat her to it. He brought his big hand down on the topmost one with a crash. Getting to his feet, he stood looking down at her, his eyes narrowed and the little lines of muscle at the corners of his lips white.

For a second they stared at each other across the desk-top, then Russ picked up the pictures.

"You won't, hanh?" he said. "Well, by the lord, I'll show you when I say a thing I mean it. You're still my daughter and what I say goes, see?"

326

Mary, seeing what he intended to do, said, "Please."

"It's a little late for that, ain't it?" he said coldly.

The mountings of the two pictures looked very white against the dark brown skin of his hands. He tore them across once, and then again, not looking down at what he was doing, keeping his eyes on her face.

"There," he said triumphantly, holding the pieces out to her. "There's my answer, Miss Lady. I want you to take this out in the kitchen and put it in the stove and I want you to do it so's your mother'll see you."

Mary reached numbly for the pieces and when Russ handed them to her, his fingers touched her skin and it was so cold it startled him. He glanced quickly at her face, but she wasn't looking at him; she was staring down at the remains of the pictures.

"I don't want to hear another word about it," Russ said, making each word round and heavy. "Not another word."

Grace looked up as Mary came into the kitchen and started to say something, but when she saw what it was Mary had in her hand, her mouth shut to on the words before they were out. Mary didn't look at her, but went directly across to the stove and shoved the heavy paper far down into the flames, poking it as deep as she could with the lid lifter. Then she went back across the kitchen as if Grace hadn't been there.

Watching her, Grace let out a sudden startled breath and then went quickly into Russ's office. She found him sitting behind the desk doing nothing, but he pretended to have been busy when he saw her.

"What did you say to her?" Grace said stiffly. "Why, her face looked like death when she came out to the kitchen."

"Say to her," Russ scowled. "I didn't say any more than you wanted me to, if you'll remember."

"Did you tear em both up?"

"Naturally."

"Well, I'm sort of sorry you tore the one with the tree,

too," she said slowly. "That was quite pretty and there wasn't anything in that you wouldn't want to be seen really."

"Oh, judast." Russ shrugged hugely. "I never in my born days saw the beat of a bunch of women. It's enough to drive a man crazy. Here I've gone and done what you got after me to do, and now you come sayin you wish I hadn't."

"All right," Grace said hastily. "I'm not sayin I wish you hadn't. I think you done just the right thing."

"Well, I should hope so," Russ said.

He sat frowning down at his papers until he heard her go out and then he sat there uncomfortably remembering Mary's face when he had torn the pictures.

WHEN she finished writing the last of the four letters, Mary straightened up with a sigh of relief. There, that was done and it was the last thing she could think of to do. That covered everything, there wasn't a loose end anywhere. And now she couldn't do anything but wait. She picked up the four envelopes, stacked them neatly between her fingers and stood them up against the base of the table lamp. For a moment she sat staring at the address on the top one, but when the words began to look queer to her, she stopped staring and got up stiffly.

The house was quiet now, but a glance at the old fashioned alarm clock, ticking away on her dresser, told her that it wasn't late enough. She went over to the window, putting her head against the glass, trying to look out, but the room behind her was too bright. The reflections in the black pool of the windowpane shut her in. Reaching over, she snapped out the light.

Her hands were shaking slightly when she put them on the window sill, but it was more reflex than any actual nervousness. She wasn't frightened any more; she felt detached, as if she were standing back watching herself and waiting, with a disinterested curiosity, to see what would happen.

Twenty-one years! You'd think in that time you might have put down roots in a place. But she'd lived here twenty-one years and it had taken exactly three hours to rub out every trace of her.

The night pressing up against her window began to make her feel as if there were something outside there, looking in at her; but when her eyes began to grow used to it, she saw that it really wasn't as dark as she'd thought. The wide fields of snow gave off a faint luminous light that had all the cold of phosphorus in water. The stars looked bright and low and big and they were bright enough to cast shadows across the snow. The shadow of the barn was an impenetrable mystery and the fingers of deep blue, whispering across the snow crust, were the branches of trees.

She could feel the cold coming in through the glass and it felt good against her face. From Russ's office window, below her and a little to the right, came a strong angle of yellow light that knifed across the darkness and stopped as suddenly as if the night had become a solid wall through which anything as soft as light couldn't penetrate. As she stood watching it, the darkness won and the light vanished. Soon afterwards she heard Russ come upstairs and pass her door.

She felt suddenly the way she had once a long time ago. They'd gone swimming at the lake early one evening, just after sundown, but before the full light had faded from the sky in the west. For a time they'd splashed around the float, shouting to each other, making a racket to hold back the night. Then Mary had climbed up for a last dive before coming out of the water and when she went under, she opened her eyes for the first time, expecting things to look as they always had, somehow expecting the slanting rays of sunlight to come down through the brown lake water as they always had before, forgetting that there wasn't any sunlight. The look of things, underwater, had turned dangerous, the deep green gloom, the furry dark square of the float, the strange distorted heavy look of things had been the most frightening thing she had ever seen.

She'd thrust her foot strongly against a rock, snatching it immediately away from any contact with this dead world, and shot to the top of water. While the others had kept on shouting around her, she'd sat shaking on the float, remembering the way it had been under water. And when she'd finally had to lower herself into it once more to swim ashore, it had been all she could do to keep from crying at the soft deceptive gentleness of the water against her skin.

The night outside the window had lost all its clarity and had taken on that underwater look that had terrified her so. And turning her back on it, quickly, she picked up the clock, set it, and thrust it under her pillow. Without undressing, she lay down on the bed, pulling the quilt up around her.

The clock exploded with a muffled whirr and Mary, sitting up in the darkness, had a moment when she couldn't think what was happening. Then she flung herself desperately on the pillow and fumbled for the clock, choking it finally. In the silence after its buzz had died, she sat holding her breath to see whether or not it had wakened anyone but her.

"Must have been softer than I thought," she muttered. Sitting there, she rubbed her hands together, trying to clear them of the thin film of sweat that shock and momentary terror had brought out on them. They were sticky with it, and felt dirty. She wiped them desperately on the blanket and then, before her resolution failed her, she got up and went quickly over to the door.

The house was quiet as she went down the hall toward the stairs. Stanny's door was partly open, and she could hear his heavy regular breathing, but there was no other sound anywhere.

After listening a moment, she went softly back to her room, changed her slacks for a heavy wool skirt, put on her coat and shut the small traveling bag she hauled out of the closet.

Then she straightened up and looked around the gray gloom of the bedroom. Her eyes, accustomed to the lack of light, took in the details of the little room, not because she thought she would never see it again, but merely to see if she'd forgotten anything.

The paler square of the four letters leaning against the lamp caught her eye and she sucked her breath in sharply. That would be all she needed, to go off now and forget them. She went over and picked them up, shuffling through to the last one. She was sure that was the right one, but she lit a match to make sure. It was. It had taken her five minutes to decide what to put on the envelope and, finally, she'd just written "Ma." She stood that envelope back against the lamp and stuffed the others into her coat pocket. Then, thinking how Grace would look when she found it, she almost picked that one up, too.

Before her hand could reach out and take it, she turned and went quietly out the door, pulling it to behind her. Downstairs at last, she took the bag out to the kitchen and left it there, turning back cautiously to the front hall. Outside the door of Russ's office, she stood listening again, feeling her own heart beating hard enough to shake her whole body.

My god, she thought, what if he should catch me now. There wouldn't be anything she could possibly say. There wouldn't be a thing. What would he do? she thought, her hand on the knob of the office door. It swung noiselessly away from her and she stepped into the little room. The smell of pipe smoke in the still air stopped her as if Russ himself had been sitting there waiting for her. For a moment she even had the feeling that he was. She shook her head angrily and went softly across the floor to the steel engraving that hung on the wall behind his desk.

What if he'd had it fixed, she thought then, trying to put obstacles in her own way. He might have had it fixed and not said anything about it. She hesitated there, almost ready to go back upstairs and go to bed. I should have waited to make sure. Maybe there's nothing in it. Maybe he used the money and hasn't had time to put it back yet.

What's the matter with you? She felt her lips form the words. This was a heck of a time to get cold feet.

Reaching up, she slid the picture a little to one side and felt the knob of the safe door cold against her shaking fingers. It opened easily and she thought with relief, Well, at least he never bothered to fix it. She reached into the safe and at the feel of the crisp edges of the bills, she felt so weak that she knew she hadn't really expected them to be there.

There were two packages, neat and tight, and she was afraid to light another match to see how much there was. She took them over to the window and stood holding them close to her eyes, trying to make out the figure. At last she traced out the two, five, o on one package and felt herself starting to shake again. All that money, she thought. My lord, what'll he do when he finds out? For a second she considered taking only half of it. Two hundred and fifty dollars was an awful lot of money, she thought; it seemed more to her than it actually was because she'd never held that much in her hand at one time. But it would go fast, she told herself, and before she could change her mind, stuffed both packages into her purse, snapped it shut, and turned back to the door.

Nervousness made her think it was already starting to get light, but it couldn't be yet. It wasn't more than three o'clock. The train left Freehold at six. That meant nearly two hours of waiting around and probably the station wouldn't be open.

She was beginning to feel sick to her stomach when she let herself out the entry door and went quickly across the frozen snow to Jake's old car. She had started to think of all the things that might happen even yet. What if it won't start, she thought. What'll I do then? She'd heard Stanny say just the other day that he'd started it up and it went like a watch, but anything might have happened since then.

She put her suitcase in the front seat, took off the stiff blanket that covered the radiator and started to throw it on the ground. Then, because that didn't seem quite right, she folded it and hung it carefully across the lowest limb of the old Red Astrakhan before climbing into the car.

The Ford was in gear and she worked the throttle twice, turned on the switch, and put her foot on the clutch, twisting the wheel until the car should have started down the little slope to the driveway of its own weight. Nothing happened.

Oh god, she thought frantically. What's the matter now? It had to start and it had to start the first time. There wasn't going to be any chance to come back and try again. She jerked strongly in the seat, trying to move the light car. Then for a moment, she sat clutching the icy wheel in her bare hands, her eyes closed, breathing hard. When she opened her eyes again, the frosty silvery cloud of her own breath in the cab made her jump. She reached for the brake, keeping one hand on the wheel, and when she found it before she'd expected to, she felt again that weak feeling of relief take her somewhere behind the knees.

She let the brake off quietly, and the car started forward, gaining momentum, until it reached the drive. She took her foot off the clutch and the sudden cough of the tinny engine made her breathe in sharply and clamp her foot down on the pedal. As the drive leveled out, the car started to slow a little and she couldn't face the grinding of the starter. Angrily, she let up on the clutch, clenching her teeth, hunching her shoulders against the noise of the motor. It caught, missed, caught again, and she swung the light car out of the driveway and up onto the tar.

When she was nearly out of sight of the house, she stopped and sat looking back at its huge bulk through the rear-view mirror. There was no sign of life and the darkness made it look bigger than it ever had before. Just to make sure, she got out and stood staring back. The mass of the old house looked implacable and smug, wrapped in its dark silence, and it made her shiver a little, thinking of all the things that might have happened to stop her, but hadn't.

When she climbed back into the car and drove away, she was thinking that it had been easier than she'd expected, she was thinking what a fool she'd been not to make certain everything was all right before she started out. When she thought of the things that might possibly have gone wrong, it turned her cold.

"I'm a fool for luck," she said softly.

By the time she reached the village, dark and deserted and like the gray ghost of a town, she'd begun to feel exhilaration crinkling along her nerve-ends. She stopped before the post office, slipped the three letters into the night box, and drove on, the blare of her lights the only sign of life. After the little car had labored up the hill and the sound of its engine died, the dark and the stillness surged in as if it had never passed at all.

IT WAS still dark when Grace and Russ came downstairs the next morning. Grace hated winter if only because it meant getting up before daylight; but Russ claimed he couldn't have slept later than five-thirty if somebody shot him at four.

"I'd wake up just the same," he'd say. "After five-thirty, I just lay there and roll around till it's time to get up."

Grace sat watching him eat for a moment getting pleasure from his pleasure, before she said, "Russ, I wish you or Stanny would take that old car of Jake's and put it somewhere where I don't have to stare at it all day long."

"I been thinking I'd sell it," Russ said, swallowing a mouthful of egg. "It's not worth much but I might get something for the junk value."

"Oh, I don't know. Somehow I don't like to sell it. Couldn't we just put it down back of the barn somewhere, where it wouldn't be cluttering up the yard so?"

"I spose so," he said, not really caring. "But I hate to think of it settin out there just rustin down when anyone might get a little out of it."

"You wouldn't get more than twenty or thirty dollars, would you? I should think you could afford to let that go."

"Oh, I don't care. I'll tell Stanny to put it around back."

He looked up at her, his expression a mixture of tenderness and exasperation. Sometimes he caught himself wishing that Grace would let go the way most women would have. If she'd settle down and have herself a cry and get it over with, she'd feel a lot better than she did. But she never had been one to let go like that. He could remember very few times when he'd seen her cry and when he stopped to think about it, it seemed to him that the things she'd chosen to cry about had been trivial.

Funny, he thought, some little thing most people wouldn't even notice would set her off. And now she couldn't cry about Jake. This was the first time she'd said his name since the afternoon of the funeral and now it was only to say something about his old car.

"Well," he said. "I'll tell Stanny when he comes down."

He could hear Stanny moving around in his room and presently he came slowly down the front stairs and appeared in the door looking hauled together and untidy, his hair standing on end and his unformed young face looking even looser and more without integration than it usually did. His grandfather was right behind him. He was having one of his silent mornings because he went over to the stove and poured his coffee as if there were nobody else in the room.

"Stan," Russ said, getting up from the table. "As soon as you finish your breakfast, go out and move Jake's car round back of the barn, will you?"

"Do it right now," Stanny said.

"You'll do nothin of the sort," his mother stopped him at the door. "You'll come back here and eat your breakfast. Come on, now, so's I can get cleared away."

"Oh, well." Stanny sighed and came back to the table. Grace watched him eat for a second, but she just couldn't stand it.

"For heaven sake, Stanny, how many times do I have to tell you not to gulp your food down that way? It won't do you any good at all, and besides it's not polite. For the lord sake, you're nearly fifteen years old, you ought to know how to behave yourself by now."

"Well, gosh, look at the time." Stanny cast a frenzied glance at the clock, "If I got to eat and do all the things anyone wants done around here, I have to hurry, don't I? My gosh, I can't fiddle away all my time. I don't want to have to walk way downtown this weather. If I don't hurry I'll miss the bus."

"If you'd stop talking and eat," Grace pointed out firmly. "Why, you wouldn't lose half the time you're wasting right now."

Nat stared sympathetically at Stanny and stuck his little finger out straight, hoping to make him laugh but Stanny's injury was too deep.

In silence, Stanny finished his breakfast, taking great pains to let Grace see how politely he was eating, and how slowly. When he'd finished, he piled his school books on the corner of the table, pulled his sweater on over his head, and went out. Grace heard him banging around in the entry as he wriggled into his wind breaker. Then he pulled open the outer door, but instead of going on out to the car, he turned and came back.

"What is it now?" she said patiently, as he came in.

"Hey." Stanny's eyes bugged out a little. "Jake's car's gone."

"Gone?" she echoed blankly. "Well, it can't be."

"Well, my lord," Stanny said. "I can certainly tell whether that car's out there or not, and it ain't."

"Isn't," Grace said mechanically. She went over to the window and stared out. Undeniably the car was gone. "Russ," she said, as if he could hear her. Leaving Stanny open-mouthed in the doorway, she went quickly in to the front room.

"Russ, Jake's car—"

"What about it?" He glanced up. "What's the matter? Can't the kid start it?"

"It's gone."

"Gone?" He sounded as blank as she had when she'd repeated the word after Stanny.

"It's not there."

"It was last night," Russ said.

"Well, it's certainly not now."

"Pete sake," he said. "Somebody must've stolen it. But I don't know why anybody'd take the risk for that junk heap."

He stopped suddenly and Grace, staring at him, thought she could read his mind. As if she didn't realize what she was doing, she put her hand up to stop the sudden jerking of the little muscle at the corner of her mouth. All at once she remembered another morning and another missing car. Russ got up slowly and came over to her.

"Go up and see if she's in her room," he said. "Anyone might have stole that car, sittin there the way it was."

Grace didn't answer him. She went heavily out to the foot of the stairs, but she couldn't seem to make herself start up them. Russ was standing in the door watching her and she looked piteously at him.

"Russ, I can't. You go."

"All right."

He went past her and up the stairs two at a time. She just stood and waited after his big figure passed out of sight. She heard him open Mary's door and then there was only silence and she stood hoping it might be because he'd closed the door behind him and she just couldn't hear what he was saying.

When he came in sight again he was walking slowly, turning something over and over in his big hands. She could see it was an envelope as he started down the stairs and it made his hands look large and brown.

"What is it?" She tried to speak in her natural tone, but the words came out in a whisper.

"Well, I guess it's for you," he said uncomfortably. He tore the end off the envelope, read the single sheet inside hastily and passed it down to her. Feeling his eyes on her, Grace could hardly make herself read the short note. When she'd finished it, she looked up at him again, blindly, and as if she wasn't quite sure he was standing there.

"Wait," Russ said. "I'll see if it's true."

He went by her and along to the office. Unable to stay where she was alone, Grace followed him and stood in the door watching him push aside the familiar old steel engraving. He pulled open the safe door and peered into the dark hole.

"Ayep," he said. "It's gone. Every penny of it."

"I—I never thought one of them would steal."

"By the lord," Russ said. He stared at her in complete angry bewilderment. "Grace, what ailed those kids? Can you tell me that? What was wrong with em?"

He saw that Grace wasn't listening to him. She stood looking down at the sheet of paper in her hand.

"My lord," she said softly. "I'm glad she took it from you, if she had to steal. I'm glad she did it that way."

"Does that make it any better?" he said loudly, his eyes wide with rage. "Stealin's stealin, any way you look at it. By god, it's lucky for her she never said where she was going.

I'd haul her back here quicker'n I can wink. She knew it, too. That's why, if you'll notice, she never said where she was going."

"Where is there for her *to* go?" Grace's lips felt stiff and she had to make a separate effort over each word. "I don't see where she could possibly go."

"I dunno," Russ shrugged. He turned to his desk, and Grace saw that he intended to put Mary out of his mind just as cleanly as he had put Gene and Jake. "I don't know where she went and I care less. But all I got to say is, she better not show around here again. If she ever comes back here thinking we'll take her in—well, I hope she tries it!"

He slammed his fist down on the old desk.

"Just let her try it," he said heavily.

Grace turned and left him. When she came back into the kitchen, Stanny was standing by the door, still, but he was breathing hard, as if he'd been moving fast.

"Was you in there listening to us?" His mother looked at him sharply.

Stanny's eyes slid easily away from her hard stare.

"No, I been right here," he said. "I been wondering what to do. If I don't hurry, I'll miss the bus, and then I'll have to walk."

"All right," Grace said. "Get along with you."

"But where's Jake's car?" Stanny eyed her curiously. "What happened? Someone take it?"

"Nemmind about Jake's car," Grace said. "Just don't worry your head about things that don't concern you."

"Okay." Stanny picked up his books. "I was just wonderin, that's all."

He went out whistling, and Grace went to the door to watch him down the drive. She stood there, poised to duck back into the house if he should turn and see her. But somehow she felt as if she had to watch him. Now he's the last one, she thought, and felt as if he might vanish before her eyes. He's the last one of my kids I've got left.

She nearly called after him, just to make him turn and wave to her, but didn't; and when he crossed the road and stood there waiting for his bus, she dodged back quickly so he wouldn't see her and know she'd been watching him. When she came back into the kitchen, she needed somebody to talk to but her father had gone. His empty coffee cup stood there on the table—except for that, he might never have been in the room.

The mailman stopped at her box so seldom that Hat, when she saw him stuff something into it that morning, didn't wait to put on her coat. She thrust her arms through the ragged sleeves of her old gray sweater and went, bare headed and bare handed, down the path to the mailbox.

It was one of those cold clear frosty mornings when winter smelled every bit as good as spring to her. And though it was so cold, it was one of those days that gave her strength to believe the winter would be over soon. Somehow, on days like this, everything looked gentle, almost soft, although the cold was buttoned in over the countryside like a blanket. But there was something as elusive as a feeling, something that might have been no more than a breath in the still air. It made her feel as if maybe the earth under the snow had begun to get warm and was giving off a thin elusive odor almost like that of plowed land.

There was only one letter in the box and she took it out, turning it over to find out who it was from; but the only writing on it was her own name and address.

"Hmph," she said aloud, realizing that she'd started to talk to herself lately. "Probly nothin but a bill and I come traipsin all the way down here to the road after it."

It wasn't a bill and she knew it because she had never in her life run a bill anywhere. But it amused her to wonder, before she opened it, what it might be. It was a rare enough occurrence when she got mail and she liked to draw out the pleasure as far as she could.

Holding the unopened letter in her hand, she went slowly back up the path toward the house, noticing the way the young spruces were beginning to grow out from the edge of the woods. She could remember the time when, from the back porch here, she could look down across the fields, through the thin young growth, to the village; but these last years it seemed as if the whole field had sprung up suddenly until she could see only as far as the edge of her own potato piece. The snow, now, seemed to make the little trees stand out more. In the summer, with green beneath them, too, they blended back against the larger trees, and you didn't notice them coming; but in winter with nothing to hide their advance, they made her feel as if they'd take another quick stride toward the house when she turned her back.

It was like a game they'd played when she was a girl. She'd forgotten the name of it, Giant Steps, or something like that, she thought. Whoever was It, stood with his back to a row of players and counted twenty. During the count, the others were supposed to get as close to home as they could; but if the person who was It, turned at the end of the count and caught anyone moving, the incautious player was forced to go back to the beginning. And the way the spruces crept up on her made her think of it now.

"I spose I ought to have them cleared out," she said, tapping the letter thoughtfully against her large front teeth. She stared idly at the little trees. "I won't yet, though," she decided, her hand on the latch of the back door. "They're real pretty. It's a cussed shame to go rootlin them out."

She put her letter down on the freshly washed oilcloth-covered table where she could see it as she went back and forth. She wouldn't open it till she got her housework done and got ready to have her dinner. It would give her something to look forward to. Maybe it would be something exciting and nice when she did open it.

When she came downstairs at eleven-thirty to get her dinner, the delivery truck from Parson's Grocery was just hauling up to the door. She went to hold it open while the shockheaded boy brought in her carton of groceries.

"Set it down right over there on the chair," she directed, and went over to check through the list with him to be sure nothing had been forgotten. When she'd made sure everything was just as she'd ordered it, she went slowly to the cupboard and took down the pewter teapot.

"How much does it come to, this time?"

"Lessee." The boy consulted a slip in his notebook, carefully, the tip of his pink tongue showing a little. "That's three-fifty-seven."

Hat counted out the exact change into his hard young hand, doling out the last two pennies. When he'd gone, she stood there, the teapot in her hand, staring into it as if by the mere force of her eyes she could make its contents multiply. There'd been ninety-seven dollars there last fall and she'd been sure it was enough to take her through until she could start earning for herself; but the way it dwindled away under her fingers was beginning to scare her. It scared her when she stopped to think about it, so she didn't very often. But sometimes it crept up on her and then she found herself devising schemes, some of them wild enough to make her smile, others not so wild but uncommonly unpleasant to think about. There was one, tucked away in the back of her mind, that seemed about the most sensible thing she could think of to do. But whenever she found herself coming back to it, she could feel herself shy off again, knowing what people would say, what Grace would say, if she ever tried to do anything of the sort.

"Nemmind," she said, putting the teapot back on the shelf and going hastily over to the table. This was certainly the time to read her letter. Maybe it'd take her mind off her troubles.

She stuck a stub of pencil under the flap of the envelope and ripped it untidily open, pulling out the two folded sheets of paper. She never looked at the signature of a letter first for the same reason she wouldn't have thought of reading the end of a book first. But she always went so fast in the first reading to get to the end and find out who the letter was from or how the book ended, that she never made a great deal of sense out of it and had to go back and re-read it after she was satisfied that she hadn't cheated.

"There, for the land sake, Mary," she said, and went back to find out just what it was Mary'd had to write her a letter about.

Her second reading, slower and more careful, was punctuated with nods of agreement and small exclamations of pleasure. She read the postscript twice. It said, You can have any of the pictures I left there, if you want them.

"Well," Hat said. "I'll bet it *did* do some good, me talking to her that day. I'll miss her," she said. "But she'll be better off."

Think of that, she thought, her wanting me to have them pictures. She went happily out to the little room in the shed and got the two pictures she'd decided long ago were her favorites. Bringing them back into the kitchen, she stood for a moment wondering where to put them. She didn't cotton to the idea of putting them in the parlor because that meant she wouldn't be able to see them without going out of her way. She wanted them where she could enjoy them whenever she happened to look up. Finally, not without a sigh of regret, she took down the big Columbian Rope calendar over the kitchen table, and getting her hammer from the trash drawer, proceeded to nail the two small canvases up in its place.

If she's got the nerve, Hat thought, standing back to look

343

at her paintings, to go away like that with nothing to go on, then I guess I got the nerve to do what I've got to. I will. Yessir, the next time Pa comes up, I'll talk to him about it. Grace can say what she wants to, it won't make a mite of difference. Then it occurred to her that Grace didn't have to know what she was going to do until it was done. She grinned, thinking she'd certainly taken a leaf out of Mary's book. Well, that was the only way to get things done, just don't tell anyone till it's all over.

ON HIS way home that night, Aaron stopped at the mailbox and, as he went up the drive, fighting the jerk of the wheels in the frozen ruts, the mail lay on the seat beside him. He didn't bother to look at it until he got into the house. Then he stood, shivering a little in the cold kitchen, sorting out the ads from anything that might be worth opening. The two letters for Ralph he threw on the table, the three ads, one from a patent medicine company, one from a book agent, and the third from a man who had some miraculous tulip bulbs, he put on the top of the dead stove. His own letters he thrust into his hip pocket.

He went over to the wood-box and picked over the kindling carefully, choosing three or four soft pine sticks. Then he stood by the stove whittling one side of each stick into thin shavings that he didn't quite detach from the stick. He laid the fire carefully, using the three circulars for tinder.

He'd thought when he went out this morning that the fire might hold through the day. There was nothing he hated more than coming into a cold house at night, with no fire and no sign of food. You could certainly tell, with one glance at this kitchen, it'd been a long time since a woman had been inside it. Somehow things seemed to get in a hell of a clutter.

It wasn't dirt, it was just things lying around. It was a lot easier, at the moment, to put a thing down wherever you were when you stopped using it. That way you'd know where it was when you wanted it again. But his system broke down, because when he went back to find whatever it was he'd been using, he discovered he'd used a lot of other things since in the same place, and there was always a pile of culch to paw through before he could find what he'd started out for in the beginning.

He hadn't realized, until he'd started trying to do for himself, how much of a comfort it was to have a woman around the place, if only for the picking up she did. He could remember how he'd teased Annie about being poison neat, how he'd told her he could never lay a hand on a thing when he wanted it because she followed him around picking things up and putting them away where nobody'd ever think of looking for them. But now he was beginning to see why she'd done it.

Gosh, he thought ruefully, standing there waiting for the roar of the fire to tell him it was time to put in the heavy wood, I don't know but what I'll have to get married again. Ralph wasn't any help. Last night he had been sitting beside the sewing machine in the warm corner near the stove, greasing his high hunting boots. Aaron hadn't seen him doing it, but there were the boots beside the chair, their tops lying over limply; there was the round can of grease, its cover with the moose head on it, half put back, right on top of the pile of sweaters one of them had left lying limply over the leaf of the machine.

After he'd got the fire going, he went over and picked up the grease can, put its cover on securely, and put it away carefully in the drawer where they kept shoe polish and machine oil. Then, feeling virtuously that he'd made a step in the right direction, he got the potatoes and put them on to boil, shoving the teakettle forward on the stove so it'd be ready to make tea when Ralph got home.

He was sitting in the other room looking at the paper when Ralph came in. He heard him go over to the table and put something down. Then there was a silence while Ralph must be looking at the letters. Aaron could hear the slight sound of paper tearing, and he got up and came out into the kitchen.

"Hi." Ralph looked up from the letter he was reading. "I got us some hamburg for supper. How d'you want it?"

"Anyway that's easiest," Aaron said. "Anyway you like it."

"Fix it in a minute," Ralph said. He looked down at the letter. "Pa," he said suddenly, and the unaccustomed rough sound of his voice made Aaron jump.

"Somethin wrong?" He glanced sharply at Ralph.

"My girl friend's skipped out on me." Ralph looked up at him, his wide face pale and a little puzzled. "She's gone away."

"Mary?" Aaron stared.

"She don't even say where she's goin." Ralph looked hurt. "All it says is she's goin away. You'd think she'd say where."

"Probly didn't want Russ to find out where." Aaron went over and poked uselessly at the fire so he wouldn't have to watch Ralph. "That's too bad, kid. I'm sorry."

"So'm I," Ralph said. He couldn't seem to understand what he'd just read and when his father looked at him, he was reading the letter again. "If it got tough," Ralph said, "she knew all she had to do was come to me. I'd have fixed things up somehow. It would have been all right. She didn't have to go away like that."

"Maybe she wanted to," Aaron suggested.

"But where'll she go?" Ralph said, suddenly, his voice thinning out. "She won't have any place to go. My god, what'll happen to her?"

"Don't you worry," Aaron said easily. "She's a nice girl, but she's a Walls and they always land on their feet."

Ralph put the letter down carefully on the table.

"That's all you can think of, isn't it. I don't believe you've let it out of your mind for one minute what Russ did to you. I believe you been stewin it over all these years.

"Well, hell," he said helplessly. He reached down and touched the letter with one finger. "I wish she'd a told me what she was goin to do. Maybe I could've helped. I would, too," he said fiercely as if his father had denied it. "I'd a done anythin she wanted me to, see?"

He went across the kitchen hastily, as if he'd thought of something he had to do, and Aaron heard his feet pounding up the back stairs.

Well, he thought, it's too bad. That's what it is. He took the spider out of the warming oven and put it on the back of the stove. Might's well start the hamburg, he thought. He'll be back down and hungry as soon's he smells it.

WITHOUT thinking, Grace poured out Nat's tea right along with the others—she'd been doing his separately for so long she nearly did it from habit—but she missed today. She'd been thinking about other things, anyhow—and she found a lot of things to think about nowadays. Somehow, a woman standing helplessly by watching her own children go away from her, found a lot to think about. She did a lot of wondering about whether or not she'd brought them up right. Maybe it would have been better, as Mary'd said, if she and Russ hadn't given them everything they wanted. But it seemed to her from the first minute Gene had been born, her whole life had been nothing but a planning and a devising of ways to get the kids something they wanted or something that would please them.

In the beginning that obtaining had involved a good deal of scraping around and pinching a penny here and a penny there.

347

In later years, she'd been able, thank goodness, to give them things without denying herself, but thinking back, she wasn't sure it hadn't been more fun when she'd had to go without things for herself to give them something. Of course, the kids themselves didn't appreciate it and they were certainly proving it to her now; but it had meant a good deal to her.

She could say with satisfaction that her kids had never wanted for anything, not once in all their lives had they ever asked her for anything she hadn't been able to squeeze out for them—when she saw sense in the request. She'd never bothered with the foolish little fads they had, she'd figured all kids had those streaks of wanting this or that just because they saw another kid with the coveted article.

There was another thing about her children too, that had always given her a good deal of satisfaction and that was that none of them had ever worn hand-me-down clothes. Her own childhood had been a misery to her because of the hand-me-downs. Hat had always been bigger than she was, although Hat was younger. And Grace, even as a child, had been so fastidious that the idea of wearing anyone else's old clothes had made her miserable. She'd always been sure that people recognized Hat's outgrown dresses, even though her mother had always taken great pains about making them over. They were, and always had been, Hat's clothes and she'd never felt at home in them. None of her kids had ever worn so much as a shirt that hadn't been his when it was new and his until it wore out.

She could still remember how discouraging it had been to try and dress Mary up. It seemed to Grace that Mary's whole growing up had been a battle between them about the clothes she'd wear. Grace would go without a new dress herself to get some pretty little frilly thing for Mary, just the thing a girl would be tickled pink to have—all doshed out with little ribbons and sprigs of flowers and lovely to look at. Mary would start off in the morning looking like something right out of the catalog. But when she got home at night it was a different story. Grace, looking up from whatever she happened to be doing, would see Mary's head poking fearfully around the corner of the door, just the top of her head as far as her eyes; and the eyes would look apologetic and a little scared. Grace would know immediately that something had happened to the new dress, something that would be pretty impossible to repair.

At first she thought Mary did it on purpose—it hurt her to think one of the kids would do a thing like that, deliberately destroy something she'd gone to a good deal of pains to get for him. But after a while she began to realize it wasn't purposeful destruction—it was a sort of inspired thoughtlessness and lack of care. Mary just never stopped to think about her clothes, she always bulled it right ahead and did what she wanted to, whether it was playing ball or stealing apples and neither one was a pastime that kept clothes in good repair. Grace had tried—she'd tried hard. She used to take Mary in and stand her in front of the large mirror in her bedroom.

"There," she'd say. "I want you to stand there and take a good look at yourself. I want you to look at that nice new dress I put on you right out of the box this morning."

Mary, speechless with horror at the realization, would stand looking in silence until her lack of speech made Grace want to grab her and shake until she said something, anything.

"I want you to tell me," she'd say, holding her patience, it seemed to her, with both hands. "I want you to think of what you looked like when you went off to school this mornin, and I want you to tell me what you'd do to any little girl who was as careless with her lovely new clothes as you are."

Mary wouldn't say anything, but Grace would see the large tears beginning to form in the corners of her dark eyes and somehow the sight of them made her want to make the child cry. Perversely it satisfied something inside her, if Mary would only cry.

"I want to tell you," she'd say. "I wanted a new dress myself and I needed one, too. But I didn't think of myself. I
don't go out much and I can get along. So I denied myself to
get you that lovely new dress and look what you've done to
it and now neither one of us is any better off."

"Well, I never meant to do it." Mary's voice would shake
a little.

"You never meant to! I should hope not. It's just that
you're a bad careless girl and you never think of anythin but
yourself and your own pleasure. You never think of the way
your poor mother and father work and slave to give you
pretty clothes so you won't be ashamed when you go to
school—how we scrimp to keep you kids looking decent. No,
all you thing about is doin some foolish thing that comes into
your head.

"And that's another thing. I don't see what fun a little girl
gets out of goin stealin apples with a gang of boys. In the first
place, it's rough and rowdy and not for ladies to do. In the
second place, it's not honest. Stealin! Is that the way I've
brought you up?"

"No." The tears had started falling now.

"I should hope not," Grace would say. "I should certainly
hope not. Why won't you be mother's little lady and play
with nice little girls. Why, when I was a girl, I used to spend
hours playin house. I'd get my dolls and dress and undress
them by the hour and be perfectly happy. Why won't you
act like that? Why do you always have to be runnin off with
a gang of boys?"

Mary, by this time, would be capable of only a sort of
choking gulp.

"There," Grace would say. "Now, stop your cryin. I
haven't said anythin to make you cry. I'm just tryin to impress on you what it means when you ruin your clothes like
this. Money doesn't grow on trees and you keep it in mind.
If I didn't think so much of you, big as you are, I'd give you

the trouncing of your life. And I will next time. Now, you go take that dress off and I'll see what I can do with it. But when I get it fixed, you're going to keep it for good. You can just wear your old dresses until you learn how to take care of the good ones."

But it never seemed to do any good and they were all alike. She could talk to the boys, too, until she was blue in the face and it never seemed to have a mite of effect on them. They'd turn around five minutes later and do the same thing all over again.

There had been one Christmas when things had been pretty tight. Lobsters had been scarce all winter and just before Christmas, Russ's old engine had let go. He'd been expecting it for weeks, but it finally let go just before Christmas and he came home to tell her it'd take two hundred dollars to fix the old kicker up and all they'd had that year between them and starvation was two hundred and fifty. Grace remembered getting out the bankbook and sitting up nearly all one night trying to figure out how she could wangle some sort of a Christmas for the kids. Russ had shaken his head when she had asked him what he thought.

"That engine's got to be fixed if we want to eat this winter. That'll leave us just fifty dollars and I don't dare take any of that for Christmas. We'll just have to tell them things are tight this year and there won't be any Christmas. They're old enough to realize how things are."

"Kids are never old enough to realize that about Christmas," Grace had said. "I don't know but what I'd rather take the money and give them a good one this year than I would see it get poured back into that cussed engine. Seems to me that boat takes every penny extra that comes into this house."

"Well, you can choose between that and starvin," Russ said angrily. "Personally, I'd rather see them with their bellies full any day in the week than give them a lot of junk they'll just bust up the day after and then have em go hungry for the next six months."

"Well, I don't know."

"Oh, lord," he said with rough tenderness. "I know you'd rather starve than disappoint those kids in anything."

"Well, yes, I don't know but I would."

"All I got to say is, it's a good thing you got me around to handle things. Because I'd rather eat. Now, you just tell them that it just can't be managed this year."

"I take notice," Grace said tartly. "You always leave it to me to tell them the unpleasant things."

In the end, though, he'd taken the two hundred dollars and had the old engine patched up. Grace had looked at the bankbook a long time before putting it away in the desk drawer with a sigh. Russ was right, of course, they couldn't draw out their last fifty dollars just for a thing like Christmas. But, by Christmas Eve, she hadn't managed to tell the kids and she'd found Jake going through her bedroom closet apprehensively. He'd wanted a tricycle. He wanted it badly. And he couldn't find any packages at all. As far as he could see, there was nothing at all in the line of Christmas presents hidden anywhere.

At the age of eight, Jake had one of the fattest reddest faces she'd ever seen on a little boy; but it was the worried look that got to her. He went out of the room past her without a word, but she'd stepped to the door a moment later and there he was in the hall, looking back at her, his face a pucker of worried wrinkles.

It was three o'clock then and the bank closed at three-thirty. But that was before they'd moved up on the Ridge and she had just time to get there and draw out the last fifty dollars before the window closed. She took it all, leaving just two dollars to hold the account open.

To this day she couldn't forget the look on Russ's face when he'd come in the door and seen the things there under the big tree waiting for morning. He'd been late getting in that night and it was nine o'clock before he got home and the kids had been tucked away for an hour. She'd just finished putting the things under the tree and Jake's tricycle stood there in all its glory.

The sudden change in the quality of the silence in the house had made her look up to see Russ standing there in the door behind her. For a moment she thought he was going to smash the whole thing. He looked as if he wanted to. He hadn't, though.

But on Christmas Day, he got up and went out before anyone else was stirring, as if it had been any day, and had been gone until late that night. Grace hadn't cared, though. It had been worth every bit of it to see the kids's faces when they came down that morning and found the tree waiting. Jake, particularly, had looked relieved.

Two days after Christmas, she remembered now, he'd left the tricycle alongside the road and Jay Turner's wood truck ran over it and smashed it flat. Jake hadn't cried, but Grace had.

Now, though, she was glad she'd done it. Whether it had been right or wrong didn't matter now. Every bit of it she was glad she'd done.

She'd got thinking back over the things she'd done for the kids and how careless they'd always been, and she got so engrossed she forgot that her father couldn't bear his tea scalding from the teapot the way she and Russ liked theirs. So she filled his cup full and Nat, expecting that she'd remembered to cool it off as she always did, got a good swallow of it before he realized.

He uttered a strangled squawk and let go of his cup. At the crash, Russ stopped eating with his fork in midair, and stared. Nat, clutching his throat with both hands, got up and started for the door.

"My lord," Grace said, aghast. "I clean forgot to cool his tea off for him."

"Yes." Nat turned in the doorway and stared at her balefully. He gasped for air once or twice and pointed a trembling finger at her. "You must want to see me dead before my time. It's a little enough I ask you to do for me and you can't even remember to do that."

"I'm sorry, Pa," she said smoothly, trying to calm him.

"Sorry!" He snorted twice, loudly.

"Calm down, Nat," Russ said. "Accidents'll happen."

"I wish I was as sure as you are it's an accident," Nat howled. "I think she's tryin to drive me out. She's tired of havin me around. Tryin to drive me out. I got a good mind to go off and live with Will Hutchins."

"Go on, you old fraud," Russ said. "You know you an Will ain't said a civil word to each other for twenty years."

"Well, I know what to expect from him," Nat scowled. "When he goes stabbin you in the back, you ain't surprised. An it'd be better livin with him—no women around."

Grace started to get up to go to him, but Nat waved his hand at her.

"No, no," he said testily. "I'll go off somewhere until I stop bein on fire. I'd rather be alone. I don't want you to go puttin yourself out none for me." He stumped off into the other room and a moment later they could hear him going slowly up the stairs.

Russ jerked his head, grinning.

"He waited in there to see if you was comin," he said to Grace.

"I know he did." She stared ruefully after her father. "I'm real sorry it happened. I always try to remember and I usually do. I got thinkin about something else, I guess."

"Well," Russ said, a little testily. "I don't know's there's any need for his actin like a baby when you *do* forget. After all, he isn't the star boarder, is he?"

He reached over and picked up Nat's empty cup gingerly by the rim. The handle had broken off when the old man dropped it.

"No need for him to go smashin up the china either, is there?"

"Oh, nemmind it, Russ," she said. "It's an old cup."

"Humph," Russ said grumpily. "He sure made a devil of a mess of things. Enough to make you lose your appetite. Look at that place!"

Grace said "Ts," and went to get the dishcloth. Russ waited until she'd taken away Nat's plate and sopped up the spilled tea, before he said, "Guess your whole family's acting a little queer."

Grace stopped suddenly and looked at him.

"I don't know what you mean. You know Pa always acts like that when I forget about his tea."

"Oh, I didn't mean him only. I was thinkin about this latest thing of Hat's."

"Hat?" Grace said, giving the impression that she said the word carefully. Russ hadn't mentioned Hat's name since he'd told Grace that she'd refused to come down and live with them. Grace had taken pains not to mention it herself, because he'd seemed so upset by Hat's refusal. Now his amused blue eyes gave her pause, wondering just what was in the wind.

"Thought maybe you knew about it," Russ said.

"Whatever it is, I don't. Hat ain't been near me for months now. I haven't seen her since last fall."

"Things must be gettin kind of slim with her," Russ said thoughtfully. He reached over with his fork and speared a couple of the fried potatoes in the dish and ate them. Watching him, Grace could see that he was watching her, although he didn't seem to be looking at her.

Seeing that she wasn't going to ask him any questions, Russ fished into his pocket, brought out his billfold, fumbled around in it maddeningly, and finally passed her a folded sheet of ordinary white paper.

"That was up in the post office," he said. "Been there near a week, I guess. Everyone who'd be interested must have seen it by now, so I took it down to show you. I figured you'd like to know what kind of a rig she's runnin up there since the old lady died."

Grace took the sheet of paper as if he'd handed her a snake and she didn't like snakes. She squinted at it hopelessly and then gave up and went to get her glasses from their usual place on the shelf in the dining room.

"I swear I'm gettin blinder'n a bat," she muttered, half to herself, coming back into the kitchen. She put the glasses carefully in place and the instant she let go of the bows, they slid down on her nose. It made it necessary for her to tilt her head back slightly to see at all.

"Auction Sale," she started to read aloud, but after the secon word, her voice faded off and she read through the rest of the hand-printed sheet silently, with her lips moving slightly over each word. When he'd read it through, she put it down on the table, flat, and looked up at Russ as if she thought he'd been fooling her.

"Russ Walls! That thing has never been up in the *post office*."

"It has. For the last week." Russ nodded.

"For the lord sake," Grace said. Her mouth fell open slightly and she sat staring at him as if he'd turned into a complete stranger right there before her eyes. "I—I—my lord, Russ, what's she up to now?"

"God only knows." Russ shrugged and got up to go over and peer into the stove. He took a stick of the well-cured birch from the wood-box and pounded it into the stove with the lid-holder, before he turned to look at her again. "When single women get to be Hat's age," he said pontifically—and Grace knew if he hadn't been talking about her blood relation, he'd have said "old maid"—"I suppose anyone's got a right to expect all sorts of queer actions from them."

"But—Hat's never been queer."

"That's no sign, is it, she can't begin now? I have always said it warn't good for her, livin there in that great ark of a house all alone with nobody to keep her company but that sick old woman. Time and time again I've said to you, right in this room, Grace, she ought to get married. Why, she should of married years ago and had kids as big as yourn by now if she'd done the right thing." He stopped to see if she were going to say anything more, but Grace's complete amazement held her silent.

"It's not as if she never had the chance, either," Russ said. "There was a time, years ago, when she could have had Bill Martin—all she ever had to do was wink. And look where she'd be now, sittin right in a butter tub."

"Well, you know how she felt. She never felt it'd be right for us both to run off and leave Ma alone. Course, there was Pa, but he never was much good around. And I *did* get married and out of it."

"That's no excuse. If she'd taken Bill and you married to me, why, we all could of chipped in and hired somebody to take care of your mother as long as she lived. Might even have had her to live with one of us. I'd a been willin. I never give anyone the chance to say to me I was willin to neglect my duty, and I would a considered that a duty."

"For the lord sake," Grace said again. She could feel her mind going round in circles and always coming back to the same place.

"Yup," Russ said heartily. He thrust his hands into his pockets and rose slightly on his toes. "There's no question about it. Take women livin alone like that, they get to be queerer than Dick's hatband. I wouldn't be surprised to see her go crazy, sooner or later."

"Fiddle-diddle," Grace said sharply, stung into active cham-

357

pionship of Hat. "You know as well as I do, Russ, there never was a saner person than Hat. If she's crazy, it happened in the last few weeks and people don't go crazy like that. No, if she's doing anything like this, there's an almighty good reason for it and I'm going to find out what it is."

"I would if I was you," Russ said. His face looked sober, but Grace knew him well enough to realize that he was getting a good deal of amusement out of her confusion. "Why, there's no knowin what people will think if she starts carryin on like this."

"What I can't understand is—" Grace started to ignore him. "What on earth has Hat got to sell." She picked up the handbill again and sat looking at it. "Household goods, furniture, hand-hooked rugs." Each word, as she read it off, sounded like a word she'd never heard before, a word Hat might have invented for all it meant to Grace.

"Sounds to me," Russ said thoughtfully. "Sounds to me like she's sellin everything but the house right out from under her."

"Why, this thing isn't anything but an invitation to every pokin tom, dick, and harry who wants to, to go in there and have a good look at everything," Grace said suddenly, realizing for the first time what the bill meant. "Why, my lord, there's people in this town'd give their eyeteeth for a chance like that at anyone else's house. Why, I don't see what she's thinkin of, I don't see how she can stand it."

She looked down at the paper and saw that her hand was shaking.

"Why, she must be goin to work and sellin every one of them lovely hooked rugs mother made during her last years. And that beautiful old oak furniture! If she ever sold that, I'd never forgive her. Besides, she hasn't any right to sell those things. They're half mine."

Russ, who had heard her say time and time again if she had to stay under the same roof with that oak furniture one year longer than she had she'd have gone crazy, lifted one eyebrow

358

and said nothing. Grace herself had forgotten completely that she'd ever said she couldn't see how Hat lived with it without screaming.

"Some of that stuff is heirlooms," Grace told him. "I planned on seeing it handed down in the family. Well, that settles it. I'm going right up there and see what ails her. Why, she must be out of her mind!"

"Ayep," Russ said.

"When is it she plans on making a fool of herself? Grace verified the date. "Why, it's this very afternoon. I should think you might have told me about it sooner so's I could have stopped her in time. I believe you didn't on purpose. You just wanted her to go ahead and see what happened."

"No. No, I never—" Russ tried hard to keep his face straight. "I knew perfectly well, if I just told you about it, you'd never believe it and I didn't want to take the poster down for fear Hat'd find out about it. There I was, between two fires. So I figured the best way to do was the way I did."

"Humph." Grace could put more meaning into a disgusted snort than anyone he knew. "Well, I'll never believe that, anyhow, Russ Walls. I guess I've lived with you long enough to know how you work. You just did it to get me rucked up at the last minute, so I'd go boilin up there. Well, all right. That's just what I'm goin to do."

"Well, you hurry up and I'll wait and take you up before I go downtown."

"You won't do anything of the sort," Grace said snappily. "You've had all the fun out of this you're going to get. You needn't think I want you around when I talk to her. The lord knows what you said to her the other time you was up there. She hasn't been near me since and I haven't heard a peep out of her."

"All right." Russ shook his head—a man who could not understand the way a woman's mind worked. "All right. I'm perfectly willing to stay out of it. I'll go along, I guess."

359

"I guess you better," Grace said. She got up from the table, clutching Hat's notice tightly. Her wide cheeks were bright with suppressed anger and her eyes flashed behind the sliding glasses. "I guess it'd be better for all of us if you just forgot about the whole thing. Hat's my sister and I'll talk to her when there's any talking to be done hereafter."

"All right," Russ said again.

He enjoyed the spectacle of her anger so much that he wouldn't even let what she was saying get under his skin. He knew quite well that she considered him in some way responsible for this second-hand invasion of her privacy and he would have felt completely justified in making a point of it; but he didn't want to take her attention off Hat. He wanted things to carry through the way they'd started, just for the fun of seeing what would happen. He vanished strategically into the front room and sat there while she cleaned up the kitchen. He heard her go up the stairs fifteen minutes later and the sound of her steps moving about in their bedroom directly above his head kept him pretty well posted as to what she was doing.

Finally he heard her coming down again. Getting up, he went softly over to the hall door and was standing there when Grace reached the foot of the stairs. She stopped on the bottom step and stood looking at him silently. For a moment Russ stared back, then he grinned a little.

"My lord," he said. "You certainly are a fine looking woman when you get togged out like that."

"All right," she said shortly. "I ain't in any mood to put up with your foolishness this afternoon, Russ."

He kept on grinning but said nothing more and she went on by him and out the door, closing it behind her with a slam that shook the glass panes in the long sidelights. Russ formed a whistle, but kept it to a mere whisper of sound. He went back into the front room so he could watch her out the window. She was going down the drive like a full-rigged ship under all the canvas it could carry and then crowded. But she

360

was a fine looking woman, he'd meant that. He could still sense in the air the faint odor of what the kids used to call her mad perfume.

Don't it beat all, he thought, the way a woman works. Now, if she was just going up there to see Hat about how much milk you use in a cake, she wouldn't any more bother to tog up like that than the man in the moon. But you get her good and mad, and look at her! All dressed up like the Queen of Sheba. It had always been that way when she was going somewhere she didn't want to go, or to see somebody she'd didn't like. She'd spend hours getting dressed just right. But you let her be going to see a friend and she scarcely even bothered to comb her hair.

He watched her big neat navy-blue back receding down the drive, dark against the thin scattered snow. She certainly was a woman any man could be proud of when she got dressed up like that. He'd never for a minute regretted marrying her, even though they'd had their differences. The only thing was, he supposed it would have made things considerably easier for him if she'd been a more sociable woman than she was—she never had been one to go out much and it might have helped him a little if she had. But when he stopped to think about it, he figured he'd gone just as far on his own as he would have if she'd been different.

Grace herself was thinking much the same thing as she went quickly down the drive and started up the Ridge Road toward Hat's house. Under the first layer of anger and shock, she was thinking back, trying to remember how long it had been since she'd got dressed up in the afternoon to go out anywhere. Doing it now made her realize suddenly how seldom she did it; she realized, too, that there were very few houses in this town where she would have felt free to go in the afternoon without waiting for an invitation. Hat's was about the only one.

Thinking that made her see that, apart from her immediate

family, she was actually a lonely woman. I haven't got one real woman friend to my name, she thought, leaving out Hat because they were sisters and anyone expected sisters to be friendly. It would be going some, she thought, regaining her anger, if I wasn't welcome in my own sister's house. It's part my house, too. I was born and brought up there as well as she was, and I don't know's there's any reason for Hat to take it for granted that house and everything in it's hern to do what she wants to with, without an ah, yes, or no to me.

She told herself tartly, it wasn't so much that she didn't want Hat to have the things or the place, but she didn't like her taking it for granted she could go ahead and do things like this. Mother had never said which one of them was to have such and such a thing—everyone had understood that Hat would go on living there and have the use of the things. Besides, there was Nat. He was the actual in-name owner of the house and everything in it.

In spite of herself, Grace started to enjoy the day. The high brilliant sky arched over the Ridge like a great dome swept clear of clouds. The spruces looked like purply-bronze trees against blue and white. And when she turned to glance back over the town, she caught her breath suddenly, thinking how *far* everything looked. Things had a look of great distance, as if they were off at the end of nowhere. And the way the water went off and off made her feel, queerly, as if there were nothing beyond it, as if it might go on forever, steely and bright and blue. It was reassuring to her to see boats moving in the harbor.

She could see, too, the long line where the black back of the breakwater was beginning to thrust itself above the surface of the ocean like some long-submerged animal coming up—it was like the abnormally straight backbone of a serpent—it was like something that should never have become visible and the light patches that she knew were men along it might have been huge barnacles. Well, she thought, tightening her lips

362

unconsciously, he may be right and that may be what they need to make that a decent harbor, but it certainly don't do much to improve the appearance of things from up here.

She turned her back on the harbor and went on up the road. Before she was in sight of Hat's house, set back the way it was, she could see the cars parked along the road. My soul, she thought, there must be crowds of people there! And that made her mad all over again. If only nobody had come to her silly sale; but she might have known better. Picture the people in this town passing up a chance like this to do a little prying, and with the owner's permission! At the owner's invitation, she amended.

She went in through Hat's white gate and up the front walk. Even before she opened the door, she could hear the voices. It sounded as if Hat had her whole flock of hens right there in the front room with her. Grace hesitated a moment, steeling herself, before she found the strength to push the door open and go in. Most of the chatter seemed to be coming from the big front parlor, but there were three women standing talking in the hall and when they saw Grace, they stopped, suddenly.

Yes, you tittering old busybodies, Grace thought, eyeing them. I *would* if I was you.

"Afternoon," she said and, without apparent effort, mustered up a smile.

They made a subdued murmuring of sound, carrying out the illusion of a disturbed hen-roost, then settled back into their conversation. But she was sure what they talked about now had no connection with what they'd been saying when she opened the door. She went on past them to the door of the front room.

My lord, she thought, if mother can see any of this going on, she certainly *will* be spinning in her grave.

Every table Hat had in the house must have been lined around the walls of the otherwise bare room and, spread out upon the tables, were things Grace hadn't seen for years. Entire sets of dishes, she could remember from her childhood; sets of four and six hand-painted plates she remembered had hung on the walls in her mother's bedroom; vases; an old chocolate set she had never seen used, the long spout of the pot just chipped a little; an ornate cut glass fruit bowl that her mother had always set great store by; things that she had forgotten completely. But seeing them here, spread out for the curious eyes of anyone who bothered to look, Grace told herself there wasn't a thing there it wouldn't have killed her mother to part with.

She made a circuit of the room, looking everything over carefully, so engrossed that she paid no attention to the people who glanced at her and got quickly out of her way. As far as she was concerned, they might not have been there at all. She didn't even see them.

She reached the door of the dining room and looked in, telling herself there could be nothing worse to see there. But the sight of her own sister acting like a common salesman was almost too much for her. If she hadn't been so mad, she might have said what she was thinking right then and there and disgraced herself for life. She was always thankful afterward that her anger almost strangled her.

Hat was standing in the middle of a heap of rugs, holding one after the other up to point out its respective merits.

"This one." She picked up an oval braided rug. "This one's pure silk and, believe me, it'll wear just like iron. Now this one, this hooked one with the picture done into it, it's one hundred per cent wool."

She glanced up, momentarily, caught Grace's eye, and her firm full voice faded slightly. But it came back to her completely and she went on as if Grace hadn't been standing there.

"I'll have to get twenty dollars for the hooked one. The braided one, I'll let go for fifteen."

Urban Jellison and his wife were standing in the little knot of observers. She leaned forward, a little mouse-colored woman, and fingered the braided rug. She glanced over her shoulder at her husband and then turned to the hooked one, holding it up to get a better look at the picture on it. Grace, looking over her shoulder, saw the small white house with its path winding along beside the baby-blue river and remembered the amount of discussion her mother'd had over whether the house should be white or not.

"I spose it'd be sensible to get the braided one, wouldn't it, Urban?" Mrs. Jellison turned to her husband, who glanced down at his hands, embarrassed in the face of so much female consideration. "I don't know, though, the hooked one's awfully pretty and I do like that picture."

"Get that one, then, if you like it."

"I don't know. It seems an awful lot to pay."

"Couldn't you come down a mite?" Urban looked at Hat, his ears red with the effort it took him to ask the question.

"Well, I guess I could knock off two-fifty," Hat said. "But that's the limit."

"I'll take it." Urban reached into his pocket and there, before Grace's scandalized eyes, counted out the cash into Hat's outstretched hand from a greasy looking leather wallet.

When they went out, Grace heard the woman say, "It's almost too pretty to use. We could hang it on the wall till it got dirty and put it down then."

Hat hesitated, made as if to pick up another rug from the heap around her ankles, but stopped then and looked up at Grace.

"Did you want to see me?" she said evenly.

"Yes, I'd like to have a word with you," Grace said with acerbity, "if you can bring yourself to let folks pick out their own rugs."

Hat, flushing brightly, led the way in silence out through to the kitchen and sat down. Grace stood in the door looking at the old familiar room and she actually felt a twinge of homesickness for it, although, she told herself, it wasn't arranged half as conveniently as her own kitchen at home and she would never have been able to get used to things here again.

"Well—" Hat looked up at her with a rueful grin. "Sit down, Grace. You might's well, now you're here. I spose you've come loaded for bear."

"Is it all right for us to talk here?" Grace looked over her shoulder. "You sure one of your customers won't come poking out to take a look at the stove?"

She sat down stiffly on the very edge of one of the straight chairs, folded her hands, and looked squarely at Hat.

"I might've known you'd take it like that," Hat said slowly. "But I didn't hardly expect you up here today. I either thought you'd come before or wait till it was over."

"I thought it'd be a good idea to come today to see if there was anything I could save out of the wreckage," Grace said.

"Well, now," Hat said, in the soothing tone she would have used to an animal or to her hens. "I don't know as it's as bad as all that."

"Bad! Hattie Hanna, how can you sit there with a straight face and look me in the eye, I cannot see. How you could put poor mother's things right out in the face and eyes of the world, like that. If there was one thing she hated it was to have people fingerin and pokin over her things."

"I guess you've kind of forgot, ain't you? Them things won't do Ma any good where she is. And the money'll help me out a lot."

Grace gasped and sat up straighter in her chair.

"Well!" she said.

"Well what? I'm not ashamed to admit I can use money. I don't know's there's many people can get along without it."

"Yes, but," Grace began. Then she remembered that it was Hat who was in the wrong, not her, and her tone sharpened. "Nearly every busybody in town's in your front room right now, tryin to see what they can see."

366

Hat sighed and then smiled.

"Yes," she agreed. "And them that ain't there now have been and gone."

"Why, it makes my flesh crawl to think of everyone that wants to comin in here and pickin over my own mother's things. Hat, I don't know what you can be thinkin of. And besides, think how people'll talk. What gets into you, anyhow? Did you ever stop to think about the rest of the family?"

"Yes," Hat nodded. "I thought a long time. But I couldn't see any other way out of it. People'll buy these things and pay hard cash for em. I figured it'd be a lot less disgraceful for the rest of the family if I did somethin like this than if I starved to death."

"Hat, I—I didn't know. But you're foolish. All you would have had to do would be come to Russ or me."

"That's just what I didn't want to do," Hat said. "I've come to you and Russ too often. I had to when Ma was alive. There wasn't anythin else to do. Now they's just me an I can take care of myself."

Watching the purposely calm face Hat turned on her, Grace felt suddenly like screaming. She wanted to grab Hat and shake her until she was blue in the face. With an effort she made her voice cold.

"I spose it never occurred to you that you didn't have the right to sell those things? After all, Pa's still alive and the place *is* his."

Hat looked down at the table and started tracing the patterns in the bright oilcloth with the short nail of her stubby forefinger. For a moment Grace thought she wasn't going to answer. But Hat looked up again, shaking her head.

"I spoke to Pa about it," she said. "I told him what I had in mind a week ago. He knew it."

Seeing that she had betrayed irrevocably the fact that Nat hadn't mentioned it to her, Grace took another tack.

"I'd looked forward to seeing those old things of mother's

handed down in the family," she said icily. "But I spose neither one of you thought of that."

"Well, after all." Hat began to bristle a little. "As you said yourself, as long as Pa's alive they're his things. He has a right to do what he wants, hasn't he?"

"Well," Grace said again, on an explosive breath. "I certainly never expected you to take this attitude, Hattie. I thought you'd at least have the grace to be a little sorry."

"Sorry I'm keepin myself from starvin?" Hat stood up and Grace noticed with a slight catch of her breath that Hat was even taller than she was. "Well, I've had enough, Grace. Enough out of you and Russ, both. Now I'm goin to tell you somethin. I think you've got an awful lot of nerve to come up here like this and treat me as if I was a baby. I know perfectly well what I'm doin. And I ain't doin a thing without permission of the rightful owner. I am heartily sick and tired of you and Russ thinkin you own me an I'm going to do everythin in my power to see to it I never have to take anythin from either of you again. Is that clear?"

Hat lost her temper very seldom, but when she did it was an awe-inspiring sight. She didn't get shrill—her voice grew deeper and her full cheeks flushed a bright red as Grace's own did. But she seemed to grow tall—to tower.

"All right," Grace said stiffly and got up to head for the shed door. "If that's how you feel, I'll see to it it won't be necessary for you to take our charity again."

"I'd be pleased if you would," Hat said. "And you better not go out through the shed, Grace, all dressed up like that. Things is a mess out there. I'll go to the door with you."

In silence they went through the house. Grace refused to look either to right or left. She kept her eyes straight front. Just inside the door, Hat hesitated and turned.

"Wait a minute," she said and disappeared into her bedroom. When she came out, she was polishing something on her apron. "Here." She stretched out her hand. "I saved this for you. I know you always liked it."

Grace stood staring down at the little ivory figurine Hat was holding out to her. All the years she'd been growing up it had stood on the mantel in the front room—a little scrimshawed sailor with a perfect intricate parrot perched on his shoulder. Looking at it, Grace could feel tears starting to grow in her eyes. Because she didn't know what else to do, she took it and went silently out the door Hat held open for her.

"Hat," she tried once more. "Sometimes I think you haven't got a mite of pride."

"I haven't," Hat said. "Not the kind you mean. I can't afford it. That kind of pride's for people with money in the bank."

She shut the door and Grace, finding herself suddenly alone and out where people could see her, went on down the walk clutching the little sailor firmly in her big hand and trying not to cry right out there where everybody and his brother could see what she was doing. She started to get mad again, thinking back over what they'd said to each other, and that helped. She didn't feel so much like crying.

That Urban Jellison, she thought. The very idea of him spending that much money on an ordinary old hook rug when they've got a bill as long as your arm down to Parsons's store.

JOE HASBROUCK, although he was as much a part of the Ridge as any other man who'd ever lived there, had very seldom been there in February. In fact, he could remember only two occasions—once when his father had died. Before his death the old man had conceived the idea that he wanted to be buried there in the Ridge and, being the sort of man he had been, his wishes were as accurately carried out after his death as if his entire family could feel old Joe's eagle eye bent terribly on them from some particularly righteous Hasbrouck heaven. The second time had been on the occasion of his own honeymoon, which Joe remembered with a certain wry amusement. His reactions had been similar on both occasions.

Now he was here again, ostensibly for a vacation. He certainly needed a rest after the winter he'd put in. But he felt a proprietary interest in what went on here and he wanted to see just what was happening. Rumors of more than passing interest had reached him.

Joe Hasbrouck's status in Christian Ridge was a peculiar one. He was, beyond a doubt, summer people, and he knew it. He was quite aware of the attitude of the natives toward the summer people, that peculiar mixture of distaste and reverence. He knew that there wasn't a man in Christian Ridge who didn't look down on the summer people as strange creatures with too much money and too much time, and he drew an amusement from wondering just what most of those men would think if they could see the bankbooks of their supposedly more fortunate brothers and sisters.

But, while he was summer people, there was a very real difference between the Hasbroucks and the people who came to the hotels and the big shore cottages. Joe Hasbrouck still came to the house his grandfather had built when Bar Harbor was nothing but the hopeful beginning of a town. He was third generation, one of the aristocracy, and there were few enough of them left. Joe, looking around him at his summer neighbors, felt a good deal the way the year-round residents felt when they looked at him.

There was another fact that he resented and couldn't understand. He could not see why any cheap down east fisherman could move into one of the little hovels down by the fish wharf and be immediately accepted while he, whose family had known this town for three generations, he who could call every man in town by his first name and had all his life, was still the outsider.

He was thinking about that as he put his big sedan skillfully down the shore road, thinking it so resentfully that his thick red face was twisted slightly out of its customary good humored lines. His wife, who was sitting silently beside him, glanced across at his scowl and permitted herself a fleeting cool smile.

"You certainly don't look as if you were enjoying this pilgrimage to the scenes of your childhood," she said, letting her full voice out a trifle.

Joe looked at her slim, well-kept figure with no feeling whatsoever.

"I was thinking," he said slowly, and stopped.

The car rounded the last wooded point of land and he could look suddenly out across the narrow arm of water to the opposite shore where his own huge gray green roof thrust up through the blued spruces.

"What's the matter?" he asked, not taking his eyes off the harbor. "Don't you really like it here, Lucia?"

"Oh—" She managed to give the impression of shrugged shoulders without moving in her place. "It's all right, in a primitive sort of way. All this stark winter scenery." Her voice underlined the last three words satirically. "It makes me feel as if I'd just stepped into the middle of a copy of *Ethan Frome*."

"Good god," Joe said, genuinely startled. Then, because he couldn't think of anything else to say, he kept quiet. He didn't feel like quarreling with her and he knew all he had to do to precipitate one of their icily polite exchanges was to say something about the Ridge. She'd always hated the place, ever since that first February, ten, no, twelve years ago. Thinking about the twelve years, Joe nearly said good god again, but restrained himself in time.

Well, he thought, looking at the slowly darkening stretch

371

of water and the heavy metallic spruces, she can be as smart as she likes about it; it's one lovely place. There was something in the tautness, the sparcity of the late winter afternoon that almost hurt him. The light over the tops of the spruces, maybe, or the still lucent way the water in the harbor lay between its rocky shores. In this particular light, everything had a sad sort of violet look that he liked whether she did or not. It made him think of pictures, the kind of pictures he would have had in his house if it hadn't been for Lucia.

The road ended abruptly in the wide parking space and Joe pulled to a stop beside the other car that was parked there.

"Be darned," he said. "I didn't think anyone'd be here."

He got out, not bothering to ask her to come too, because he knew she wouldn't want to, and made his way clumsily down the bank to the backbone of the breakwater. He noticed that there was a good deal of it visible at this particular tide. And then he found the other occupant of the silence and the purple afternoon.

Russ was standing with his back to the land, looking out across the water, and there was a possessive look about his wide shoulders that made Joe smile. But his face was completely serious as he went slowly up the shore to stand beside him.

"Russ," he said easily. "What d'you think of it?"

"Well, Mr. Hasbrouck," Russ said. He stuck out his big hand and pumped Joe's heartily. "They was sayin you was in town."

"Yes," Joe said. "Came down for a little rest. Getting along, I guess. Find when you reach a certain age you have to begin taking things easier. Thought I'd take a run down and see what was going on here."

"Well, now." Russ gave the judicious impression of a man well pleased. "I'm real glad you did. Does me good to see the summer folks takin interest in what goes on here. Now, you'll see right away—" He turned and waved his hand at the line of rock as if he'd just that moment called it up out of the deep. "This breakwater's goin to be the makins of this harbor."

"Hm," Joe said. He nodded. "Yes."

"Why, lord," Russ said heartily. "You'll see the time when you can leave your boat in the harbor in a rip-snortin notheaster an never think a thing about it. Way it has been, of course, it ain't really safe. You heard about the damage done in that October storm we had?"

"Yes," Joe said again. "Of course, it really won't make much difference to me. About the boat, I mean. My mooring's up inside the pool and pretty well sheltered by the trees; but I imagine it'll make a difference as far as taxes go."

He raised his thick light eyebrows and glanced sideways at Russ.

"Well, now, Mr. Hasbrouck," Russ said placatingly, "the little mite of difference this'll make in your taxes ain't goin to be enough to keep anyone awake nights. Why, I should think you'd be happy to see progress without worryin about a tax increase as small as that one'll be."

"I hear"—Joe was unable to resist taking a slight dig—"you ran into a little trouble out there."

Russ's face clouded momentarily.

"Fool of a surveyor missed that deep-hole. Couldn't have expected it to be there anyhow. Fellers in this town been fishing out of this harbor now for years. Nobody ever heard of there bein a deep-hole there. Surveyor said it looked to him almost like a made channel. Only it wasn't, because a made channel out there would of silted in long before now."

"Added considerably to your cost, didn't it?"

"Well, it would of in any case."

"Yeah—the only trouble is people're going to think there's something fishy, aren't they?"

"Not if I tell them different." Russ's voice was a little less outgoing than it had been. "Well, live and learn. Any rate, the breakwater's there and that means progress."

"Progress, eh?" Joe grinned. "Well, I'm like the lot of them. Progress is all right in its place, but I'm damned if I like it when it costs me money."

"Now, now, now," Russ said, drawing the words out until they sounded like a hum. "That's no way to look at it. Why, you been comin here long enough to see what this town's like. Of course, I don't expect it's much different than any other place. But sometimes it seems as if people here was almighty slow about takin up anythin new. Why, you know's well as I do, what happened about the water supply here. You know how much that's cost us, an all because it was somethin new and nobody went for it."

Joe remembered it well; he remembered it so well that he felt his face grow a little hot as he tried to keep his eyes level on Russ's. He hadn't had any vote or any actual personal means of putting himself on record at the time the privately owned water supply system of the Ridge had been offered to the town at what had seemed to him too high a price. But he'd had his say, along with others, and the result had been that the town, in special meeting, had turned down the offer which had been taken up immediately by an out-of-town company which had been doing well with it ever since. Wondering with sudden discomfort, if Russ knew about his part in that deal and was, perhaps, laughing just a little, Joe looked at him quickly. Russ's face was perfectly sober and there was no sign of laughter in his eyes. Joe's self-esteem reestablished itself quickly.

"Yes, I see what you mean," he said. "Well, learn by experience, as you say. No matter how much talking you do to people, it isn't going to have any effect at all until they find out for themselves."

"Just exactly what I feel myself," Russ nodded. "You take

374

this town. I do a lot of gassin about how mad it makes me, but when you stop to think of it, if you got any big city down to the size of this town, it'd probly be jest exactly like it. Why," he warmed visibly to his theme. "That's one of the wonderful things about this country. Our cities ain't nothin but grown up small towns. If only anyone could know enough people in a city, why he'd probly find just the same proportion of em mean as in a small town. See what I mean?"

"Perfectly." Joe nodded.

"You got to remember," Russ said. "A town like this is a whole lot more than just a small town—it's the whole darn country on a small scale, yeah. You got everythin right here. The way you think an act, that's the way the whole country does—because the whole country's jest small towns. I dunno, maybe the whole world. The difference between Russians and Americans, for instance, on a bigger scale, could be the difference between the way I talk and the way, say, a New Yorker does, see?"

"That's true," Joe nodded pontifically.

"Yes, like I say, progress," Russ said reverently.

Since there was no possible answer, Joe was silent. For a moment they stood there, side by side, looking at the breakwater.

"Oh, Russ," Joe said suddenly, remembering. "Heard about your boy."

"Ayeh," Russ said. He moved his shoulders slightly. "Poor Jake. He was only twenty-three."

"Makes you stop and think when they go that young. It's a shame. I was sorry to hear it."

"Those things happen," Russ said soberly.

Suddenly he thought: Jake. And momentarily it was as if he could see him—for the first time since the funeral, Jake seemed real to him, as if he had been an actual person with an actual existence and, for the first time, he felt a sense of loss.

Jake was my son and he's dead. Twenty-three was young, so young that Russ, thinking of it, felt harshly aware of the waste, the sense of mortality that dead youth gave more poignantly than dead age. The death of the young made you feel as if you were a trespasser in life.

The sensation was uncomfortable but fleeting—and as it died away from him, Russ caught himself taking in, out of the corner of his eye, every detail of the younger man's carelessly correct sporting clothes. They were so well-worn and so comfortable looking that he caught himself wondering if the ads for clothes like that read "already broken in." He had an idea they looked a good deal like that when they came from the store.

They turned and went up the beach together, talking heartily. And Joe, even with his acute feeling about the summer people, didn't realize that there wasn't another man of his age in the entire town who would have talked to Russ the way he did. Not, man to man, the way they were doing. Joe felt none of the unacknowledged inferiority that young men often feel for older ones. But he felt it in a different way when they reached the steep bank and he found himself puffing heavily over the ascent that Russ took easily in stride.

"Good lord," he said, windily, at the top. "Your physical condition must be something to make the doctors go out of business."

"Pretty good for an old one," Russ said, not too complacently. "Knock on wood."

He stood watching as Joe climbed into his car. Then Russ went over to the far window and spoke through the glass to Mrs. Hasbrouck. Seeing who he was, she put down the window and shook hands with him.

"Real glad to see you both," Russ said. "How d'you like it here in winter, Missis Hasbrouck?"

"Lovely place," she said. "Really lovely."

"Tis, ain't it?" Russ said. And then, because it was getting on for his suppertime and he was hungry, he let the conversation go. The uncomfortable silence strung out until Joe started his engine and leaned across his wife to say good night to Russ.

"Come an see us again soon," Russ said and stood watching as the big car circled the parking space and disappeared up the road. When it was well out of sight, he started to grin, merely a suggestion of amusement around the tight corners of his mouth, got into his car and followed the other one up to the corner.

In the car ahead, Joe Hasbrouck, who had forgotten all about his difference with his wife, and who was bathing in the responsive glow Russ could start when he chose, was saying, "You know, Lucia, there's a man you have to admire, even if you do know he'd take your eyeteeth if he could get em without letting you know."

"Admire?" She accented the word deliberately.

"Yes, admire," Joe insisted stubbornly. "He's progressive, but not too progressive. He's old stock and the flower of it. He's a man who's been content to make the most of his material—and a good job he's done, too."

"He's a man who can pull the wool over your eyes anyhow," she said.

"Hell," Joe said, stung. "You make me tired. You couldn't see good in anything if it up and hit you. But I'll tell you this, my good woman, if we had more men of his caliber in this country we wouldn't be in the bloody awful mess we're in right now."

"If you start talking politics now," she said calmly, "I shall scream."

Joe clenched his teeth and drove the rest of the way home in silence, seeing the gray weathered shingles of his cottage with relief. He stopped in front of the door, waited for her to get out and then, without saying anything to her, went on to the garage.

DRIVING up the Ridge Road, Russ began to feel unaccountably depressed. It must be the weather, he thought, all this cold. You'd think you'd begin to see a few signs of it letting up, this time of year.

He had just turned the corner by Andy Galley's when his lights picked up the plodding figure that had dodged out into the ditch just ahead of him. He pulled to a stop and leaned over to open the door.

"Goin home, Stan?"

Stanny climbed into the front seat beside him and Russ, looking at his shadowy bulk realized with a good deal of surprise that Stanny had grown a lot this past winter. His shoulders had somehow lost the spindling look that Russ hated and were beginning to take on a surprising fullness, at least they looked full in the heavy jacket he wore.

"Howcome you're gettin home so late?" Russ glanced at him. "Get kept after school or something?"

"Not this time," Stanny said surprisingly. "Had to stay for basketball practice."

"That so? What d'you play?"

"Why, uh, right guard," Stanny said cautiously. "Second team, though."

"Second team, hanh?" Russ said, but there was no hint in his voice of what Stanny had been afraid of. "Like it?"

"So-so."

Seeing that Stanny was going to let it go at that, Russ found himself casting about in his mind for something else to talk to him about. Judast, he thought, I ought to be able to think of something to say to my own kid.

"Hey," he said suddenly and Stanny jumped. For a moment, feeling the involuntary motion, Russ had a quick reflex feeling of distaste. "Matter? You nervous?" he said.

Stanny made a noise that tried to be no.

"Well, I was thinkin," Russ went on quickly before he could change his mind. "Jack Welman, the station agent up to Freehold, called me up this mornin. Said Jake's car was setting up there in the station yard. Been there for a couple weeks now. He said he thought I might like to know about it."

"That so?" Stanny turned his head just enough to make out his father's profile against the faint light left in the sky. He was bursting to ask questions, but he didn't quite dare.

"Yeah," Russ said. "I was thinkin. It ain't any more'n a pile of junk, but if you want to take the trouble to go up and get it, why you could have it."

"Omigosh," Stanny said. "You mean, it could be *my* car?"

"Why not?" Russ began to feel expansive before the excited voice.

"But, well—judast priest," Stanny said, forgetting his nervousness in the larger emotion of excitement. "Gosh, I haven't got a license."

"Well, so what?" Russ said impatiently. "You're near fifteen. You can get one then."

"Yeah, but—" Stanny's voice cracked a little. "I mean about bringin it down. If I get picked up, what'll I do?"

"Oh, hell," Russ said. "You get picked up, you just tell the cop to come to me. Don't worry about that. I'll take care of it. Besides, there's never anyone between here and Freehold."

"Holy cats! When can I go get her?"

"Whenever you want to. Tomorrow."

"What about school? I got to go to school, haven't I?"

Russ started to say never mind that, but changed his mind before the words were out. No use giving the kid any big ideas, he thought.

379

"Go after school," he said. "What's the matter with that? Can't you wait that long?"

"Well, sure, sure. I never thought."

"It's time you started thinkin, then," Russ said, but even that couldn't damage Stanny's enthusiasm. Russ felt as if he were sitting beside a firecracker that might go off at any minute. He could feel himself beginning to grin a little, remembering the first car he'd ever owned. Well hell, he thought, got to give the kid a few breaks.

He stopped and let Stanny out at the back door before taking the Buick around to the barn.

"Gee," Stanny said. He got out and stood with his bony young hands clutching the door. "Gee, thanks, Pa. Thanks a lot."

"Forget it," Russ said. He waved his hand and Stanny turned and ran for the house. Nat was sitting by the kitchen window when he went in.

"Oh, Stanny," he said. "You busy tomorrow night? Radio says we're in for a thaw. I didn't know but we oughta go git that ice boat. I don't blieve there'll be much more chanct to use her this year."

"Gee," Stanny said. "I can't make it tomorrow night, Gramp. Pa and me've got a deal on. I got to do something for him tomorrow night. Maybe later on."

"Well, sure, there's no hurry," Nat said. He watched as Stanny, with a new dignity, took off his jacket and hung it carefully on the hook behind the door. "Anythin important?" he asked finally.

"Well," Stanny glanced at him. "You know how it is. We got a deal on, that's all."

THE LAST WEEK in February was pneumonia weather. The days limped after each other, damp, foggy, unpleasant. Everything that stood upright dripped water and dampness seeped through wood until even the bedding felt clammy when Grace turned it back at night. She would stand thoughtfully, feeling the sheet, wondering if it was sensible to let anyone sleep in a bed like that.

For a week, the Ridge was dim and unreal, its cutting outline softened till it looked like a great dark mass of feathers instead of trees. The trunks of the trees themselves were damp and black looking and the snow, under the thaw, sank in upon itself, a sodden gray blanket, fast showing the rips and tears where the ground poked through. Out across the lower field, where the slush stood in gray puddles, it looked fallen in, like a face when false teeth have been removed.

The salt water ice that winter had formed across the harbor, in the lees, and up in the land-locked pool where the summer boats were moored three months of the year, stood the thaw better than the snow had. The jagged, castle-like ramparts, thrown up when the tide went out letting rocks thrust their way up through the ice, melted and fell; but the ice itself, porous and yellow and deceptive, held until the first big blow of March took it out on a low drain tide.

Wires, telephone pole crossbars, and bare tree branches, everything that ran parallel to the ground, had a row of tiny, glistening drops of water along its lower edge—it was as if the winter had driven the frost deep into the marrow of all things, animate and inanimate, and the thaw was forcing it out now, like clear colorless blood.

The first day of March was like that; but on the second, the proverbial March storms began. Wind came pouring in a raw dank flood out of the northeast, bringing more snow, and by nightfall a roaring blizzard had set in, closing up the harbor. It grew a little warmer as the night wore on, and the snow changed to sleet and rain. Then, toward morning, the wind veered into the northwest, and the cold came down again. It wasn't the bitter, nail-driving cold of winter, but a more tentative, more augmentative cold, a personified cold that almost seemed aware of its own fleeting qualities, as if it knew itself for what it was, a last peevish lash of winter.

Town Meeting Day, the third of March, dawned clear and crisp.

Russ, going to the door, stopped, took one look, and turned back to the kitchen to call Grace to come and look, too. In a few sheltered spots the snow still lingered, particularly sad and gray looking in the clash and glitter of the morning. Everywhere, where there had been water the day before, there was ice now. It was like a world of steel and glass, static and immovable. Each separate blade of last year's dead brown grass, each separate needle on the spruces, each smallest twig on bush and tree, had an importance out of all proportion to its size.

The least breath of the warming wind stirred up a cacophony of brittle clicking and the poverty birches in the pasture had already started to crack their glaze and the sun, picking out each prism, shot out colors almost too bright to bear against the eyes.

"There," Grace said after a minute. "You know it *is* beautiful, Russ. In spite of the trouble it causes, I'm kind of glad we had just one sleet storm before the winter was out."

"Hmmm," Russ said. He squinted at the sun and tested the wind uneasily. "I hope to god it melts and they get out with the sanders before Meetin time. They don't, there won't be enough people there to make it worth havin."

"Don't worry." Grace looked at him fondly. "You always get as nervous as a cat before Town Meetin, and then there's never any need for it. They always vote you right back in again."

"Oh, it's not that," Russ said testily. "There's just some

things I want to see go through right, that's all. I'm not worried."

He went back into the house, put on his larrigans, and went out to the barn. For a moment he stood looking thoughtfully at the car. Now in the old Buick he never would have dreamed of using chains; he always said he'd just as soon have skates on each wheel as chains for all the good they did. He's always figured they *acted* like skates. But with this car he didn't know, he still didn't quite trust her; she had none of the familiarity of age and long usage that had given him confidence in the old one. And he wasn't a good enough driver to get the feel of a car quickly. It would be months before he'd be able to get into this car and be sure she'd take him where he wanted to go without having something happen.

Grace watched him go skidding and slipping down the drive and held her breath when he almost took a complete spin where the drive met the main road. But she breathed easier as he straightened out and gained speed. They must have·sanded, she thought. The sander must have come up by here before daylight—she'd been up ever since then and hadn't heard or seen it.

She was glad to have him out of the house at last. The morning of Town Meeting Day was always a trial. Russ claimed he wasn't nervous and she knew he never went a step out of his way to do any electioneering. But the night before, he'd go to bed as calm as a mill pond and the next morning he'd get up as touchy as a bear with a sore head, and not be fit to speak to until the day was over.

Well, she thought, thank the lord he's out of the house and I can turn around without falling over him. It seemed to her she hadn't turned all morning without finding Russ at her heels about something.

If it wasn't this, it was that. He couldn't find a clean shirt and why didn't she put them in his drawer where he'd be expected to look instead of hanging them on the rack in the kitchen. He couldn't find his glasses and who the devil was there to use them except him and why couldn't people leave his things alone. There wasn't any cream for the coffee and he should think she might put herself out just a little to see that he at least got the cream for his coffee the way he liked it.

Realizing what was wrong with him, having seen it work the same way for the past ten years, Grace had, with apparent patience, tended out on him until he finally got ready to go. Then she came back into the kitchen, poured herself some coffee from the big pot, and sat down at the table with a sigh of relief. Nat, who had retired early to a chair behind the stove, well out of the way, looked at her with a gleam of amusement.

"That's over," he said.

"For another year, anyhow." She shook her head. "Every time I tell myself I *cannot* stand it one more year, then I go ahead and do it."

"You'll stand it," Nat said philosophically. "You'll probly have to for the rest of his life. Or yourn," he added as a sort of afterthought.

"He looked quite nice when he got all ready, didn't he?" she said, more to turn her father's train of thought than for any other reason. But he *had* looked nice, she realized. He always did when he got dressed up. She did wish, though, she could get him to the place where he'd wear shoes instead of stuffing the pants legs of his good suits down into those old larrigans. She thought that was why the cuffs of his good suits always wore out first, and it got them so dirty and greasy, too; but it never did any good to say anything to him about it.

THE BIG front door of the Masonic Hall was open when Russ got downtown, but he went in the smaller door and up the stairs to his office. That door was still locked and before he got out his key to open it, he took a quick look at his watch. It was all of eight-thirty and high time Florence should have been there. He'd taken the trouble to tell her specially the night before that he'd want her early this morning.

Women, he thought, opening the door. It seems as if I spend most of my time fiddling around and waiting for some woman or other. They're all alike. Not one of them's got any sense of duty. If it's not one thing, it's another.

He went into his office and started riffling around in the papers on the desk. He actually had nothing pressing to do because he did things before they reached that stage; but there'd been some letters he'd wanted to get off before the Meeting started.

Fifteen minutes later he heard Florence come into the outer office and take off her coat. There was a subdued jingle as she hung it in the closet, setting the row of wire coat hangers swaying. Then, as he sat waiting, there was absolute silence outside his closed door. His look changed to an aggrieved stare. What the devil was she doing out there, anyway? Probably just something to take up her time and keep him waiting when she knew perfectly well he *was* waiting.

He opened his mouth to let out a roar, but as he did, he saw the door of his office start swinging in slowly and he shut his mouth again quickly and sat watching. The door swung half open before she put her hand on it and he saw the four red nails like four drops of blood just above the knob. Beginning to wonder if she'd suddenly gone completely crazy, he sat waiting to see what she intended to do. A moment later the side of her head and one eye appeared around the door jamb, gazed at him for a second, and withdrew.

For pete sake, Russ thought, I always knew she was queer, but I believe she's gone completely off her nut this time.

The hand disappeared, too, and for a second the silence was

385

unbroken. Then she pushed the door completely open and stood there watching him.

"Oh," she said, with much the tone she would have used if she hadn't seen him before. "I wasn't sure you were in here."

"Well, do you know it now?" Russ stared at her, feeling his glare become stiff.

"I can see you," Florence said sullenly.

"I spose you've forgotten I told you yesterday I wanted you here early," he glared at her savagely.

"No. But I had to do some shoppin and the store doesn't open till eight-thirty." Florence came hastily across to the desk. "What was it you wanted?"

"If you can manage to spare the time," Russ said sardonically, "I would appreciate it deeply if you could take down a couple of letters for me."

She didn't have her notebook with her, but she sat down in the straight chair, snatched a couple of sheets of office stationery and a pencil from his desk, and settled herself nervously at the corner.

"I'll just take them down on this to save time," she said hastily.

When he'd finished the two letters, Russ glanced at his watch, saw that it was nearly nine o'clock and jumped for his hat, leaving her there at his desk.

"Go ahead and type them," he said. "I'll sign em this noon when I get back."

"You goin to the Meetin?" Florence asked.

For a second astonishment held him silent. He stared at her wondering how the devil her mind worked.

"Naturally I am," he said. "Don't be such a damn fool."

Florence flinched delicately at the word. That ought to hold her, he thought, going rapidly down the stairs. Of all the fools. Why, they couldn't have the Meeting without him there.

They had already begun, though, when he came in. The

moderator was just going up to the platform. He saw that they'd elected Joe Daniels as usual and the usualness of it was reassuring. Though he knew he didn't have anything to worry about anyhow, it was good to see Joe starting up to the platform. He and Joe had been going it together since the beginning ten years ago. First Joe'd get elected moderator and then Russ would get elected First Selectman. He had come to the point where he looked on Joe as a sort of talisman.

He could feel the little stir in the crowd as he went rapidly down the hall and took his place in the first row, the seat he always had and which was left for him whether he came late or not. Aaron was in his usual place beside Russ. He looked up and nodded shortly. Looking beyond Aaron's sharply marked brown profile, Russ saw that Andy Galley was sitting next to him. Andy was running for Third Selectman for the second time. He'd tried it last year without success, but Russ had an idea he might make it this time. He wasn't displeased at the prospect. Andy was a good capable man and Russ was getting just a little tired of the hide-boundness of Guy Abel who'd had the job for the last four or five years. Guy was sitting on the other side of Andy and he leaned forward to look across him at Russ and wink his eye. Then, chuckling richly but silently, he sat back in his seat and dug Andy over the ribs with his elbow. Andy glanced quickly at Russ, grinned slightly, and looked away.

Russ didn't blame Andy much for looking embarrassed. Guy was behaving naturally and his very naturalness was enough to make anyone cringe. Sometimes Russ wondered if Guy had the brains to be anything but natural. But if Guy lost out this trip, Russ was going to have to take a little action next year. He always relied on Guy to do his nominating for him and if Guy should lose his job, he might be able to figure out it was partly because Russ thought he'd had it long enough. Even a man with Guy's particularly unintricate brain might work that out and if he did he certainly wasn't going to go out of his way to nominate a man who'd helped him out of as easy a job as the one he had now.

Lester Bunker, the chairman of the warrant committee, was sitting at a small table a little behind Joe Daniels's stand and Russ, looking up suddenly, caught his eye, distorted and dull in the dim light from the old flies. Lester pretended studiously he hadn't been staring, but Russ knew he had, and sat staring himself until Lester was forced to look up again. Then Russ smiled and nodded his head cordially.

Russ hunched his shoulders, leaned comfortably back in his chair, and fumbled for his pants pockets. Joe read the first article and Guy, caught half-asleep, staggered to his feet. Yes, Russ thought, listening to his thick voice, I'll have to do something different next year. With satisfaction, he heard his name seconded from the back of the hall somewhere. Somebody else nominated Pete Elkins and that name, too, after a hesitation long enough to make Russ grin, was seconded faintly.

"Any more?" Joe lifted his gavel and started bringing it down again, taking it for granted that there would be no more nominations. He stopped the downward swing, though, before the gavel hit the stand, and his mouth dropped open a little.

"Nominate Bill Martin." The voice was loud and sounded nervous.

"Second it," Aaron said easily.

Russ, taken completely by surprise, was too amazed to turn and see who'd put Bill's name into the voting. He didn't even turn his head to look at Aaron. The surprise wasn't obvious to anyone looking at him. He sat still, slouched in his seat, and his eyes hadn't lifted from the toe of his right larrigan. But his eyes had narrowed slightly and he was turning this new development over in his mind with alacrity. Pete Elkins was all right. He was a small fisherman from over the back side of town and his nomination was merely a sop to convention. But Bill Martin was another kettle of fish and the whole thing was completely unexpected.

Never before, in all the years he'd been Selectman, had Russ ever found himself facing an opponent who might stand a chance of beating him. He wasn't sure that he faced one now. But Bill was too important to be dismissed without consideration.

Russ turned his head just enough to catch Aaron's eye and found Aaron already watching him. He raised one eyebrow quizzically and Aaron looked away. Guy Abel leaned out excitedly to look past Andy again. He shrugged and mouthed something Russ couldn't make out.

"He wants to know," Andy hissed incautiously, "what the devil this is all about."

Aaron was looking straight in front of him as if he hadn't even heard the whisper.

"Aaron knows more about it than I do," Russ said, his voice low. He was smiling slightly when he glanced from Andy to Aaron. "If Guy wants to know, let him ask *him*."

Joe's gavel hit the stand with a crack. Russ sat up in his chair, beginning to feel the tautness of anticipation spread pleasantly through his mind. Something was coming now, it had to, and he was more than ready for whatever it was.

The same voice that had nominated Bill Martin now demanded the floor in no uncertain terms. Art's scared, Russ thought. I wouldn't have known his voice at all. He's nervous.

"There's a few questions I'd like to ask Mr. Walls before we vote on this article," Art said.

Russ got up out of his chair, rising slowly to his full height, because when he did it slowly people were apt to be more impressed. He nodded at Joe and turned to face the hall. Art's perfectly round, dun-colored head looked like a pale bowling ball, lifted a little above the level of the others around him. It was pretty hard for Russ to realize that Art was standing as tall as he could. He nodded again.

"I'm always open to questions," he said, letting his voice out till it filled the hall, making Art's sound colorless and small.

"That's all right," Art said. "And now we'd like a few answers."

"That's perfectly okay with me," Russ said gravely. "But you'll have to ask the questions before I can answer them, Art."

He stood listening to the wave of tittering laughter and watching Art's brown face turn a dusky red. That was all right. If this was anything important, it wouldn't hurt to have every advantage he could and he figured if he could make Art look a little ridiculous or make him lose his temper, it would be all to the good.

"I want to ask some questions about this breakwater," Art said.

"Well, that's good. I'm glad that's been brought up," Russ said. "I got one to ask first. Did any of you notice the difference in that easterly we had night before last an yesterday? There wasn't any damage to speak of, was there? And that was every mite as bad as the one we had last fall."

"I'm not saying it isn't a good thing to have there," Art said loudly. "What I *am* sayin is that it seems to me it's costin us a good deal more than we understood it was goin to."

"I admit that." Russ smiled but there was no humor in it. "But you can't hold anyone responsible for an act of God, can you? You were told all about it at the time."

"It sounds like a darn queer yarn to me," Art said. "Findin that drop-off there. An besides, if you'd give the contract to a feller submitted a flat bid instead of this foolishness about cost-plus, then wouldn't it a been up to him to stand the expense?"

"I hope you don't think I gave that contract to anyone," Russ said. "It was awarded by the Board of Selectmen. Not me personally. We figured out who'd give us the best value for our money and they got the job, that's all."

"Well, that drop-off was a mighty convenient and darned expensive act of God, if that's what you want to call it."

"Before I ask you what you mean by that," Russ said icily, "I want you to understand this. If the contract *had* been awarded to a contractor who'd submitted a flat bid, there would have been a clause in it to cover any contingency like this one."

"Well," Art stumbled, hesitated, and said desperately, "ain't it the truth that Aaron Billings submitted a flat bid that was under the price we're payin these people's doin the job?"

"That's true," Russ said. "But, if this business about the deep-hole hadn't come up, Aaron's price would have been higher. We took everything into consideration and we had bad luck, that's all. As it is, I honestly think we've got a better piece of work out there now than Aaron could of done. That's my opinion and I'll stick to it."

"Now we're gettin to it," Art stiffened visibly. "Somebody made a mistake and this time I guess it was you. It seems to me it's mighty queer, here we been fishin out of this harbor for years and never in all my life did I ever hear about there bein a drop-off between the shore and Hall's Shoal."

"I don't know anyone's got X-ray eyes," Russ said. "It's not wide, it's just deep, almost like a made channel. It's there an you're welcome to drop down an see it any time you want to."

"You can be as comical as you want to," Art said. "The fact remains, all we got to go on is your word it's there. I for one don't believe it is. And I'm askin you right here an now, warn't it made good an worth your while to see to it that bid was awarded the way it was?"

The audible silence in the auditorium after Art's voice stopped, it seemed to Russ, came up around him in waves. For a minute he was almost too angry to speak. He started to say something hot, hesitated, thinking, Steady, boy. When he began to talk, he started slowly, carefully, picking each word.

"There's nobody here in this hall hasn't known me for a good many years. I don't believe there's many here would suspect me of a thing like that. And if you're sayin it here in public, Art, without proof, why, it's a dangerous thing to do."

"You always was a good talker," Art said. "But it ain't goin to work this time. I don't want any slick talk from you. I want a straight answer."

"All right." Russ straightened his shoulders. "I'm not gettin a red cent out of it. Now, I want to know where you get any reason for thinkin I am. And can you prove what you jest said?"

"I ain't said anythin that needed provin. I just asked you a question."

"Well, all right. I've answered it."

Art started to say something more, but evidently couldn't think of anything and subsided into his seat. Russ, watching the crowd, saw the stir in a far corner and then recognized Bill Martin's voice.

"Mr. Moderator," Bill said and then, without waiting for Joe to recognize him, launched into what he had to say. "I didn't put my name in because I particularly wanted this job. I just figured this way. We been goin on now for a good long time with a man you could say a thing like this about and have people believe it. I ain't sayin he did or he didn't stand to make anything out of seein that contract awarded to a certain company. I don't know. But I know there's been a good deal of talk about it lately. And I'm tired of seein this town run and owned lock, stock, and barrel by any man who might be capable of doin a thing like takin a bribe."

"I don't know what I've got to do to make you fellows see what happened," Russ said angrily. "Do you need a blueprint, or somethin? Look, I had this all out with Aaron himself and if you ask him, he'll have to tell you it's true. And I'll tell you just what I told him. I value my job. I wouldn't take a chance on a thing like this even if I wanted to. And I don't."

Suddenly they all looked like strangers to him. There was no face in the long rows of faces that he could remember having seen before. What was happening was so unbelievable that he couldn't feel as if it was happening to him. Standing there, he experienced a sensation he hadn't felt for years, not unintentionally. For a moment he couldn't recognize the honesty of the feeling and when he saw that he'd lost his temper, it was too far gone for him to hold himself back.

"I don't know what's the truth of it," Bill said. "Far as I can see they ain't any way it can be proved one way or the other. But the way I feel is this. If anyone can say that about a man and have people believe it, then the man's capable of it."

Russ took a step toward Bill and had the satisfaction of seeing a flicker of apprehension cross the smooth brown face. There was a brassy taste in his mouth and he knew he was going to say the wrong thing and couldn't stop himself.

"If you want to believe that," he said, "go ahead. By god, after what I've done for this town, the way I've worked for you's, go ahead."

He turned to look at Joe Daniels who was staring at him, round-eyed, as if he'd never seen him before.

"I want to withdraw my name from the voting," Russ said in a voice he didn't know for his own. He started rapidly for the door. There was a tentative boo, but it died instantly and he went the rest of the way in silence.

There is an expressive quality to the silence of a big room with a lot of people in it. It's a silence that makes you think everyone is holding his breath. That was the silence Russ left inside. Waves of it vibrated behind him like the wake of a boat in a shoal water. And when he closed the big front door, Joe Daniels jumped up and dropped his gavel. Heavily, like a man moving in his sleep, he stooped and picked it up again, his fingers fumbling clumsily with the handle.

"After all," he said suddenly. "We don't know it's true and if it ain't, I can tell you, you've gone to work an lost an almighty good man for the job."

"Maybe——" Art Ferguson got slowly to his feet. "Maybe you're right, Joe. But just knowin a man's capable of pullin a thing like that makes you wonder."

"How d'you know he's capable of it?" Joe said loudly. "He didn't act like a man with anythin on his conscience."

"Well." Andy Galley got up. "I move we vote on his name, just the same. Me, I'm convinced."

"Hell," Joe said. "You oughta know you can't do that. You heard him withdraw, didn't you? I don't believe you can vote a man into office if he does that."

Momentarily the thread of sense was lost in a rising tide on general conversation. Joe glared and slammed his gavel on the table lustily. The voices died away reluctantly.

"I for one," Joe said. "I don't believe a word of it. I've known Russ Walls as long as any of you has and I don't believe it. By judast——" Joe's righteous fervor overcame him. "I'm not goin to have anythin to do with such a bunch of damn fools. Anyone wants this job can take it."

He flung down the gavel, which bounced off the table with a crash, and stalked down the steps to Russ's empty seat in the front row.

After a moment's hesitation, Lester Bunker stepped forward and picked up the gavel.

"If none of you's got any objection," he said, "I guess I can do it, though probably I won't do as good a job as Joe."

"No," Joe said loudly, "you probably won't. And you probably won't elect anybody'd do as good a job as Russ done, neither."

"I'd like to have the floor." Andy Galley got up. "It looks to me like a bunch of you got together and cooked up this whole mess. Well, maybe Joe's right and you can't vote on a man's name after he's withdrawn it. I don't care. I nominate Russ Walls and I move we vote on his name just the same."

"What if he won't take it?" Joe snapped.

"If he don't," Andy said, agreeing without question on the outcome of the vote, "why, it'll just go to whoever gets the second place."

Looking at Russ at the breakfast table the next morning, Grace marveled at the way he sat there putting away his food as if nothing at all had happened—or as if something exciting had happened.

When she'd heard the night before from Stanny just what had taken place at the Meeting, she'd expected Russ to be beaten and defeated. He had looked tired when he'd come in last night. But he hadn't said anything at all about the Meeting. Instead he sat down at the table, ate his supper, and had then gone off into the other room as if nothing at all out of place had gone on.

Now he looked like a man who was interested and excited, almost as if he'd found a completely new interest in life.

When anything happened that affected the family the way this probably would, Grace usually waited until after they went to bed at night before she mentioned it to Russ. The kids had heard them discussing their problems down through the years, their voices nothing but a low mumble of sound off in another room somewhere. But last night there had been none of the kids to hear them but Stanny, and Nat, slightly deaf and off in his back room, couldn't have heard if he'd wanted to.

Russ went up to bed a little earlier than usual, and after waiting long enough to let him get to sleep if he wanted to rather than talk to her, Grace went up herself. She went reluctantly, hating the thing that had happened, wondering if there was any truth in the rigmarole Stanny had told her, wishing it had never happened. She knew, better than most,

how much his job meant to Russ, and she knew that the pres-
tige it gave him meant a great deal. Now he'd lost the whole
thing, lost it in such a way that there wasn't a person in the
whole town who wouldn't look after him curiously, satisfied,
amused, scornful.

It was going to be his pride more than anything else that
would be hurt. And her own, too, she had to admit. It was
going to be hard for her to think of him as an object for scorn
who had been so long a man to look up to. There was a catch
phrase her mother had been fond of—"he was the soul of
honor"; the old lady said it about any man she happened to
admire. And that phrase had always made Grace think of
Russ, not the things he did or the way he was—but his actual
physical appearance, the way he looked. But there must have
been a feeling of falsity about it to make her accept so readily
the idea that he might have taken money to do somebody a
favor.

She went quietly upstairs, quite ready to believe that he
had done it, and stopped outside the bedroom door to listen.
Against hope, she stood hoping that he might be asleep and
listening for some sound to tell her he wasn't—but if there was
a sound she couldn't hear it through the door.

She stood listening to the silence of the great empty house
and it seemed to her like something inimical and dangerous,
something that was closing in upon her as she stood there and
she had no defense against it. For a moment she hated Russ,
thinking suddenly, It's his fault things turned out this way
and he wasn't satisfied with driving the kids away. She
couldn't bring herself to add, even in her thoughts, "and kill-
ing one of them."

And now this—on top of everything else, there was this.
Sometimes it seemed to Grace as if a woman felt more than
a man did and she thought that if one more thing happened,
no matter what it was, big or little, she simply would not be
able to bear it. It seemed to her that happiness was something

like a road and nobody could go beyond a certain point on it, because after that point the road just disappeared, dissolved, and if you stepped over the edge there was nothing but darkness.

I was too happy, she thought. Here I was with my kids all grown up and here with me and beginning to be company for me, and Russ happy and doing what he wanted to; now look at it. Everything gone!

Actual and complete realization struck her for the first time with all its force. For the first time she realized exactly what this winter had done to *her*. She didn't think of events as singular ones happening to other people, but as an accumulation of tragedies all personal to her.

She pushed the bedroom door open, stepped into darkness, and knew instinctively that Russ, although he didn't move or speak, was lying there wide awake, waiting for her. The knowledge that he still needed her was comforting, and finding that there was still somebody for her to mother made her feel so much better that she forgot what she'd been thinking and thought only of him and what he must be feeling.

"You all right, Russ?" she said.

Instantly he reared up in bed and threw the clothes back to get up.

"All right?" She could almost see the expression that went with that tone. "All right? Of course, I'm all right."

"Well, I just thought," she began a little helplessly, having expected anything but this particular reaction.

"Who's been feedin you the lowdown on what happened?"

He had started to pace the floor slowly. She could see him, a tall dim white shape, passing between her and the faintly lighter window, regularly as a pendulum.

"You ought to know this town well enough by now. Whenever anything happens they're always ready to call you up and tell you all about it. Anything excitin."

"Hah, well. I guess they got what they were lookin for today."

Grace sat down wordlessly on the edge of the bed and started taking off her shoes and stockings. Russ kept up his pacing and didn't say anything more until she finished undressing and crawled into bed. She lay there, stiffly, wondering if he'd gone completely out of his head, thinking, maybe the shock was too much. He certainly didn't sound like a man who'd lost a job he wanted and lost it the way he had.

"Well." He turned his head to look toward her. Grace could see the faint light blur of his face. "Why don't you say somethin?"

"Because I don't know what to say, I guess."

"Aren't you even curious?"

"Yes." Grace sat up suddenly. "Yes, I am; and there's just one thing I want to know."

"Well, out with it."

"I want to know if it's so. Now, wait a minute an don't go flyin off the handle; and don't lie to me. Just say yes or no, so I'll know whether or not I got any right to hold my head up any more."

"My god," Russ said. "That's the last question I ever expected *you* to ask. Why, good lord, what kind of a life have I led, anyway—even my own wife not to know whether I'd do a thing like that."

"That's no kind of an answer to give anyone," Grace said tightly. "I've got to have somethin better than that to go on. The things that've happened this winter, well, I don't know whether I'm comin or goin. Seems as if the very devil has got into this family, every single one of them. I wouldn't be surprised to have the whole house come down in pieces right around my ears."

Russ came over to the side of the bed to look down on her, although there couldn't have been much for him to see in the darkness. When he started to speak, Grace knew instantly that his mood had taken a new and unexpected turn. Instead of being angry he had become tender and it was so unusual that she felt tears start in her eyes.

"There," he said. "I guess I ain't had time to think about anyone but myself, Grace. I never realized before, I guess, what you've gone through this winter. Maybe I haven't said as much to you as I should have."

He stopped almost as if he expected her to say something, but Grace couldn't. If she'd tried to say a single word, she knew the tears would get the better of her and she didn't want him to see her crying.

"Livin with me hasn't always been very easy for you, has it?" he said slowly.

"If only you'd sit down once in a while." Grace conquered the tears. "The way we used to and talk things over. If you'd only listen to me."

"We haven't really done much talkin, have we?" Russ sounded thoughtful and a little surprised. Lying there, Grace could feel the bed sag as he climbed into it and she rolled gratefully against him for warmth. "I don't know," he said. "It's almost like you get out of the habit of talkin when you have to do so much of it unnecessarily. I spend most of my time talkin. I guess I forget you might like to do some, too."

"What're you going to do now, Russ?" she said, wanting to pin down his mood, to find out why he seemed happy when he should have been depressed.

"I don't know, not really." His voice sounded thoughtful. "But it gives me something new to think about, anyway."

Suddenly, before she had time to answer him, she felt his big hand on her shoulder and sensed, rather than saw, his head above her. Surprise and pleasure held her silent until, if she had said anything, it wouldn't have made any difference to either of them.

NOW, facing him across the breakfast table, she was thinking, My lord, who'd have expected that to happen when I went up there last night? Russ looked up suddenly, caught her eye, and grinned, and Grace could feel her face grow warm and knew she was blushing. Russ got up slowly and stretched and, watching him, it seemed to Grace as if he filled the room. There was a vitality and an aliveness about him that was not new to her but had been growing increasingly rare as he got older and more settled.

"You're blushing," he said looking down at her.

"It's a darn good thing I can't read your mind," Grace told him tartly, "or I probly would more."

"Probly," he agreed.

Nat looked from one of them to the other and started to say something to Stanny; but just looked at him instead and shut his mouth firmly on the words. I've got to watch myself, he thought. I'm gettin old an forgetful. Sometimes I forget he ain't a full grown man.

"Well——" Russ stuffed his hands into his pockets and went over to glance out the window at the weather. He yawned mightily and turned to face his family. "Seems kind of nice," he said, "not to have to go running off downtown first thing every day." He frowned a little, defensively, against the three pairs of eyes, and turned his back. Grace could hear the loose coins in his trouser pockets starting to jingle and when he did that she always knew he was turning something over in his mind. She could almost see the wheels beginning to work.

She sat for a minute watching him, noticing the long, still-tight lines of his back and his long legs, admiring the way he stood—looking as if his feet were planted solidly on the ground, but not solid enough to hold him stiff.

Stanny got up from the table, gathered his school books from the chair beside the door and went out; his good-by floated back through the door.

"Hm," Russ said. He cleared his throat. "Well, guess I'll

go out an take a look around the place. Been a long time since I have. Dunno but what I might wait around to see if they's any mail."

"Well, all right." Grace got up. "If there's anythin that looks as if it might be interesting, I'll call you."

"For pete sake," Nat said, after the shed door had closed gently behind Russ. "I never in all my borned days seen the like of that guy."

"I know it." Grace knew what he meant before he said it.

"Here, just yesterday, he was makin everyone's life miserable because he might not get re-elected." Nat shook his head. "An now look at him. My lord, the way he acts, you'd think he never wanted that job an was goddam good an glad to get rid of it."

"All right, Pa." Grace looked at him sternly. "That's enough of that kind of talk."

"Where Russ in concerned," Nat said stoutly, "all there is for anyone to do is swear. Nothin else fits."

"Hm, well." She smiled, a tight unwillingly amused smile. "I don't know but I see what you mean. I can tell you, there've been times when I wished I could have."

"I'll bet," Nat said, deeply appreciative.

"But I don't know." Grace stopped and looked thoughtfully at the shed door. "When I stop to think, I'm real glad I took him. Things always seem to be goin on where he is. There's always something happening."

"Yes." Nat nodded his head. "Yes, I guess that ain't very far from the truth. But, honest to god, Grace, I wouldn't believe it when I stop to think. Why, I remember the time he started lobsterin out of the Ridge here. He an his whole family was always poorer'n Job's turkey. You take Russ's father now, he was a good man an a good worker, but he always seemed to have the cussedest luck.

"There warn't a man in town you'd rather have with you in case somethin went wrong than Jake Walls. But he never seemed to get any furtherer. Folks always figured Russ was just like him.

"Why, when he started lobsterin, he didn't have nothin but his father's old pea-pod. Big clumsy thing she was—and he was so cussed poor he used to wear his oars down until they warn't more'n an inch through where they hit the row locks. It's a wonder to god he ain't nothin but picked bones out around the Hamor Shoal somewheres."

"He's come a long way," Grace said. "But I wish I knew what we was goin to do now. All I'm afraid of is, he'll take to sittin around doing nothing—he's getting along. If he does that, why he'll be an old man in less time than it takes to tell. And he'll drive us all crazy into the bargain."

Her father pursed his lips.

"If I was you, Grace," he said, "I would never in god's world worry about Russ Walls sittin around doin nothin. If I know anythin about him, he's hatchin already. I seen him stand around that way before, sort of twiddlin them quarters in his pocket. Soon's he stopped twiddling, things always started to happen."

"Yes, I know it. The only trouble is, I guess I'm kind of scared to see him start. I'm kind of scared of what he might do next."

"Nothin would surprise me," Nat said. "Nothin at all."

"That," she told him emphatically, "is just exactly what I mean."

THE MAIL truck came at about ten o'clock in the morning and usually Grace was watching for it and saw it come in sight at Aaron Billings's mailbox, down the road. This morning, because she was so anxious for it to come, she missed it and heard its heavy grinding before she even looked out the window. But the noise didn't stop and at first she thought it had passed them by; until the sound of the big motor started getting louder instead of fading away.

For heaven's sake, she thought, and went to the window to find the big yellow and red truck right outside the dining room window. She could see Henny Parker's thin anxious face concentrated on something in the seat beside him; then he got out and came over to the door, his hand full of envelopes.

Grace met him in the entry.

"Hi." Henny looked at her and because she was a little sensitive, she thought he looked at her sheepishly and with a good deal of evasive curiosity.

"You always deliver the mail right to the door?" she said tartly.

Henny gulped and looked even more ashamed, making her feel ashamed for having spoken to him so sharply.

"No, ma-am, but there was this here for Russ." He thrust a long envelope at her, his eyes agonized with shyness. "See? Special delivery."

"Well, there." Grace took it and smiled at him, seeing that she'd been wrong about what he'd been thinking. I ought to have remembered how bashful he is, she thought. "Thanks a lot, Henny. It was nice of you to bring in the rest of it, too."

Kindness only made Henny worse. His homely face turned a brilliant pink. He bobbed his head twice, convulsively, and backed out of the shed. A minute later she heard the big truck bucketing down the drive.

She looked down at the envelope, her fingers feeling it carefully. Russ's name was written hugely across it, taking up most of the white space that wasn't already covered by stamps. It wasn't a hand-writing that was familiar to her and she turned it over, but the return address was a post office box number and told her nothing. She saw that it had been mailed at the Ridge Post Office and was dated early that morning.

"Humph," she said and taking the envelope gingerly between her fingers, went out to the barnyard door to call Russ.

He must have seen the truck because she found him in the barn door looking expectantly toward the house.

"Well, here's something," she said shortly because she hadn't been able to learn anything from the envelope.

He crossed the yard to her, took the envelope and tore one end off. He read the single sheet carefully and then, evidently, went back and started all over again. Watching his face, Grace could have killed him. There wasn't a flicker of expression to tell her what he was feeling. Without saying anything to her, he folded the letter back into its original creases and put it into the envelope again. When he looked up at her, his face was completely sober, but the sight of her concerned and slightly perplexed face seemed to set off a convulsion somewhere inside him.

For a moment she didn't know what he was doing and watching the shaking of his shoulders she began to be frightened. That was too much for Russ and he put back his head and let out a yell that drove her back up the steps to stand at the top clutching the rail and staring at him as if he'd gone out of his mind. She really thought he had. She hadn't heard him laugh like that in years. Finally, when he was reduced to a sort of breathless whoop, she came firmly back down the steps and held out her hand.

"You give me that letter. If there's anythin that's funny right now, I need to know about it as much as you do."

Russ handed her the envelope, bringing out his handkerchief at the same time.

"Guess I better go downtown and find out what went on at that Meetin yesterday," he said. "It would appear that I ought to know what they did."

"My lord," Grace said, her eyes taking in the words. "My lord. They never believed a word of it. For the lords sake, Russ, them fools voted you right in again."

"Whatta you mean, fools?" he bristled.

"Well, I mean, how do they know that yarn wasn't true?"

"That's the funny part of it," Russ said, beginning to grin. "They don't know and apparently it wouldn't a made the least bit of difference. Don't that beat the devil, though. Well——" He turned away and the words floated back over his shoulder. "Well, guess I better go down an see what's goin on. Maybe I'll take the job. Bein drafted like that—makes a man feel pretty big."

He was still laughing when he went by her in the big Buick. Grace stook there in the doorway shaking her head and then went in to tell her father what had happened.

Nossir, Russ was thinking, they don't even know whether that yarn was true or not. It sure beats all.

For a moment, looking out across the trees toward the village, he thought he could make out the beginnings of buds on the trees; they had that hazy look, that blurring of clear outline. There weren't any buds, he knew—it was only March. But there was a smell of spring in the air.